Praise for DUSK

"I read *Dusk* in a couple of days, unable to put it down. I *like* this guy—he's made himself an utterly convincing world which is wholly his own. There are echoes of folk such as Erikson—that hard-edged, unflinching way with a story—but he's a unique voice. There are so many things to pick out—the Machines, the Red Monks, the Shantasi. His towns and cities—Pavisse, Noreela City—are places where I can imagine a hundred other stories waiting to be told, and I was almost disappointed when they were left behind—but then began the trek across a blasted land which is committing suicide. Lebbon has a way of throwing staggering images at you which you almost have to pause and think about before you can fully grasp. This is fantasy for grown-ups—and the ending made my jaw drop. This is an excellent book, and I would not say that unless I meant it." —Paul Kearney

"*Dusk* is a deliciously dark and daring fantasy novel, proof of a startling imagination at work. Lebbon's writing is a twisted spiral of cunning, compassion, and cruelty." —Christopher Golden

"An exquisitely written, unique world is revealed in this novel, a world inhabited by flesh and blood people rendered with often brutal honesty and clarity of vision. It's rare indeed to witness the conventions of fantasy so thoroughly grabbed by the throat and shaken awake the way Tim Lebbon has done with *Dusk*. Even more enticing, this first novel in the series concludes with a jaw-dropping finale, and for what it's worth, such a reaction from me is not a common occurrence." —Steven Erikson

"A gripping and visceral dark fantasy of five fugitives in flight from terrifying pursuers through a decaying world brutalized by the Cataclysmic War. In *Dusk*, Tim Lebbon has etched a powerful new version/telling of the traditional magical quest, whose tortured twists and turns will (alternately) disturb and electrify its readers." —Sarah Ash

"*Dusk* is dark, twisted and visceral, with a *very* shocking sting in the tail—the perfect jolt for anyone jaded by the creaking shelves of cuddly, rent-an-elf fantasy. Tim Lebbon is an important new voice in the fantasy field. Bring on the night!" —Mark Chadbourn

"Tim Lebbon writes with a pen dipped in the dark stuff of nightmare. The world he creates is eerie, brutal and complex, and the story abounds with action and menace." —K. J. Bishop

"Totally original. I've never read anything like it.... New wonders at every turn... One might subtitle it 'A Riveting Work of Staggering Imagination.'" —F. Paul Wilson

"A compelling, if harrowing, read. I was hooked straightaway. It is dark, nasty, and visceral and yet a real page-turner. The characters are well developed—so good that even when they are not likeable, they are comprehensible.... Lebbon also manages to create a world which is convincingly corroded. Surprisingly quickly, I found myself reveling in a world of decay and disruption—like Viriconium or New Crobuzon, like Hawkwood's world, Noreela is a world where life is hard and yet at times rewarding.... The ending is both effective and jawdropping.... I found shades of Cook and Erikson here in the book's violence, Miéville in its contemporary weirdness and perhaps most strongly Paul Kearney here, in that combination of horror, decay and squalor, though Lebbon is clearly his own voice. His proficiency as a writer means that in the end the style of the story wins through to create a book which is imaginative and memorable, and if you can handle it, definitely worth reading." —sffworld.com

"Well-drawn characters and a literate way with the grisly distinguish this first of a new fantasy series from Stoker-winner Lebbon.... Many of the well-handled action scenes are from the bad guys' point-of-view, an unusual perspective that helps round out the author's fantasy world. The climactic battle, a variation on the classic raising of the dead, offers an ambiguous outcome that presumably will be resolved in the sequel." —*Publishers Weekly*

"Dark, gripping swords-and-sorcery noir... Lebbon's medieval world is well-developed.... The bleak tone and setting, which includes drugs and whores aplenty, counterpoint with dark effectiveness those fantasies that focus on highborn royalty and knights in shining armor. If any armor shines here, it's because it's covered in blood. A promising departure for horror novelist Lebbon." —*Kirkus Review*

"Bram Stoker Award–winning Lebbon begins a new series with a coming-of-age tale featuring a sharp-witted, youthful hero and a group of unlikely allies that includes a thief, a warrior, and a witch. Engaging storytelling and a solid backstory make this a good choice for most fantasy collections." —*Library Journal*

"Lebbon is an author so skilled he definitely belongs on auto-buy.... His prose is alternately poetic and flesh-slicingly real. His characters always strike a nerve and have the sort of heft that makes you feel as if you might have met them or the real people they were based upon—even if they were not in fact based on real people. And finally, for me the killer, Lebbon's novels offer places you can go back and visit.... [*Dusk*] will cut deeply, without remorse." —Agony Column

"Incredibly good...a masterful job...*Dusk* is a great read and another reason for me to point to Tim Lebbon as one of the most talented authors working today. Though it may be billed as a fantasy book, the trappings that come along with that label are all but naught here, and a world is created that I know I want to hear more from as soon as possible." —thehorrorchannel.com

"A riveting adult fantasy." —*Rocky Mountain News*

"The exhilarating story line paints a dark, gloomy Poe-like atmosphere throughout, especially when the adversaries take center stage. The key characters, in particular the teen and his champions, are unique individuals that make their realm seem even more nightmarishly real. Tim Lebbon paints the darkest *Dusk* that will have readers keeping the lights on until dawn breaks." —*Midwest Book Review*

ALSO BY TIM LEBBON

NOVELS

Dusk
Hellboy: Unnatural Selection
Mesmer
The Nature of Balance
Hush (with Gavin Williams)
Face
Until She Sleeps
Desolation
Berserk

NOVELLAS

White
Naming of Parts
Changing of Faces
Exorcising Angels (with Simon Clark)
Dead Man's Hand
Pieces of Hate

COLLECTIONS

Faith in the Flesh
As the Sun Goes Down
White and Other Tales of Ruin
Fears Unnamed

DAWN
TIM LEBBON

BANTAM • SPECTRA

DAWN
A Bantam Spectra Book / April 2007

Published by Bantam Dell
A Division of Random House, Inc.
New York, New York

This is a work of fiction. Names, characters, places, and incidents either
are the product of the author's imagination or are used fictitiously. Any
resemblance to actual persons, living or dead, events, or locales
is entirely coincidental.

Bantam Books, the rooster colophon, Spectra, and the portrayal
of a boxed "s" are trademarks of Random House, Inc.

Library of Congress Cataloging-in-Publication Data
Lebbon, Tim.
Dawn / Tim Lebbon.
p.   cm.
ISBN-13: 978-0-553-38365-2 (trade pbk.)
I. Title.
PS3612.E245D39 2007
813'.6—dc22
2006031849

Printed in the United States of America
Published simultaneously in Canada

www.bantamdell.com

BVG   10 9 8 7 6 5 4 3 2

For Mum

18/10/'37–30/5/'06

You did a good lot.

Acknowledgments

Thanks once again to the Night Shade guys.
A big thanks also to Steven Erikson, Paul Kearney,
Chris Golden, Sarah Ash, K. J. Bishop, F. Paul Wilson,
Mark Chadbourn, and Steve Calcutt.

And, of course, Anne and everyone at Bantam.

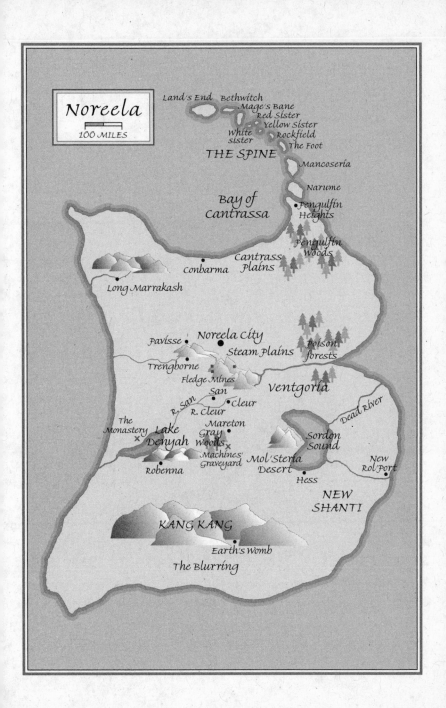

PART ONE
Every
Moment's End

knew she would return, the heat of revenge was growing brighter within her heart.

The people of Robenna had driven her out, poisoned her and murdered her unborn child. Given time, their descendants would pay.

"Dreaming of death and vengeance, Lenora?"

Lenora looked up into Angel's eyes. The Mage had crawled back along the hawk's spine and now sat astride its huge tail, her face a hand's width from Lenora's. She was beautiful. Whatever time had done to her, she had undone. The might of new magic flickered behind her eyes, and its potential seemed to light her from within.

Lenora tried to speak, but she was lost for words.

"Don't worry," Angel said. She drew closer still, until her blazing eyes encompassed the whole world. "So am I."

"Mistress . . ."

"I frighten you?" Angel raised an eyebrow.

Lenora averted her eyes.

"That's only right. Fear is good, Lenora. You remember the first time I touched you, casting out your pain and driving away death on that burning ship? You were filled with fear then also, but it was fear of the Black. I saved you from death to serve me, and you've done so ever since. But you've become casual about your fear, as S'Hivez and I have become blasé about our desires. We've always wanted to regain magic, but maybe pain grew to suit us better. Perhaps we became too used to life as outcasts." The Mage looked off past Lenora, back the way they had come. "Do you think that's true, Lenora?"

"No, Mistress. You've always been Mages, with or without magic."

Angel smiled, and Lenora felt a brief stab of jealousy—she was aware of how she looked with her bald head, scarred body and black teeth—but she cast it aside.

"Lenora, you need never lie to me. You're almost one of us. You came with us out of Noreela three hundred years ago; you think the same way about this accursed place, and you want the same thing. So we're *almost* the same . . . except you don't have this." She reached out and touched Lenora's forehead.

At first, the point of contact burned. Then the sensation changed from heat to one of intense cold—a chill that would freeze air and crack rock—and Lenora's eyes closed to accept whatever Angel was handing her.

There was one single image: the death of Noreela. Lenora viewed it at the speed of thought, north to south, east to west, passing over mountains and valleys, deserts and lakes, and everywhere finding the stain of destruction on the landscape. A city lay in ruins, buildings burned down into ruined heaps, streets strewn with smoking corpses, waterways polluted with rotting flesh. Farms and villages were equally devastated, their inhabitants laid out in neat lines and fixed to the land by wooden spikes. An army lay dead on a hillside, muddied armor already rusting beneath the blood spilled from the thousands of corpses. A great river was home to a hundred boats, all of them submerged, each of them filled to their watery brims with naked corpses.

And all the while, Noreela itself was suffering great traumas. A mountain range swam in fire, only the highest peaks still visible above the flames. On an endless plain the ground was cracked open, but instead of fire and lava rising up, the land's innards rolled out across the grass, giant coils of molten earth and stone hardening in the twilight and venting scampering things the size of the largest hawk. The air turning to glass, the ground melting away, water bursting into flame . . . The whole of Noreela was in chaos, and at its center pulsed a magic grown darker than ever before.

"There, at the hub," Angel's voice said. "That's us." And Lenora saw. The fleeting visions slowed, settling toward a huge wound in the land. The wound bled. In the center of this sea of blood, floating in a boat forged from the bones of countless victims, writhed two ecstatic shadows.

The Mages, joyous with the victory of vengeance found.

Angel removed her finger from Lenora's head.

"The future?" Lenora gasped.

"No one sees the future. I showed you what I *want* of the future: Noreela drowning in blood. And with your help, S'Hivez and I will make it so." Angel paused, looked down at her hands, then continued. "You have no idea of this *power*, Lenora! It's like being dipped in molten metal, yet knowing you can send that heat anywhere, to do anything. S'Hivez and I have been communing with shades, and they are working for us already. I can see what's happening in the land because the shades tell me! We know that the Monks are dead back in the valley, and the machines are still once again. We know that the Duke's army is weak and formless in Long Marrakash. We know that night is here for Noreela, and it is *our* night. I can step from one side of the land to the other simply by closing my eyes."

Lenora was speechless. The energy came off Angel in waves, and the whole of Noreela pivoted on the Mage's every utterance.

"Our army is yours," Angel said. "When it lands at Conbarma, you will be there to welcome it in and arm it with the greatest weapons we can make. And then you will take Noreela."

"You're leaving?" Lenora asked, aghast.

Angel turned to crawl back along the hawk.

"But where are you going?"

"You question me?"

"Of course not."

Angel laughed, as if dismissing Lenora's query and her own stern answer. But she said no more, leaving Lenora wondering what the next few days would bring.

War, for certain. More bloodshed and death than she had ever imagined. But with the Mages leaving the Krote army to its own devices, Lenora found doubt stoking her fear.

————

SHE SOON LOST track of time. The constant twilight was unsettling, as if some angry god had swiped the sun from existence. To begin with, Lenora had been able to keep step with time as it drifted by. But as that day passed and they flew on into the steady night, she became confused. She found herself glancing to the west, hoping to see the smudge of a bloodred sunrise, but there was only twilight. As the Mages had taken daylight from the world, so had they removed night, leaving the land perpetually in between: no sun, no stars. Only the moons remained.

The life moon was a silvery disc, low down to the horizon in the east, nervously peering above the edge of the world. The death moon, bright and dusty yellow, rode high in the north. They flew toward it, and it seemed to leak some of its sickly hue across the landscape. There were those who believed that the moons were the remains of ancient gods, banished to the skies by a mutual hatred and destined to gather as many souls as they could in an eternal competition. The life moon was losing, and the death moon was yellow with the swell of wraiths. Soon, moon-followers believed, it would burst.

Lenora had no time for such phony religions. She knew her gods, and they rode this dead beast with her. And now that the Mages were here, Noreela had no room for alternative beliefs. She was lucky; few people ever spent time with their deities of choice.

They flew on, heading northward for Conbarma and the landing site for the Krote army. The Mages let nothing distract them. Noreela was a banquet spread below them, waiting to be plundered and pillaged just as they had dreamed about for three hundred years. Lenora could see larger towns now as they went farther north, splashes of illumination across the shadowed land, and twisting ribbons of light where caravans traveled the surrounding countryside. She would have so loved to land, take on one of these groups and show them the true meaning of fear. Since the battle for Conbarma, the whole land had changed, and she craved the feel of an enemy's blood on her skin once more. But the hawk carried them on, its dead tentacles trailing behind them, gas sacs still gushing to keep them afloat, and Lenora knew that the Mages had a more encompassing revenge in mind.

There would be slaughter, and blood would be spilled. But first they had an army to welcome.

———————

IT HAD BEEN dusk when they left the machines' graveyard, and when they sighted the Bay of Cantrassa below them, Lenora guessed that it should be dusk again. They had been gone for almost two full days, and she hoped that her warriors had prepared Conbarma for the arrival of the Krote ships. They would be only days away, perhaps even now passing the northernmost reaches of The Spine. Time was moving on, and war was close.

As S'Hivez guided the hawk down to follow the coastline to Conbarma, Lenora found herself eager to dismount. She craved some time away from her masters. She was tired, her skin was burned by the cold wind and she felt dizzied by the power she had been close to for so long. The Mages exuded a force that sent Lenora's tired mind into a spin. They were like holes punched in reality, so alien that even she, their servant and lieutenant, could barely endure their presence.

For a while, the voice of her daughter's shade whispered in her mind. Lenora shook her head and Angel glanced back, the Mage's eyes a piercing blue against the twilit sky.

"Conbarma," S'Hivez said, the word like broken glass against skin. He spoke so rarely that Lenora had forgotten his voice.

She leaned sideways and looked down at the sea to their right. The surging waves swallowed the death moon's yellow light and spread it like a slick of rot. To their left she saw the port of Conbarma nestled in its own natural bay. She was glad that the fires of the battle had been extinguished.

S'Hivez delved deeper into the dead hawk's neck and brought it down, curving into a glide that would take them to Conbarma from the sea. They passed just above the waves. The hawk's trailing tentacles skimmed the water, throwing up lines of spray, and by the time they reached the harbor there were several hawks aloft, their Krote riders armed and ready to repel an attack.

Lenora managed a smile. How their moods would change when they saw what this thing brought in!

S'Hivez landed the hawk on the harbor's edge. He extracted his hands from its dead flesh and flicked fat and clotted blood at the ground. Lenora wondered whether he saw the symbolism in this, but she guessed not. Angel had always been the one for that.

The hawk deflated beneath them, spreading across the ground like a hunk of melting fat, and immediately its stink grew worse. Lenora glanced at the dead boy lying between the Mages. She wondered why Angel had brought him this far.

Lenora slid from the hawk, but had trouble finding her feet. Nobody came to help. She looked up, hands on her knees, cringing as her legs tingled back to life, and then she realized why. None of the Krotes were looking at her.

The Mages were kneeling side by side on the ground. Their hands were pressed to the dusty surface before them. S'Hivez seemed to be chanting, though it could have been the sound of the sea breaking against the mole. Light began to dance between their fingers. Dust rose. Stones scurried away from their hands like startled insects.

Dozens of Krotes—those with whom she had flown from Dana'Man, and fought for Conbarma two days before—gathered around, faces growing pale in the moonlight as they saw who had arrived. One or two glanced at Lenora and then away again, back to the Mages, fascination overpowering the fear.

It's good to be scared, Lenora thought. That was what Angel had told her. The Mages had always been a formidable presence, but now they were so much more. There was something so dreadfully wrong about the exiled Shantasi and his ex-lover that Lenora found it difficult to look at them. It was as though light were repelled from their skin. She thought of the shapes she had seen in her vision: two wraiths aboard the bone boat on a sea of Noreelan blood.

The ground started to glow beneath the Mages' hands. The last of the smaller rocks flitted away. They stung Lenora's lower legs, but she dared not move. This was something she had to see, because she knew now what the Mages were doing: displaying their power to the Krotes. They could have landed and talked to the warriors, but discussion of the magic they now possessed was nothing compared to a demonstration.

Lenora stepped back several paces. Her heart fluttered a few beats, and the many wounds on her exposed skin tingled with something approaching excitement. *This is when we see,* she thought. *This is when they really show us what they can do.*

The Mages began to stand, hands maintaining contact with the ground as though stuck there, then slowly they straightened their backs, raising their arms and bringing part of the ground with them. Each hand was lifting a column of fluid stone. The ground vibrated. Rock growled and crumbled, and strange rainbows shimmered in the dust. Angel laughed, and S'Hivez's muttering became louder, the words revealing themselves as something less complex than a spell. *It's all coming back,* he said, again and again.

Lenora could feel heat from the molten rock, and she saw other Krotes stepping back as their skin stretched and reddened. The Mages began to mold it and, between them, something took shape. Sharp edges appeared from nowhere; curves hardened; a globe of rock rose up on thin stony stilts. Angel laughed again, and Lenora shivered.

The Mages backed away from each other, allowing the thing room to grow. More rock flowed from the ground, urged on by a simple gesture from S'Hivez, and they molded this around the form, thickening the trunk and lengthening the limbs. They added more, and then S'Hivez stepped back and lowered his hands.

He looks tired, Lenora thought. *They have their magic, but they're not used to using it.* S'Hivez looked at her through the heat haze, and she saw the black pits of his eyes. He scowled. She looked away, skin crawling, scalp tightening as if the old wound there were about to reopen. A thought came, and she could do nothing to hold it back: *He can hear me.*

"Lenora!" Angel called. "A present for you, and it will be ready soon." She pointed at the sea and a huge geyser rose, glinting silver and yellow from the moons' contrasting light. Krotes scattered as the water fell into a wave, tumbling across the ground until it broke around the glowing sculpture.

The stone hissed as its framework was suddenly cooled. And as the steam died away, Angel appeared by Lenora's side. She leaned in close, her breath hot. "It's yours," she whispered. "Your machine, your ride, and soon I'll give it life." She turned away and surveyed the assembled Krotes. "You'll *all* have one! Machines of war, for you to do what you've trained for: take Noreela. Soon the ships will be here, and your fellow Krotes will follow you east and south and west. I name every one of you here a captain, and Lenora is your mistress. You answer to her, and she will answer to us. And the rewards at the end of this war will be beyond imagining." She turned back to Lenora. "I'm giving you my army," she said. "Use it well. I know your intentions, Lenora. I know your aims." She came close so that only Lenora could hear what she said. "I know what you hear and what speaks to you, but ignore that calling until you've fulfilled your purpose. You're here *for* me, and *because* of me."

"Yes, Mistress," Lenora whispered. *Not long to wait,* she thought. And she hoped that the shade of her dead child could hear the promise in those words.

"And now, life for your machine." Angel walked to the fallen hawk with the dead boy still on its back. She laughed. "Oh, S'Hivez, even *you* must appreciate the symbolism of this!"

The Mage laid one hand on the hawk and the other on the dead farm boy's arm. Beneath her hands, the flesh of both began to shimmer and ripple, and soon the stench of cooking meat once again permeated the air. She moved back slowly, melted flesh flowing like thick honey, then she swiveled and thrust her hands at the sculpture.

Flesh flew. Blood misted the air as if blown by a sudden gust of wind. Bones cracked and ruptured, impacting the rock, delving inside and crackling as they fused back together. The flesh of the boy and the hawk melded and filled the fighting machine, flooding hollows within its rocky construct, then building layer upon layer around its outside. Blood greased its joints. The dead hawk shrank as more of its flesh was scoured away. The boy's corpse was no more.

Angel lowered her hands and stepped back. Lenora saw that she was panting slightly, her shoulders stooped a little too much, and she wondered again at how much this new magic was draining the Mages. But then Angel looked at her, and behind her smile Lenora saw a strength she had never witnessed before. Not just physical strength—Angel had always been strong—but a strength of purpose. There was no doubt in Angel, and no fear. She was unstoppable.

"Here it is," Angel said. She pointed back at the machine. "And here you are."

Lenora fell to her knees. She clasped her hands to her head and pressed, trying to squeeze out the thing she felt inside. She was intimately aware of the strange life that had just been created, and even as she felt Angel's calming touch and heard her soothing words, she knew that this was something never meant to be.

Take care, Angel whispered in her mind, *you're strong, Lenora, and this is feeble and weak—a machine, a tool for you to command and use. It lives like an animal down a hole, not like you, not like a proud Krote come to conquer and claim. Its half-life is less than a hawk's shit, but you are linked to it now by this touch.* And Angel withdrew from her mind, leaving that link in place.

Lenora took a deep breath and opened her eyes. She was looking directly at the machine where it stood awaiting her touch. She sensed its unnatural shade drawing back in fear.

The machine moved.

The Krotes gathered across the harbor gasped. *This is the first time they've seen magic,* Lenora thought. She was the only one here, other than the Mages, who had been alive during the Cataclysmic War. These other Krotes were fifth- or sixth-generation descendants of those who had fled Noreela, tall or short, dark-skinned or light, the blood flowing in their veins merged with that of the many tribes they had found on Dana'Man and its satellite islands. They were fighters, warriors, true to the Mages and faithful in their pledges. But they had only ever heard of magic, never seen it. Never *touched* it.

Lenora looked around at her captains and saw their fear, and realized that this was a defining moment in the history of the land. Everything had changed when the Mages caught the boy, took his magic and stripped his soul, and now that change was about to envelop the whole of Noreela. What she did now would dictate her own part in that change, and what would follow.

Lenora walked forward, approaching what she perceived to be the front of this machine. As she drew closer she saw that it had the semblance of a face. She closed her eyes and took a deep breath. When she opened them again, the machine was staring at her.

It had several eyes, placed at various points around its bulbous head. Two of them were looking at her. It was too dark to see their color, but she knew that they were not the eyes of a hawk. She lifted her chin and glared back.

The machine lowered itself, stone underside settling on the ground, and Lenora climbed onto its back. It stank of something more elemental than scorched flesh. It smelled, Lenora realized, of magic.

She sat astride the machine's back and rested her hands on two bony protuberances on either side of its head. *Stand*, she thought, and the machine raised itself on several stone legs. It shivered beneath her, the vibrations traveling up her thighs and into her stomach. It gave a strange sexual quality to her fear, tingling her skin and causing her old wounds to ache as if craving the knife, the blade, the arrow once again. *Walk*, she thought, and the machine took its first hesitant steps. She could feel its inner workings throbbing beneath her: no heartbeat, but something that felt like a fire being stoked; no breathing, but gasps as gas was blown out and air sucked in. *Turn*, and the machine paused at the edge of the harbor, a step away from tumbling into the sea, and rotated to face her Krotes.

The Mages watched. Even S'Hivez seemed to be smiling.

Lenora sensed the power at work beneath her. This was not just a thing of stone and flesh and blood, it was also imbued with the Mages' magic, awash with a deadly potential that she had yet to realize. The possibilities were thrilling. *Fire*, she thought, and a ball of flame formed from one of the machine's mouths. She held it there, its roaring echoed by the gasps from the assembled warriors. Then she turned the machine and flung the fire far out to sea. It seemed to burn even as it sank, and for a few seconds the whole harbor's surface was illuminated from beneath.

My gods, she thought, *what have you created?*

Lenora turned the machine and stood on its back, and from there she could see right across Conbarma's waterfront. Every surviving Krote—almost fifty of them—and the Mages were watching her. She felt the power in that, and smiled.

Angel smiled back.

"There's work to be done!" Lenora said. "More machines to be built, more preparations to make. The sun has fled, and the twilight it's left behind will be filled with the death cries of Noreela. This is your time: the time you've lived for from the moment you became Krotes." She paused, looked down at the head of the machine with its mad eyes and slavering mouths. "I once saw the northern shores of Noreela awash with blood, and that memory has always been bitter, because the blood was my own. Now it's time to stain the land again, this time with its own blood. Noreela will fall; there's no doubt of that. It's the manner of that fall I look forward to seeing."

More fire, she thought, and the machine formed several balls of flame and sent them to hover above the heads of the Krotes.

The warriors cheered, the fire reflected in their eyes. Lenora walked the thing among them, letting them reach out and touch its cool stone and cooler flesh. The fires faded, but in the twilight they all became familiar with this thing that would help them win the war.

Lenora smiled at Angel and S'Hivez, and she saw that they were pleased.

Chapter 2

ALISHIA KNEW THAT she was dreaming, yet she could feel the books coming to life.

Her stroll through the library seemed to last forever. She could not recall where she had begun, and she had no inkling of where she was going. There were only walls of books. There was no ceiling, only hazy heights where the weird light that suffused the air at ground level faded away into a colorless dusk. Beneath her feet there was the ground: stone and dust here; worn timber boarding there. She had passed through one book-formed alley where the ground was comprised of uprooted grave markers laid flat. She had knelt and touched the carved stone, but the engravings had been in a language she did not know, all the names strange to her. Beside these markers, the book spines revealed intimate histories of the unknowns buried there. *A Moment on the Road for Shute,* one read. *A Thought in a Cave at Whimple,* said another. She had run her fingers along the worn spines, but she dared not remove a book and start reading in case she became trapped in one moment forever.

Sometimes the stacks were built straight and tall, and they

converged in the distance until it almost looked as though they were touching. Perhaps if she walked fast enough she would reach a point where the walls met, spines converging, pages overlapping, and then she would become one more tome of history in this vast place.

At times, the giant shelves seemed ready to fall. They curved left and right, tilted outward or inward, and on several occasions she found herself moving through a tunnel of books, stacks meeting just above her head, histories propping one another up, and she wondered what would happen were she to remove a book. Would it cause a whole wall to tumble down upon her? Would it start a fall throughout the library, burying her and re-sorting history into a random mixture of old books and new, good and bad? Would it destroy order?

She thought not. And dwelling on this she realized that there *was* no order around her, only assembled chaos. The books were not sorted into sections; they were random. There were occasional groupings—such as those applying to the owners of the grave markers—but as Alishia fingered her way along the assembled spines, these soon blended into other areas, other times. A kiss became a turning wheel became the one-hundred-and-seventeen-thousandth stolen thought of a skull hawk's life. This was history built as it had been made, like a collection of random thoughts in a mind too huge to contemplate.

And they were coming to life. Alishia had known this for a while—in the confused memory of her walk through this place, the exact instant of knowing was obscured—but it did not frighten her, and it did not surprise her. All her life she had known that books were living things, not just a convergence of concept and ink, intellect and paper. They did not breathe or think, but they grew and gave a sense of potential so much larger than whatever was written on their pages. She had often lain awake in her room at the edge of Noreela City and tried to imagine one book in her own darkened library, what it looked like at that moment with no one there to view it, how the words read with no one there to read them. Its pages would be closed and the spaces between leaves dark and inscrutable, but the words were still there, telling their truths and hinting at so much more. Sometimes she believed that true magic could only take place with no one there to see it. Her own interaction with a book would change it, and someone else reading it would alter it yet again. That idea had always disturbed her, yet she kept it alive. Like a person, only a book could ever really know itself.

She walked past a wall of books with instants in time on their spines, illustrated with hastily drawn pictures from a child's hand. The books seemed to shift in her view, as if rearranging themselves every time she blinked, though the spines always told the same story. She could feel the history behind the books, and she wondered whether she could remove one from the shelves and peer through the gap into a time she had never known. But in all this dreaming she had yet to open a one, and she felt that there was a special moment ahead. A special moment, and a special book.

Alishia moved on, and the books began to turn into something more. Their power spilled around them, exuding potential like slicks of light, hazing the air and causing Alishia to wave her hands before her face to find her way through. Her hands and arms disturbed drifting moments of history, and she suddenly knew them: a Mourner, chanting down the wraiths of a whole village and fearing something that lived in a hole in the ground; a man and woman journeying into the depths, passing through new cities and entering older places; a young boy standing on a cliff somewhere in the west and looking out at the forest of masts spiking the sea's horizon. Each image was imbued with the emotion of the moment, and Alishia went from fear to excitement to angst in the space of several seconds. She closed her eyes and ran.

She crossed her arms and held her hands beneath her armpits, but experiencing these spilled moments was nothing to do with touch.

Alishia stopped then, dropping to the worn timber floor, realizing suddenly where she was: this was a dream, and she was floating in Noreela's rich and varied history. She was awash with it. She could walk forever, but she would find no walls. She could try to climb the stacks, but she would not find their summits, because they probably rose endlessly. Every truth lay here, every event, every lie and deceit and murder and rape, every meaningless moment and whispered oath lost to the winds of time, and if she wandered forever, perhaps she would know it all. History tumbled down around her and became the air of this dream library, and each time she breathed in she knew something more.

Knowledge had always been Alishia's drug, and she closed her eyes and breathed deep.

But something was wrong. Beyond her dream the world had changed forever; something bad had come into the land. She could remember seeing Rafe taken out of the flying machine by the Mages. She could still feel the blast of heat and light in her mind that his going had inspired, and she was beginning to realize that, in a very real way, she was a vital part of this dream library. Alishia could wander here forever and never find what she was looking for, but she was not simply a visitor. This was not a random dream brought on by recent events. She was the librarian.

She gasped and awoke back into the dream. Reality had been drawing her away, and a sensation of cold came in from some-where. She stood and shook her head. To her left the alley between book stacks curved away, disappearing. To her right, it opened out into a wide reading area. There were several tables and a dozen chairs, all with worn wood and upholstery frayed by years of use . . . or neglect.

Alishia frowned, hating the idea of that. There were books lying open on tables, but she was not sure whether they had been placed there, or whether they had simply fallen from stacks and dropped open.

She walked into the reading area, and as she left the space be-tween stacks she saw the shape sitting in the far corner. Cliffs of books rose on all sides, and the light here seemed subdued. She had no idea of the source of this light, but something seemed to swallow it. The book stacks were a deep red, as though smeared with blood that had long since dried. The floor was dusty, but the dust seemed to move. The shape sat in a deep, wide chair, almost swallowed by the soft padding, and in its lap rested a heavy book. The cover was made of polished wood, the binding sewn with horse's hair, and the figure turned the heavy pages one by one.

It was not reading the book. It was staring at Alishia. Its eyes glinted as it blinked; she knew that it was reading her.

Get out of my library, she said in her dream, and her skin turned cold.

Already found what I need, a voice said. The figure was still turning pages. It was almost halfway through the thick book now, and it must have been sitting there for hours waiting for her. *This no longer means anything to me.* It looked down at the book and its hands grew still, one supporting the tome, the other laid flat on the open page.

Alishia stepped closer and saw that the page was blank. She knew that they were all blank. Unlike everything else in the library, nothing came from this book, and it held no weight.

Where did you get that? she asked.

The figure looked up at her and something happened to the light. Its source—invisible and mysterious—shifted, and she could make out more of the thing's face. Its features were rugged and beautiful, skin rough and attractive, and its eyes held the weight of ages. *I brought it with me,* it said. *It's a new history, whose truth is yet to be forged.* It stood up, and cool blue flames seeped from the book in its hands.

Alishia stepped back. She felt coolness on her skin again, a tingle on her cheek and down her left arm. The fire flowed out from the book, flaring to the floor and seeping between old floorboards, lighting the space below. Alishia dropped to her knees and pressed her face to the pitted timber. *It'll spread,* she thought, *it'll move down there, it'll* flow, *and everywhere and everywhen it touches will be destroyed.* She looked through a knothole and saw the dark space beneath illuminated by the new blue fire. Shadows danced, and they seemed to be growing closer, rising quickly from whatever depths they had been banished to.

Alishia sat up and stared at the strange figure. *How dare you!* she said.

It shrugged. And then it threw the book.

The flaming tome of blank pages struck the book stacks and exploded. Each page drifted somewhere different, the fire writing its own fiery truth on the stark white blankness. The conflagration suddenly turned from cold blue to blazing orange. Books erupted into flame, fire licked its way between covers and into the dark spaces between pages, and old truths went up in smoke, casting ash into the air and disintegrating when her panicked gaze fell upon them.

No, she thought. *This can't be happening. I won't let it happen again! This is my library, and there's so much more to know . . .*

A wall of books tumbled and spilled toward her, and the figure laughed as it ran away. The books struck her, but the impact did not hurt. Fire roared from their dry interiors and caressed her face, but

there was no pain, and she walked through the flames to the space
between stacks. She ran from the flames and they reached after her,
though they had no effect.

As the librarian of this place, Alishia was after all still just an
idea.

———

AS SHE BEGAN to wake up, Alishia could smell the mysterious
scent of Kang Kang on the breeze. Floating somewhere between
dream and reality she sensed the acidic tang, turned left and fell
into a wall of shelving. She closed her fist around a spine and pulled
out the book. It thrummed in her hand, begging to be opened, and
she knew that its insides were crawling with the mysteries of that
mountainous place. She was afraid of Kang Kang. She did not want
to open the book. The smell hinted at memories that would come
flushing back, but they were not her own. They were the memories
of the land.

"Got to keep them closed," she whispered.

"Open your Mage-shitting eyes!" a voice said. Alishia looked
around, ducking low to avoid the smoke that was rapidly filling the
library.

"Kang Kang," she said, squeezing the book in her hand.

"Almost," the other voice said. "I can smell its wrongness from
here."

The fire suddenly retreated, the smoke cleared from her lungs
and Alishia sat up and opened her eyes.

"Ahh," the second voice said. "The sleeper awakes."

"Hope," Alishia said.

The witch was sitting beside her, wild hair pointing at the dusky
sky as if berating it. "I just know I'll grow to hate the irony of that
name."

Alishia looked around. She saw Kosar sitting a few steps away
with his back to them, head bowed. Closer, on her left, Trey was
kneeling and smiling at her, though the smile was dark in his eyes.
There was no Rafe. There was no A'Meer. Of course not. That was
finished now. A'Meer was dead and Rafe was gone. She wondered
how long ago the flame of destruction had been lit in the land.

She looked up and saw the death moon hanging heavy and fat.
It gave light, but she did not like the feel of it on her skin: it reminded

her of the light of those library flames. The darkness seemed false and unreal. Wrong.

"Where are we?" she said. "What . . . ?" She trailed off, noticing the shattered ribs of the great machine that had borne them aloft. Beyond them, shadows lay close to the ground. They were no longer moving.

"We came down," Hope said. "The machine faded and we came down."

"My face," Alishia said. She touched her cheek and it was warm, not cool. Her arm still tingled. She wondered whether she had been burned in her dream.

"Sorry," Hope said, sounding anything but. "I slapped and shook you to wake you up. You were screaming and shouting, and there's no saying what's out there to hear. Besides, you've been asleep too long."

"What's too long?"

"Almost a day," Trey said.

Alishia looked at the fledge miner, smiling, and was grateful to see the smile returned. His eyes were wider than she had ever seen them. She supposed this subdued light suited him well. "It was sunset when we left the machines' graveyard," she said. She looked up, and though she saw no sign of the sun smearing the horizon, still it did not appear to be fully dark. The weak light was flat and unnatural, like the light in the library of her dream.

"It's about that time again now," Trey said. "But . . ." He trailed off, sketching in the dust with his finger.

"They took Rafe," Alishia said. "He's gone. He's dead."

"He's not dead!" Hope snapped.

Alishia closed her eyes and felt the weight of what he had left her. It was an alien presence in her mind, contained yet filled with potential. It shied away from the dark. The more she sought it, the farther away it seemed to go, as if scared of what it would see through her eyes.

"He is dead," she said, "and the magic he carried has been stolen."

"He *can't* be dead!" Hope said. She shook her head and looked at each of them in turn; Alishia, Trey, Kosar's back. "It *can't* just end like this."

"The Mages turned the sky dark," Trey said. "We flew south for a while, then the machine just seemed to lose its power. It drifted lower. Its ribs started to crack and crumble. The ground shook. We dragged you into the center and sat there, and we landed here a little while ago." He continued shaping dust and stones with his hand, as though building something new.

"But it's dead," Kosar said. It was the first time the big thief had spoken, and though he stood he did not turn around. He was staring out between two of the cracked ribs that had protected them for a while, silhouetted against the pale yellow light of the death moon. "It brought us down gently, but died the second it touched the ground. It's not a machine anymore. It's a lump of mud and rock that doesn't belong here, and *we* don't belong here, either. I don't think we belong anywhere in Noreela."

"There's always hope," the witch said. Alishia did not like the look in her eyes. There was madness there, just below the surface, a madness that seemed to shift and shape the witch's spiraling tattoos.

"Hope has gone," Kosar said. He turned around and looked at Alishia, but there was no interest in his eyes. He came closer and sat beside Trey, his movements weary and slow. "If there ever was hope, it was in that boy. Rafe. That poor boy."

"We can't be so sure he's dead," Hope said. "Why would they kill him? Why would the Mages come so far just to take him away and kill him?"

"They wanted what he had inside," Alishia said.

"Of course they did," Hope said. "Magic. But by killing him—"

"It was *inside* him, Hope," Alishia said. "Not really a part of him. Disconnected, a thing waiting to be born, and they opened him up and took it out."

"Opened him up," Kosar said, staring down at his feet.

"And how can you know all this?" Hope said. Her voice was rising, aggression showing through, and Alishia knew that the witch was terrified.

"You know how I know, Hope. You all do." She looked at her hands, held them up to the sky to catch some of the weak moonlight. "I'm getting younger," she said.

"It's that *thing* inside you," Hope said. "That *shade*. It's *you* who ensured that he'd die, you know."

"That thing's not inside me anymore."

"How can we know that?"

"Because I'm telling you."

"And you expect us to trust you?"

"I expect nothing, but I hope you do." Alishia closed her eyes. "I had a dream," she said.

"What sort of dream?" Trey came close and touched her arm, and Alishia was so grateful for the contact that she almost cried. She smiled at Trey and leaned toward him, the movement speaking volumes.

"Bad dreams," Alishia said. "As though I have something priceless that I can't look after forever."

"This is all so fucking pointless," Kosar said quietly.

They fell silent, and in the distance Alishia heard a skull raven calling into the darkness. She wondered what it had found sleeping, whose dreams it may be stealing and whether there was a volume in her dream library that would contain the knowledge of its victim.

She relished Trey's touch, yet something felt so wrong about her body. She wondered if he could perceive that simply by touching her. She was not hungry, for a start, and her throat was not dry, and she did not need to urinate. They said she had been asleep for a whole day. The dream felt like a lifetime, but her body seemed not to notice. She was growing younger, and the tide of time seemed to be changing with her.

"It's not pointless," Alishia whispered at last. None of them answered—Trey merely squeezed her hand tighter—so she went on. "I've dreamed, Kosar, of something vast and priceless and in danger. That something is in me, and it wasn't in me before. And I just know it's from Rafe. He knew he was going to die. Perhaps he'd known right from the beginning. And it was his last act of defiance to pass it to me, because he knew he was also passing along his last scrap of hope."

"So magic is fucking with us," Kosar said. "It seeds itself in Rafe, dooms him to die, then passes itself to you. But it kills A'Meer in the meantime, and leaves us to sit and rot here. Lets itself be taken by the Mages and twisted into whatever they want. That's good. That's all good."

"Magic lets nothing happen," Alishia said. "Rafe told us that. It was so young, so passive, it was fighting to stay alive. But there's so much below the surface of things that we can never see or understand, and I think what Rafe passed into me was an idea. A knowledge that only I can carry."

"Why only you?" Hope said, and the envy in her voice was obvious.

"Because I'm a librarian," Alishia said.

Hope laughed. It was a horrible sound, loud and guttural. The skull raven called again in the distance, as if in response.

"Something's wrong with me," Alishia said. Trey shuffled closer until she felt the heat of his flesh. "Trey, something's wrong, and I know it's all going to end so soon."

"It's ended already," Kosar said. "Noreela will change, that's for certain, and anyone they do leave alive will have to change along with it."

"But I'm trying to tell you, Kosar, that there's hope in me."

"What sort of hope? Magic?"

Alishia shook her head, but she knew that was neither right nor wrong. "Not magic, but a route there."

"How do you pretend to know this?"

"It's what I feel. It's what Rafe told me before he was taken. I don't know; this is all so *strange* to me. All I know is I have dreams, and something unnatural is happening to me. There's a reason behind that, and hope within it."

Kosar stared at her for a few heartbeats, his eyes unwavering. "The land has turned stranger than ever, and now you've turned too. I don't believe a word."

"You've given up."

The thief looked down at his hands, touching fingertips together as if welcoming the pain.

"Then perhaps I'll go to Kang Kang on my own," Alishia said.

"Kang Kang?" Trey said.

"It's where the machine was taking us."

"We were heading south," Hope said, "but that's not to say we were going *there*. Nobody wants to go *there*."

Alishia tried to stand but her legs were weak, her muscles fluid. Trey was by her side, helping her up instead of telling her to sit down. She leaned against him, her arm around his shoulder, his around her waist, and looked south. The landscape faded into darkness, but even against the dark sky she thought she could make out the jagged teeth of mountains on the horizon. They were low down, barely visible, yet she was certain she could see Kang Kang. The sight made her cold, but still she heard its call.

"I need to be there," she said. "There's something there, a place where I'll be safe, and maybe—"

"There's nowhere safe on Noreela anymore!" Kosar said, standing and kicking at the ground. He turned away, passing between two shattered ribs of the failed machine and walking out into the long grass.

Alishia wanted him to stop and turn back, sigh, shake his head, admit that he may be wrong and she may be right. But he became a shade in the poor light, and just before he faded from view she saw him sit and merge with the shadows gathered on the ground.

———

THE MAGES MADE more machines.

Lenora's concerns about their strength were unfounded, for each new act of creation seemed to make them stronger.

They dragged rock up from the ground with a flick of their wrists, molded it, dipped it into the sea or brought the water up onto the harbor to cool and cast it into shape. Some of the remaining hawks were slaughtered and their flesh and blood put to use, clothing the machines and lubricating the joints between the stone limbs. Angel used metal from the frontage of one building to cast one machine, giving it spikes and barrels to shoot forth stones and molded metal balls when it was brought to life. S'Hivez broke down a storage hut and used the timber to make a spiderlike construct that would carry its rider low to the ground, its many legs making it fleet. The stench of magic hung across the harbor. Each time a machine was completed a nervous Krote was called forward, connected to that machine as Lenora had been attached to her own, and then they mounted and rode along the harbor wall. Unnatural silhouettes were splayed across the water, cast by the weak light from the taverns and other buildings along the harbor.

The creation went on for a long time. Angel and S'Hivez made the first few machines together, merging ideas and raw materials to make several similar constructs: four legs, tall as a Krote, fire vents and slots that could eject sharpened discs. Then Angel suddenly jumped into the harbor, sinking beneath the water and raising a wave that crashed against the mole. When she lifted herself back out on a column of steam, she drew a ruined ship up from the depths along with her. Its timbers bent to her will: its rusted metal twisted and shed its coating. Ropes and chains swirled about her head, and she clothed her new machine in a dead hawk's hide. It seemed a mess, but when she motioned a Krote across and joined her with the new machine, its ropes began to whip and its chains to flail.

The Krote stood on the thing's back and urged it toward a timber house at the harbor's edge. In the space of a few heartbeats, the house was in ruins.

As Angel moved on to another creation, the waterfront was soon lit by various fires as the Krotes experimented with their weapons of war. A couple of buildings erupted into flames, but mostly the warriors kept the fire to themselves, learning how to manipulate their machines' limbs, bodies or other parts — juggling flame, swiping with cutting things, becoming accustomed to the poison vents in their mounts' hides or the places where discs and arrows could be loaded and ejected. The whole scene was cast onto the water as grotesque, dancing shadows.

Lenora walked her own machine amongst her Krotes, already comfortable with how it felt beneath her, and how she could touch its most basic mind with her own. But this was far different from the hawks, she realized. This thing was not really alive. It had not evolved or grown out of nature: it had been created, and it had no purpose other than to follow her bidding. It would not require food or water, sleep or rest. Lenora thought back to the final days of the Cataclysmic War. The Mages' machines had been mighty, but there had been something missing from them that was already evident in these new constructs: a spark of consciousness. The war machines of old, driven by magic though they were, had relied on their riders to initiate every move, gears and magical power routes cast into their bodies and often subject to fault or damage. Now these new machines were part construct, part animal. They had the stone and metal, flesh and blood of the old machines, but these conjoined elements were more than just building blocks; they made the machines whole.

The Mages had twisted their new magic even further than before.

———

WITH EVERY KROTE now riding a new machine, Conbarma was in ruins. Much of the harbor had been torn up, buildings were leveled, traces of hawk flesh lay across the ground and the sky itself seemed to be burning from the fires erupting around the town. The Krotes were reveling in this new experience, and the Mages seemed content with that.

Lenora maneuvered her machine in front of a tall, striding thing and questioned the Krote sitting high above her. "Have you seen the Mages?"

"No, Mistress."

Lenora frowned and looked around. The fires lit the sky and deepened shadows. Every Krote was now mounted on his or her machine, and there was no sign of anyone walking.

"Mistress . . . I never knew it would be like this."

Lenora looked up at the Krote. He was young, tall and dark-skinned, only slightly scarred by battle. "What *did* you think it would be like?"

He shook his head. "I had no idea. I'd heard all the stories, read the histories, but this is such *power*." He lowered his voice and leaned closer, as if that would hide his next comment. "How can the Mages give all this to us?"

"They've given us nothing," Lenora said. "Only a taste of what they have. We control the machines, not the magic that made them. Never forget that."

"But I can *feel* it!"

"*Never* forget that!" Lenora said again, harsher than she had intended.

The young Krote's eyes flickered down, then he looked at her again and nodded. "Mistress."

"Now go on your way. I'll be issuing a call to meet soon enough. Practice with your mount. Get its feel, discover its movement and limitations, if it has any." She examined the machine, trying to make out details in the flickering light. "It's tall, so it should be a good runner. And those legs are barbed and sharp. You'll be able to cut down our enemies like fields of corn."

"I've never seen corn," he said.

"You will."

She saw the Mages then, emerging from between two squat stone buildings farther along the harbor. They watched the Krotes, and though they were illuminated by various dancing fires, still there was a darkness between them, darker than twilight and immune to the fires shining from a dozen different angles. Even from this far away, Lenora could see the twinkle of Angel's eyes, but the shadow hanging at her side gave away nothing.

Lenora steered her machine their way, walking slowly to match their pace. S'Hivez stared up at her, his expression unchanging, and it took only heartbeats for her to avert her gaze.

"It's quite an army we're building here," Angel said.

"Unbeatable," Lenora said.

"Of course." Angel nodded and stared at her lieutenant. Her face was young, the skin barely marked by time, and she seemed to glow with some inner truth only just discovered.

What the fuck is that? Lenora thought. The air between the Mages seemed to belong somewhere else. It was dark and calm, untouched by fire or moonlight, but flowing with its own particular threads of illumination.

"A soul unborn," S'Hivez said. "Aborted by nature and cast aside."

"It's a shade," Lenora whispered. The thing held no real shape, though occasionally it seemed to find form for a few heartbeats. Each form was familiar but unrecognizable, as though Lenora was viewing dreams long forgotten.

"It's part of a shade that we've brought into the world," Angel said. The shadow slipped around her shoulder and down her front, pooling at her feet. "We're leaving this with you, Lenora. Soon S'Hivez and I must go, but there's a lot more work to be done for our main army's arrival. There are plans to be made, and machines to be built, and—"

"Why are you going?" Lenora said.

"Don't question our actions," Angel said, her voice low and even.

Lenora looked down at her hands. The machine settled slightly below her, as if it too was cowed by the Mage's words. "Mistress."

"We have our reasons, just as we have reasons for leaving this shade. It has a touch of our magic. Just a touch, but enough to draw up machines and carry on our work."

"I could do it," Lenora said. The Mages were silent, so she continued. "I could give life to the machines, make our army. With magic." Her words terrified her, but to have even a *hint* of what they had, an *echo* . . .

I could help my child, she thought. Her daughter's shade, floating out there somewhere, abandoned and never alive. *What I could do with that!*

S'Hivez growled.

"We're here to fight a war with Noreela," Angel said. If she knew what Lenora had been thinking, she gave no sign. "If we hand magic to any living thing, that thing becomes our enemy."

"I would never—"

"You wouldn't be able to help yourself." Angel and S'Hivez started to walk away, leaving the shade flexing its shadows across the ground.

"Is that it?" Lenora said.

Angel glanced over her shoulder and smiled. "Almost. Watch."

The Mages parted and paused at the entrance to a road leading into the heart of Conbarma. The Krotes had seen their approach and quietly moved away, giving the Mages room to work. There was a sense of anxiety in the air, a promise of change.

Angel and S'Hivez knelt and pressed their hands into the ground. The rock there quickly began to glow, radiating burnt orange spears of light which arced across Conbarma and sizzled out in the darkness. They crawled backward on their knees, increasing the distance between them and enlarging the spread of boiling rock. The surface broke into liquid, and a bubble rose to the surface and burst, sending molten stone pattering down around S'Hivez. He seemed unconcerned, and if any of the lava touched him, it caused no wound.

Farther back, farther, and when the Mages eventually stood and brought their hands from the ground, they left a pit of fire fifty steps across. Angel glanced back at Lenora and smiled. "From here, the shade will raise machines," she said.

She and S'Hivez left the lava pit and approached an area of open ground where the mole was rooted into the mainland. It was here that Angel had first touched Noreelan soil after three hundred years in exile, only two days before but seemingly an age ago. *How slowly time passes*, Lenora thought, *without day or night to mark it.*

The Mages touched the ground again, but this time they hauled rocks up and out without melting them, piling them around the perimeter of the excavation, deepening the hole with every touch. It took only a dozen heartbeats and then they moved back again, S'Hivez's shoulders sagging as if the effort had tired him.

Angel came back to where Lenora still sat astride her machine. "And that," she said, "is the flesh pit. It needs filling, Lenora, before the shade can get to work. It has a touch of magic, but still it needs raw materials."

"Will that thing listen to me?" Lenora asked.

"Shades take no orders from anything alive. But we've ensured that it knows its purpose."

Lenora looked at the shadow low to the ground, like a wound on reality. "You control it?" she asked. *Is that what my daughter is now?* she thought.

"We gave it a promise," Angel said. "There are many like that one, and they will work for us across Noreela. We'll give them what they crave, in time."

"Life?"

Angel grinned, and her smile was one that Lenora wished never to see again. "Is there an element of personal interest in this conversation?"

"My interest is to serve you, Mistress."

"Then build me my army, Lenora, and do to Noreela what it did to us so long ago." Then Angel and S'Hivez departed, melting away into shadows cast by looming buildings.

Lenora steered her mount between two burning houses. She found a curved alley, emerging into a shadowed courtyard lit only by the sickly light of the death moon. The place seemed undisturbed since their landing here a couple of days before. There was a long table that had been set for a meal, though the food had never been served, and birds or other creatures had tumbled the bottles of rotwine that had been opened and left to breathe. Yet even here there was evidence that Noreela had moved on. It was apparent in the way the moonlight struck the plates, shadows stalked from beneath the table and plants drooping from wall baskets seemed to be shedding their tiny leaves. A few floated to the ground as Lenora watched, fluttering at the air like dying beetles. Noreela belonged to the Mages now, and the dusk they had brought down across the land was their first brand of ownership.

Lenora stepped from her machine and walked to a chair that had been tipped over. She righted it, sat and began to shake. Her skin was warm, her head clear, and yet she could not prevent the shivers passing through her from toes to scalp, left hand to right. She sat on her hands and bent low, as if presenting less of a target would fool the shivers into leaving. She mumbled a plea to the twilight, trying to ignore the smells of heated flesh and fresh magic that wafted in from the harbor. Such stenches flashed old memories in her mind: the beaches of The Spine, Noreelan war machines cutting down Krotes left and right, the wounds she had received and the gouge to her shoulder delivered by a machine walking on legs of fire. Her flesh burning . . . the magic, ripe and rich in the Noreelan that sought to kill her, its sickly sweet smell . . .

"Oh by the Mages, what's wrong with me?" she whispered, and her tears startled her. She shook her head and watched them speckling the ground.

Not long to wait, a voice said.

Angel knew of her lost child; perhaps she had known forever. Did she suspect that Lenora would betray their cause for her own petty revenge? Was that why the Mages had given her their army, as bribery to stay?

Was she really that important to them?

"I *will* avenge you," she said. Though her voice was quiet, it was firm. "But not yet. I have duties."

It's cold, I hurt, I can never have you back, the voice said, and there was the truth, that muttered phrase from a thing that had never had the chance to live.

"I can never have you back, either," Lenora said. "Not even if I go to Robenna and kill everyone there, all the descendants of those bastards who whipped me from the village, poisoned me and slaughtered you in my womb before you'd even drawn a breath or given me a smile. I can never have you back."

But I can feel better, the voice whispered.

Lenora nodded. "And so can I." Her memories of Robenna were so vague as to be little more than faded dreams, but there was one image that presented itself to her again and again: a house on stilts, a stream running beneath it and a tall man in a white robe standing on its balcony, watching her being whipped with poison-tipped sticks as the villagers drove her out. Pregnant out of wedlock: that had been her crime. The man watched, and perhaps it was only her fervent dreams of revenge that put pity in his eyes. He had been the village chieftain, and the father of her child.

"I need no fucking pity," she said to this silent courtyard, over three hundred years and four hundred miles away. And she closed her eyes, imagining the man's robe turning red as he was hacked to shreds.

————

A NOISE FROM the harbor shocked her from her daydream. Lenora stood and looked around, glancing at shadows as they seemed to dart away. Dreams, fading into the Mages' dusk.

Another roar sounded, so deep that it vibrated the ground at her feet. Her machine did not move, but two of its eyes glittered as it watched her. She ignored them—there could surely be no expression there—mounted and urged it upright. The shakes were gone now, and her eyes were dry. Perhaps dreaming of revenge could melt away the tears.

She steered the machine from the courtyard, through the alley and out between the two burning buildings, and then she saw what had made the sound.

Both Mages stood on the mole that stretched out across the mouth of the harbor. They were constructing another machine, but this was larger than anything they had made yet. Twice the size of the largest hawk Lenora had ever seen, it seemed to float above the choppy waters, held upright on thick columns of steam. Angel and S'Hivez worked their hands into and around the rock, twisting and molding it to their needs, pumping fresh magic into this miraculous creation. The rock dipped and a roar of steam sent ripples across the harbor. It rose again, the Mages went back to work, then the surface of the water began to bubble and burst as dozens of sea creatures were sucked from beneath. Fish, octopus, a foxlion, shelled creatures and something five times the size of a Krote with more teeth than skin—they all flapped through the air and landed on the red-hot machine, melting into it as the Mages manipulated their flesh and scales, bones and teeth, adding to their creation every second.

Wings sprouted from its sides, one pointing inland at Noreela, the other stretching above the wilder waters beyond the mole. Eventually, with the machine complete, Angel and S'Hivez cast it down into the waters to cool into its final shape.

When it rose again, they mounted its huge back, and it lifted them high above Conbarma.

"There's so much left to do," Lenora muttered.

The monstrous flying machine flapped its wings, sending clots of flaming feathers groundward.

"Where do I start?"

It rose higher and higher, and soon it was simply one shadow among many. Even the light from the moons failed to reveal its bulk.

Now we are both alone, her child's voice whispered, and Lenora shook her head.

"Mistress?" a Krote said.

Lenora looked at her warriors mounted on their machines of war. They looked intimidating, terrifying, lost.

"Mistress, what now?"

"Now," Lenora said, "I need you to find a stock of rotwine and food. Post sentries at the town's perimeter, but the rest of you will drink and eat with me, and we'll plan the days ahead."

Lenora smiled, suddenly eager for the fight. And quietened the voice in her mind, telling it there was all the time in the world.

Chapter 3

AS HE APPROACHED another nameless village, Lucien Malini was hoping for a fight. Terribly wounded though he was from the battle at the machines' graveyard, still he relished the prospect of wetting his sword again. His skin raged red.

The battle in the graveyard was a day behind him, and with every breath since then he had known that the Mages had won. Magic was back, they had taken it for themselves, and yet blood pumped through his veins, clotting around his wounds, drawing rent flesh back together, stiffening fractured bones, feeding on the rage that was stronger than ever before. In the constant, unnatural twilight that had marked the Mages' return he felt a sense of cool defeat, but deep down Lucien still had a burning purpose driving him on. He had seen the dead Shantasi melt and flow across the ground, and the implication of what that could mean drove him on. His whole life had been directed toward one purpose. The fact that he still lived, weakened though he was, gave him a sense that could have been hope.

He moved on toward the village. It was a motley collection of

huts and shacks—triangular constructions built low to the ground
to weather the storms blowing in from the Mol'Steria Desert. No
dwelling rose higher than his head, and it was only the contours of
the land that prevented him from seeing right across the village.
That, and the dusky light. It should be dawn—all of his senses suggested that—and yet dusk still clung to the sky. There were no
smudges of the sun hidden behind the clouds, and the death moon
sheened the land with a sickly illumination. In this light, Lucien's
blood was black.

The Mages' first effect on Noreela, with the magic he had sworn
they would never again possess.

From the village came the scrape of metal on stone. Lucien
paused. He could see no movement, but the sound was shifting
slowly from right to left. He tried to silence his breathing but could
not; his injuries were too varied, their effects too harsh.

He could smell death here, but he could sense fear as well. It
was manifest in the silence, the stillness, the way that no door
opened even a crack as he approached the village from the west. In
the light of the death moon the villagers would see him walking
along the rutted road. They would see his sword, his torn cloak and
the wounds that still seeped blood. Some of them might even know
of the Red Monks, and the cause that drove their madness. Yet
today . . .

"Failure tastes bitter," Lucien muttered. He spat a mouthful of
blood onto the road and ground it down into the dust. The scrape of
his boot was loud in the eerie silence hugging this village.

Not even the sound of an animal, a bird, a plant shifting in the
breeze coming in across the desert.

"I don't fear you!" Lucien shouted, blood bubbling heavy and
thick in his chest. He spat again, up at the sky this time, and welcomed the blood pattering down on his face. It gave him back his
color.

The sound of metal on stone came again, from two directions
this time, and below it he could hear something dragging across the
ground, like an echo of his foot grinding blood into the dust.

"We can lose, but you can never win," he whispered. And he
still believed that. Through everything that had happened over the
past few days, he still believed in his cause. He had to. If he lost faith
now, his body would give in. His faith gave him power.

The first shape emerged from behind one of the low houses,

crawling slowly into view. He could not tell whether it was a man or woman. In one hand it seemed to be holding a sword, and its legs were clad in metal. Each time it moved, it moaned.

Another shape crawled toward him out of the darkness. This one held two swords and wore a metallic mask, shiny in places and smeared with blood in others.

The Red Monk stood his ground and hefted his own weapon, but he sensed no fight in these things. They were not coming for him. They were simply moving, because to stay still was to submit to the pain of transformation. As the first shape came closer, Lucien saw that they were not holding swords at all.

Their hands had turned to metal. Legs too, and faces, flesh blurring to silver. And this close he could hear their moans more clearly, tell that somewhere behind that human sound of pain was an inhuman clicking and rattling as things inside milled together.

Lucien could see human eyes moving behind the metal facade of the second shape's face. They held nothing sane.

He stepped back, avoiding these crawling monsters. They must have started changing before the Mages' victory, yet still he blamed the magic. It was the cause of everything wrong in the land, and these travesties were more examples of a bad world growing worse.

Lucien dodged past the half-human things and ran through the village. Here and there he saw a glimmer of metal beside the low dwellings, but he did not pause. As he passed the outskirts he saw the remains of a huge old machine half buried in the ground, and the death moon reflected from fresh breaks in the various metallic limbs. Perhaps it had spread like a disease.

He ran, ignoring the screams of his wounds, and for a long time after he checked himself all over, searching for the first spikes of metal forming from within.

———

THREE HUNDRED YEARS ago, Jossua Elmantoz had helped force the Mages from Noreela and felt magic forsaking the land. Now, crossing the mountain range southeast of Lake Denyah, he knew that they were back. Magic had returned, changing the world into a constant state of twilight. The only explanation for this that made sense was that the Mages once again had magic for themselves. They had found the boy Rafe Baburn and extracted the seed of magic he carried; forced it to bloom to their own calling, twisted it once again to their own desires. The very thing he had spent his long life trying to prevent had happened. He had failed. The Red Monks were lost. They would die and fade into obscurity, reviled and cast as demons, when in reality it was this that they had been striving to prevent all along.

The end of Noreela.

Jossua walked on because there was nothing else for him to do. He still held on to hope, because without hope there was only death. But everything felt empty and pointless, each movement without meaning and every thought existing only to drift away and be lost to history. Nobody would know if he lay down and died in these mountains. He would become food for scavengers. Or perhaps the carrion creatures would eschew his old, rotten meat—too tough for them, too strange—and leave him to rot into whatever the land was becoming.

Noreela would change. The Mages were not here for control or power. This time, they came for revenge.

But his rage roared on. His anger at the Mages, his fury at his own Monks' inability to halt magic's path across the land—a boy, it had only been *one boy*!—drove him onward. That, and the faintest idea that hope could never be fully extinguished.

Something slinked out of the night and came toward him, a wild animal stinking of old dead flesh and growling deep within its throat. Jossua paused and scanned the shadows; his eyes were bad, and dusk stole what vision he still retained. He saw a shadow within shadows, and when it moved it was huge.

The creature growled, and Jossua growled back.

Footsteps scampered away into the night. Jossua growled again, to himself this time, and he relished the sense of fury filling him, flushing his face with blood, singing into his sheathed sword and demanding that something wet its pitted metal.

He continued on toward Kang Kang. His aims were changed now, but his final destination must surely be the same. There was only one place left on Noreela where perhaps he could find answers, and where hope may yet dwell: the Womb of the Land.

And he had a map.

———

KOSAR HAD NEVER felt so wretched. His thoughts lay with A'Meer, and Rafe, and how he had let them both down. He should have remained in those woods with A'Meer, and perhaps together they could have fought their way to the machines' graveyard, covering each other's retreat. And Rafe . . . if Kosar had jumped at his legs and held tighter, or launched himself at the Mage, or fought with no regard for his own life, maybe then the boy could have been saved . . .

He knew that neither of these scenarios would have been possible, yet he played them out perpetually in his mind. He and A'Meer fighting their way through the woods, ducking sword blows from dozens of Monks, jumping from tree to tree and scoring hits without being wounded themselves. A'Meer's face, grim yet determined. Blood splashed on her pale skin. Her dark hair loose from where a Monk's sword had sliced through the band.

If they'd gone toward New Shanti instead of following Rafe's suggestion that had taken them to the graveyard, maybe they would have survived. Kosar sighed. "The Mages would have found us in the open," he whispered. "Come down on their hawks and cut us to ribbons. Or the Monks would have reached us first and slaughtered us out on the plains, or at the edge of the desert. At least back there, we had a chance." He shook his head. *What chance? A chance to follow chance just a little while longer, only to see it snatched away?*

He looked up at the sky. The death moon hung full and heavy, and the life moon skimmed the horizon. Their combined light gave the land a dim illumination, bright enough for Kosar to examine his wounded fingers. They were still bleeding. He used to welcome the pain because it told him that he was still alive. Now the rest of his body hurt more.

"She's asleep again," Trey said.

Kosar jumped. He had not heard the fledge miner approach. "Good."

"You're being unfair to her."

"She's talking Mage shit, Trey. We're beaten. Just look around; you can see that. You may be used to darkness, but we live in daylight up here, and we welcome it."

Trey sat beside him, and Kosar welcomed the companionship. "Last time I traveled with fledge, Alishia exuded the same blankness as Rafe. There was something in her that pushed me away."

"The same as Rafe?" Kosar asked, trying not to sound interested.

"The same. The two of them shared a lot without any of us knowing, of that I'm certain."

"None of us know anything," Kosar said, "other than the fact that the Mages are back. There'll be a second Cataclysmic War, and this time Noreela will lose. They could be gone in ten days, leaving nothing behind but the bodies of every dead Noreelan."

"Is that what you believe?" Trey said.

"I don't know."

"Don't give in so quickly, Kosar. There are the Shantasi! They'll put up a fight, won't they?"

"Against magic that can turn day to dusk?"

Trey was silent for a few moments, staring up at the sky as if to discern the truth in its darkness. "Well, I trust the girl," he said. He rose to walk back to the lifeless machine, but Kosar stood and stopped him.

"If you trust her, tell her to show us something. Rafe brought that boat up out of the river; he cured A'Meer. Tell Alishia to show us something, and maybe I'll believe as well."

"It's not like that," Trey said. "She's not like Rafe. She told me he was never born." He shrugged Kosar's hand from his shoulder and walked away.

Never born, Kosar thought. He did not understand. He wished A'Meer were here, someone he could truly talk to. He sat down again, but this time he looked south toward the mountains. He had been as far as Kang Kang's foothills once, and he'd vowed never to go there again.

"Am I being a coward?" he whispered. "Can I be so wrong?" But the night remained silent, offering no easy answer.

———

RAFE WAS NEVER *born*, Hope thought. *This girl was. And yet she says she's growing younger.* She watched the sleeping girl until Trey rose and went after the thief. Then she shuffled closer. She lay down so that she could feel the girl's heat through her own clothes, and whispered in her ear, "What are you?"

Alishia did not answer, and gave no sign of having heard.

"What are you carrying?"

Still no response. Hope looked after Trey and Kosar, shadows against the darkness. They had their backs to her. The big thief had never trusted her, but she supposed he now believed there was no reason to keep up his guard.

The witch laid her hand on Alishia's forehead. The girl was hot, and a slight shiver passed through her body. Hope closed her eyes and bade magic enter her, but there was nothing, no sense of power or promise or worth. She took her hand away and cursed.

But she's growing younger, Hope's inner voice chimed in, and she nodded. The big thief didn't care, the fledge miner didn't understand and Hope was the only one ready to deal with what this could really mean. *I'll take her wherever she wants to go,* she thought, *because there's something of the boy in her.* Because Rafe was never born. He was the offspring of the Womb of the Land in Kang Kang, just as the old prophecy passed down to her from her mother and grandmother had predicted. And now Alishia wanted to go there, and maybe it was the Womb she sought.

"I'll take you," she whispered in the sleeping girl's ear. "With or without the fledger and the thief, I'll take you into Kang Kang."

Hope lay down beside the girl once again and breathed in some of her stale breath, hoping that Alishia's exhalations would talk to her. But there was nothing.

———

TREY PAUSED AT the edge of the grounded machine and looked in at Alishia and Hope lying together. He was still unsure of the witch. She had seemed as concerned as any of them about Rafe's well-being, but there were signs that she had her own interests at heart as well. He had passed her by several times on his fledge trips, never confident enough to touch on her mind but more than aware of the stew of emotions residing there. Hope was unsure of herself, confused, and her mind was in such conflict that its effects spilled into the air around her. Trey had sensed her confusion, and it worried him.

Now, with Rafe gone and Alishia looking like their final hope, the witch seemed to have found a cause once again. There she was, curled up before Alishia, eyes closed but mind still undoubtedly running away with itself. Trey wondered how he and Kosar figured in her daydreams.

The witch's face flexed, her tattoos merging to cloud her skin.

"Are you asleep?" Trey whispered. Hope did not move, but that meant nothing. He stepped between two of the thick ribs and quietly hefted his disc-sword, slinging it onto his back. He had tried wiping Monks' blood from the blade, but it had stained. The luster had gone from the metal, probably for good, and he hoped that he never had to face another Red Monk. Perhaps next time the blade would be less effective.

He knelt beside Alishia and touched her forehead. He moved her toward him slightly, away from the witch, holding her head up off the ground so that she did not scrape her face. She was warm. Her skin was slick with sweat. He put his ear to her mouth until he could feel the subtle caress of her breath, but she was silent in her sleep. Whatever was going on inside her head remained there, enigmatic as ever.

"Just tell us everything," Trey whispered. "You need Kosar's trust, and you can get that by showing him what you mean. You need Hope's loyalty, and perhaps you'll get that in the same way." He glanced at the witch, and in the twilight her face seemed darker than normal. He moved his hand beneath her nose and felt for her breath, afraid for a moment that she had simply given up on life.

The witch opened her eyes and stared at Trey.

"Throttle me in my sleep, will you?"

Trey snatched his hand back. "Of course not. I was checking that you were all right."

Hope's face relaxed and she looked at Alishia. "Of course you were," she said. "And I'm fine. I was trying to sleep, but my dreams won't let me."

"What do you dream of?"

"Kang Kang," Hope said.

"What of it?" Trey looked past Hope, beyond the fallen machine at the dark peaks on the horizon.

"Alishia says that's our aim, so I'm going to take her."

"So am I," Trey said, committing himself.

"It's a long walk," the witch said, sitting up. "And a dangerous one. Kang Kang's nothing like the rest of Noreela."

Trey tried to read the witch's strange smile, but it barely touched her eyes. It was as if those tattoos swirling across her cheeks and dipping into her mouth had tightened, drawing her cheeks up into a grotesque parody of a grin.

"Trey?"

He looked at her, startled by her unaccustomed use of his name.

"We're on the same side. We may have different ideas of what's happening, and differing reasons for being where we are today, but we're both here for Alishia and whatever she carries, and we're both against the Mages. Anyone in Noreela must be against them, sane or otherwise. There's no alternative. Do you understand?"

Trey nodded, not sure that he did. Was Hope trying to form an alliance with him, or simply confuse him more?

"I'm pleased you want to come to Kang Kang," she said. "We can help each other. As for Kosar . . . I think he's lost to us."

Trey looked at the shadow of the thief. *Maybe,* he thought. *Or maybe he'll do things his own way as well.*

"We need to go soon," the witch said.

"We should wait until she's awake. And I want to try Kosar one more time."

"The thief's doubt and mistrust will cause us trouble," Hope said.

"He's the one who brought us this far."

She raised her eyebrows but did not respond.

She thinks it's her, Trey thought. *She thinks she's the leader of this pathetic little gang.*

Trey went back to Kosar, and all the way he knew what the answer would be. The big man barely glanced up. Even as Trey stated their aim and said they would be moving soon, Kosar only looked at the horizon and nodded. "I'll not be going with you."

"Where will you go?"

"Some corner of Noreela where I can be forgotten."

Trey wanted to say more. He so wished he could think of something stirring and affecting that would make Kosar rethink his decision and join their continuing journey south—something about trust and loyalty, and pursuing any scrap of hope that might still exist. But he followed Kosar's gaze and saw the landscape swathed in unnatural twilight, and he knew that it would not take long for the plants and animals to die.

"I don't think such a corner exists," he said. Then he turned away from the thief and walked back to Alishia and Hope.

———

WHEN KOSAR STOOD and looked back, the others were mere shadows. He could see Trey standing within the fake protection of the dead machine's ribs, and on the ground at his feet Hope and Alishia seemed to be huddled together. There was an implication of ownership in Hope's pose that he did not like. She had been the same with Rafe. *We'll have to watch her,* A'Meer had whispered to him one night, and yet in that final, useless fight, Hope had been as strong as any of them.

He guessed that she missed Rafe more than anyone as well. With him had gone her lifetime of dreams and desires. It was no surprise that she was willing to hang on to any fragment of hope that remained, however false.

Is Alishia really something special? Kosar wondered, and he realized that, yes, she probably was. She was certainly no longer a normal girl, if she ever had been. But he no longer cared. A'Meer was dead, and day was night. *Useless,* he thought. He turned away from Trey, Hope and Alishia and looked east.

He wanted to be on his way. Hope put him on edge, Alishia disturbed him and Trey was somewhere he was never meant to be. The fledger had used the last of his fledge a couple of days before, and already he was showing signs of withdrawal. It was difficult to tell in this weak light, but his skin seemed to be growing a paler yellow, the whites of his eyes clouding with burst blood vessels.

Kosar craved his own company once again, and the idea of wandering Noreela seemed the only thing to do. He would explore, as he had done so long ago. He would find the corner of Noreela that Trey said would not exist, and perhaps he could live out his life there, hidden away from the glare of the Mages' influence.

And if they burn the land? A'Meer asked in his mind. *Send out armies, kill everything, spread disease?*

Kosar shook his head. She had always been so practical. "Leave me alone," he said. "I'll mourn you well enough, but don't start talking back at me, A'Meer."

It's you doing the talking, just using my voice.

"And is that the voice of reason?"

Maybe.

He shook his head again and touched the sword at his side. "Fuck."

A large bird passed overhead—a moor hawk, perhaps—and Kosar watched it drift away in the night. It had flown northeast. With no real idea of where he wanted to go, he decided to follow.

———

A'MEER'S VOICE REMAINED silent as Kosar took his first steps away. He expected guilt to crush him, regret to pick at his limbs and turn him around, but his steps felt fine, his legs surprisingly strong.

Perhaps the last few days had welcomed him back into the life of a traveler once again.

He waited for the shout that would bring him to a halt, but none came. He did not look back. If he turned and saw Trey watching him leave he would have to return, try to explain once again why this was all so hopeless now that Rafe had gone and dusk had fallen. Kosar was a good man, and even though he was finding the going easy, he guessed that guilt was only a step or two behind. He had no wish to let it catch up.

The moor hawk had disappeared into the night but he heard it calling—a doleful, lonely cry. Kosar wondered who or what else could hear it. Trey undoubtedly, and Hope and Alishia if they were awake. But perhaps there were others out there, camping down under the oppressive weight of the night, and the sound of the moor hawk would surely make them feel more isolated and alone than ever. He wondered whether the Red Monks had followed the flying machine on foot, even though their purpose was gone. Perhaps any surviving Monks would be roaming the land, madder than ever before.

He walked on, and in time he was far enough away so that he would not hear Trey even if the fledge miner did call after him. There was scant comfort in this, but beneath that was a sense of betrayal that Kosar did his best to smother. The time would come for that, he knew. Perhaps when he was witnessing the Mages' armies burning villages and towns, raining down destruction from their hawks, riding monstrous new creations across the landscape . . . Perhaps then he would truly taste his own bitter betrayal of the only people he could call friends. Or maybe it would take the imminence of death to bring home his true treachery. Perhaps he would be dying beneath the leather boot of a Krote, staring up along the length of a bloodied spear, before he would truly appreciate how unfair he had been.

I led them here, he thought, and he hated the idea of that. Kosar had always been a loner, not a leader. But Rafe's damned magic had steered and coerced them down the center of Noreela, dangling free will and then snatching it away at every opportunity. They had been driven here like a horse guided by its rider, except that their rider had been acting through the mind of an innocent boy.

Now you're talking Mage shit, A'Meer's voice said. *You led them, and you know it.*

"My words, your voice?" he whispered. The night offered no answer. "Damn, A'Meer, I miss you so much."

Kosar thought about where he could go, and as he began to examine the possibilities, each idea brought buried memories back to life—times and events he had not thought about in years. The experience was strangely comforting, and he enjoyed living these moments again. They were a distraction from the present.

If he carried on in this direction, he would soon come to the Mol'Steria Desert. North of that were the Mol'Steria Mountains and then Sordon Sound, the great inland sea that bordered New Shanti. He had never been as far as the desert, but A'Meer had often told him about it, sitting in the Broken Arm nursing a mug of rotwine as she relayed tales of sand demons and flaming trees, roads of glass and the huge, lumbering grinders that spent their unknowable lives turning rock into sand. It had all sounded so enchanting to him, the seasoned traveler, and he had promised A'Meer that he would go there one day. He'd seen an excitement in her deep, dark eyes as she talked about this place so close to her homeland. And though she denied it, he had always believed that she harbored a secret desire to go home. At the time, he had put her unwillingness to return down to some family problem, or an underlying wanderlust that she had yet to quench. Since then, he had discovered the truth.

Kosar paused and looked ahead. The dusk hid much of the land and turned the rest a pale silver, light from the moons splashing in seemingly isolated patches. There were rolling hills and hidden valleys, a landscape of shadows and shaded peaks, home to anything from a man to a herd of tumblers. The Mages' army could be hiding within five thousand steps of where he was, and he'd have no idea until he stumbled upon it. And with that thought came the very reason he should not head for New Shanti: the Shantasi were the only people likely to raise a serious defense against the Mages, and New Shanti would become a battleground.

Kosar glanced behind him but saw no signs of pursuit.

If he went due east, he would walk into New Shanti across the plains, arriving eventually at Hess, the Shantasi Mystic city. Even before he knew that she was a warrior, A'Meer had told him about her youth spent out on those plains, patrolling the approaches to New Shanti along with others of her age. It was a rite of passage, ten thousand young Shantasi at any one time complementing the Shantasi army that made the plain its home. It was their most vulnerable point, and much of the year she had spent there had been in training for possible attack from the rest of Noreela. Kosar had scoffed at such an idea, but A'Meer had been grim-faced and serious. "Do you have any idea of where the Shantasi come from?" she had asked. Kosar had shaken his head, still trying to maintain his smile but failing beneath A'Meer's glare. "Slavery," she had said, and his image of the thousands of Shantasi children camped across that plain suddenly changed. Freedom was a luxury with a price. The Shantasi paid for freedom with their childhood.

Later, A'Meer's revelation of her true nature—as a Shantasi warrior sworn to find and protect fledgling magic—had altered Kosar's perception of her people even more. Now he imagined them as a fiercely independent race, lost and yet making their home here, on Noreela, and willing to give so much for the ground they had. A'Meer, he supposed, had scared him.

So that way lay New Shanti, and plains swarming with Shantasi youths willing to prove themselves adults. Their chance would come soon, Kosar knew. The Mages would be forming their armies and preparing to march. War was the only certainty in Noreela's future.

Kosar turned away, a sickness punching at his gut. It was shame and self-loathing, but it was also a delayed reaction to what had happened. Fear, biting deep. Guilt, sinking teeth into his insides. He knew that it would never let go. He could walk forever and pass through Kang Kang, into The Blurring that many said lay beyond, and perhaps he would even reach a southern coast that no one had ever seen . . . but guilt would still be there, turning in his gut like a constant sword. A'Meer had died protecting what she thought was right, and now he was running away to save his own skin.

"No!" he said. *Yes. There's nothing heroic here. Nothing symbolic. It's cowardice. I can't face the dark future with others, so I'm trying to do it on my own.*

Trey and Hope think they have a chance to fight the future, A'Meer's voice said.

"They know nothing," Kosar said. It felt strange talking to the dark, but it acted like a mirror, turning his words back on himself. He was talking to his own shadow, berating a solitary shape that stood here in the darkness while Noreela prepared to crumble. He touched his sword and felt sick at the thought of violence. Didn't he have the right to be scared? He was a marked thief, and his fingertips stung as he touched the sword's handle. Any success he'd had fighting the Monks had been a reflection of A'Meer's bravery, skill and determination. He was just a useless wanderer. A middle-aged waster who could not even steal anymore because of his brands. No one trusted him.

A'Meer did, A'Meer's voice said. *And Trey, and Alishia, and Rafe. As for Hope . . . that damn witch trusts no one but herself.*

Kosar closed his eyes and squeezed his fists, grimacing at the pain from his fingers but hoping it would drive A'Meer's voice from his head.

"I'm just hearing things," he said.

And then the ground began to move, and he was seeing things as well.

To begin with, he thought he had something in his eye. He lifted his eyelid and blinked rapidly, trying to expunge the hazing from his vision. Then he closed his eyes, and when he looked again the same effect was there: a blurring of the ground around his feet, as though the grasses and stones had lost their sharp edges. The death moon yellowed the scene and gave the undefined ground a creamy texture, and Kosar suddenly felt sick from the sense of movement.

He fell to his knees and vomited, and when he opened his eyes the ground was alive. It stirred beneath him, parting around the warm puddle between his hands, undulating as though the ground itself had turned fluid. He stood quickly, and for a few seconds he could make out the shapes of his hands in the soil before the shifting surface moved in to cover them.

"Oh fuck," he whispered, because now he knew what these things were, and he remembered the last time he had seen them. They had presented a warning then, forming themselves as Red Monks into which A'Meer had fired several useless arrows. These were mimics. Knowing them, Kosar felt a vast, alien intelligence focusing upon him.

He wanted to run, but he was afraid of stepping on the mimics. Would he hurt them? Would they translate his fear into aggression? He closed his eyes and heard them shifting through grasses, passing over fallen leaves, moving around and beneath small stones, sending up whispers that seemed to blur the air as their bodies blurred the ground. His stomach still churned. He wished A'Meer were here with him.

Kosar tried to perceive a pattern or meaning to their movement.

He could make out no particular direction. It was as though each mimic acted independently, fulfilling its own aim. Whatever communication might pass amongst them seemed to dictate no combined purpose. He wondered if they were eating or sleeping, talking or conspiring, and then the ground broke before him and a shape began to rise.

It formed so quickly that it was fully there before he had time to truly comprehend what he was seeing.

A'Meer stood before him. But this was not A'Meer as he had ever seen her. There was no smile on her pale face, no mischievous twinkle in her dark eyes, no sign that she saw or heard or recognized anything. The mimics had formed her upright, but this A'Meer was dead. Kosar had no doubt about that: her legs were gashed, her stomach and chest a mess of protruding flesh and bone, her throat gaping like a screaming mouth. Even her head was cleaved down to between her eyes. He could see her shattered skull and exposed brain. The mimics were meticulous in their detail. This was A'Meer as they had last seen her, lying dead back in the Gray Woods while he was probably still running up the slope to the machines' graveyard. They had seen blood pulsing from her throat, and they copied that action now. They had seen her right eye ruptured and leaking onto her cheek, and that image repeated itself here. She was dead, his beloved A'Meer . . . and yet her mouth moved, as though she were trying to inhale one last time, or expel one final word.

"A'Meer," Kosar whispered, though he knew it was not her. Still, seeing that image, her death hit home like never before, and Kosar started crying. Tears blurred the vision, and then the scene distorted some more as A'Meer came apart before him—flesh flowing, bone melting away—and sank back into the uniform mass of mimics shifting across the ground.

Kosar tried talking to them, asking what they wanted and why they had shown him this, but the mimics suddenly flowed to the east as fast as a man could run. The movement upset his senses and sent him tumbling to his left. He fell, rolled, and when he looked down, the ground was itself again. The mimics whispered away.

"A'Meer," he said again, but no more thoughts were spoken in her voice.

Yet as the impact of viewing her death hit home, Kosar began to wonder what message the mimics had been trying to convey. By showing him a vision of A'Meer, what could they possibly have been trying to communicate? And why?

Before, they had revealed themselves to Rafe, the carrier of the land's new magic. But he was simply Kosar. He did not understand. He could not attribute intelligence to such small things. Hive organisms, Hope had called them, their whole effect the sum of their parts. They had shown him A'Meer, dead and bleeding, her mouth working at the air . . .

"Final words?" he said. "Final wish?" Or perhaps the mimics themselves had manipulated her image for their own ends.

The darkness seemed deeper than before, and more filled with unknown things. Kosar had never been too proud to admit fear, and he was scared now—more of the things he did not know than of the things he did. Rafe's marking by magic and his subsequent loss must have affected the land far deeper than Kosar could have imagined. The mimics' appearance, and the fact that they seemed to be offering help, was as disturbing as it was shocking. He had never even heard of their existence before a few days ago. Now they were trying to send him a message.

What else could be stirring across the land?

He stared into the distance, and suddenly the blank twilight offered him a revelation: the mimics had cause to deal with him! Rafe was dead and gone, and yet they still bothered with a cowardly thief fleeing something he did not understand.

Something he *could* not understand.

They still had cause to appear to him!

He started running back the way he had come. He had been gone for an hour, maybe two, and he hoped that they were still there. *Don't be gone*, he thought. *We need to talk. In the name of the Black, we need to talk now more than ever before!*

Stomach aching from his bout of vomiting, hand still giving him pain, Kosar ran once again, feeling the weight of Noreela falling heavier on his shoulders the closer he came to the fallen machine.

———

THE OTHERS WERE gone. The space between the shattered ribs was devoid of life, as though the machine had stood here for a thousand years and its insides had long since rotted away. Kosar stood panting, just outside the circumference of ribs, staring at the emptiness within.

Gone! He had come unerringly back, navigating through the twilight by instinct alone. It had only taken him half an hour at most, but in that time Hope, Trey and Alishia had left, abandoning this site of Kosar's betrayal and heading south for Kang Kang. He looked in that direction and saw its peaks on the horizon, low and distant and yet menacing even from here.

"Mage shit!" Kosar thumped a rib with the heel of one hand and it crumbled, sending creamy shards to the ground. So strong before, now so weak; he was amazed that magic could change so much. He circled the machine, trailing his hand along the ribs and the hardened skin that still hung between some of them, thinking about the short time this thing had been aloft and what it had been trying to achieve. At first it had simply moved them away from the danger: the Monks, the fighting machines, the Mages and their Krote warrior. But after that, when the danger had seemingly passed, it had turned south and continued on that course, so definite in its direction that it must have been intentional. Rafe had said that he needed to go to Kang Kang, and Kosar had assumed it was so he could hide. But perhaps there was something else. Maybe he was missing the simple truth, too eager to let fear and confusion cloud his judgment.

Now Alishia wanted to go to Kang Kang as well.

Kosar hung his head and tried to catch his breath. He was no longer a young man, and lately he had been doing a lot of running. Running, and fighting—and every waking second spent with those Red Monks trying to kill them. At the time fear had driven him on, but now that he'd had time to pause and reflect, his muscles had stiffened, his legs turned to planks of useless wood. He closed his eyes and kneaded his thighs, hissing with the pain.

"Damn you, Hope. Damn you, Trey."

"Damn *you*, Kosar!"

A blade settled on Kosar's right shoulder and pressed to the side of his neck. He felt the tension in the blade, wound and ready to spin. "Trey!"

"Why have you come back?"

"I need to talk to you and Hope. I saw something—"

"You didn't want to talk earlier."

Kosar pushed the disc-sword from his shoulder and turned. "I wasn't ready then," he said. Trey was staring at him, and the fledger's face was yellow as the death moon. "What's wrong, Trey?"

Trey smiled. Then he leaned forward, laughter buzzing through him rather than bursting out. He was too tired to laugh properly. He stood after a while and wiped moisture from his eyes. The smile was a grimace now, and his shaking had turned into a shiver he could barely control. "What's wrong, Kosar, is that the Mages have won. I'm starting into the fledge rage, which may last for days or even longer, and I'm nowhere near any fledge mine that I know of. It could well kill me in the end. You ran, and we thought you were gone for good, saving your own skin and leaving us out here in the dark. Alishia walked for a while, but then she collapsed, shouting about burning books and truth turning to ash, and I haven't been able to wake her since. Hope is with her now . . . and Hope has her own reasons for being here, so I don't trust her for a moment. I can still hear my mother's cry. I can still smell Sonda's blood, spilled underground. I can feel the Nax in my mind. And you ask me what's wrong?"

Kosar reached out, then dropped his hands again. Trey stepped forward and rested his head on the thief's shoulder, weeping, his thin arms snaking around Kosar's back and hugging him tight.

Kosar closed his eyes and felt the fledger's anger and hate and fear flowing into him, soaking his shoulder with tears, feeding his flesh with heat, filling his mind with a bitter shame that he thought might never go away. It was almost as bad as being in those Gray Woods again, having those things feeding on his darkest secrets and dragging them up for contemplation. *Almost* as bad. But not quite. Because Trey was a friend, and even though Kosar had abandoned him, now he had returned. Kosar hugged Trey, and realized that strength such as this went both ways.

"Trey, I saw something out there," he said. "Mimics showed me A'Meer as she was when she died, and there's a reason for that. There *has* to be."

Trey stepped back. "You're looking for reasons?" he said. "A couple of hours ago you wouldn't listen to *any* reason."

"No, not back then," Kosar said. "I admit that I went, and that I had no intention of returning. Everything feels so hopeless . . . I thought we should part, be on our own. I can't explain it without . . ."

"Without telling the truth: you don't care."

"I do care, Trey!"

"Really?"

Kosar looked away from the sick fledger and turned south. "Where are Hope and Alishia?"

"That way, not far. Alishia is weak. Whatever's happening to her is bleeding her strength."

Kosar glanced at Trey. "And *you* look terrible."

"I've never gone a day without fledge in my life. And being up here seems to make it all worse. I can't understand how any fledge miners manage to stay topside."

"A lot of them get sick," Kosar said. "Is there no mine around here that you know of?"

"If there is, how would I know? My home is hundreds of miles from here." Trey dropped to his knees, sighing as he touched the damp grass. "So, are you staying?"

"I'm not sure," Kosar said. "We need to talk, all of us. Hope knows of the mimics, and I suspect she may have an idea of what just happened—and why."

"Did she talk?"

"Who?"

"A'Meer?"

"No." Kosar shook his head, remembering the way her mouth was opening and closing as blood gushed from her wounded neck. *Final words? Last wish?* He glanced up at the life moon still rising above the horizon. He thought he saw something pass briefly across its face, or perhaps it was a fleck of dust in his eye. "Let's go find Hope and Alishia."

———

THEY AGREED TO build a small fire and camp behind a fold in the land. It protected them from a chill breeze that had come in from the north, and it would also partially hide them from prying eyes. There was the risk that they would be seen by anyone or anything approaching from the south, but they needed warmth and something hot to eat. Trey had found some fat grubs beneath the moss on the rocks that formed this natural dip, and he pierced them and went about cooking them over the fire. Kosar wondered whether the witch had used chemicala to start the fire, but she showed him the flints in her hand. *I have nothing left,* she had said.

Alishia lay on her side, pressed into the shelf of rock and covered with a blanket Hope still carried. The girl was very quiet. Her scalp was bleeding. She had fallen soon after leaving the machine and struck her head on a rock.

Hope sat close, brushing hair away from the wound.

Kosar told Trey and Hope of his experience with the mimics. Hope's eyes were wide, her tattoos reflecting her interest.

"And there was only one image of A'Meer?" she said.

"Yes, only one."

"And she was cut up, dead?"

"Yes." Kosar stared into the fire, seeing a hundred strange dancing shapes within its flames. When he was a boy he had dreamed of living inside a fire, exploring the molten caves of wood and coal, but he had never considered what the heat would do to him. He sometimes wished he still possessed that childlike naiveté.

"They went east?"

Kosar nodded. "It was like having the land pulled from under me."

"I think today we can all feel like that," Hope whispered. She looked down at Alishia and brushed the unconscious girl's hair again, letting her finger trail through the drying blood. She raised her hand and tapped her finger against her lips, staring into the fire.

What is she doing? Kosar thought. The witch licked her lips and glanced up at Kosar, and for a second her mistrust was obvious.

"We need honesty now," Kosar said. "More than anything we need to tell one another everything. Don't you agree, Hope? If there is something that Alishia has, something she can do—"

"Didn't you run away?" Hope said.

"I saw no reason to stay."

"And now you do?" She touched Alishia again, lifted a strand of her hair. "Now you want to help this girl, instead of leave her—and us—to whatever fate may befall us?"

Kosar nodded. "The mimics came to me for a reason. That's why I came back, Hope. And I came back to hear what you know of the mimics. You're a witch. You pride yourself on such knowledge. I need to know why they showed me what they did, and what message they were trying to convey."

Hope gave a smile that lit her face. "I think the message is obvious. You're to go to New Shanti to tell the Shantasi about Alishia. Trey and I are to take her south, to Kang Kang."

"And what's in Kang Kang?"

"You think I know?"

"I'm sure you do."

Hope looked down at the fire again, and Kosar wondered just what she saw in there. *I see the echoes of childhood adventure, scorched away by the heat of the real world. What does an old witch see in a campfire?*

"I can tell you only what I believe," she said. "What I know for sure is so much less."

"I'm sure your beliefs are educated," Trey said.

"They are at that, fledger."

"So," Kosar said. "The mimics. Kang Kang. New Shanti."

"All linked, and all coming together very quickly," Hope said. She shifted and sat up, hugging her knees. She glanced down at Alishia, then back up at Trey and Kosar. Even now there was a scheming look in her eye, and Kosar looked away, unnerved.

"How so?" Trey said.

"The mimics—from what I know of them—can be everywhere," she said. "They pop up here and there, but do they really move? I don't know; nobody does. They're as difficult to communicate with as the moons, or the Sleeping Gods. They're part of Noreela, but no part that we're used to. The mere fact that they're intruding into our world, and our problems, makes it obvious that their presence is significant. That was no chance meeting, Kosar. They knew who you were, and they knew who A'Meer was to you. It was a very definite message they wished to convey."

"For me to go to New Shanti," Kosar said. He thought of the mimics melting down and flowing east, and there was no other meaning he could read into that.

"Why would they be interested?" Trey said. "If they're so remote from us, why would they be bothered with Kosar running, A'Meer dying?"

"Noreela is their world as well as ours," Hope said. "We've named it and farmed it and all but destroyed it, but they live here too. I suppose they know how the new magic has already been distorted by the Mages, and they can foresee the effect this will have on them as well as us."

".They showed us the Monks," Kosar said.

"They wanted Rafe to survive."

"They wanted his magic?"

Hope shrugged.

"How can you read their message?" Trey said.

"It seems so obvious to me."

"But you're saying that they know about Alishia?"

"Yes."

"Well, if *they* know about her, what about the Mages?"

Hope stared at Trey, then at Kosar, and in the shifting firelight her tattoos seemed to be twisting across her face like a hundred baby snakes. "Maybe they know also," she said.

For a second the fire seemed to burn brighter, but Kosar put it down to a gust of wind from the north. Buried embers glowed hotter, flames wavered higher and a chill fingered his spine. "No," he said. "I don't think so."

"What makes you so sure?" Hope said.

"Whatever may be happening to Alishia started before the Mages took Rafe. If they'd known then, they would have made sure she died too."

"They didn't have magic then," Hope said. "They were still looking for it."

"Well, they have it now," Trey said. "Kosar's right. If they knew about it, we wouldn't be sitting here in the cold talking about this."

Hope looked up as though expecting to be plucked from the ground that very moment. Kosar saw her tattoos picking up reflections from the life and death moons, and neither seemed to suit. *She's a strange woman*, he thought, and as if in response she stroked Alishia's wound again.

"Do you think her blood has power?" Trey said.

"What?"

"Alishia. Her cut head. You keep touching it, and I'm wondering if it's because you think her blood has power."

"Of course not, miner."

"Then leave her alone!" Trey moved to the prone girl's side and stroked an errant strand of hair from her face.

"Neither of you owns that girl," Kosar said. Hope glared at him, and Trey glanced up with his doleful yellow eyes. Kosar smiled at Hope. "So, what's in Kang Kang?"

The old witch sighed and prodded at the fire with a stick. Kosar saw his caves collapse and new ones form, and the future was a whole different story.

"There's a place there," she said, pausing as if unwilling to divulge any more. But the two men were silent, giving her time, and eventually Hope carried on. "It's called the Womb of the Land. I heard about it from my mother and grandmother, but no one I've met since has mentioned it. Long ago, I began to think that maybe I dreamed them telling me of it, but the telling was so significant to what has just happened that it must be true."

"Significant how?"

"It was a prophecy," she said. "An old one, rarely spoken, and written in languages not used for generations. It said that the future of magic would emerge in a child unborn, one that came from the Womb of the Land in Kang Kang."

"Birthed from the land?" Kosar asked.

"I assume that's what it meant. I don't know what this place looks like: a cave, a field, a lake. Rafe was never born, Kosar. He had no navel, and his parents were not his own."

"And you think he was from Kang Kang?"

"Yes."

"And now Alishia wants to return there," Trey said. "To the land's womb."

Hope nodded. "And she's getting younger."

"Or so she claims," Kosar said. "She's been through a lot. The shade in her mind, ripping her up like that. How can we say what that did to her? How can we even begin to understand?"

"We have to take her," Trey said.

Kosar moved closer to the fire, taking fresh comfort in his childish memories. But every speck of the fire seemed to move independently, each flame flickered a different way, and he wondered how close the mimics were, all the time. "I suppose our decisions are made for us."

"They always were," Hope said.

"She'll never be able to walk that far," Trey said.

"Then we carry her. Or drag her. Either way, we all have some walking to do."

"I could steal you a horse," Kosar said, but he knew immediately that would not be so easy.

"Not anymore, thief. And not out here. We're within pissing distance of Kang Kang, and not many people choose to live here. Those that do must have very good reasons. And with the dusk, everyone will be on their guard more than ever."

"You're right." Kosar nodded. "But I've been here before, and farther. These aren't good places you'll be going through, Hope.

Why not come to New Shanti with me? The Shantasi will take us in, and then we can go to Kang Kang with protection."

Hope shook her head. "The way's clear, Kosar."

"You always hated the Shantasi. You always shunned A'Meer."

Hope looked away, and for the first time Kosar thought she looked ashamed. "I never really hated her," the witch said. "The Shantasi wish for everything I wish for." She stood and walked away, and Kosar let her go.

"You support this?" Trey asked.

Kosar nodded. "It seems the only way. The Shantasi are powerful, and I'm sure they'll help. And Hope's right; if we all go to New Shanti, we risk Alishia's safety even more. If there really is hope, we need to keep it alight."

"I feel so ill," Trey said. "So tired and weak."

"Perhaps in Kang Kang there'll be fledge."

"Perhaps," Trey said.

And what will fledge from that place be like? Kosar wondered. Right now, that was something he did not wish to consider.

"Keep your disc-sword handy," Kosar said. "There are tumblers in the foothills."

"And what else?"

"I never went deeper."

Hope returned, and an uncomfortable silence hung over the camp as the three tried to bed down. They were all exhausted, and they needed their strength for the journeys to come.

But none of them could sleep. Kosar looked to the sky and wondered whether it was day. Hope lay on her side and stared at Alishia, breathing in the sleeping girl's stale breath. And Trey closed his eyes and shook, clearly trying to journey, seeking here and there for even a hint of the fledge that would keep him alive.

Time passed, but everything remained the same.

Chapter 4

O'GAN PENTLE STARED at the moons and craved a sign of hope. He searched between the shades of dusk for the shapes of stars he knew, and perhaps those he did not. But there were no stars to be seen. And though the sound of panic had been prevalent in Hess since the sun had failed to rise, he refused to submit to its lure. It would be too easy to curl up and cry, find a dark corner in which to await the inevitable doom. That act took no courage, only resignation. It would gain him nothing. The Mystics had been following events and divining news from the sun and stars, and the fall of dusk had been the clearest sign of all. The Mages were coming, and when they attacked New Shanti with their inevitable army of Krotes, death would make equals of them all.

O'Gan had been atop the Temple for the last two days. Other Mystics had come to begin with, sitting with him and trading ideas, fears, hopes. They walked the Temple's roof and inhaled the Janne plants, breathing in their mystic pollen and closing their eyes to read the visions it inspired. Most of them ended up frowning and sniffing again. Their collective mind remained blank, as though darkened by whatever had stolen light from the day. O'Gan had conversed with many other Mystics, and though his conviction that the end was not yet here remained as strong as ever, eventually the others had slipped away. He was sad to see them go. Many of them were friends, and he felt a certain betrayal at their desertion, but there was also unease at being the only one to remain up here for so long, waiting for a sign. Was he wrong? Was hope truly lost?

Two hours ago, one of the Elder Mystics had come to talk to him. She had been told of O'Gan's solitary watch on the Temple platform, and came to see for herself. It was the first time she had climbed those steps for years, and he heard her coming from a long way off. Her breath was harsh, her groans of pain loud as bones ground together in her knees, and O'Gan moved to the head of the steps to welcome her up. He believed that this was a turning point for the Mystics. He looked out over Hess—still burning lights proudly into the dusk—and a sense of immense pride flooded him. It warmed him against the dark, emboldened him against the terrible times to come, yet as he held out his hands to help the Elder Mystic onto the Temple's highest point, her voice slashed him like a knife.

"You're a fool, Pentle, to even think of hope."

He was so taken aback that he could not respond.

"The Mystics are fleeing Hess, those who have not already taken their own lives. The Guiders have already gone. Politicians!" She shook her head. "The future is a place darker than the Black, and to stay here will be to call doom onto your shade."

"My shade is strong," O'Gan said. "We've lived with fear forever, and only now will we let it defeat us?"

"There's a difference between bravery and stupidity. We've lived bravely, O'Gan, but Hess is no place to make a stand. It's a Mystic city, not built for war. And the Mages . . . the Krotes . . ." She trailed off, dropping to her knees near the edge of the Temple and trying to catch her tears as they fell.

"We can't just give them the city without a fight!"

"They'll *take* it without a fight," the Elder said. "It'll be a slaughter! They'll ride across the desert, fly in across Sordon Sound, and anyone left will be butchered. Back in the heart of New Shanti, in the hills of Mallor where O'Neakin stood, that's where we'll make our stand. Not here on the edge."

"But you can't just give up. Hess is our home!"

"We have no true home on Noreela. We're merely borrowing this place."

"A thousand years of history and you still feel misplaced." O'Gan sighed. "That's why I never wish to become an Elder. Bitterness like that must eat at you. Do your insides melt under such sourness?"

"It's history, and history is a fact, O'Gan."

"History can wallow in my waste."

The Elder looked up, and the darkness seemed to hold its breath. "Ahh," she said, "the true wise words of a Mystic." She stood and started back down the steps. They curved around the outside of the tall Temple, like a giant snake wrapped around a column.

O'Gan walked to the edge of the roof and watched her go. He should call down to her, he knew, and talk of hope and defiance in the face of the Mages' return. They should discuss how their army should be placed, where the fight would be best entered into, how many Shantasi warriors would come back to their homeland from across Noreela now that dusk had fallen and war was close. But the Elder shuffled onward, and in her determined gait O'Gan saw no room for thinking of this sort. She believed that every step brought death closer. He was not the one to shake those beliefs.

Since then he had been walking the circuit of the flat Temple roof. This was the most holy site in New Shanti, the place where the hundreds of Mystics spent much of their time watching for signs in the heavens and discussing Shantasi business, both political and spiritual. The stone was worn smooth by centuries of footfalls, and here and there had taken on a deep, oily sheen.

O'Gan wished that more Mystics would come to see him. He possessed a faith that he had so far failed to share, try though he had. He believed that hope would never be fully extinguished, and that the Mages would always have a vulnerable point. He had been shocked over the past day to discover just how little the other Mystics were willing to share in his conviction. *I cannot be alone in this*, he thought, but with each passing hour it seemed more and more that this was so.

He knelt at the edge of the roof and looked down into the streets. The Temple was ten stories high, and from here the people looked like beetles scurrying through cracks in the ground. Shantasi hurried to and fro, some of them pushing or pulling small carts, others walking their families east toward the edge of the city and the long open spaces that lay beyond. They were ill equipped for such a journey: not enough food, not enough water, too heavily laden with weapons or possessions. Panic had scarred their minds. It was the calling of the Mystics to ease such panic and guard against rash actions, but O'Gan could see the several robed shapes of Mystics in the streets as well, making their own shameful escapes.

He stood and walked to the center of the Temple roof, sat down, then stared up at the sky.

He remembered his first time climbing the steps to this lofty place of rumination and spiritual enlightenment, almost fifty years ago. He had been a humble young man then, keen to begin training the Shantasi warriors who were sent out into Noreela to await magic's return. He had done his best to hide his excitement, standing patiently at the foot of the tower, careful not to look up and betray his awe. Everyone knew what he was feeling—Mystics smiled as they made their own way up the tower, and even people in the streets seemed to sense his restrained enthusiasm—but temperance was part of the ceremony, and he had no wish to fail. He had stood there for several hours awaiting his turn, and when that time came he had started to climb.

Most other buildings in Hess were one or two stories high, their walls built from thick layers of intricately carved stone, roofs usually lined with timber and waterproofed with dried mud and reeds from the banks of Sordon Sound. Many walls were plastered and decorated with vibrant colors depicting family histories. Windows were formed of thick glass shaded against the heat, and here and there were communal gardens, fed by underground springs that kept them luscious and green all year round.

The Temple was a different building entirely. More ceremonial than functional, its base housed a huge hall where the Mystics would gather when the weather prevented them climbing to the roof. The base itself was over a hundred steps across, buried deep in the bedrock of the land and giving support to the thousands of carved rocks that went to make up the walls. Above this a circular building rose, narrowing slightly until, at ten stories high, the flat stone roof provided the main area for the Mystics' work. Around the building curved the staircase, stone slabs fixed at regular intervals in the walls to provide a narrow, steep climb to the roof. People had fallen from here, and some had died. The Shantasi had a strong belief in the whims of time, and if that was the way for them to find the Black, so be it.

O'Gan had begun the climb with his whole body shaking, as though cold. Each step had seemed a hundred steps above the previous; his feet were heavy, his thighs burned and the climb had taken forever. He glanced to his left often, viewing Hess from an angle and height he had never seen before; spotting familiar landmarks had enabled him to feel grounded, real, still there. Climbing the Temple was such an unreal experience that he valued that feeling. He was born in Hess, he was a part of Hess, and climbing up and out of that place in no way lessened his commitment to the city.

And then the wide roof had opened up before him, startling him with its expanse. There were no railings around its edges, only the thin stems and scant blossoms of the legendary Janne plant, whose unique seedlings had been brought from Shanti so long ago.

O'Gan felt as if he could see forever. He stood on the final step for some time, trying to come to terms with the view and the fact that he was here at last, until an Elder Mystic took his hand and guided him onto the roof.

He had remained there for three days, smelling the plants and welcoming visions. Descending had been like entering a strange new life. The buildings of Hess had taken on a darker hue, the people's faces held more mystery than enlightenment and the air always seemed to carry a hint of the Janne pollen. Ever since then, the Temple was where he had felt most at home.

Now home was a strange concept. Dusk hung low over the city when it should have been day. Birds were silent, and many had been seen tumbling from their perches, as if shocked to death by the confusions of light and dark. Livestock in the meat markets were unsettled and flighty, and one herd of sheebok had kicked their pen to splinters and escaped into the wilds. A lantern hung above every door, all windows were lit and the smell of burning oil drifted across the Mystic city, corrupting the usual aromas of street cooking and spice. The people of Hess were doing their best to hold back the night, but the real battle had not yet begun.

Fear, O'Gan knew, would be the Mages' greatest ally. If they waited before venturing to New Shanti, her people would crumble and fall without lifting a weapon.

Perhaps it was like this all across Noreela. He hoped not.

He looked north, out over the misty Sordon Sound, and a great blackness seemed to hang there like a weight ready to fall. There was no telling what was happening right now in the north of Noreela. Most in Hess believed they were already at war, but they could not know for certain, and it was the not knowing that chilled O'Gan most of all. The Mystics had tried for much of the previous day, sniffing the Janne until the purple blossoms started to shrivel and fade, sitting spaced across the roof or huddled in warm groups, opening themselves to visions. But the world of their collective mind was blank. And perhaps it was this more than anything that had eventually driven them to flee.

Magic was a fickle thing, so one Elder had said. There was no knowing what it would do, or could do, nor how the Mages would handle it. The future was a mystery darker than the blackest night, and O'Gan wished for a sign that would give illumination to the dark.

He sat in the center of the Temple roof, searching the darkened heavens for hope. He closed his eyes and wished for a happy dream, but the cool breeze singing in across Sordon Sound offered only tales of woe.

"We can't just give in," he said. "We have to *fight*!"

And then the sign he had been hoping for finally arrived.

———

AT FIRST, O'GAN thought it was the breeze, blowing sand from the Mol'Steria Desert and dusting it against the side of the Temple. He closed his eyes tighter and hugged his legs to try to present less of a target for the incoming storm.

Then he realized that there was no breeze, and no sand pricked his skin.

Yet the sound continued. O'Gan kept his eyes closed, hoping that this was the beginning of a vision. He had not breathed Janne pollen for several hours, though sometimes visions would come as the effect of the pollen wore off. But this was sensory: he was *hearing* the hiss of sand. His mind was devoid of vision as ever, and as he opened his eyes he saw the sign that he had been waiting for finally present itself.

A shadow rose above the edge of the Temple roof. It came a hand's width higher than the roof before falling and flowing across the stone. And it kept coming, like dark water pouring up instead of down. O'Gan stood and backed away, checking behind him to make sure the shape was not rising all around. His heart stuttered, skipping beats. He pressed his hand to his chest and breathed deeply, trying to calm his nerves. *Not the Mages already*, he thought. *Please, not so soon!* But then a true vision took root and bloomed, faster than any he had ever felt. Whole new vistas opened up to him, blank for now, but begging to be filled. Something spoke through the vision, asking him to open his mind.

"What are you?" O'Gan whispered. This high above Hess, his voice seemed loud. From below came the continuing sound of underlying panic in the streets: voices raised higher than usual, children crying instead of laughing, the clatter of wheels and the steady clomp of shoes on stone. Up here was silence, but for the whisper of this shadow and his own muttered response. His question remained unanswered, hanging in the air like a shape waiting to find itself. This thing had not harmed him—the distant vision suggested that there was no harm here—and yet it was dark, and O'Gan Pentle feared this darkness. Shadows moving within shadows only posed more questions, and however peaceful its intent, O'Gan could not calm the fear he had of this thing.

He moved back until he felt a Janne touching the bare skin of his neck. He felt the kiss of its blossom, but it was cool and moist, rotting rather than growing. The Janne reveled in sunlight and now they were being starved. *This will happen everywhere*, O'Gan thought. *Grasses and herbs, trees and shrubs, our spice farms, they'll all start to die. This will become a world of rotting things.* The spreading shadow paused, as if listening to his thoughts.

"What are you?" he asked again. "What do you want?"

The shadow whispered and flexed like thick water, darker waves forming on its surface. It flowed closer to O'Gan but paused several steps away. He could smell nothing, see nothing other than the shadow, and yet he heard the constant whisper, as though a sea of sand were being stirred by an unseen hand.

"If you're here to help, then I'm ready to listen," O'Gan said. "The other Mystics have given up on Hess, but there is fight left in the Shantasi."

The shadow began to rise higher before him, taking on depth and tone. It formed the shape of a person, and gave it color and character: the dark rents of wounds, the fading light in its eyes.

Her mouth opened and closed as if trying to speak or breathe.

She was Shantasi. And O'Gan knew her. "A'Meer Pott!" She had been one of his first students over fifty years ago, before going out into the land and never returning. Now here she was again, a living corpse rising before him, showing him her wounds, shouting a plea he could not hear.

She did not react to her name. Her eyes did not change, and her mouth continued opening and closing, dripping lines of dark blood and clear saliva silvered by the moonlight. She had lost teeth, and an eye was gone. Her head had suffered a terrible injury. She was surely dead.

Yet this was no vision. "A'Meer, are you there, can you hear me? Are you A'Meer's wraith? Have you come for me to chant you down?" Her one good eye glittered with tears. "Are you really there?"

O'Gan reached out. A whisper, a hiss, and her image retreated across the roof before him, remaining a steady five steps away. He walked faster and still she retreated. He stopped and backed away, the image of A'Meer following as though bound to him.

"What is it?" he said. He squinted, trying to make out what A'Meer was saying or whether she was actually saying anything. Her mouth fell open, cheeks sucked in, lips pressing together before the whole movement began again.

O'Gan backed away to the edge of the roof and turned to sniff at a Janne. He chose a bloom that had withered and died, and the smell that came from it was one of rot and surrender. He winced, turning to the next plant in line. This one was tall, its blooms few, and a couple of them still seemed to be drawing strength from the ancient stone in which it was buried. He pressed his face to a bloom, closed his eyes and breathed in.

Hope . . . a voice whispered, but it was like no voice he had ever heard before. It was a breeze through the bare branches of a tree, the wash of foamy waters on the shores of Sordon Sound, the whispered exhalation of a lover passing seed and giving life. It was the language of the land.

Panting, he breathed deeply of the bloom. He felt the pollen abrading the insides of his nostrils and the sting of rupturing blood vessels, and he tasted the blood that dripped over his top lip. But he did not hear that voice again. He moved to another bloom and inhaled its pollen, glancing back at A'Meer's image, upright and dead, listening for the single word that had been breathed to him from the first intense vision.

"Hope!" he cried, his mind buzzing from so much pollen. He walked toward A'Meer, swaying across the Temple roof and falling to his knees. "Hope? Is there still hope, poor dead A'Meer?" To see her like this was distressing, but to hear that word uttered at the moment of her death, to *feel* it, seemed to justify every Shantasi death. "Hope!" O'Gan screamed, and for a few seconds the bustle of the streets below the Temple died down, and he imagined pale faces looking up to see who dared shout this word.

A'Meer began to grow indistinct and hazy and O'Gan reached out to save her. She was coming apart before him, fading as though she were a painting splashed with water. He moved forward quickly, and this time the image of the dead Shantasi did not drift away. His fingertips reached her and passed inside, pressing against her fragmenting chest and finding a subtle resistance that surrounded his hand, like a thousand flies alighting on his skin. He gasped and pulled back, and for a second a smear of A'Meer came with him, dropping from his arm and merging with the shifting shadow at his feet.

The whisper came again, and the shadow filtered back over the edge of the Temple. O'Gan sat nursing his hand and repeating that word again and again, hoping the repetition would imbue it with some power, some truth.

There was hope. He had not been wrong. Now he only had to spread this knowledge.

———

WALKING DOWN THE steps from the Temple, O'Gan entered a world he no longer knew. He had been on the roof for almost two days, and in that time Hess had changed forever. It had once been a city of contemplation and consideration, a calm place where street markets sold food and drink to the many people lingering in the communal gardens, musing on the problems of life and death. Mystics had wandered the streets, eyes closed and hands folded as they considered the meaning of a vision from their last time on the Temple. Sometimes they would pause and begin to talk, using their Voice to gather an audience. Their words would have depth, their depths would give meaning, and a dozen people would move on possessed of more knowledge than before. The Mystics were the brain of Hess, the rest of the Shantasi living there its blood. The

Mystic city troubled some; its atmosphere did not suit everyone. But of all the places O'Gan had been in New Shanti, Hess had always felt most like home.

Now it was strange to him, and he was a stranger within it. Halfway down the Temple staircase he paused to look down into the streets. He could make out more detail than had been possible from the Temple roof, and he could see just how much Hess had changed. Not only the city itself, but the people. Panic had overtaken contemplation, fear had usurped thoughtfulness and the streets had grumbled with the last of Hess' population of half a million fleeing. He had been watching from the Temple for some time, but this close he could make out individual expressions and hear muttered curses rather than apologies when people walked into one another. One family pulled a large cart behind them, their belongings piled high, and they shouted at people to move out of the way, tugging the cart through a street barely wide enough to contain it. The father kicked a market stall aside, pushing it against the wall and stomping on spilled fruit so that the cart would not be slowed. The mother argued with the fruit seller, while two children sat wide-eyed in the back of the cart, surrounded by what their parents believed were their whole lives. Lamps still hung outside most buildings in an attempt to drive away the night, and the flames gave the children's eyes a haunted look.

Many Mystics had joined in the flight. He still could not understand. "There's hope," he said, but he wondered how he could make them believe.

At the foot of the Temple, stepping down onto the ground for the first time in two days, O'Gan realized that the land itself had changed. It felt different beneath his feet, as though ages had come and gone. It was strange to him now, the rock beneath him unknown, the sand between his toes unfamiliar.

"Mystic," a voice said. "Mystic!"

"O'Gan Pentle," he said, already turning to confront the voice. A woman faced him, the hood drawn over her head barely hiding the bruising around her mouth, the dried blood beneath her nose. "What happened?"

"Mystic Pentle, I can't leave the city," she said. "It's my home. My children's home. Always here, always been here, and now this, this darkness that brings such madness . . ." She was barely coherent.

Her eyes were jumping in their sockets, as though not wishing to focus on anything.

"What happened to you?" O'Gan asked.

"My husband wanted to leave. Said it wasn't safe here. Took the children. I went after him but they're lost to me now . . . I fell, and the crowds walked on me."

"No one helped you up?"

The woman nodded. "An Elder Mystic. Then she left me bleeding and crying." She suddenly seemed to find focus, eyes locking on O'Gan's, pleading and desperate. "What's happening? Where is everyone going?"

"They want safety, that's all," O'Gan said. "Your husband did what he thought was best. Your children . . ." But O'Gan could not finish. Mystics did not have children, and he could never hope to understand.

The woman looked up at him, tears slipping down her cheeks and reflecting flickering light from a nearby lantern. "I know he's right," she said. "That's the worst. I know he's right, and still I can't leave." She held her face in her hands and started crying, real tears that rose from deep within and shuddered her shoulders.

"There's still hope," O'Gan said, touching her face. The tears were hot, and neither his words nor touch seemed to help.

He moved past the woman and approached the door to the Temple's huge inner hall. It was ajar. A sliver of darkness peered out—no light, no evidence of candles or lanterns burning within. He tried to drive away the bitter disappointment. Coming down, he had started to believe there would be Mystics gathered here, ready to plan the defense of Hess. Now it seemed that he had been wrong, and that the Elder Mystic had been right. Fleeing the city was the only plan they had.

He shoved the heavy wooden door with his foot. The hinges squealed, weak light filtered in and what O'Gan saw shocked him to the core. It was Elder Garia, a woman five decades older than O'Gan with whom he had often spent time on the Temple. She had enjoyed his company, and she had been close with several other Mystics, her natural disposition one of companionship and friendship.

But Elder Garia had spent her last moments on Noreela alone. She was splayed on the tiled floor just inside the door, as if at the last moment she had changed her mind and sought help. In her right hand was the knife that had opened her wrists; in her left, a clutch of Janne blossom, stolen from the roof, rotten and rank and bleeding black sap between stiff fingers.

"Oh no," O'Gan said. He closed his eyes, but that did little to hide the image. He thought of the other corpse he had just seen—the image of A'Meer—and the word she had given him in her silent plea: *Hope*. However that vision had been brought to him, whatever that shadow had been, he had to believe it was true. If not, then Mystic Garia's fate was perhaps the wisest choice she had ever made.

O'Gan fled the Temple. The crying woman had crumpled to the ground, and he knew that he should help her, offer guidance through her confusion. But if he helped her, there would be another, and another, and eventually he would be drawn into hopelessness. He could help one, or he could help one million.

He closed his eyes and moved on. He often walked this way through the streets, continuing his inner dialogue as he moved, but now his dialogue was confused and the streets were unforgiving. He bumped into a man after a dozen steps. "You're going north, Mystic," the man said.

"And which way should I be going?"

"South, away from those damn Mages and whatever they've brought to Noreela!"

"I don't think they brought anything," O'Gan said. "I think they came and found it here."

"Either way, magic's theirs now," the man said.

"Who told you that?"

"It's the word everywhere!" The man lowered his eyes, uncomfortable at talking this way to a Mystic.

"There's hope," O'Gan said. "That's another word—my word—and I want you to spread it. Will you do that for me?"

The man glanced up, frowning, looking over O'Gan's shoulder at the tall, empty Temple. "Hope when all the Mystics flee with us?"

"Not all," O'Gan said. He thought of Elder Garia dead by her own hand.

"Some are dead," the man whispered, awed. "My brother saw them down by the coast, kneeling in the sand and drawing their swords and—"

"Mystics?"

"A dozen of them!"

"Your brother lied to you."

The man's eyes narrowed, but even in such a time he could not express anger at a Mystic.

I hope, O'Gan thought. *I hope he lied. I'd have known if so many had died; I'd have felt it. Our collective mind would have screamed and railed against it . . .*

And his mind when he breathed in the Janne pollen was a blank, devoid of life.

"He lied," O'Gan said again, more to himself than the man.

"Forgive me," the man said. He moved past O'Gan and hurried away.

There must be some of us left, O'Gan thought. *An Elder Mystic, someone I can tell about the appearance of A'Meer. Someone who'll know what that means, and what to do. Where to go.*

A group of Shantasi warriors trotted past him heading north, going against the flow. Their long dark hair was tied, pale skin made paler by the poor light, and their extensive weaponry was worn so precisely that it made no sound.

"Good," O'Gan said, and the last warrior in line turned to look at him. O'Gan saw terror in the woman's eyes.

He walked on through the streets, looking for someone who could tell him what he had seen.

Chapter 5

FLAGE WAS BORN over fifty years earlier, when he was twenty years old. When he died.

Only a privileged few can remember the moment of their birth. But perhaps such crushing exposure and agonizing animation is best left forgotten.

He retained a vivid memory of that birth and the moments that led to it. He was a rover, prowling the northern extremes of Kang Kang with his small rover band, always traveling east to west to make sure they kept Kang Kang to their left. Left was the evil side, right the good. If they turned around and headed east, Kang Kang would be to their right, and its neutral influence on their roving group would change without warning. Right would become wrong, and Flage had seen the results of rovers traveling in the opposite direction—the shattered wagons and the torn bodies, the strange sigils carved into murdered men's chests and the insides of dead women's thighs—and he had no wish to meet whatever had done that. Some said that Kang Kang was a mother with countless children, and each and every one of them served her without thought or question. They lived in the valleys of her flesh and the folds of her guts, and when called upon they emerged into the sunlight and made it their own. No one had ever seen these children of Kang Kang, so their appearance was conjecture and myth: the height of ten men, the girth of a horse, hands of stone and heads of bone, eyes lit by timeless fires from the roots of the mountains where dark things gathered around the meager light there was.

Every year, Flage heard fresh whispers of these demons, and each time their appearance was more terrifying than ever.

They had been roving and camping across the plains north of Kang Kang for a couple of years, gathering furbats from caves and canyons and milking them of their rhellim. Once every life moon, a group of rovers would travel north or west with the rhellim, trading with small farming communities or the larger villages around The Heights. They would return with food, drink and tellan coins, and news of the outside world that barely interested the rovers. Their lives were their own, and though they shared the landscape with others, that did not mean that there was any need to interact with greater Noreela. The land was dying, but they barely looked further than the next day.

When finally they reached the western extreme of Kang Kang there was an important choice to be made. They could turn north and head toward Lake Denyah and The Heights, perhaps adapting their trade on the way. Their chieftain had heard that there were still fodder being bred and eaten in the wild villages in and around The Heights, and he suggested that they could begin their own small business, breeding and selling these unfortunate beasts. *They can rove with us*, he said, *eating the best meat and roots, drinking the best mountain water, then when their time comes they'll command a good price*.

Flage and others objected. *They're people*, he said. *They're fodder*, the chieftain responded, and the rovers entered an argument that lasted two days and caused several vicious knife fights. Flage had escaped the violence, but spent several days afterward nursing a wounded woman. Shurl had gone against one of the biggest men in the group, throwing herself on him when he had called her a fodder-fucker, and in a drunken rage he had pulled a knife and lashed out. Shurl escaped that first attack, but drawing her own knife had been a mistake: the fight was made, the other rovers drew back and within a few heartbeats Shurl was writhing on the ground with the man's knife stuck in her right thigh.

Flage helped her back to her wagon. When he drew out the knife, she screamed and held him around the neck. The wound bled profusely, and he had to press a bandage to it, pushing hard while Shurl strapped it around her leg. He kept the pressure on the wound, and now and then when Shurl moved he felt the soft hair between her legs brushing the back of his hand. He could feel the heat of her. Glancing up he caught her looking at him. She smiled, and he reached for the canteen of rhellim hanging from the cross support of her wagon.

Three evenings later the chieftain called another meeting to discuss where to go next. He urged caution and peace, saying that he had dispensed with the idea of becoming fodder farmers. But when he mentioned another alternative, a hush fell across the several hundred rovers. These people were rarely silent. They enjoyed music and talk, they loved and slept and danced in the open, they shared the most intimate aspects of their lives with everyone else in the band, and to be in the presence of so many silent rovers was an experience Flage would never forget. It made him want to scream at the life moon where it hung low in the north. But Shurl was holding his hand. He glanced at her, and she was serious and scared. Her eyes were wide. She too could barely believe what the chieftain was suggesting.

They could turn slowly southward, he said, passing between the mountain range's westernmost hills and the sea, and then eventually turn east once again, keeping Kang Kang to their left as ever. That would take them south of the mountain range, into regions where no one had traveled before. That very fact should have inspired a sense of adventure in the assembled rovers—their life was after all one of exploration and travel—but instead, a palpable sense of fear embraced them. The silence was broken only by something calling far away, a soulful hoot from the mountains to the south.

The Blurring, someone said.

The chieftain stood his ground. *No one has ever been there,* he said, *not even the ancient Voyagers. It's called The Blurring because nobody knows what's there. There are no maps of the land south of Kang Kang . . . there may be a whole new world down there! Kang Kang may merely be the gateway to places we can't begin to imagine!*

People have *tried this before,* Flage said. He stood, shaking off Shurl's grasping hand. *Travelers have gone down there and never come back. I don't want to know why.*

Maybe because they found somewhere better, the chieftain said, sounding desperate.

The crowd started to murmur, then talk, then the shouting began again. Steel glinted in the darkness.

The chieftain screamed a halt, and the rovers calmed down. *Tomorrow,* he said. *In the light of day, when we can see Kang Kang and hear its reply to our ideas, we'll put it to the vote.*

Flage and Shurl walked away from the group, climbing a rise until they found a rocky overhang offering protection from the breeze and prying eyes. They sat close together, sharing warmth and sipping rhellim and rotwine, and when the fire of the drug reached their centers they tore at each other's clothing and made love beneath the life moon.

Later, Flage was musing on the decision to be made the following day. He lay atop Shurl, still hard inside her, and she was smiling up at him when he died.

THE TUMBLER CAME from nowhere. Flage was looking down into Shurl's eyes as they changed from smiling to fearful. They turned dark as something smothered them with its huge shadow.

Tumbler! she said.

Flage raised himself, still feeling Shurl's muscles holding him within her, and then something landed on his back and crushed him. Their teeth cracked together. His nose broke against Shurl's cheek. The heat of her flesh was suddenly so sweet and wonderful, and he would feel it forever, smell her musk and share his heat with her.

Then he felt thick, sharp spikes piercing his body.

There was no pain at first. He sensed his skin being pierced and the barbs driving in—his left heel, right thigh, right buttock, the small of his back, two more beneath each shoulder—and their invasion was cool and numb. The tumbler was twisting back and forth on his back, driving the barbs deeper and pressing him down onto Shurl. Her head had turned and she was screaming, but he could not hear her above his own shout of shock, fear and agony.

The pain came in a huge wave, rushing through his body from

his feet, culminating in the back of his skull as he felt himself punctured there with one more barb. It drove in deep and fast, severing his spine and stealing away all sensation. His eyes went wide, his mouth drooped, and he watched Shurl fall away as the tumbler reared back and started to roll. Shurl disappeared beneath him. The peaks of Kang Kang fell away, the sky swung by above him and then the ground came up and punched him in the face. The tumbler moved on, crushing Flage's body and driving its spears farther into flesh and bone.

Sight began to fade, and with every impact Flage became less of himself and more of the tumbler. Hearing was the final sense to leave. He heard his bones crunching as the tumbler rolled, a regular *crump, crump* as he was crushed again and again.

He was dying, but there was something waiting for him on the other side. He found it in his mind as his bodily functions ceased, leaving him as a broken hunk of meat on the tumbler's outside. It was a presence that he should not know, but did. It was an oasis of safety that he was scared to accept, a welcoming warmth that tried to swathe his free-floating consciousness as he drew back toward a darkness that hung behind. He knew what that darkness was—the Black—and his wraith stood before it, bemused and scared.

We'll chant you down, the presence said, and he recognized it: a dozen wraiths, a hundred, all of them together and existing within the heart of this tumbler. *We'll chant you down to us.*

You can't chant me down, Flage said, and the act of talking without speaking drove him even closer to the darkness.

The wraiths started to hum, whisper and sing. He experienced the words and tunes without sensing them in any way. The music became a part of him as the countless wraiths sang, and he could not help but be drawn toward them and away from the dark. *But wraiths are sung into the Black.*

This is so much better, the presence said.

Dead, adrift, Flage let himself go free. And eventually—hours or years later—he was a part of the tumbler that had killed him.

FLAGE COULD STILL remember his name, though he had long ago ceased thinking of himself as an individual. His wraith was part of the whole now, an element of the tumbler—one spark in the flame of consciousness that surrounded its original, strange mind like rings in a tree's trunk. Before, life had been difficult. Since his death and welcoming into the tumbler, there had been no such anxieties. While its physical self took sustenance from the bodies speared onto its hide, its composite soul became stronger with every wraith gathered.

There were wraiths of people who had been alive long ago, but Flage was not interested in their stories. Here was important, and now was the time. And here and now Flage knew that something was wrong.

It was not fear, but a sense that the tumbler's existence was about to change. Deep at its core, the root mind was troubled.

It had been into Kang Kang and beyond, existing south of that place for many years, when the call came for it to head north. Flage felt the call arrive, and it hurt. It struck the tumbler like a psychic scream. Its mind quivered and shook, and Flage and the others were flung outward by the force of the tumbler's shock. All around him came murmuring and singing, the wraiths chanting themselves back down to peace.

When the mind finally settled, and the tumbler passed between an endless mountain and a bottomless ravine, its wraiths combined to form the question. And when the tumbler answered they fell silent for a while, existing and thinking more as individuals than they had for many years. *Something has changed*, the mind had said. *It has grown dark, and there's danger again.*

The wraiths echoed those words: *Something has changed . . .*

Still the fear was held away, but there was something in the tumbler's answer that set the wraiths on edge.

Flage probed outside and knew only darkness.

The tumbler moved north into Kang Kang.

LENORA SAT ALONE on a cliff east of Conbarma, watching for the first Krote ship. Looking down and west she could make out the town along the coast. The Krotes down there were preparing for the arrival of the main force, clearing buildings and making sure the harbor was not blocked by sunken ships or dead hawks. They were using their machines, and Lenora was delighted at how quickly the warriors had adapted. She had seen machines before, during the Cataclysmic War, but the rest of the Krotes had only stories to go by. Trained though they were—bred to fight and loyal to the

Mages and their cause—they had never seen anything quite like this. True, there were the snow demons on Dana'Man, the foxlions that grew far larger in cold climates, and a century earlier the Krotes had fought a brief, bloody war with an army of creatures that rose out of the seas north of Dana'Man on icy chariots. But the machines were different because they represented the very thing that the Krotes had spent their whole life waiting for: magic. And while snow demons and creatures from the deep were living things that could be beheaded with a slideshock or stabbed with a sword, magic was unknown to them.

The machines had given the Krotes purpose. They cleaned and talked to them. In truth, it was magic that made and maintained them, but the Krotes had all developed attachments which Lenora did nothing to discourage. If fear was still present—and Lenora suspected that it was, however brave a face the Krotes wore—then it was a healthy fear. It made them stronger.

For the last two nights, Lenora had dreamed of the whole Krote army riding south on such machines.

Her own ride stood beside her, silent and motionless. Its eyes stared at her unblinking, and its limbs were tucked in to its sides. It would rise to her command the instant she touched it, and that gave her an awesome sense of power. What blood those limbs would taste! What slaughter those eyes would see!

And yet . . . the Mages had gone. That troubled her, even though they had left her as mistress of their entire army. She was humbled by their trust. The responsibility was immense, and if she conducted herself well and succeeded in her charge—taking Noreela, and destroying any resistance without mercy—then she would quite possibly be as powerful as the Mages themselves. If she was lax in her duties and the rout became bogged down in a costly war, then the sole responsibility would lie with her. There would be no pleading, no begging for mercy, no appealing to the Mages' more understanding side. They would kill her, and over three centuries of exile they'd had plenty of time to invent some terrible ways to kill. Lenora knew that her survival was in the balance for the foreseeable future. She had nothing to fear from Noreela, but the Mages terrified her.

They had left her without a hint of magic. Instead they had left an aborted shade, imbued with a touch of their magic, and it was down there now at the harbor, sitting between the fire and flesh pits and waiting for the first of the Krote ships to arrive.

Lenora had never seen a shade, and she found this one terrifying. Not only because of what it was but what it had. The Mages trusted it more than her.

She was not jealous; she was too loyal to the Mages for that. But she was unsettled.

She sighed and looked north. The twilight gave the sea a whole new texture, skimming the heads of waves with reflected light from the moons and hiding the troughs in shadows deeper than ever before. She had sent Krotes north on hawks to keep watch for the first of the ships, telling them to instruct the captains to light lanterns so that Conbarma would see them coming in. She had sent hawks instead of a flying machine because she did not wish to startle the incoming Krotes. Best that they catch their first glimpse of magic on land.

The sea was a soporific whisper against the foot of the cliffs, and Lenora had caught herself nodding off several times. Each time her eyes closed she saw daylight, and when she opened them she heard the echo of a dream voice.

When she saw the first hint of light on the horizon her old heart skipped a beat. *So soon!* she thought. She stood, climbed aboard her machine and ordered it to stand. The added height gave her a better viewpoint, and she could definitely make out a splash of light far out on the ocean, blinking on and off as the sea swelled and dipped.

"Back to Conbarma," she said, and the machine began the journey down. Already it felt natural beneath her, though its speed unsettled her so close to the cliff. The ride back to Conbarma was fast, and she passed the perimeter guards with a nod.

"First ship's coming in," she said. The guards sat up, and their machines twitched beneath them. "I'll send relief after it arrives. There'll be plenty for you to see."

"Yes, Mistress." *Mistress.* It would take her a while to get used to that.

At the harbor the shade was still sitting between the two pits, but the flesh pit seemed to be glowing.

"There's a ship coming in," she told one of her captains. "What's been happening down here?"

The captain rode his machine—a tall, spidery construct—to her side. He sat higher than her, and he seemed almost embarrassed looking down. "That . . . thing plucked some animals from the sea," he said. "They came up like a living wave, splashed across the harbor, and it gathered them into the flesh pit."

"Gathered them how?"

"It pushed with its shadows."

Lenora nodded. "Good. It knows the ship's coming and it's preparing."

The captain stared out to sea, obviously pleased to have something else to draw his attention.

———

THE SHIP SLOWED as it approached the harbor, the great paddle wheels on either side almost still, turned by the vessel's momentum rather than the efforts of the Krotes belowdecks. Sails were dropped and tied. Lanterns hung from masts, forming flaming eyes on the carved figurehead: the snarling likeness of a snow demon. *I'll never see one of those things again*, Lenora thought.

The ship bumped against the harbor. Lines were thrown and secured, and the gangway was eased across the gap and fixed into place. The Krotes on the ship crowded along the gunwale, their faces a uniform yellow in the reflected light from so many lanterns. Some of them cheered, but most merely stood there, staring at the warriors on the harbor then looking around the town itself.

A few saw the pits and thing that stood between them, and Lenora saw their eyes widen.

"Welcome to Noreela!" she shouted. "Where's your captain?"

"Here." A shape hobbled from the shadows beneath the forecastle and stood at the head of the boarding ramp. Short and thin, her pure white hair was bound in two plaits that hung to her thighs. The end of each plait shone with a sliver of sharpened metal.

"Ducianne!" Lenora said. "If I'd known you were to captain the first ship I'd have had a barrel of rotwine waiting for you!"

"I haven't had a drink in days, Lenora," Ducianne said. "Fuck with me and you lose an eye."

"You and whose army?" Lenora said. She smiled and made her way up the ramp. Ducianne hobbled down to meet her—she'd lost half her foot to a foxlion ten years before—and they embraced. Lenora felt her old friend's scars, hard knots of flesh against her own. "It's good to see you."

"And you, Lenora. Where are the Mages? Has there been any fighting yet?"

"The Mages have gone and left me in charge."

"Gone where?"

"You think I'd question their intentions?"

Ducianne grinned. "I suppose not. So you're the mistress now, eh?" Her eyes shifted briefly, but it could have been a lamp swaying on the ship.

"There's more," Lenora said. "Lots more. But let's get your Krotes off the ship first. And tell me, this darkness: Does it extend far out to sea?"

"It was day, then night, then day again . . . and at midday, as we passed Land's End on The Spine, darkness fell quickly. No clouds, no setting sun, just a fading of the light. It spooked us all. Half of our sheebok jumped into the sea."

"You look hungry," Lenora said.

Ducianne nodded. "My warriors need food and drink, Lenora. It's been a hard journey. Storms. Cold. And an attack by sea taints rotted our food and soured the water. But there was always the fight at journey's end to keep us going." She flipped her head, sending the barbed hair plaits toward Lenora's face.

Lenora caught them in both hands and tugged. "You're a mean one, Ducianne."

"Why else would I be a captain?"

They walked up onto deck. The Krotes were eager to leave the stinking ship, but they bowed to Lenora.

"Don't bow to me," she said. "Soon, others will bow to you." The warriors rose, and this close Lenora was shocked at their condition. They looked gaunt, their eyes too large for their heads, and old wounds of war glowed pink in the subdued light. "The journey was never that long!"

A big Krote spoke to her, his manner deferential but defensive. "We've never undertaken a sea journey like this," he said. "And there was a bad storm. We've all been sick for days."

"Then you need fattening up," she said. "Off the ship, now. You first. Go into the town and my captains will take care of you." She turned to Ducianne. "There are machines," she said, "and there'll be one made for every Krote aboard."

"Machines!" Ducianne said. "How?"

"The Mages left a shade."

Ducianne's eyes widened, but she did not deign comment or ask more.

The Krotes left the ship in a long, slow line. Each of them looked at the shade, and skirted as far around it and its factory pits as they could.

"That's a fucking abomination," Ducianne said as she walked alongside Lenora.

"It's the Mages'," Lenora snapped. "And it's magic."

"So they truly have it? They really did get it back for themselves?"

"Of course. It was easy." Lenora thought back to the fight with the Monks and machines, the attack on the huge flying machine that had tried to protect the boy, the ferocity of his protectors' defense. "Easy."

———

LATER, LENORA AND Ducianne sat alone in one of Conbarma's taverns, drinking rotwine and listening to the shade making machines. Some of the braver, less exhausted Krotes from Ducianne's ship had seen the machines of war around Conbarma, and shunning rest they had approached the shade to be equipped with their own. Lenora had watched the first construct melded and merged from the pits, then she dragged Ducianne away from the spectacle. There was talking to be done, and planning, and it felt good having a friend with her once again. Though Noreela had always been their aim, still she felt a thousand miles from home.

They could hear the gasps of amazement from outside, the sound of flesh being ripped from the pit and magical fire melding it with stone and metal, and then the unnatural footfalls as the machines took their first, confident steps. The sounds from the Krotes changed slowly from astonishment to triumph as each of them was given their own weapon of war: flying, crawling, running, stepping, crushing and spitting—all of them knew that they were being granted more power than they had ever possessed before.

Walls fell, and explosions of noxious gas parted the air. The Krotes were already in training.

Lenora sat with her back to the window and Ducianne kept glancing over her shoulder. Her eyes reflected the fiery truth of what was happening outside.

"It feels strange," Ducianne said. "Good, but . . ."

"Unnatural?" Lenora asked. She shrugged. "We've been used to

82 TIM LEBBON

doing everything for ourselves. We mine and refine and cast metal to make swords, raid the islands south of Dana'Man for timber to make our arrows, clear the ground of snow and ice, dig the soil, plants crops, watch them mostly freeze and rot in the ground. Life is harsh for every Krote. Has been ever since we left this land three hundred years ago."

"You were there," Ducianne said. "What does it feel like coming back?"

Lenora stirred her rotwine with one finger. "It feels like revenge."

"But those things out there," Ducianne said, and again she could not finish her sentence.

"Very soon, they'll feel right," Lenora said. "I never rode a machine during the Cataclysmic War, but I saw them, and I knew them. And these are so much *more*! Back then they were tools, but now they have more than a spark of life. I know for sure once the Krotes ride them into battle they'll feel as comfortable with them as with one another. They'll be an extension of your arm. Or in your case, your foot."

Ducianne lifted the stump of her right foot and thudded it down on the table. "If magic could grow this back for me, *then* I'd be impressed!"

"I'm sure it could," Lenora said. "But when you have your machine, you won't need it anymore."

Ducianne drained her cup of rotwine and poured more. "I look forward to it."

"There's plenty of time. Let's sit and talk, let your Krotes get theirs first. We've got some planning to do."

"And a war to fight!" Ducianne said, grinning. "I can still hardly believe we're here. No fucking snow demons stalking the perimeter, no icicles hanging from my nose. There was a time on the way here when the ice floes disappeared. I can't remember passing the last one: one moment they were there, the next time I looked there was only open sea. That's what brought it home to me the most, Lenora. The change in the sea."

"And the sky growing dark."

Ducianne's grin faltered. "That too. It scared a lot of us, but we knew what it had to be. It was a victory. It shouldn't have made us feel like that."

"A lot of what happens over the next few days will affect us in different ways," Lenora said.

Ducianne nodded. "So where have they gone?" she asked quietly, as though the Mages were listening from the shadows in the unlit fireplace.

Lenora shrugged. "I have no idea. They raised themselves a huge flying machine and took off. They left me in charge of the army and told me to take Noreela."

"A minor responsibility, then." Ducianne covered her smile with another draft of rotwine.

"Something I never expected," Lenora said. "I thought after all this time that they'd want to lead the army themselves. They have so much anger inside, so much hate." She looked around the deserted tavern and closed her eyes. *I have to stop talking about them like this,* she thought. *They'll know. They'll see.*

"And so do we," Ducianne said. "This is the reason we've lived our lives, all of us. This is the finest day ever!" She drained her rotwine and threw the mug at the bar. It shattered against the wall and spilled its dregs like a splash of dark blood. "First blood to the Krotes!" she shouted.

"First blood," Lenora said.

"So, tell me about the battle to take this place. I saw an old church earlier, looked like there'd been a bastard of a siege there. Defenders? Villagers? Tell me, Lenora."

Lenora smiled and thought back to their landing at Conbarma. But then she looked forward, and something sighed deep down in her mind. "Let's talk of the future, not the past. There are battles to come that will make this one look like a fart in a storm. And now that you're here, it's time to organize. The Mages made each of my Krotes a captain, but you're to be my lieutenant, Ducianne."

"So what are you giving me?" the short woman said. Her voice was low, filled with anticipation.

Lenora stood and walked slowly to the bar. She smiled. She could feel Ducianne simmering behind her.

"Damn it all to Black, Lenora!"

Lenora laughed and turned around, holding another bottle of rotwine. "I'm giving you Long Marrakash," she said.

Ducianne gasped. "The Duke?"

"The Duke, and whatever armies remain around him. Find

them and destroy them. Bring me his head, Ducianne. Kill the Duke of this shitting land, and stick his head on the front of your machine."

"My machine . . ."

Lenora nodded. "I think it's your turn."

———

THEY WALKED TO the pits together. Lenora left her machine squatting outside the tavern, venting hazy gas from several stumpy horns. She felt its eyes follow her as she walked to the harbor with Ducianne.

The limping Krote lieutenant went forward until she was within twenty steps of the shade. It spun and flexed in the air, existing within its own set of laws. One moment it looked like a giant heart, bare and beating to the rhythm of the land; the next it was a glass ball, its insides bottomless, outside opaque and mysterious. As Ducianne paused before it, the shade was barely there at all.

"So show me," Ducianne said.

The shade sunk into the ground and rose again in the flesh pit. It brought with it a stew of living stuff: blood and brains, bone and skin, flesh and cartilage, rising as though forced upward by a slow explosion of gas from the stinking mass of dead-but-living flesh. The shade was a space between this stuff, filled only by shadow.

Ducianne took only one step back. Most Krotes withdrew several steps, and some had fallen to their knees, but Ducianne was brave. Lenora could see her old friend's shoulders shaking and her bad foot tapping at the ground in a reflex motion, but the lieutenant remained facing forward.

It knows she's my lieutenant, Lenora thought. *It's making her something special.*

Stone and flesh, soil and bone, fire and water mixed and twisted and flexed together, and a dozen heartbeats later the shade shrank down and drew back, leaving the new machine as an offering to the Krote. Ducianne was staring at it, her foot still tapping the ground, when the shade joined them. She slumped, but did not go to her knees. Her hands stole to the two short swords at her belt and touched the hilts, taking comfort from the contact. She turned around and searched for Lenora. Her face visibly relaxed when she caught sight of her friend.

Lenora nodded at Ducianne's new mount.

The machine was huge. Four thick, stumpy legs, a wide body with a dozen arms, each of them tipped with curls of sharpened bone that seemed to echo the Krote's hairstyle. The thick flesh of its back was protected from below by a congealed slab of stone, melted and re-formed to provide a heavy shield. Its arms were bone and flesh, stone and fire. It gushed hot air from openings in its upper body. As Ducianne approached, the machine lowered itself, its stone stomach scraping against the dock, and one of its long arms came down and bent to form a step.

Ducianne climbed its arm and sat upon its back, smiling when she realized that it had been shaped precisely for her. She looked at Lenora and the smile widened.

The machine stood.

Ducianne sat there for some time, running her hands over the strange construct's bony and stony carapace, finding glimmering metal levers and handles set into its back. Closing her eyes, she thought her first command.

The machine reared on its hind legs and then jumped, leaping a hundred steps and landing lightly on the roof of the tavern.

Lenora watched in amazement. She saw her own construct turn slightly as though watching Ducianne's, then the lieutenant issued her second order and the machine jumped back down to the harbor. It strode quickly toward Lenora, halting a step away so that she could hear its insides grinding and clicking together, smell the heat that could have been its breath.

"I like it," Ducianne said.

"I'm glad," Lenora said. "And now, Lieutenant, there are some battle plans to discuss."

———

AFTER THE PLANNING and talking, the excitement and anticipation, Lenora walked to the end of the mole. She passed the ship that had come in earlier that day and knew that it would never be sailing again. The shade had already stripped most of its metals, and it groaned as the sea's swell nudged it against the harbor wall. Bracings were failing, and struts were popping out without their metal straps to hold them in place.

The fire and flesh pits were denuded. The shade had made almost two hundred machines since the ship docked.

At the end of the mole, Lenora sat down and looked out to sea.

There was nothing but darkness out there, but just over the horizon more ships were coming this way, bringing with them thousands of Krotes. The idea chilled Lenora, but it made her proud as well. The thought of revenge—the Mages' and her own—had often been the only idea that kept her going through those long, dark years on Dana'Man.

She was old. Sometimes she forgot that. She was old, and she would have been dead centuries before were it not for Angel and her strange touch. *I have a touch of magic in me even now*, she thought, *keeping me alive, driving away the effects of these wounds, time, age. Angel made me live for her, and even when magic went away I was still alive. So it's in me, and it always has been.* She did not know how right or wrong she was, but the concept gave her comfort.

She ran her hand over her bald head, feeling ridged scar tissue of wounds that should have killed her. Her shoulder and neck were equally damaged, and sometimes when she heard the sea, these wounds ached at the memory of their creation. But not here, not now. Now she felt fit like never before.

And that voice was there more than ever. An echo here, a random word there, holding no meaning yet still making sense. *There's plenty of time*, Lenora kept thinking, trying to quieten the shade of her murdered daughter. But sometimes that voice almost became frantic, and Lenora was beginning to wonder just how much time she really had.

Chapter 6

THEY HAD PARTED company with Kosar half a day before, and already Trey believed that they would not reach Kang Kang alive. The mountain peaks seemed no closer, still evident as ragged shadows on the horizon. The landscape had flattened into one vast plain, with few places to shelter from the chill breeze that seemed to constantly blow from the north. And Alishia had spent more time asleep than awake.

Trey had carried the librarian most of the way. At first the feeling of her flesh against his had pleased him: he could sense the warmth of her through their clothing, enjoying its immediacy. He carried her on his back, her head resting on one shoulder and legs slung over his arms by his side. He could feel her breasts pressing against him, though they were smaller than he had imagined, and the touch of her thighs under her rucked-up dress was both a shock and a pleasure. Sometimes he had been certain that she was awake; a twitch of her limbs, or a flick of her hair against his face. But the farther they went, the more Trey came to believe that Alishia was merely dreaming. When she did wake, she asked to be put down, hugging herself to the ground like a newborn sheebok.

Adult though she appeared, Trey found her incredibly light, as though she were being hollowed from the inside.

Worse, the fledge rage was upon him. It had been almost two topside days since he'd had his last crumb of the drug, and the effects of its withdrawal were beginning to tell. His mind wandered of its own accord, drifting to the past or into the hazy future as though determined to travel on its own, without the drug to guide it. He had sore feet and heavy hands, and his joints ground as though rock dust had been poured into them. He had seen the effects of fledge withdrawal several times underground, and it was never pleasant. In the world of the fledge miners, it had been used as a punishment. Whenever they stopped, he would search through his shoulder bag six or seven times, looking for crumbs of the drug that he may have missed. He knew that shreds that small would have turned completely stale by now, and would likely do him more harm than good, but the need was upon him. If he put the mouth of the bag around his face he could breathe in and smell fledge, and even the memory started to take him away. Never far, though. There was always the terrible here and now to draw him back.

At least the withdrawal served to divert his attention from the pain of carrying Alishia.

Hope knew what was happening to him. She never mentioned it outright, but her look spoke volumes. He would find the witch staring at him when he reined his mind in from vague wanderings, her gaze switching back and forth between Trey and the girl on his back. When she realized he had seen her, she would look away, but he did not like her expression. Her tattoos did not help. Trey did not understand them. He resolved to ask her, but the time never seemed right.

Hope was carrying his disc-sword. He had been unsure about that to begin with, but the practicalities of carrying the sleeping girl as well as his weapon had soon proven impossible. The witch hefted it over her shoulder as though she had carried one her whole life. It made her appear more dangerous than ever.

"We just don't seem to be any closer," Trey said. He paused, lowered Alishia to the ground, then slumped down beside her.

Hope walked on a few steps before sitting. "Kang Kang is always misleading," she said. "Maybe it doesn't want us there."

"It's a mountain range," Trey said.

"It's much more than that." Hope plucked something from her deep pockets and started to chew. She offered some to Trey, but he shook his head. One taste of her dried meat had already put him off it for life. When he'd asked where it came from she had smiled and turned away. For all he knew it was the flesh of a child.

"I don't know how much farther I can carry her," he said. "She's lighter all the time, but she feels heavier with every step."

"If you weren't craving that fucking drug you'd be stronger."

"I can't help it," he said, hating his appealing tone.

"Fledgers are all the same, useless without their fledge."

"Hope . . ." But Trey trailed off. There was no arguing with the witch. She had never liked or trusted him, and her brief talk about them being on the same side now seemed ages ago.

"I'm going to look around," Hope said. She stood and walked away, staring at the ground and kicking at the grass as she went.

"She's not safe."

"What?" At first Trey thought he was hearing things. Perhaps desperation for fledge was putting false echoes in his mind, talking to him from the shadows of his need. He turned left and right, listening for a voice but hearing none, then he saw that Alishia's eyes were open. They were glazed and creamy like ruptured eggs. Open, but vacant.

She was still asleep.

"She's not safe," Alishia said again. Her jaw moved strangely, stiff and mechanical.

"Alishia?" Trey leaned in closer and waved his hand in front of her eyes. She did not blink, but her eyelids drooped slowly shut. A tear ran down one cheek.

"Her book speaks volumes of danger," Alishia murmured. Her mouth kept moving but soon the words became distorted, and the sound drifted away to a mumble, and then to nothing.

Trey moved closer to the librarian and held her hand. It was cool, like the hand of a doll. His mother used to make dolls for children in the home-cave, heads carved from light snowstone, bodies woven with reeds brought down from topside. She had painted the faces herself, and Trey had always been amazed by the life she could bring to those things—eyes filled with light, simple smiles that gave away so much. It was as if his mother saw real potential in every doll. They all attracted their own name and personality purely

through the expressions she gave them, and different children preferred different dolls. But that had been years before, back when his
mother could still work with her hands.

Alishia's expression was less lifelike than any doll Trey had ever
seen.

He leaned over her and turned his face, feeling her stale breath
tickle his cheek. It was cool and shallow. He touched her skin, turned
her head, smoothed the wrinkle between her eyes, touched his finger to her lips and felt their dryness. Her cheeks were filling out,
nose flattening, and she seemed to be turning into someone else.

Growing younger, Trey thought. *How can that be?* He lifted the
front of her dress and let go, and it settled down onto her slight
frame. When he first met her on the slopes of the Widow's Peaks,
she had filled that dress. He'd thought she was a young girl at first—
the way she spoke, the things she said—but when he'd become
used to the sun, he had seen that was not the case. Now she was
turning into that girl he had first imagined.

"Hope," he whispered into her ear. "What about her? What
book? Does she have it in her bag?" In the poor light, with birds
fallen silent and the breeze pausing every few seconds, his whispers
seemed incredibly loud.

Alishia's eyes opened a crack and she muttered something.

"What?" Trey leaned in closer, unable to hear. He pressed his
ear to her mouth, and felt it grow cool as she took in a breath to
speak again.

"Hope's book . . . not yet scribed . . . new, bad chapter . . ."

Trey frowned, straining to hear. But Alishia said no more.

He sat up, closed his eyes and felt a sickening punch to his
stomach. Mage shit, he so needed some fledge.

"Did she speak?" Hope asked.

Trey jumped. He hadn't heard the witch approaching, and now
she was standing just a few steps away. "No," he said. "Where have
you been?"

The witch patted her pocket. "Harvesting."

"We need to move on, Hope," Trey said. "I don't think she's
well."

"Are you up to carrying her again?"

"I'll have to be." Trey stood and bent down for Alishia, lifting
her into a sitting position. She was not as limp as she had been be-

fore, and he thought maybe she was trying to help. Her eyes were still closed, though, and her head rolled on her neck.

Hope helped him lift Alishia and then she led the way, walking ahead and looking left and right, down at the ground and up at the sky. Trey liked to think that she was watching out for dangers, but he thought it was more likely that she was searching for things she did not want him to see.

Her book speaks volumes of danger, Alishia had whispered. If only Trey understood what that meant.

––––––––––

HOPE FELT MOVEMENT in the deep pocket of her coat. She slapped it hard, stunning the spider into immobility once again. As soon as she found some hedgehock she'd be able to dope it, but in the meantime she was doing her best to avoid being bitten. It was a risk, but she needed to arm herself. And there was no harm in having an advantage that the fledger did not know about.

She should be able to smell hedgehock before she saw it, but her senses felt strangely numbed by the darkness.

Over the past few hours, Hope had been looking everywhere for the light of dawn. This endless twilight had started to feel heavy, squeezing her heart, crushing her lungs so that she could barely draw breath, and she was so desperate to see a sliver of dawn that she felt like running at the eastern horizon until it appeared. As a witch and a whore she had spent much of her life conducting business at night, and she had only just begun to realize how much she missed the daylight. The landscape was silenced by what had happened. It was as though Noreela was in shock at the Mages' audacity. Several times she had to close her eyes and breathe long and deep to prevent panic from settling in.

Hope had spent so long with nobody in her life but herself. Since her mother had died decades ago, she had been on her own, a witch without magic, and anyone who did come into her life went out of it just as quickly. Following Rafe had given her a purpose, and someone else to care about. In him she had seen the possible realization of her own potential. Magic would have brought much of what was missing from her life. She had lived her whole life craving to fulfill the promise of the name "witch." She had the ways and means, the knowledge and experience, the hexes passed down through her family line. She had an open mind, and the understanding of the land that would have allowed magic to embed itself comfortably in her life. Many others would have been scared of it, and some would have run from its influence. But in Rafe, Hope had seen her entire future.

Now he was gone, and Hope had another child to follow.

Alishia carried something different, but whatever it was had come from Rafe. Hope felt her own life drawing to a close—this darkness seemed like a precursor to her own light fading slowly away—but there was still one chance, in Alishia. And however unlikely it may be, all she had left to believe in was this girl.

The obstacles were beyond measure: the Mages, with magic twisted to their perverted use, and the Mages' army that was undoubtedly readying to assault Noreela. And Kang Kang. But Hope had nothing left to live for. Alishia, and whatever she carried, was all that mattered to her now.

The spider in her right pocket jumped and squirmed. Hope flicked the outside of her coat and the creature fell still once again.

Hedgehock! she thought. *Where's the Mage-shitting hedgehock?* She walked faster, pulling away from the fledger and Alishia, and then that familiar warm, herby smell hit her.

It was as though Fate had guided her this way.

She knelt down, plucked the shriveling leaves of the hedgehock plant and proceeded to tear them into tiny shreds.

———

ALISHIA'S LIBRARY WAS still burning, but she was immune to the flames. The books were not. She could smell the tang of blistering paper and warping card, and the stench of ancient inks released a smoke that she knew to be hallucinatory. But could she hallucinate when she was already in a dream? She breathed in deeply to find out, and a staircase took her down to another level. The stairs curved down to the left, spiraling beneath the library but never leaving its identity behind. Books still lined the walls, all with titles she did not, or could not, understand. Even though she could not speak many old languages, still she usually recognized them for what they were. These were all unknown to her. She took out one book at random, sat on the stone step and rested it across her thighs. It was bound in thick red card, its color still vivid even though she was sure it had been shelved here for hundreds, or thousands, of years. When she opened it, a flattened spider fell from between the pages, shattering to dust when it hit the floor. The smell of age wafted out. She turned the pages, not recognizing any of the words or the language they formed, but still distressed at the way they looked on the brittle paper.

She closed the book and shelved it again, moving farther down the staircase. She thought perhaps she was going deeper into her own mind, but at least the flames were only burning above her now. They were eating away at history, but something told her that the history that really mattered to her—the stories from the past that could help her future—were stored down here. She hoped that the staircase would not act as a chimney and suck the flames down.

There was another library. This one was in a cave rather than a building, its ceiling hanging with stalactites of ancient paper that had petrified into solid carvings. She saw forms that did not bear seeing, and shapes that hinted at more terrible things she could never know. She looked up, expecting floorboards, but the roof of the cave was impossibly lined with books. The floor too, row upon row of spines facing upward, and wherever she walked she heard the crackle of old bindings breaking beneath her feet.

She knew where she was going. The book she plucked from the wall was not as old as many of the others, but its spine was worn and the pages weathered as though it had been read thousands of times. She checked inside the front cover, but there was no marking to show that it had ever been taken from the library.

"That's because this isn't really a library," Alishia said, and the books seemed to lean in disapprovingly.

She sat on a pile of books leaning against one wall and opened the new volume. *One Afternoon in Pavisse*, it was titled, and the first page told her about a witch called Hope who had stilled a man's heart with a long, thin knife while he was rutting with her. The witch had smiled and welcomed the gush of blood across her chest. The description of his penis shriveling within her as he died was long and detailed, the sensations lovingly rendered in words. Alishia closed her eyes and turned a few more pages, reading again, seeing how the witch had eaten a meal from a plate resting on the cooling man's back and then carefully used her fruit knife to carve away a tattoo that covered one side of his scalp. She would paste it to one of the small windows in the basement room to dry, and later she intended to sell it for information. There was no mention of the information the witch sought. The book ended with the witch preparing to dispose of the body.

Alishia slammed the book closed and reshelved it. *We're in danger,* she thought. *She never was out for us; she's only for herself. She'll kill us as easily as that man, and cut out anything she needs.* She stood and walked to the other side of the room. She did not know which book she was looking for, but she *did* seem to know the ones to discard. She ran her fingers along many spines and received a rush of sensation. She felt disgust, fear and revulsion, and mixed in with that was a brief moment of ravenous hunger. *Just moments in her life, been and gone, done with now. No threat to us.* But they *were* a threat, she knew that, because every book in this new cavernous library told Alishia what a desperate woman Hope really was.

She plucked a book from the shelf without reading the spine. She remained standing this time, not wishing to settle down to view something from Hope's life, but when she opened the book she realized that only the first page had been used. It was an illustration with a few notes beneath. The picture was of a spider, fat and orange, and the caption read *gravemaker spider*. Underneath, the words read: *stilled for now, numbed with hedgehock, but a pinch of salt will wake it.*

Her book speaks volumes of danger, Alishia thought. Then she said it as well, but smoke from the fire above had started to seep down the staircase, and her throat was dry and sore.

She ran back up to the main library and lost herself again amidst the towering stacks of books. There was more here that would help her, she knew, much more. All she had to do was find it.

———

KOSAR HAD SPENT many of his younger years traveling across Noreela, working and stealing and living his life as he wished it to be lived. He had seen many worrying, wicked and strange things, and almost all of them had happened during the day. It seemed as if the rot setting into the land gave weirdness more audacity, so that it was no longer relegated to dark places. Daylight had slowly become an alien place.

The dark had always been simply another part of Noreela. Nothing fearful hid there, because it no longer needed to.

But now the constant twilight was squirming beneath his skin, setting him on edge and starting to affect his judgment.

To begin with he was certain that he was heading east, but as more time passed his doubt began to grow. The toothed shadow of Kang Kang silhouetted against the sky had faded over the horizon to his right, yet it still felt as though he was traveling in the wrong direction. He ignored the sensation initially, looking down at the ground before him and walking on. Then he started pausing, looking back the way he had come, wondering whether his senses had become so confused that he was actually walking exactly the wrong way.

The moons offered him no clues, and all certainty was fleeing him.

When he came to a copse of trees, he examined the trunks and exposed roots, looking for moss or sun bleaching so that he could tell direction. But the trees seemed to swim in his vision, swaying as though his eyes were watering. When he wiped his sleeves across his face and looked again, the trees had changed position. They hissed and spat.

He stood and backed away, looking up into their canopies. Leaves had shriveled and already started to drop, and the exposed branches looked like skeletal fingers reaching for the moons. They waved at the sky and groaned as they rubbed together, and Kosar turned and ran.

In his panic, he tripped and banged his head. He lay dazed for a few heartbeats, rolling onto his back and looking up at the blank, black sky. No stars with which to plot his position; no sun to chart his course; just a uniform darkness, so distant and yet so heavy and close that he felt it crushing him into the soft subsoil that was the skin of Noreela itself.

"Fuck!" Kosar leapt to his feet and drew his sword. "Fuck! Fuck!" Shouting scared him—the sound was loud across this silent landscape—but it also made him feel better. The blade could do nothing against darkness, but his words could penetrate the silence. He shouted again, mixed curses and pleas, and in the distance something crashed through some trees and bushes and took flight. He saw a shadow heading up into the sky, and though he did not know what it was, it did not frighten him. It was something of Noreela, not of the dark. It was just as afraid as he.

Kosar backed away from the trees and headed across the landscape again, wiping a dribble of blood from his temple. He touched it to the sword to sate the metal and resheathed it. It was A'Meer's sword. It had seen some blood at his hand, but not much, and he wondered at its history. She had told him it was her father's before her, but that was all. She had kept so much truth from him.

Going to New Shanti suddenly seemed a comforting idea. There he would see many more Shantasi, and he had no doubt that they would remind him of A'Meer. He remembered her pressing against him in a stranger's house as a Red Monk passed by outside, the heat of her flesh on his, the fear transmitted through her body and breath. *She was a warrior, but she found it easy to rely on me.*

He walked on. He wondered whether those strange trees had been turned that way by the Mages' twisting of the new magic, or whether they were simply another factor of the land's long decline. Or perhaps Kang Kang could affect the land even this far out. It was not a good place. He was shamefully pleased that he was not going there, but he pitied Trey, who had become as near to a friend as Kosar had ever had.

And Hope. The witch, the whore, someone Kosar had never trusted. She was going with them.

Hess was maybe a hundred miles from here. At a push he could walk it in two days—if there were no interruptions along the way—or he could try to find a village or farm and steal a horse. He touched his fingertips together, winced at the ever-present pain and wondered whether his stealing days were over.

———

SOMETIME LATER, KOSAR realized that he was being followed.

He did not stop or glance back; the feeling was so intense that he did not want to give away the fact that he knew. He sped up slightly, but could hear nothing in pursuit. And yet his blind sense prickled: the hairs on his neck stood up and his balls tingled. His sword was a comfortable weight on his belt rather than an annoyance. *It's tasted Monk blood,* he thought, but the idea of a Red Monk following him was not one he wished to entertain.

The landscape was becoming more hilly, bringing the horizon closer and providing more valleys and dips in which the darkness could hide. Moonlight still gave the land a monotone splash of weak illumination, but great lakes of darkness lay here and there, as though the light was not heavy enough to penetrate that deeply. There could be anything on the floors of these valleys. Perhaps they had been this dark for a long, long time. Where he could, Kosar decided to keep to the hills.

He climbed a long, slow incline, panting with the effort and realizing how hungry he was. He had a water pouch that was half full, but he had not thought about food for a while. He would have to stop soon and set some snares, maybe see if he could find some berries or roots to strip and eat. But the plants were dying. Leaves were shriveling and drying, and when he passed a clump of common black bushes there was an unpleasant odor underlying everything, as though the ground itself was slowly going to rot. *Maybe this is how it will end*, he thought. *Maybe the land will just fade away and die. It may take a year, but the Mages have been waiting three centuries for this. Less effort for them. And a weakening land would never fight back.*

There was a sound behind him, a distant thud like something dropping to the ground. Kosar paused, head tilted to pick up anything else. He realized that anyone or anything watching would now know that he had heard them, but the pretense could do him no good. Perhaps whatever it was would not reveal itself.

Kosar held on to the sword and felt comforted at the way it fit his hand.

He carried on walking, reaching the top of the hill in one final hard climb. He was sweating and panting now, shaking with the exertion, but stopping for a rest would help bring his follower closer. He could smell rotting plants again, and to his left he saw the outline of a huge old machine rusting into the ground. Yellow moonlight from the death moon bathed its interior and made it more defined than anything Kosar had seen since darkness fell. He had often heard it said that the death moon favored the dead with its light.

He turned around and stared down the hill he had just climbed. For a few seconds he saw the shape way down the slope, struggling upward like a huge beetle. Then whoever or whatever it was must have seen him silhouetted against the moonlit sky, because the shadow grew still and merged with the ground.

"Come on!" Kosar shouted. "Don't be a coward!" *Should be running, not shouting*, he thought, but terror had brought out a new bravery. If he was to confront whatever this was, he'd rather do it now than have it follow him at a distance. "Come *on!*" But the shadow remained hidden.

He looked across at the machine and considered hiding within its rusted embrace. But then he thought of those old machines rising to fight in the graveyard, the flesh and blood flowing to them from out of nowhere, and quickly moved on.

HE FOUND THE village in a fold in the land. The landscape dipped and rose, and it was maybe a quarter of a day after leaving the hilltop machine that he first saw the faint glow in the distance, all that time aware that someone or something was on his tail, fearing attack from behind and equally afraid of what might lay before him. The darkness was bleeding the strength from him, much as it was killing the plants.

At first he thought it was moonlight reflecting from a huge lake—the life moon had risen higher now, pale, wan and defiant—but as he drew closer across a ridge he realized that it was light rising from a deep wound in the land. A crevasse or a crater, carved into the bedrock by particularly violent waters. He had never been to this part of Noreela before—New Shanti and its environs were generally not high on a wanderer's list of destinations—and he tried to envisage a map of the area. The darkness still confused him. The Mol'Steria Desert should lie to the north, Sordon Sound to the northeast, and as far as he could recall, there should not have been a river anywhere near here. And yet Kang Kang still lay to the south, hidden by a horizon brought closer by the dusk. Perhaps in the strange years since the Cataclysmic War, one of its rivers had broken out from underground and torn the land.

At the highest point of the ridge, he turned back to try to see his follower. He saw no shadows running for cover, no shapes falling still out of the corner of his eye, but that could mean that the follower was becoming more careful. In this poor light it could be standing motionless a hundred steps away and Kosar would never see it.

It took him an hour to walk down the hillside and approach the edge of the ravine. The glow barely rose above the ground surrounding it, but it lit Kosar's way for the final few hundred steps. It was a refreshing change being able to see the grasses part around his feet, but he also saw the withered remnants of mollies and chloeys, testament to the dark, and he wondered whether the sun would ever return.

Kosar paused frequently to look back, but nothing else emerged from the darkness.

The light came from a fire. He could smell the tang of burning wood, and a haze of smoke hung low in the air, mostly hidden from sight but detectable by smell and taste. *Hangman's wood!* Kosar thought. It was often used on the Cantrass Plains to smoke fish and other meats, because it burned slow and not too hot. Its smoke was spicy and almost as mouthwatering as cooking meat, and he increased his step almost without realizing.

At the edge, looking down at the ravine floor two hundred steps below, he realized how foolish he had been.

There was a village down there, built in a huddle against the sheer cliffs on either side, and through its middle flowed a stream. From this high up the water looked black. The area around the village was illuminated by two huge fires, one built at either end of the settlement. He could make out maybe two dozen buildings, and between them the shapes of people going to and fro.

The fires had not been there for long. Everyone in Noreela must be reacting differently to the fall of dusk; these people were digging in for a fight.

And he had walked right up to the edge of their territory like a sheebok to the slaughter.

Something approached from behind. Kosar spun around, hand on sword, and he just had time to glimpse three dark faces before a heavy blow crunched into his nose, and all he saw was light.

A'MEER WAS LOOMING above him, and he thought that the mimics were back. But when he opened his eyes and looked past the pain he saw that she was smiling, not gasping, and her dark hair was parted into the usual plaits instead of being cleaved by a sword blow, and when she opened her mouth he knew that she was going to tell him it had all been a mistake, that Rafe was fine and Kosar was just coming out of a long unconsciousness after that final terrible battle in the machines' graveyard.

"Wake, yer scummer!" A'Meer splashed across his face, and she tasted of piss. Someone giggled and was cut short by a harsh grunt. "Wake, scummer. Or I'll cut yer throat where you lay!"

Kosar opened his eyes. The bright pain had vanished and it was twilight once again. He was lying on his back, and above him stood two men and a woman. They had dark skin, long hair formed into elaborate sculptures and fixed with dried, painted mud, and their faces and bodies glittered with dozens of metallic piercings. Breakers. Kosar had run into them once before. They were even further removed from Noreelan society than the rovers.

He groaned. His face was hot and sore, his nose streamed blood. One of his teeth had broken. He could feel the stump of it with his tongue, and shards had buried themselves in his lip. He turned his head and spat blood and tooth. His neck hurt and his head throbbed, and he wondered whether there was more damage he had yet to discover.

"He's spying on us. We should take his eyes," the woman said.

"And his tongue," a male voice added.

Kosar looked up at the three Breakers. One of the men was buttoning his fly after pissing on Kosar. He seemed to be the one in charge; he stood close to Kosar while the other two hung back, side by side for security. "I'm no spy," he said.

"Then what in the Black are you?" the lead Breaker said.

"A thief." Kosar slowly raised one hand to display his marks.

"And so?" the Breaker said. "Why should I trust a thief any more than a spy? And one that's got caught too. Yer no thief, yer a fool, and fools deserve to have their throats aired."

"Maybe he came to steal from us, Schiff," the woman said.

"I didn't even know you were here." Kosar rested his head back on the ground and closed his eyes, trying to fight off the sickness welling in him. "What did you hit me with?"

"Magic," the Breaker said.

Kosar's eyes snapped open and he looked at the thing in Schiff's right hand. It was a club, a mad merging of stone and metal and wood held together by dried mud and twisted grasses. There was no magic about it, and if the light had been better he would see it decorated with his blood. "No magic there," he said.

Schiff squatted beside Kosar and thumped the club down beside his head. "Yet this bastard'll open up your skull easy enough," he said. "Open it up like magic!"

"I know why it's dark," Kosar said. *Got to be careful here*, he thought. *Got to feed them just enough, but not too much.* The Breakers spent their lives traveling Noreela and dismantling old machines, opening up rusted metal hulks and cracking stone limbs, searching through long-dried arteries and funnels and routes for dregs of the old magic they still believed to be there somewhere. They came into towns and villages in small groups and lived apart from the local populace, setting up their own commune, growing their own food and keeping sheebok and sometimes sand rats for meat. Out in the wilds, Breaker communities often sprouted up around old mines or abandoned farms, and the centerpiece was always a giant machine. Sometimes they worked a machine for a whole generation, taking it apart meticulously and carefully, laying the component parts out to view. Magic had made the machines long ago, and now Breakers were dismantling them. They knew more about how the machines were made—and perhaps how they had worked—than anyone in Noreela.

Kosar had never heard of any magic being found, of course. And therein lay the Breakers' madness. After three hundred years of failure, they were more hungry than ever.

"It's the land," Schiff said. He stared past Kosar down into the ravine. "Noreela's been dead a long time, and now it's finally starting to rot."

"It's magic," Kosar said. "It's back in the land, but the Mages have come and taken it."

"What in the fucking Black are you talking about, scummer?" The big Breaker stood and lifted the club, letting gravity swing it into the side of Kosar's head.

It was not a heavy blow; there was no strength behind it. But the pain bled through Kosar like molten silver, and when he looked up at the life moon he saw it turning red. For a second it had eyes and a face—a mad, angry face obsessed with purpose and flooded with blood. *Maybe it really would have been better if we'd not run so fast, if A'Meer hadn't fought so well, if I hadn't loosed that tumbler to kill the Monk. If they'd caught Rafe and slaughtered him, maybe the magic would have gone with him. The Mages would have returned to nothing, and perhaps they would have been killed by the Monks. They were old, and probably mad.*

"Better if he'd died," Kosar muttered.

"What was that, scummer?"

"Better if he'd never shown us anything." Kosar's head swam, as though he'd had too much rotwine. Sickness still threatened. He wished a tumbler would come and roll him away.

"Kill him, Schiff!" the woman said. "He's mad and raging, and he's nothing for us."

Schiff knelt again and touched Kosar's belt. "He has a Shantasi sword," he said.

"So? He's a thief."

Schiff looked at Kosar, *really* looked at him for the first time, and Kosar returned his gaze. "He has something for us," the Breaker said.

"What in the Black could he have for us?"

"Don't know," Schiff said. He frowned, still looking at Kosar. Then he moved closer and sniffed. Kosar heard his piercings clinking and scratching at one another. "Maybe we'll have to cut him open to find out."

"So are Breakers butchers as well?" Kosar asked. He formed his words closely, trying not to slur and show weakness.

"I'm whatever I need to be," Schiff said. He nodded down at Kosar's sword. "Who did you steal that from?"

"It's not stolen," Kosar said.

"Then who gave it to you?"

"A friend."

"Come on, Schiff, stop playing with him. Brain him and leave him for the sand rats." The woman seemed to be getting nervous. Kosar saw her glancing around, trying to see into the dark. The glow of the huge fires down in the ravine reflected pale yellow in her eyes.

Schiff reached out quickly, nudging Kosar's hand aside and grabbing the sword handle.

Kosar sat up and closed his own hand around Schiff's, wincing as piercings in the back of the Breaker's hand rubbed against his raw fingers. "The sword's mine."

Schiff leaned forward, his nose pressed against Kosar's. "I'll have it from you like this, or I'll smash your skull open and then have it from you. Your choice, scummer."

"Aren't you going to kill me anyway?" Kosar breathed long and deep, fighting the nausea for a few seconds more.

"If you don't continue to interest me, yes." Schiff pulled hard, knocking Kosar's hand aside and drawing the sword. He ran his fingers along the blade, sniffed at it, tasted it. "You've seen some action," he said.

"Some," Kosar said.

"Who did you kill?"

"Red Monks."

Schiff fell silent, but his two companions broke into laughter, even the nervous woman. "Red Monks!" she said. "I'd have like'd to have seen that!" Her laugh broke into a cackle, reminding Kosar of Hope. *Where is she now?* he thought. *I hope she's safe. I hope she's looking after Trey and Alishia.*

"Bring him!" Schiff said. He stood and held the sword before him, turning it this way and that as he inspected its surface, its cutting edges, the designs on the hilt and the sweat-darkened leather looped a hundred times around the handle.

"It needs blood," Kosar said.

"It'll have it." Schiff tapped the sword against his face, neck and chest, creating a mess of metallic notes.

The other two Breakers hefted Kosar to his feet and shoved him toward the lip of the ravine. For a terrifying instant he thought they were simply going to push him over and let the jagged rocks do what they would not. But then he saw the path cleverly concealed behind a pile of rocks at the cliff edge and, their way illuminated only by the flickering light of the two huge fires, they began their descent to the ravine floor.

Kosar was still dizzied from the blow to his head. He spat more blood and wondered what would become of it. Would it soak down into the sand, solidify, form part of a stone that would perhaps be found in ten thousand years? What would that finder of the future think of a stone with teeth shards and fossilized blood seaming it? They could build a story about him, and it would be far from the truth.

Or maybe a sand rat would lick up the bloody splash, teeth specks and all, and Kosar's spit would end up as rat shit.

Fate had many tricks in store, and the future felt so insecure.

Breakers did not welcome strangers. Halfway down the sloping path, Kosar became certain that if he let them reach the ravine floor he would be dead within the hour.

———

"MAGIC'S BACK IN the land," he said. "The Mages have it. I was with the boy it was being reborn into, and they stole him away and killed him and took it for themselves. They made the skies grow dark. It's the beginning of their revenge."

"Shut up, scummer!"

Kosar felt A'Meer's sword prick his back and urge him on. He winced at the feeling of metal parting his skin, and the warm dribble of blood that followed. *At least the blade's blooded,* he thought. The wound was not deep but it stung. Schiff's voice had changed. Before it had been dismissive and harsh, now there was more thought behind it. *He's going to kill me,* Kosar thought. *For some reason I scare him, and he'll kill me as soon as we get down, run me through with the sword A'Meer gave me, but he'll do it in front of his Breaker clan to show that he's protecting them from whatever new rot has set into the land.*

"Why don't you believe me?" Kosar said.

"Move on or I'll help you on your way."

"You've been looking for it forever, and now when it's actually *here,* in the land instead of rotting away in old machines that were dead before you were an itch in your father's cock, you're not even close to ready—"

The sword pricked in again, digging into Kosar's right shoulder above the shoulder blade, splitting skin and flesh, and Kosar fell forward and spun at the same time, landing on his side and kicking out at Schiff's legs. The path cut into the side of the cliff was barely wide enough for two people and, with the other Breakers behind him, Schiff had nowhere to go. Kosar was confident that one good kick would send the Breaker tumbling from the path.

His right foot connected with Schiff's left leg. Schiff did not move, and Kosar cried out as pain tore up his leg and into his hip. He kicked again and Schiff stepped back, swinging out with the sword, sweeping it across the path in an arc that would take off Kosar's foot. Kosar pulled back, cringing as the wound in his shoulder gushed. *More blood spilled,* he thought. *I can't have much left.* The sword scraped across the path and sparks flew.

Schiff grinned. He moved back a step or two, forcing the other two Breakers back behind him, and pulled at his trouser leg. It rose away from his foot and gathered at his knee, and Kosar saw the fires reflected on the metal skin of his leg. "Machines give us everything we need," he said.

"But I've seen them alive," Kosar said. And for the first time, he saw something like belief in the Breaker's eyes.

"I'm going to fucking kill you, scummer," Schiff whispered.

"Why?" Kosar said. He was bracing himself against the ground,

testing his right arm to make sure he could lever himself upward.
The wound on his shoulder was painful, but it didn't appear to have
damaged the muscles. As soon as Schiff was distracted he was going
to launch himself at the big Breaker and shove him from the path.
Easy, he thought. *Piece of piss, as Hope would say.*

Schiff seemed unable to answer Kosar's question.

Kosar glanced over Schiff's shoulder at the woman. She looked
confused, and scared. "Because with magic back, your lives mean
nothing," he said. "That's why. I've brought a truth you can't bear."

"Schiff, what's he—?"

Schiff turned, already starting to shout at the woman, and
Kosar pushed himself up from the path. A stone rolled beneath his
hand, his shoulder jarred and the wound seemed to stab at him
again. He cursed and pushed harder, tearing a muscle in his shoulder and adding to the pain already nestling there. The woman's
eyes opened wider as she stared past Schiff at Kosar. Kosar saw fire
reflected there, yellow then red, as though her eyes were slowly filling with blood, and Schiff started to turn back, sword rising, legs
bracing, mouth opening in a scream of rage and realization. *He be-
lieves me*, Kosar thought, *and I've made his life meaningless.*

Kosar stood and drove forward, striking Schiff across the nose
with his elbow and feeling the crunch of cartilage giving way.
The Breaker's piercings tinkled and scraped as they were ground
together.

Schiff roared, swinging his arm, but Kosar had pushed himself
into the Breaker's fighting circle and the sword slapped harmlessly
across his lower back. *Five heartbeats*, he thought, *that's all it'll
take, five heartbeats to draw back and stab in and then A'Meer's
father's sword will gut me.* He thought much, much more in those
few moments, a slew of images rather than words: Rafe raising the
boat from the River San; watching A'Meer in the Broken Arm without her knowing he was there, the way her plaits swung, her constant wry smile; running across the plain toward the Gray Woods,
fearing the Monks behind them and having no idea of what they
were about to face; the machines, rising; the Mages, falling out of
the sunset; the darkness. And he realized that he had never been
this close to death before.

The other male Breaker screamed.

Kosar looked over Schiff's shoulder.

The Breaker was behind the woman, ten steps back along the

path, and he was staring down at a sword protruding from his chest. Behind him, a flash of red. And above this confusion of colors, a face, teeth bared and eyes blacker than mere darkness.

"Monk!" the woman shouted. Her voice was low and rough, as if her throat were already slit.

The Red Monk lifted the Breaker with the sword through his chest, pivoted and leaned forward. The man shrieked, waving his arms and legs, then slid from the sword and fell. When he struck the rocks his scream ceased, replaced by the thuds and crunches of his body tumbling to the foot of the cliff.

The woman backed toward Kosar and Schiff, but the Monk was on her quickly, a blur of robe and glittering sword sweeping her from the cliff path. She did not scream as she fell into the dark.

Kosar shoved against Schiff but stumbled over his own ankles, falling down again. He remembered fighting the Monk in the square in Pavisse. Now he did not even have a sword.

Schiff stood his ground. Kosar had a fleeting sense of respect for this Breaker, hefting a strange sword and planting his feet on the narrow cliff path in readiness to take on a Red Monk. But then the demon strode in, grunting as Schiff buried the sword in its shoulder, pushing itself further onto the blade until it was close enough to strike out and bury its own in Schiff's gut.

The Breaker screamed. His hands went to the wound, leaving Kosar's sword protruding from the Red Monk, and the Monk glared down at Kosar.

"I know you," it said. Its voice was deep, and belonged to this darkness.

The Monk lifted Schiff and jerked its arms, tearing the blade up through the Breaker's stomach until it reached his ribs, and all the time Schiff was screaming and crying, thrashing at the Monk standing just beyond his reach. He was hanging out over space now, with the demon standing at the edge of the path seemingly unafraid of the drop before it.

Kosar pushed himself up, ran at the Red Monk and shouldered into it. For a terrible instant he imagined that nothing would happen. He would bounce from the Monk just as his foot had rebounded from Schiff's metallic leg; the Monk would drop Schiff after his companions, turn around, place the point of the bloody sword against Kosar's throat and push.

I know you, it had said.

The Monk toppled over the edge of the narrow path. It held on to its sword lodged in Schiff's stomach, so the two of them fell together. The Breaker screamed. The Monk made no sound at all.

Kosar watched them bounce from rocks and hit the ground, their impact illuminated by the giant fires. The Monk lay with arms and legs outstretched, its robe settling around it like a dead bird's wings. The Breaker's back was broken. The sword glistened in his belly. Beside them, the remains of the other two fallen seemed to shift in the echo of flames.

Kosar looked along the ravine and saw movement there, shapes darting between buildings, several more gathered in the heart of what must once have been a giant machine. It rose around them, ribs or struts or limbs curving up out of the ground as though the machine had died emerging, or trying to bury itself. It framed the Breakers against the fire. They had spent untold years gutting and deconstructing it, and now they hid behind it.

More shapes were slipping from shadow to shadow, coming closer to the foot of the path. Even if they did try to chase him down, Kosar was confident he could make it out of the ravine before the Breakers reached him. But he had lost his sword. He had a long way to go before he reached Hess, and between here and there were untold dangers. He had never been a fighter, but that metal had made him feel safer—perhaps because it had been given to him by A'Meer.

The first Breaker reached the foot of the path and started up, and Kosar turned to flee.

But then he saw more movement below. The Monk had shifted, brought in its arms and legs and was slowly rising to its feet.

I know you, it had said.

It reached out and prised its weapon from the dead Breaker's gut, before tugging A'Meer's sword from its own shoulder. It looked up directly at Kosar. From this distance he could not see the thing's eyes, but flickering light from the fires seemed to make some connections between the two of them. And when the Monk started limping toward the village and those hiding there, Kosar found himself silently urging it on.

The Breaker at the foot of the path spotted the Red Monk coming toward him. He obviously knew what he was seeing, and sprinted back to the small village, ducking in behind the big machine and adding his shadow to the others hiding there. Above the roar of the giant fires, Kosar could hear shouting from the houses, echoing back into caves that were invisible from this angle. They sounded like the calls of an injured, cornered animal, terrified yet filled with fury.

The Monk reached the village. Kosar heard a crossbow being fired, and immediately he was taken back to Trengborne, watching a Red Monk ride into the village and slaughter every person there in its relentless search for Rafe Baburn.

The Monk grunted, then walked on.

It fell a hundred steps!

It met the first Breaker and killed her with one swipe of its sword.

When it came to the harvested machine, the Monk paused, as if waiting for magic to erupt and set the machine upon it. And then, when nothing happened, the Monk entered into battle.

Kosar sat on the path and watched the slaughter. He felt bad for the Breakers—especially when he saw several small shapes dart from a house straight into the Monk's path—but he could not forget that they had been readying to kill him. They had been brainwashed by their ancestors into believing that they could gain magic by breaking. They were, he supposed, as much victims of the Mages as anyone in Noreela. And now their harsh world had turned harsher.

The Monk fought past the machine, leaving dead and dying in its wake. Shadows emerged from houses and tried to flee, but the Monk ran them down and killed them. It crossed the stream, pushing through the waist-high water. It knocked aside crossbow bolts with the two swords, taking several hits in its torso and limbs, and then attacked those on the other side. The ones who fought back, it killed quickly; those who fled, the Monk seemed to take its time over. It was a demon, a monster, a killer risen from the ashes of dead magic, and now it fought in a world where new magic had made it redundant.

Kosar wondered what the thing was feeling and thinking right now. Was this revenge killing, a rage-filled slaughter? Or was it simply killing out of habit?

He knew he should have left. The fighting went on for half an hour, the final few minutes punctuated only by a single, mournful scream. But he sat and watched. And when the Monk emerged from the Breaker village, strode past the old machine and ran to the foot of the cliff path, Kosar found that he could barely stand. The wound on his back was sticky with blood, and his crunched nose meant that he could only breathe through his mouth. He swayed, trying to retain the knowledge of which way was up and down, as the Red Monk ran up the path toward him.

Both swords raised.

Kosar tumbled forward. In his delirium, he decided that a quick fall and death on the rocks would be better than being hacked to pieces. *I know you,* the Monk had said. So Kosar fell into space. He heard the Monk panting and wheezing, bloody bubbles bursting on its lips.

A hand closed around his ankle and pulled. Kosar pivoted flat against the cliff face, staring down at the dead Breakers spread on the rocks below, and was jerked over rough rock.

As he was turned onto his back, he stared into the face of the demon.

Chapter 7

TIME LOST MEANING. It had started when day and night were stolen away, and now their bodies had begun to rebel. Hope would sit and mutter to herself when they paused to rest, cross-legged and staring southward like a figurehead on a long-lost ship, arms jerking with muscular spasms every time she tried to lie down. She cursed and spat and spoke in languages Trey could never know. But sometimes a sense of calm came over her and she watched Alishia. Always Alishia.

The girl would wake into confusion and disorientation, blinking in the dusk like a cave rat that had never seen the light. She ate a little, drank less and found it difficult to stand unaided. She said that her bones ached and her joints felt as though they were grinding together, and when Trey went to lift her she would cry out in pain.

The constant level of subdued light should have been a comfort to Trey, but he had never felt so disturbed. The fledge rage was strong in him now. When he walked with Alishia across his back, he thought of what fledge looked like, how it smelled and tasted, how

it felt between blind hands down in the utter darkness of the mines.
He was young and still learning, but older miners had told him how
they could identify fledge from different seams through touch alone,
how they could tell whether it was fresh or stale by the texture and
moisture content and how they knew from the first touch on their
tongues whether or not it was going to give them a good journey.

Trey so wished to travel with fledge, now that all he could do
was walk. How he wanted to sit back and hover above his body, look
down and see himself spread-eagled on the ground, launch his quest-
ing mind into the twilight to discover whole truths he had never
even guessed at. He could dip down into Hope's mind and see the
volumes of danger of which Alishia had spoken. He could visit
Alishia where she slept, troubled and in pain, and ask whether this
was really the right thing to do. And he could move farther afield.
Kang Kang lay ahead of them, and it pressed against him like a
physical force, urging him to turn and flee the way he had come. It
was an impassable wall of stone in a wide-open cave, immovable
and daunting. He could explore.

With fledge he could do anything. He found himself sniffing
for it with every breath he took.

Night, night, night. He looked at the witch and knew that she
was turning mad. He looked at Alishia, twitching in her sleep and
mumbling words he did not understand. And he looked at the sky,
realizing for the first time ever how even he, a cave dweller, was in-
fluenced by the turns of the sun.

———

"SOMETHING UP AHEAD," Hope said. "Something strange."

"How do you know?"

"Can't you feel it? The air's different. There's a constant breeze
from the north, but it feels as though the ground's moving instead of
the air." Hope looked ahead, toward the shadowy mountains of
Kang Kang, and her tattoos squirmed like salted snakes.

Trey lowered Alishia to the ground, groaning as the tension in
his shoulders gave way to pain. He kneaded at his cramping muscles and followed Hope's gaze. The landscape ahead of them was a
blank: no contours in the shadows, no hint of any features, no indication that there was anything there at all. Darkness lay thick across
the ground. He sniffed for fledge, but found only a sterile odor, like
the air in a cave after a flood. Cleaned. Purged. Empty.

"What is it?" he said.

"I don't know." The witch hefted his disc-sword and he reached for it. He closed his hand around the shaft and Hope looked at him, eyebrows raised. Then she smiled and let go. "Very well, fledger," she said. She dipped her hand into a pocket and kept it there.

What does she have in there? Trey thought. He'd seen her ripping some plant and dropping it into her pocket. To feed something? Or to let the leaves dry?

Alishia rolled onto her back and her eyes snapped open, but when he knelt beside her Trey could see that she was still asleep. He waved a hand in front of her face, but her eyes did not flicker. He so wanted those eyes to turn to him and smile. But he had begun to fear that would never happen again.

"We should go on," Hope said. "We'll be in the foothills of Kang Kang before we know it. They're closer."

Trey had noticed that too. Though the repulsion he felt was still strong, the mountains had suddenly seemed to come close, pushing him away yet urging him in. He felt as though two forces were acting upon him, and he had no idea which one to obey. He stood and held his disc-sword in both hands, ready to spin the blade and take on anything that came at them from the dark.

"Hope," he said, "we haven't seen anyone. We've been walking for maybe two topside days, and we haven't seen another living soul."

"They're out there," the witch said. "Back in the small range of lead-rock hills we passed through, there was a band of rovers. They hid from us. Farther on—maybe half a day ago—we passed close to a village. They were lined against us, barricaded, ready to fight. I could smell the fear on them, and the stink of sheebok and land hogs rotting into the ground. They were farmers. Terrified. Scared of what we were and what we'd do if we found them. If only they knew our fear as well. There have been others too, hiding in shadows or lying low in the folds of the land. We've been keeping to the high places so we can see into the distance, looking for Kang Kang and keeping watch for threats. Most of the people around here are lying as low as they can."

"I heard nothing," Trey said. "I saw no one."

"Neither did I. I smelled them."

Trey thought of all the time he had spent trying to find the hint of fledge on the air.

"So what's this?" he said quietly. "It's like an open space of nothing. I see Kang Kang in the distance, but nothing in between."

"Maybe there *is* nothing," Hope said.

"What do you mean?"

"The land's been strange for so long now. Perhaps the Mages' return has quickened the rot."

"But there must be time," Trey said. "We have to have time. This can't be hopeless, can it?"

Hope shrugged and looked at the sleeping girl. "I don't think Fate owes us anything," she said. "We may make it to within five steps of our destination and then be killed in a rockfall. There's nothing looking out for us, fledger. With Rafe, perhaps his magic watched over us, but not with this one. We're more on our own than we've ever been. Can't you feel that?"

Trey shivered, nodded, and his guts knotted with a sudden craving for fledge.

"We'll go on," Hope said. "We can't stop here, not now. If you can carry her farther, we should go."

Hope helped Trey lift Alishia onto his back, then she took his disc-sword and walked on ahead once more, marking their route, looking left and right, up and down, watching for danger or searching for something more. Alishia was heavy, but not as heavy as she had been. Her thighs were thinner, her face less well defined, and her stomach had become soft with adolescent fat. *Still growing younger,* Trey thought. *She's our limit. We go this way because of what she said, but we only have so long, because of her. If we get there too late . . .*

He heard a thud and felt the ground shake. Hope paused and glanced around at him, then kept moving on. Trey followed. Another crash from somewhere in the near distance, like a giant footfall hitting the land, and again he felt the vibration through his feet.

"What is that?" he said.

Hope had paused again and was looking up at the sky. Trey followed her gaze and saw the shadows. At first he thought it was a huge storm cloud, and he would have welcomed a downpour of rain. It would be a novelty for him, and they were growing painfully short on water. But then he saw the shadows dropping out of the darkness—a mass that seemed to shun moonlight, swallowing it rather than reflecting —and he knew that this was not a rain of water.

The shadows spun groundward. They passed out of view, and seconds later came another series of thuds.

"Hope?" Trey called.

"This should be interesting," she said.

"Hope, what is it?" But the witch had moved on again, running down through a narrow gulley and heading for a small hill that obscured the land ahead of them. Trey took a final look up, saw more shadows falling away from the mass of negative sky and followed.

"HERE," HOPE SAID. "This is where we stop for now."

Trey struggled up the small rise toward the witch. She was staring south. "What is it?"

"See for yourself."

He saw the vague, massive cloud above the hillside; then Kang Kang, its highest peaks appearing above the line of the hill. And then as he drew closer to Hope he could make out the landscape that lay between them and the first of Kang Kang's foothills.

There was very little left.

"What in the Black . . . ?"

"The land has gone bad," Hope said, as if that could explain it all.

In the distance, the land had been stripped bare. Trees, grasses and plants, all gone. Above them, a mile or two up, the stew of the land twisted and rolled endlessly overhead. Closer by, at the foot of the hillside they now stood upon, the closest extreme of the fallout area was marked by a giant wellburr tree lying on its side, roots exposed and branches snapped and crushed.

"Mage shit," Trey said. "The land's eating itself."

Hope seemed lost for words.

The process must have started quite recently, because it was not yet complete. In several places the bared bedrock spewed broken columns of earth and stone skyward. Geysers of sand and gravel blasted up toward that cloud of land.

At the edges of the cloud, where the effect seemed to lessen, what went up was starting to come back down. The thuds they had heard and felt were trees and rocks falling back to Noreela, slanting away from the stripped landscape and forming a perimeter banking of refuse: timber and stone, soil and vegetation, thumping back down with murderous finality.

Trey saw a sheebok spinning end over end as it fell in the distance. Perhaps it was already dead, perhaps not, but it struck the ground and exploded, sending glistening tendrils of itself across a slew of bushes and trees.

"We need to move back," Trey said, awed and aghast.

"We'll be safe here."

"How do you know? It may spread. It might expand faster than we can run, and then we'll be sucked up into *that*!"

"Not sucked," the witch said. "Fall. Everything's falling upward. It's stripping the land to the bedrock. Taking it back down to the bare Noreela . . . taking all the hindrances away."

"What are you on about?" Trey glanced at Alishia's head resting on his shoulder, trying to see whether her eyes were open. He lifted his shoulder slightly, trying to gain her attention, but she was still asleep. "Alishia," he whispered, but there was no reaction.

"We should stay here," the witch said. "Keep one eye on what's happening, wait for it to fade away."

"Maybe it won't," Trey said. "Maybe it'll keep happening until the rock and the ground are all sucked up. Who knows what it may uncover?" He thought of deep mines and the waking Nax and legends of Sleeping Gods, and he looked down at the heathers between his feet, wondering what mysteries their roots tapped in to.

"If it spreads, there's little we can do," Hope said. "We can only hope that it stops eventually, otherwise . . ."

"Otherwise we won't even get close to Kang Kang."

"We could go around it," she said.

Trey looked east and west along the low ridge they stood upon, but both directions vanished into darkness. The cloud above them was huge, and he could discern no limits to the effect ahead of them. Perhaps it went on forever.

"We can't just sit and wait," he said. "Alishia is growing younger every minute."

"Well, we can't walk out into that!" Hope said, shaking her hand at the strange sight before them.

"You think this is the Mages, like the day growing dark?"

"For what it's worth, I think not, no. This is the land turned bad as we've seen before. The Mages will be busy in the north, destroying whatever defenses the Duke can muster." She spat at her feet. "That won't take long. So there's another deadline for you, fledger. Because the Mages won't be busy forever, and sooner or later they or their spies will find out about Alishia and what she carries."

"How could they find out?"

Hope shrugged. "Maybe they'll catch and torture Kosar. Or perhaps their spies won't be as obvious as you think. Shades. Wraiths. Other things." She grinned at Trey then, a toothy grimace that made him turn back to the ruined land. The noise was a constant rumble, interspersed with occasional thumps and vibrations as something dropped. At the base of the hill, perhaps a mile distant, the collection of debris was growing taller and wider, forming a barrier between the normal ground and that beyond.

A hissing white explosion erupted way beyond the barrier, pouring skyward and losing itself in the boiling mass overhead. Trey wondered whether this was a sacred river, revered like that one beneath the Widow's Peaks. The eruption quickly turned from white to brown as sediment was sucked up from under the bedrock. The water continued rising, bursting out from several other points and emptying itself skyward.

An hour later it began to rain, and Trey sniffed the water for any trace of fledge.

———

HE MUST HAVE closed his eyes. He was aware of the noises around him, and the heat of Alishia lying beside him on the dew-damped heather, but in his mind he was somewhere else. He was not sure where the other place was, but it felt safe and warm, insulated from the dangers he knew by the remoteness of memories. He could hear his mother singing softly in the darkness of their cave. He could smell Sonda's skin and her breath as they passed each other in the home-cave, sharing a smile and averting their eyes. He could feel the faces of his fellow miners as they broke for lunch, hear their voices, wallowing in the good humor that came from facing the constant danger of the mine together. Trey was aware of his own breathing and the tickle of heather beneath his cheek, but it was only when he opened his eyes that all those feelings of safety and contentment vanished.

Hope had gone. Alishia still lay by his side, pale and warm, and he could see her eyelids flexing as she explored something unknowable in her dreams. Trey shivered and hugged himself, wishing he had fledge to touch Alishia and see if she was all right. Wishing he had fledge for himself. His heart beat fast, his breathing was shallow, and he felt certain that everything was about to change.

He stared up at the sky. The cloud was still there but it seemed to have calmed, its feathery edges being dragged close by its continuing swirling motion. Some shadows fell away and drifted down, but fewer than before, and the noise of things impacting the ground seemed less frequent. The cloud was a nothing against the darkness, a hole he could so easily fall into. There was no light below to give it any definition, and the moonlight above slid from it as though repelled by its unnaturalness.

Trey looked away, unnerved, wondering where Hope had gone.

He pulled his water canteen from his shoulder bag and poured a few drops into Alishia's mouth. Her lips opened and her tongue protruded slightly, absorbing the moisture. Her eyes flickered open but seemed to see nothing. He leaned close and whispered her name, but there was no reaction.

Trey took one mouthful of stale water from the canteen and hid it away in his bag once more.

Still no Hope. He stood and walked a few steps along the ridge, looking down across the wide plains between them and the beginnings of Kang Kang. The ground was pale and gray, exposed rock casting back moonlight that slid beneath the cloud, and there were great swathes of shadow where darkness hid in hollows. He looked left and right along the hillside, back at the unsettling scene before him, and then he saw movement. It was like a beetle on the rough gray skin of an old pit mule, only it moved with more purpose.

Hope. She had somehow made her way through the great mountain of shattered trees and exploded rocks to start out onto the bared skeleton of Noreela. She moved carefully, glancing down at her feet yet seeming to concentrate on one single point somewhere ahead. The sky was heavy above her, still weighted with everything that should have been below, but the strange effect had ended. Trey could feel the unbearable pressure of it where he stood.

He almost called out to Hope, but realized that she was too far away. And he did not know what else could be out in the darkness, ready to home in as soon as it heard potential prey.

He rushed back to Alishia and scanned the ground around her. Hope had taken his disc-sword. Alishia stirred in her sleep and rolled onto her side, and Trey touched her to make sure she was still there.

She could have doped me, he thought. *I was lying there both awake and asleep, and she could have doped me and made off with Alishia.* He touched the librarian's hair, her neck, her back, and she was sweating and shaking as her bones and flesh faded away. *The old witch could have killed me.*

The fact that she had left him alive brought Trey little comfort. He managed to sling Alishia across his right shoulder and stand. He was amazed at her lightness. As he shifted her into a more comfortable position, she grunted and whispered something, but he could not make out the words. He paused, but she said no more.

"Not long," he said. "I can move faster with you like this. And that Mage-shitting witch isn't getting away this easily." Whatever her motives, whatever her intent, Trey had no intention of being left alone with the responsibility for Alishia. Hope knew so much, and he knew so little.

For the first time in his life, he was afraid of the dark.

———

HOPE WAS WALKING on the bare skin of Noreela. There was no evidence of time here: no buildup of soil, no rotting vegetation, no animal bones or skeletons of the unfortunate victims of Kang Kang. She saw no living or dead things marring the sterile perfection of this blank slate of the land, and she could smell nothing but the tang of exposed soil. The rock beneath her feet was dry and utterly bare. And it was warm. She could feel the warmth through her shoes. It was as though Noreela were alive, and for the first time its naked body had been revealed.

Perhaps this was a wound. She stopped and looked around, wondering what the blood of the world would look like. Above her hung the combined mess of everything fallen from here. Yet she was not falling. This strange effect had ended. She feared that soon it would reverse itself. Like the River San, the unbelievable weight of ground and rock above her would fall. Death would be quick when it came, but there would be a dozen heartbeats when she knew it was coming, and she had no wish to discover which memories would haunt those moments.

She did not look up. This was nothing compared to what she thought she had seen farther on.

She focused on where the white shape had marred the shadows, feeling her way forward with cautious steps. Occasionally she glanced down, stepping across cracks in the ground that gushed an unpleasant heat, jumping where those cracks were larger, changing direction where they were too wide to leap. The darkness within was impenetrable, as if the ground were filled with black water to its brim. She hated the warmth that rose: it reminded her of the rank moist breath of her thousands of lovers. Every breath a sigh, every sigh an unrealized dream.

She had been sitting beside Trey and Alishia when she saw the movement on the rocky plain. She was old and her eyes were poor, but she knew instantly what she had seen. The realization hit her like a solid force, a knowledge that forbore any shred of doubt, and her path was clear. Her breath stuck in her chest as though awaiting her action. She started running down the slope of the hill, her heart beating with more power and confidence than she had felt in years.

Down to the first wellburr tree, over its shattered trunk and onward; she had quickly negotiated the hills of debris, sinking to her knees in upset soil, tripping over a tangled mess of vegetation, gashing her arm on the sharp remains of an exhumed machine.

To Hope, it was the moment upon which the future might pivot.

Every few steps she remembered that white shape, how it seemed to lift out of the ground and melt back in, lit from within and exuding light when all else was darkness.

Sleeping God, she had thought, and the very idea made her feel faint.

She went on. The incredible weight of the land above drew her gaze, yet she refused its lure. If she looked, it would fall. She kept telling herself that and, though absurd, it became the truth. *If I look, it will fall.*

She leapt a crack in the ground and felt a warm breath rise within her skirts.

This was the true lay of the land. The exposed surface was Noreela in its infancy, stripped down to the blank slate upon which everything had developed: flora and fauna, man and beast, god and demon, all casting their own special places and building upon the structure of rock that was the foundation of the land.

She glanced down at the rock beneath her feet, suddenly terrified that she would see some ancient message carved there. But there was only stone, smoothed from eons of weight.

There were hollows here and there, burrows stamped down or scooped out by forces unknown. Shadows sat within them, shifting as she hurried by, and she did not pause to see whether it was her skirts making that soft hissing noise as they moved across stone, or something else.

"Sleeping God," she whispered, eyes wide in case her invocation called it back up. But the place where she had seen the movement remained as dark as everywhere else. She did not look aside for too long in case she lost her way.

The Sleeping Gods had gone to ground millennia ago, or so the stories said. They were formidable beings, demons or angels of the land that had supposedly shunned limitless power to wander the wilds, learning and teaching, creating and building but never controlling. They had taken their fill of Noreela and all it could offer and put themselves into the ground, ready to sleep eternally unless something of deep interest woke them once more. They had their worshippers and cults, and there were frequent exhortations that their time had come again. But no Sleeping Gods returned, and the cults would often wither and split to regroup again under different guises, in different places.

Since the Cataclysmic War, it was whispered that they would awake when magic returned to the land.

Hope had always doubted the veracity of that legend. When the Sleeping Gods went down thousands of years ago there had been magic, although probably none that would be recognized today. Why would the return of magic give them cause to rise from their ancient hibernation?

And yet . . .

There was always a chance, and chance is why Hope had given herself such a name.

She was closing on the place where she had seen the movement. She had marked the place well: deep pit of shadows on the right, a raised area of cracked rock on the left. Glancing back, she could just make out the barrier of fallen debris and the low hill beyond. From this distance she could not tell whether Trey was still there. There was no movement on the plain of rock, though she was aware of the shifting way above her. It shook the air, thrummed in her teeth, set her hair on end. *If I look, it will fall.*

She turned back, and for the space between heartbeats she thought the Sleeping God would be there before her, sleeping no more. She had heard a hundred descriptions of what they had looked like, and she was convinced that none of them did the Gods justice. Whatever she saw would be monumental and magnificent. It would strike at her heart with a sense of majesty, and perhaps there would be communication, an acknowledgment that she was the first living thing it had seen upon waking.

Nature going wrong will make everything right, she thought.

But there was nothing there, only the rock and shadows, and the outline of Kang Kang in the distance.

Hope slumped for a moment, confidence and optimism bled by the dusk. But then she went on, because she *had* seen it—*had* seen that shape lifting from the ground then sinking back down. Perhaps the weak moonlight had revealed it . . . but she thought that maybe it had lit itself for her.

They're as big as hawks, descended from the Constructors of Noreela, wandering its ever-changing landscape for a million years, teaching and learning, spreading and absorbing history, looking for something beyond the understanding of mere mortals.

She had heard many stories, all of them different, all of them spouted by people who swore that they told the truth. One man, lying naked on her bed while she prepared him a stew of calming herbs, told her he knew someone who had seen a Sleeping God.

A cave in the Widow's Peaks, and the God was down there, the size of ten men but with a mind so much larger, reaching much farther. It made its own darkness. My friend thought it was asleep. He touched it. He wanted some of its power for himself, thought he could just take it away. It drove him mad. He came out raging and he was never the same man again.

If he came out raging, Hope had said, *how can you believe anything he said?* The man glared at her, his whore, and she said no more.

Hope was close to where she had seen the shape rise and fall. It had curled out of the ground, like the spine of a sea creature parting the waters in the Bay of Cantrassa. The broken rocks to the left, the lake of darkness to the right . . . yes, she was almost there.

The size of a mountain, one book had said, *their eyes lakes in the land, their minds beyond and above what we can know or understand. The Sleeping Gods once walked Noreela and harvested its forests, ate of its fields and meadows, preparing the land for their descendants. We are born of the Sleeping Gods, and like concerned parents they still keep one ear to our collective voice, one eye on our progress.*

They would have come back by now if that were true, Hope thought. *Three hundred years or three days ago, they would have come back.* She slowed, her feet dragging on the bare stone, suddenly terrified of what she would find. She had heard so many legends of the Sleeping Gods, read so many stories. Lay there sweating while sailors from The Spine or Breakers from The Heights fucked her and whispered what they knew. None of them really knew anything, but she let them talk nonetheless, seeking evidence between the lines of their lies. Since the Cataclysmic War the folklore had become more diverse and myth-based than ever before. People read so little nowadays, and as Noreela regressed, so distances between places increased. Noreelans traveled less, and stories had farther to go. Each whisper changed a name or a place. Every telling exaggerated one part of the Sleeping Gods' myth, and forgot another. They had existed, but beyond that nothing was certain.

They went down because they were shamed by Noreela . . .

They await better times . . .

They will awake upon the breaking of the Black . . .

Hope had everything to fear and little to gain, yet still she went on. Would a Sleeping God help her? Would it even recognize her as something other than an insect to be crushed beneath its heel?

She thought so. They were little more than myth now, but in many stories lay a common vein of hope. They were the good of the land gone to sleep, the promise of a better future, and their most devout followers believed that their return would cure all wrongs. They were hope personified, and she had always known their name.

She walked on, and fifty steps later, as she came to the rent in the land where she had seen the shape rise and fall, the boiling soup of Noreela swirling high above finally parted. Life and death moons streamed down, and she saw what filled the hole.

Hope fell.

———

TREY WAS STRUGGLING. Light though she was, Alishia lay awkwardly across his shoulder, her bony hip grinding into his neck. A couple of hundred steps from their makeshift camp he came to the first obstacle: a mass of undergrowth, tangled and stinking of something dead. He lifted his feet higher, tramped through the fallen plants, left hand held out for balance.

He was beginning to panic. *Hope was leaving him.* Much as he disliked the witch, he could not face this journey without her. She knew so much about the land, what had changed and what might happen next. Much of what she said could well be made up, but her confidence in this knowledge comforted him. Besides, he was a stranger up here.

He looked up and saw the mass of risen ground. It was so unnatural and wrong; it grumbled and groaned like a great creature woken from some ancient slumber.

Alishia mumbled and he almost tripped, stumbling a few steps to regain his balance. He found that he'd been holding his breath. He was doing that a lot lately, because breathing seemed to feed the fledge rage burning inside. His skin felt tight, his throat constricted, his mind pressurized and fit to explode.

He sucked in air and tasted nothing.

Trey could see Hope. She was a tiny shape beyond the barrier of fallen debris, hurrying across the silvered base-rock of Noreela. *Caves down there?* Trey thought. *Fissures in the land? Fledge?* But now he could smell nothing, only a curious neutral scent to the air, as though it were all new.

His mind wandered, drawn away partly by panic but mostly by the fledge rage. Imagination tore him sideways while he forged on ahead, and he saw flashes of red, shades of white and the unmistakable smear of blood spreading across the land.

A dream, not a vision.

Alishia muttered something about books of blood, as if she could see what he imagined.

Just a dream. No fledge, no traveling. Just a dream.

He climbed the trunk of the huge fallen wellburr tree, smelling its exposed roots. Then he tackled the mound of debris, slipping and stumbling, clawing at the ground with his free hand, finally sliding down the other side with Alishia still slung over his shoulder.

His leather shoes slapped onto the bare rock, footfalls heavy with Alishia's extra weight. Behind him lay the chaos of what had once made up this land, fallen and smashed and broken, and ahead lay virgin ground, and Hope. She seemed to have paused, standing there like a frozen shadow. And then her shadow was illuminated as combined moonlight finally made its way through the debris and dust above.

Trey saw the glint of metal as she unsheathed his disc-sword.

And then Hope the witch fell forward and vanished from the world.

Trey fell to his knees and dropped Alishia to the ground. The fledge rage twisted his insides and churned his heart as his mind sought refuge somewhere deep and dark.

No travel, he thought, *no fledge*. But with the moons finally revealed again, Trey could do nothing to prevent night from flooding in.

———

THE WEIGHT OF what she saw pulled Hope down. The hollow in the rock was filled with something gray, textured, curved. The dip was perhaps thirty steps across, and a few steps below ground level the gray surface began, like a smooth, frozen lake that had lain there forever. It gave off a faint glow. It had been uncovered now, given to the moonlight. Given to *her*.

That's what I saw move, Hope thought as she tipped forward, *flexing up toward the sky, hauled back down by the power of the Sleeping God within*. As she fell, she was not afraid. Air rushed past her face and smoothed her hair. She kept hold of the disc-sword, though she realized how pathetic and petty it would seem to the God. Whatever this thing may be—a distillation of all the stories told, or something else entirely—a sliver of metal was nothing compared to its magnificence.

As she struck the gray surface, Hope did not even close her eyes. *I'll be breaking in, entering its sleep. I'll be waking it!*

The curved skin was thin, like a spider's nest left for years in a forgotten corner. Hope went straight through with little more than a rustle, wondering how it had escaped the forces stripping the ground all around. But then, the power of a Sleeping God was unknowable.

She struck something hard, gasped as the wind was knocked from her, and for a few moments she lay there, keeping a tight grip on the shaft of the disc-sword. It connected her to the world she had just left behind. It was real. It had been wetted with Noreelan rain and scorched by Noreelan sun; it had tasted blood and soaked up the fledger's sweat as he wielded it in battle. It held hints of fledge within its folded metal grain. She could not smell or taste anything, and the feel of the disc-sword was the only thing holding her in the world.

Moonlight touched strange surfaces for the first time in . . . how long? Hope had no idea. The life moon bled silver across the floor she had landed upon—too soft for rock, too hard for bone— and the death moon gave the air a yellowish tinge. Darkness seemed unwilling to seep away; it held on for a while, melting back like black ice under the weak touch of the moons. She breathed in deeply and smelled old air. It was not musty or stale, but it had been waiting to be breathed for a long time. It was weak in her lungs, and dark spots invaded her vision.

Hope raised herself onto her hands and knees, still clasping the disc-sword. Its blade scraped across the floor, like nails on a pane of smooth glass. She winced and wondered how far that sound would carry.

The witch looked up. She was a few steps below the strange skin she had broken through. The hole was ragged and wide, flaps of the gray surface swinging back and forth where they were still connected to their surroundings.

She was in some sort of tunnel, leading off to the left and right. It vanished into darkness in both directions, but she had the impression that it curved downward as well. The floor had the texture of old leather, and the ceiling above her was jagged with strange sta- lactites. She reached out and touched the wall beside her. It was damp, soft as soapstone, slick to the touch.

"A nest," she said. "Somewhere to sleep. Somewhere safe and sound." The impact of what she was seeing, and where she was, sud- denly hit her. She gasped and found it difficult to breathe. *Every lungful I take in, a Sleeping God has breathed out!*

She wondered where it was. Was she within touching distance? Was it asleep even now behind these walls, beneath this floor? Everything that had happened since she met Rafe Baburn cowering in a shop doorway seemed so meaningless and irrelevant. The peo- ple she had encountered, the miles she had traveled, the Red Monks and the Mages—all of them were so far away that even their mem- ory felt stale and faded. The Sleeping Gods were the paused hearts of Noreela, and she wanted to make them beat again.

They would rise up, spread hope, light the skies and crush the Mages like a puddle of shit beneath a sheebok's hoof.

"It's all here!" she said, and there were no echoes from the strange cave walls. Perhaps the Sleeping God was swallowing her words to discover how true she was. *See everything,* she thought. She was not ashamed. Everything she had done in her life—the good, the bad, the terrible—had been to seek out magic, to find the old lifeblood of Noreela in order to bring it back.

For you, a voice whispered. *You did it all for yourself!* She wanted to kill that voice until she realized it was her own.

Hope stood and moved off along the cave.

Moonlight seemed to stick to her. She carried it on her skin and clothes, and even when she could no longer see the rent in the ceiling, still the surfaces around her reflected silver and yellow. Life and death moons combined, as they always should, and she was pleased that the Sleeping God favored neither.

"Wake up," she whispered. "We need you now . . . *I* need you. You can rescue magic. Magic! Hear me? *Rise* up!"

The only sound was the whisper of her dress on the floor. She paused and listened for any sign of the God, a heartbeat, a breath. But the heartbeats would be days apart, and the breaths would be allied to the rhythms of the land.

The rhythms are all fucked right now, her own voice whispered in her head, and she did her best to ignore it.

The old witch moved farther along the corridor. The light remained at a low level, though there was no evident source. She sniffed, and smelled nothing alive. But nothing dead, either. Only age.

Something brushed at her face and she waved her hand before her. She heard the spiderweb splitting and felt it against her palm, strong and thick. She held her breath and waited for the heavy impact of the creature on her face, but none came. In her pocket she held the sleeping gravemaker spider, ready to use it if the need arose. The web seemed old. It was thick with dust, and rattled with the bones of unknown creatures.

The tunnel curved sharply downward and Hope followed, discsword in one hand, the other cupping the gravemaker spider. Yet she perceived no real threat. This was simply another moment in time, not a pause before chaos. She stepped carefully down the sloping cave, aware of the distance she was putting behind her.

I'll never get back up here, she thought, but she hoped that she would not have to. Once the God was awoken . . .

Hope had always looked away from herself, out into the world, seeking truths and lies that would help her. She was aware of herself at the center of things, but her attention was forever focused elsewhere. Now every moment was rich and relevant, each breath the most important she had ever taken. She was living for the present once again, and each heartbeat took her closer to the Sleeping God.

Wake, she thought, but nothing answered her call.

The floor leveled and Hope found herself in a large chamber. The walls exuded a subtle luminescence, as though set with firestones, but when she reached out and touched the surface to her left, it was cold. She pressed her hand to the wall, and the pale light shone through and showed her bones, and her veins crissing and crossing like a map of Noreela itself.

She pulled her hand away and heard a crackling behind her. She spun around, lifting the disc-sword and setting its blade spinning. Something brushed her face and at first she thought it was another web. But as she wiped dust from her eyes and moved back, she saw that the whole chamber before her was patterned with thin, delicate stems. *Like the veins in my hand*, she thought. They went from floor to ceiling, ceiling to walls, and some even stretched right across the chamber, twenty steps long. She reached out and touched one of the stems, and it crumbled into dust. She smelled her hand; there was hardly any scent at all. The dust was nothing more than gritty air in her nose.

At the other end of the chamber she could see an opening, and its shadows suggested that it led farther down. *Deeper*, she thought. *It's sleeping deeper, probably right at the bottom. Maybe thousands of years ago this place was a defense against invaders.*

She tried to avoid as many of the petrified stems as she could, but still they broke around and across her, spreading their dust to settle quickly in the still air. Once through the chamber, she turned and looked at what she had done. There was a clear path across the cavern. *Easy to follow*, she thought. Hope brushed dust from her hair and entered the opening in the wall.

THE TUNNEL OPENED up into smaller caverns, narrowed, twisting and turning this way and that, but always heading down. She wondered how far it went. The Sleeping Gods had been gone for longer than anyone knew; it could be a whole new world down here.

Search though she did, she could discern no signs at all that she had been noticed. There were no held breaths, no rumbles of movement from far away, no sudden vibrations as something huge rolled awake or sat up. If the God had awoken, it was remaining quiet.

It'll be hungry, she thought. She shook her head to clear the idea but it was there, implanted in her brain.

The ground went from leathery and hard to soft and moist, and she slipped and landed hard on her rump. She rolled, going with the lay of the land where it had suddenly shifted, trying to grab something but finding nowhere to hold on. She touched a ridge in the ground and it flattened; her fingers slid across a raised knot and it snapped off, turning to dust. She was sliding toward a long, low crack in the tunnel wall, one that looked small until she reached it and passed inside. The subtly glowing walls faded to black, and she discovered true darkness for the first time in her life. She was still slipping, holding the disc-sword close to her chest to prevent it from being snapped away, and she let out an involuntary screech. There were no echoes. She barely even heard herself.

And then she was out, falling into a cavern where the walls glowed brighter than before, the floor was covered with a bluish haze, and at its center a mass sat atop a raised platform like a statue on its pedestal.

As she struck the foot of the wall and rolled into the haze, she thought, *That's it?*

But then her mind was no longer her own, and she thought no more.

Chapter 8

"WHY HAVEN'T YOU killed me?" Kosar asked.

"I will." The Monk was kneeling several steps away, concentrating on something on the ground. He shielded the object of his fascination from Kosar. The thief did not like that.

"I killed you," Kosar mumbled. His vision swayed as his head lolled on his shoulders. *Stay awake. Stay awake!*

"I fell. I survived." The Red Monk's voice was like gravel being poured into a grave. Kosar guessed it did not have much cause to talk.

"Last Monk I killed was a woman."

The demon ignored him. Its shoulders flexed, and it moved its body to the side, as though to shed some moonlight on whatever it was doing. Kosar strained against his bonds, trying to see past the robed figure. But the knots were tight, he was woozy, and seeing would do him no good.

Whatever the Red Monk had planned, Kosar would be helpless.

He closed his eyes and rested his chin on his chest, trying to control the waves of faintness. Pain had spread through his head and neck; muscles ached, bones ground together. But Kosar knew that none of this mattered. He was going to die, and for some reason the Monk was taking its time.

I know you, it had said.

Kosar was almost certain that this demon had killed A'Meer.

His sword lay beside the Monk, still stained with Breakers' blood. Kosar wondered, after all the killing it had done, whether it could ever feel right in his hand again. If only he had the chance to find out.

"Kill me quickly," Kosar said. He bit his lip and looked up, the pain bringing him back from the edge of unconsciousness. He would look death in the face.

The Monk breathed heavily, coughing now and then, spitting blood that bubbled on the ground as if it were sap from the Poison Forests. It seemed unconcerned at the several crossbow bolts buried in its body.

"You sadistic fucking piece of Mage shit," Kosar spat. "Did you kill her the same way?"

The Monk paused, raised its head and turned to look at Kosar. Its face was not as red as it had been, though its eyes still reflected darkness. It turned back to its work.

Kosar struggled against the torn clothing the Monk had used to tie him to the broken machine. The cloth was still wet with blood. The Monk had stripped it from the Breakers it had slaughtered.

His head thumped, his chest and sides hurt and Kosar struggled every step of the way as unconsciousness took him somewhere less painful.

———

"BRING IT TO life," the Monk said.

"What?" Kosar surfaced, pulling back from the Monk standing before him.

The Monk clanged the machine with his sword. "Give it life. Wake it. Use it against me."

Kosar's head slumped back against the machine. He closed his eyes, fighting dizziness and pain. "Not right now," he said. "Maybe later."

"You can't," the demon said.

"I will. As soon as you turn your back."

The Red Monk sat down again, shifting soil and sand and rocks with the swords.

Now, Kosar thought, knowing it would do no good. *Now come to life and kill the Mage-shitting thing. Come alive now, now!* He shook his head and suddenly felt clear, strong and aware. "So what are you looking for, you piece of Mage shit? You've lost, failed. Magic is back, and the Mages have it, and it's the fault of you and yours. So what are you looking for in the bloody dust?"

The Monk rose, turned and stepped toward Kosar. It held something in the palm of its hand, a squirming insect that seemed to hate the weak moonlight. "The truth," it said.

"What's that?"

The Monk ignored his question.

Kosar aimed a kick at the demon's hand, but it moved aside and came in close, too close to kick again. He could smell it now, sickly sweet rot and body odor, the stench of something that never cleans itself, takes no care.

"Fuck off," Kosar said.

"I need to know," the Monk said. In one quick movement it brought a knife from beneath its robe and thrust it into Kosar's neck.

Kosar went stiff with shock. He could feel the knife in him, an alien object that felt much larger than it actually was, and even after the Monk withdrew the blade it felt as though it were still there, turning in his flesh with every breath he took. He gasped.

And then the pain kicked in. It overrode every other ache in Kosar's body. His bleeding nose was forgotten, the injury to his hand from the fight in the machines' graveyard, the stab wounds to his shoulders . . .

The Monk watched for a second, eyes flicking down to the wound then back to Kosar's face. Then it dropped the insect onto Kosar's neck.

He felt it. Even through the intense agony he felt the intimate contact of its tiny legs crawling up his neck, against the flow of blood, against the pain. It reached the wound and invaded his body. It was much worse than the knife, because this thing was alive. It delved and probed, passing into the rent the Monk had made and tearing its way deeper. And Kosar found himself silently begging dead A'Meer to come and take him from this terrible agony and carry him into the Black.

Then the insect stopped moving, and everything changed.

Kosar felt it growing within him. It was as though he were shrinking and the insect expanding. He was moving away from the world, sinking somewhere darker, and yet the suffering was still there. This was not unconsciousness; this was him being driven down and forced back. He fought, but there was very little fight left in him. His throat began to rattle. His mouth opened and he growled, as if attempting to speak a language he had never known.

"Why do you have those wounds on your fingertips?"

Fuck you, Kosar thought. "I'm a thief," he said. He could not help himself. He tried to bite his tongue to prevent himself from speaking more, but the thing inside him would not allow it.

The Monk smiled. "Good." It retreated a few steps and sat down, groaning as it did so. It plucked a bolt from its neck and threw it aside. Blood ran from the wound, but only a dribble. It cricked its neck and lowered its hood, revealing the bald scarlet scalp. The huge bonfires cast flickering shadows on its head.

Kosar strained at his bindings, but he could no longer feel his arms. They belonged somewhere else. The thing inside him was huge, larger than him, bursting out and becoming the center of everything he knew and believed. It had swallowed him, and when the Monk began asking its questions, the insect regurgitated the answers from Kosar's stiffened mouth.

"Who are you?"

"Kosar."

"Where are you from?"

"Trengborne."

"The village where the boy came from?"

"Yes." The insect squeezed, white fire consumed Kosar's bones. "He wasn't *from* there, but he *lived* there."

The Monk regarded him for a while, stroking the side of its nose with the tip of Kosar's sword. "The boy had magic?"

"Yes."

"He used it?"

"It used him."

The Monk nodded, musing on this. "Where is he now?"

"The Mages took him." Kosar did not have to fight against the truth in this case; he *wanted* to tell it. "They took him, stole the magic, and they have it now."

The Monk looked away, simmering.

Kosar bit his lip. Fresh blood flowed into his mouth but the pain was immaterial. It lifted him nowhere, purged nothing from his body except for more blood. He looked to the sky to see why it was darkening, then at the fires, and he realized that his vision was fading. *About time*, he thought.

"Where were you going?" the Monk said.

"To . . . to . . ." He fought, but the insect crushed him down. "To Hess."

"Why?"

"To tell the Mystics about Alishia."

"Alishia? Who is she?"

"She has something . . ." Kosar closed his eyes and raged against the thing controlling him. He thought of A'Meer and her determination, her pride, and he thought about how Rafe had changed in the space of a few days. But his mouth opened, his throat flexed and he could not swallow the words. " . . . something of magic within her."

The Monk stood and came forward, holding the sword out before it. "You cannot lie to me."

"I can't lie."

"Then there's still a chance," the Monk said. "Where is Alishia?"

Still a chance?

"Going . . . to . . . Kang Kang . . ."

The Monk turned and walked away, its shadow dancing behind it. It sheathed its sword and threw Kosar's aside.

It sees something of magic as a chance?

The Monk disappeared beyond one of the huge fires. Kosar felt the insect rip itself away from his spine and claw from the wound in his neck, saw it tumble down his chest and land in the dust. It was on its back, legs flailing at the night, and a hundred thin white tendrils swirled around it, licking at the air as if trying to find nerves once more.

With all the strength he could muster, Kosar lifted his foot and brought it down onto the struggling beetle.

He came back to himself in time to feel life fading away. *The Monk left me to die*, he thought. *At last . . . at last . . .*

———

BUT DEATH IS no easy escape, and the pain of life brought him around once more.

Kosar had no idea how much time had passed. The great fires had burned down somewhat, so it must have been several hours, but the moons still hung in the sky, it was still twilight . . . and the Monk was still there. It sat at a distance, close to one of the fading fires, its cloak hugged tight around it and its hood lifted back over its head. It had its back to Kosar. It seemed to be asleep.

He was still tied against the broken machine. His chest was tight and sore, and he stood on shaky legs to ease the pressure on his shoulders.

I should be dead, Kosar thought. He swallowed, wincing at the pain that slight movement brought. He turned his head left to right and felt something on his throat, something in him, and for a second panic rose again. But he could still see the remains of the crushed insect on the ground beside his foot. It had burst when he crushed it, spilling a puddle of his blood merged with its own.

Something ran past him. He held his breath and did his best to keep still, tracking the shadow as it darted low across the ground. It was a sand rat, large as a small sheebok, scaly tail waving at the air as it buried its long snout into one of the dead Breakers.

Kosar looked at the Monk, but the demon seemed unconcerned.

The sand rat pulled back and took something from the body. It hurried back past Kosar, glancing at him as it ran by with the Breaker's heart in its mouth.

Kosar slumped against the machine and cried out at the bindings chafing his wrists. They had rubbed the skin raw, drawing more blood and tightening each time he moved against them.

"You!" Kosar called. The Monk lifted its head, staring into the fire as if believing the call had come from there. "Haven't you killed me yet?"

The Monk stood slowly. Kosar noticed several arrows and bolts on the ground by its side, evidently picked from its body while it had been sitting beside the fire. Its red robe bore many darker patches. *Their rage keeps them going*, he thought. *Perhaps now they know they've lost, they'll just die away.* But the Monk shrugged its robe higher onto its shoulders and pulled its hood lower over its face, and when it started out for Kosar it was with purpose.

I told it about Alishia, he thought in despair.

The demon walked past the bodies of several Breakers, paying them no attention. Its feet kicked through sandy soil darkened with blood. When it came to within a dozen steps of Kosar it paused, raised its hands and lowered its hood slowly, as if uncertain of its actions. It looked above Kosar at the machine. It looked down at the puddle of blood at his feet. It looked anywhere but at his face.

"I haven't killed you," it said. "I saved your life. Clasped the wound shut. Stopped the bleeding." Its voice was rough and low, and Kosar saw the terrible scars on its face and neck for the first time. "I am Lucien Malini," it said.

Kosar was taken aback. Was he still unconscious? Was he dreaming? He swung his hand forward and imagined a sword cleaving this monster's head in two—revenge for sweet A'Meer—but his arms remained tied to the machine.

"You have a name?" he asked.

"Everything has a name. Even the Mages."

"Then why tell me? You killed the woman in those woods, didn't you? Before the machines' graveyard?"

"Yes. We fought and I killed her. And then later . . . when I went back . . . I saw her . . ."

"If you let me down from here, I'll kill you."

The Monk raised its eyebrows, forehead creasing into a scarred frown.

"Do you believe I'm telling the truth?" Kosar asked. "Don't need your filthy truth beetle for that, do you? I'll wipe the name from your lips and stamp it into the bloody dust. Then I'll cut you open and sit close by, so I can watch the sand rats eat you slowly. You'll end up as sand rat shit."

"The woman ended as more," Lucien Malini said.

"What do you mean?" Kosar could not help the question, though he did not want to engage in this demon's banter. *But it said there's still a chance.*

"She went," the Monk said. "I returned to her and she went. Disappeared. Before my eyes."

"You returned to her?"

"I had seen defeat, and I sought revenge on her corpse."

Kosar closed his eyes and the world swayed around him. He had no wish to imagine what the Monk's revenge would have been, yet the images forced themselves upon him, crowded out in moments by the mimic's presentation of A'Meer's final breaths. *A whispered word, or a gasp for air?*

When the world steadied and Kosar opened his eyes again, the Monk had come close.

"Leave me alone, demon!" Kosar whispered.

The Monk reached out and touched his throat. Its fingers were rough and a flame of pain circled Kosar's neck. Something shifted there and his head was jerked to one side, pulled by a subtle movement from the Monk's hand.

"Leave me!"

"If I leave, you may bleed to death."

"Then let me bleed to death. Or are you toying with me? Maybe you're taking your revenge on my body because A'Meer denied you that?"

The Monk stood back and stared at Kosar, as though looking for truth in its victim's face. "I don't want you to die," it said.

"I don't believe you."

"I put clasps in your throat. Sand rat teeth hold your wound together. I want you to live."

Kosar tried to turn away but felt the obstructions in his neck. They pulled at him, stretching skin and holding the sides of his wounds together. There was no fresh blood running down his chest. And the Monk asked no more questions.

"Why?" Kosar asked.

"You spoke my words in your sleep," the Monk said. "When I sat by the fire, taking arrows from my body, I heard you repeating my words. As if you could not believe them."

Kosar spat at the Monk. He was weak and his mouth was dry, and the bloody spittle landed on the ground between them. "Your kind don't believe in hope."

The Monk came forward again. Kosar kicked out but the demon simply slapped his leg aside. It seemed unconcerned at his struggles. Kosar saw it close up; deep, black eyes, the fresh wounds and older scars, the ragged teeth in its mouth, nose split in some fight. Surely there could be no hope in a thing like this?

"You'll sleep," the demon said. "I'll have time to think. And when you wake, we will talk some more."

It pressed something into Kosar's mouth, a sweet plant mulched and mixed with something more meaty. Try as he did, Kosar could not keep from swallowing. And once he'd swallowed the first speck he opened his mouth and welcomed some more. It took him away, soothed his pain, made A'Meer fade for a time into a shadow of a memory rather than a raw, bloody loss. As he felt the Monk loosening his wrist ties, Kosar stared into the failing fire and saw sunlight once again.

———————

WHEN HE FOUND the Elder Mystic sitting alone in a square on the outskirts of Hess, O'Gan thought he had discovered an ally.

He stood at the edge of the square, hidden from view in the shadow of a giant wellburr tree. He liked the feel of the tree's bark against his shoulder. It had been here for several thousand years, weathering storms and reveling in sunlight, sucking water from the ground that seeped in from the inland sea of Sordon Sound. It had grown up alone in a wild landscape, witness to histories that O'Gan could not imagine and would barely believe. When its seeds fell they were carried away by the Elder Mystics and planted far afield, taking all the history of the tree with them to give to the fledgling plants that might sprout several centuries from now. Sometimes, those carrying them were given visions when their palms were pricked by the seeds' spiky skins. And sometimes those visions gave stories that were told on the Temple, bizarre tales of histories that did not belong to the Shantasi. This land had been a stranger to them when they arrived many centuries before, and there were those who believed it was a stranger to them still.

He leaned his head against the skin of the tree and closed his eyes. His mind was still affected by the Janne pollen, blood still trickled from his nose and he sensed a comforting warmth somewhere within the tree's ancient trunk. It was the certainty that a greater mind than his was pondering events. He sighed, and an echo from centuries before bled through the bark and made him open his eyes.

The Elder Mystic was sitting on the edge of a stone water fountain. The water seemed black in the weak light. It rose in three single sheets, parting as it reached its zenith and then splashing back down. The splashes sounded like nothing at all.

The Elder trailed one hand in the water, swirling it back and forth like a paddle. She remained where she was. Even with her eyes closed, O'Gan was certain that she traveled nowhere.

Her other hand held the hilt of the knife buried in her stomach.

"Elder!" O'Gan said. He stepped from the shadow of the wellburr tree and crossed the small square to the fountain. They were alone. The square was on the western outskirt of Hess, its air heavy with scents from the Mol'Steria Desert farther west.

The Mystic raised her head and turned to look at O'Gan. She seemed surprised to see anyone here. She was very old, her pale skin wrinkled into leathery folds, her black hair streaked with silver as though it caught light from the life moon.

"O'Gan Pentle," she said. "I heard you were still at the Temple."

"I was. I saw something. I came down, and everyone was fleeing or . . . or dead." He looked at the knife in the Elder's stomach. Her hand was clasped firmly around the hilt.

"Death is the only escape," the Elder said.

"Elder Darshall, I don't understand."

The Elder shook her head, winced, and her hand made irregular patterns in the water as she shivered with pain. "I did this," she said, looking down at the knife. "But I lack the courage to finish it. I pull the knife up, empty my guts, twist it and pierce my heart, and I'm beyond their reach. Forever free, lost to the Black, and all the Elders' wraiths will combine to chant one another down. No way the Mages can reach us in the Black. No way they'd *dare*."

"We can fight," O'Gan said.

Elder Darshall shook her head. Her hand went back to drawing shapes in the water. "There is no hope."

O'Gan sat before her on the edge of the fountain. The stone was colder than usual, its heat long since sucked away by the twilight. "I *saw* hope," he said. "On the Temple, hope came to me and showed itself!"

The Elder looked up, and O'Gan was shocked to see a smile on her face. "You young Mystics," she said. "You're always so filled with optimism. You don't appreciate how much the past steers the present. Every breath you take pushes your body in a certain direction; through choice, and experience, and the way that breath informs your heart and mind. The things it plants there. The things it takes away. And likewise, every event of the past makes the present what it is."

"I don't understand." O'Gan looked at the knife, the Elder's hand, her leaking blood. He wondered at her uncertainty. Was it simply pain causing her to hold back, or fear of the Black? Or was it something else? "You can't deny hope at a time like this."

"I know what hope brings!" the Elder hissed. She leaned forward at O'Gan as if to bite him, and crying out when the movement shifted the knife in her gut. She moved back and looked down again, and sat there motionless for a while, concentrating on the knife.

If she does it now, she truly knows no hope, O'Gan thought.

Elder Darshall looked up at him and smiled. "You've been sniffing the Janne, even now."

"If you're seeing inside me, then you know I speak the truth."

"You're thinking about madness, that's all," Elder Darshall whispered. "You've seen phantoms in the dark. Things . . . perhaps sent by the Mages to finish us off. Who knows what's out there now? Who can understand?" Her eyes drifted past O'Gan and became fearful, darting here and there as though following a bat's flight.

"I heard of Elders killing themselves," he said. "I saw Elder Garia, dead by her own hand."

The Elder Mystic nodded. "Garia always was a braver soul than me. And she always understood the truth."

"What truth? None of us know the truth. It's the thing we always seek!"

Elder Darshall's stare was loaded with the wisdom of her years. O'Gan forgot about the knife and blood, and her hand stirring the waters of the fountain. For a moment the whole world was in her eyes. "The truth that we Elders kept for ourselves," she said. "The truth of the Mages, and what they did to us. And what they will do again." She started to cry. Her tears shocked O'Gan because they were born of sorrow, not pain.

"Elder . . . let me help you." He reached forward to touch the knife but the Mystic pulled back, hissing and almost slipping into the fountain.

"Don't touch me! O'Gan, don't touch me. Freedom of will is everyone's right, and I have mine even now. You have yours also, though I think this darkness is driving you mad. But I'll tell you. I'll help you to decide your course of action."

"I'm going to fight!"

"No. You're going to kill yourself and join your ancestors in the Black. And I'll tell you why.

"O'Gan, even the Mystics have a beginning. Before the Cataclysmic War the Shantasi examined and explored magic through their minds. We viewed magic as a philosophy rather than a tool, a way of life rather than a way to make life our own. And then S'Hivez went too far. He was banished, and he and Angel met and fell in love and the rest is known to everyone, but only in detail to a few. And nobody knows everything that happened during the Cataclysmic War. It was a short war but it was fought right across Noreela. Its main battles were along the path of destruction from Lake Denyah and the Mages' Monastery, north across Noreela to The Spine. But there were other battles, and many of them have faded from consciousness because most were won by the Mages. History is written by the victors and survivors. But sometimes history becomes a part of the land."

Elder Darshall's head nodded forward and her hand paused in the waters.

"Elder?" O'Gan asked, fearful that she had bled to death.

"I'm thinking," she said. "Remembering. Memories can hurt, you know that, O'Gan? They can physically hurt. I can still feel the agony from the first time I was pricked by a wellburr seed." She sighed.

"After the Cataclysmic War, history faded into itself. Time began again. Noreela picked itself up and dusted itself off, and much of it remained where the War had left it: on its knees, bereft of hope, societies shattered and its people growing apathetic and resigned. Magic was gone. Machines lay dead across the land, many of them taking their decayed cargo of people with them. The bones of the dead mingled with the cores of the machines, and history soon became something of dreams more than reality.

"You know the stories, O'Gan . . .

"It took over a hundred years for the new Mystics to arise in Hess. I was one of them. I was one of the first. I was born after the War, and my path led me here, my parents herding sheebok from village to village. Hess was a ruin then—from the War, and a battle that few talk about anymore—but there were some who wished the Mystics to rise again. They could see beyond the next bellyful of food and mouthful of water. They could see beyond the absence of the old magic. They were few, and they refused to be slaves to history as our people were slaves so long ago.

"So they took us children from our parents with the promise of wonders, nurtured us and planted Janne seeds that had been harvested from plants destroyed during the Cataclysmic War. And soon, when the first of the new Mystics were barely in their teens, the Janne urged us to look to the wellburr trees for answers to old questions: What had happened to the Mystics during the War? Why were they never seen or heard from again?

"So we went to the trees, gathered their falling seeds . . . and they bit us." The Elder trailed off.

"Elder?"

Darshall grunted, nodded. Her hand still gripped the knife. O'Gan could feel the tension there, as though every heartbeat urged the Elder Mystic to finish what she had begun.

Tell me first, he thought. *Tell me why the Elders refuse to see any hope.*

Darshall nodded again, and continued. "The pain was beyond compare. We were Mystics without magic. You've heard of the witches that still work in the land, mainly in the north? Witches with no magic . . . false magicians, using potions and chemicala to dupe the ignorant or fool themselves. We were similar, except that our minds were lessened by magic's loss. Those Mystics who came before us had magic to dwell upon, while we only had its absence. So instead of examining what magic meant we spent our time looking for signs of what it *could* mean. We searched for clues to its reappearance, signs in the stars, the way water ran downhill, the shape of a sand dune after a storm in the Mol'Steria Desert. We sat on the Temple and talked long days into longer nights, many of us secretly harboring jealousy for those Mystics that existed before the Cataclysmic War. We wanted their minds, their thoughts, their lives. We wanted to be able to immerse ourselves in the magic they had access to, view it from inside and out. We wanted our days and nights to be filled with magic, not its ghost.

"And then the wellburr tree . . .

"It all happened in one night. There were perhaps a hundred Mystics then, and a dozen of us had been chosen to harvest the seeds of a wellburr tree. *That* wellburr tree, in fact . . . the one you were hiding beneath, watching to see whether I would live or die. So we came here and set about our work.

"This square was not here back then. This was almost two hundred years ago, a little more than a century since the Mages were driven from the land. Much of Hess was still a ruin. The rebuilding began, but here and there remained pockets of destruction, and this square was one of them. There was very little here, only an open area of rubble and crushed buildings. And the stake at its center.

"The stake is what I need to tell you about. It's what we saw. We were all aware then that these pools of destruction around

Hess—untouched since the War, the only things still standing the
stakes of wellburr wood buried deep in the ground—marked the
scenes of a terror beyond compare. But the truth of it had vanished
into the past, melted away with those Shantasi who survived the raz-
ing of Hess as they eventually succumbed to age, or disease, or simply lost their desire to live.

"We avoided these places. All of us, not just the new Mystics. We
ignored them. They stank of age and time gone off, and sometimes
things came up out of the ground, sniffed at the air and went back
down. We never knew what they were. Occasionally we watched, but
we left them to themselves. They never came out, and we never went
in, and over time even the wellburr stakes began to rot away."

Elder Darshall drifted off again, her hand stirring the waters of
the fountain as if searching for something beneath its moon-slicked
surface.

"Elder Darshall? The wellburr seed?"

She nodded. "The wellburr seed. It showed us. It gave us a
glimpse of history. And ever since then, we've been trying to forget.

"We all had the same vision. Not only the Mystics whose palms
were pricked, but those who were back at the Temple as well, waiting patiently for our return. That has never happened again. It's as if
the Janne our ancestors brought out of Shanti mated with the wellburr trees, and their offspring was this one single vision. A warning?
A prophecy? Perhaps both.

"That night, six Mystics threw themselves from the Temple and
died on the streets below.

"I was standing close to the trunk over there, and when I felt a
seed's spines enter my palm, everything turned white. For a while it
was complete shock. The pain was so deep and sudden that it did
not register, and I had time to look around and see the other Mystics
around me looking the same way: eyes wide, mouths agape, hands
closed around the seeds and dripping blood. I saw their pale faces
turn dark as our blood changed and flowed faster. And then the
pain surged in, and the world lost all direction.

"The wellburr tree put us there, in that old Mystic's place. It
was showing us the history it had experienced, making us a part of
that past so that we understood. That's why I want you to kill yourself. It's too terrible. Too awful. And it will all happen again."

Elder Darshall's hand stirred the water faster, forming bubbles
that burst in the light of the death moon. The fountain pool had

turned a dull yellow now that clouds covered the life moon, and the Elder's skin had taken on a similar hue.

"The stake?" O'Gan said. He was impatient to hear the rest of the story, yet he knew that an Elder should not be rushed. Even with a knife in her gut, this two-hundred-year-old Mystic let time go by at its own pace. "Elder? The stake, the Mystic, the wellburr tree?"

"I want you to kill yourself," she whispered. And she finished her story.

"HE WAS CAUGHT by two shades.

"His name was Delgon, and he was helping to organize the defenses on Hess' western flank. They had been expecting the Mages to send a battalion of their Krote warriors across the Mol'Steria Desert to attack New Shanti, but instead the enemy used their stranglehold on magic to raise sand blights against Hess. The defenders believed they were being hit by a sand storm to begin with, and that's why Hess fell so quickly. By the time they realized the truth, the sand blights were already taking down buildings and crushing the Shantasi defenses to a pulp.

"Delgon fought on, regrouping close to here with some Shantasi warriors and their own machines of war. But another cloud of sand blights came in across Sordon Sound, picking up water as they came, and by the time they arrived they were so sodden that being caught in the open was like being struck by blocks of rock. The blights would breeze in and strip people to the bone in seconds. Delgon retreated, and was caught not far from here. The shades had been waiting. Immune to the storms, they entered Delgon together and carved their way into his mind.

"He fell, screaming. He watched his warriors rush past him, leaving him for dead, and then a sand blight ambushed them and shredded them within seconds. And then it moved on, ignoring Delgon because he was doomed.

"His mind was penetrated and laid open. The shades made it their home, finding life and experience and an existence they had never known . . . because they were not right. Not only the echoes of souls as yet unborn, these were shades aborted by nature because they were *wrong*. The Mages, of course, had put them to their own use.

"I felt Delgon's pain, and then time passed and he was in the center of an area of ruins. He was standing with his back against a stake of rough wellburr wood, arms wrenched from their sockets and shoulders dislocated so that his hands met behind the stake. They had been melted together by some blast of unimaginable heat. The flesh had flowed, and on cooling his hands had merged together, the bones fused. The pain from that . . . Delgon could barely scream. Any movement jarred his hands. His shoulders were on fire.

"He was hungry and thirsty, and he had soiled himself.

"He realized then that the battle had ended. Hess was a ruin around him. The sand blights had gone, leaving behind the remains of a city blasted with the bloody remnants of its previous inhabitants. The ruins were black with dried blood. The sky was clear, and Delgon realized that several days had passed.

"The shades had gone, but they had left something of their eternal damnation inside him.

"Most of all, when he closed his eyes and imagined the scent of the Janne blooms, he knew that magic had left the land.

"I felt Delgon's terror, and more time passed. His skin was burnt and crisp from long exposure to the sun. His vision was obscured by a gray haze, and he knew that the sunlight was making him blind. The pain in his hands had eased, but his shoulders felt as though someone was keeping a fire alight in them. Each slight movement aggravated the flames. He had slumped to his knees, his chest was tight, his stomach was distended from dehydration and an intense hunger he had never experienced before.

"And then the screaming began. He had believed himself to be alone, but the first cry came from behind him, back toward the heart of the city, and he recognized the voice of another Elder. It was quite obviously mad. Other screams started up then, spreading back and forth across Hess like echoes looking for a home. Delgon added his own voice to the cacophony. It was as if they had all believed themselves to be alone, and now the only way they could communicate was to scream.

"The screaming went on until nightfall, and as the sun went down and dusk hid the worst of the destruction, Delgon wondered again why they had all been left here like this.

"An execution, O'Gan? Or an offering?"

"I have no idea," O'Gan said. "Something bad."

"Something bad," Darshall said, nodding. "Delgon could not

sleep. Tiredness swamped him, but the pain kept him awake, and the certainty that something terrible would stalk through the red-strewn streets to eat him. Magic had gone, and he would die.

"So he stayed awake for three more days, watching the sun rise and fall on the screamed agony of the sacrificial Mystics of Hess. It was not until dusk of the fourth day that he realized he was already dead.

"I felt the pain he went through: the pain of being dead. It's like nothing I've ever felt before, and I never, ever want to feel it again. I can barely think about it now . . . hardly talk about it . . . but imagine: you feel yourself rotting. You smell the rank stench of your flesh growing bad, your blood hardening in your veins, your eyes being pecked from your skull by birds. You feel the teeth of sand rats as they gnaw at your stomach, opening you up so that they can get at the organs inside. You feel your heart being ripped out . . . and you feel it being eaten from a hundred steps away, the dozen tiny mouths of a sand rat litter shredding it and fighting over every morsel.

"Then you feel the action of their stomach acids, the pain of being broken down and shit out and lying in the sun to dry . . .

"Eventually the weight of his torso ruptured the already weakened shoulder sockets and Delgon fell onto his face in the rubble. This was three weeks after the end of the War. The sand rats were shunning him now because he was too far gone even for them. But he felt the pain of decay in every part of his body. His wraith was trapped within a rotting corpse, unable to move, still attached to the land with all his senses even though his eyes were gone.

"He suffered there for a long time. Eventually he came apart, and parts of him went underground. Suddenly possessed of movement, his hands crawled from the weakened elbow sockets and retreated down into the dark, his feet shifted themselves in opposite directions, and still he felt every wound to his body, every rip and tear of flesh, every bone prised from its socket . . . he felt them all, and his wraith started to wander this place looking for escape. Even if there had been someone to chant it down to the Black, the Mages' magic had set it adrift and given it its own appalling doom.

"S'Hivez had exacted his own vengeance upon those Mystics who banished him from New Shanti.

"Delgon's body rotted away, but parts of it remained mummified. They shift here and there, peering aboveground on occasion and showing themselves to anyone who happens to be looking.

There was no helping Delgon and the others, so we ordered that these places be paved over and a fountain placed at their centers. Small tribute to such suffering. A paltry symbol."

She looked up, waved her hand around, dripping water into the dust. "His wraith is here now, and he still suffers the agony of death, and perhaps he always will. And we became the Elder Mystics. We swore that we would keep such unbearable truths to ourselves."

————

"WHY?" O'GAN ASKED. "Why not tell us? Why hide that part of history?"

"We needed Hess to live again. Who would have wanted to dwell in a city haunted by such things?"

"So you're giving in? Every Elder is giving in just because—"

"*Just because?*" Elder Darshall shouted, and the effort clenched her stomach muscles and extended the wound. She winced but continued through the agony, perhaps ashamed at feeling pain from something so negligible. "You have no idea, O'Gan," she said, shaking her head and at last lifting her hand from the water. She stared at it for a few seconds, perhaps expecting it to be coated in Delgon's blood. "You cannot imagine the pain . . . the time . . . every second an eternity." She drifted off, still staring at her hand, mumbling something that O'Gan could not make out.

"I won't just roll over and die!" he said.

"Heed my wisdom! It's the end of the Shantasi." Elder Darshall's gaze went to her hand once more. "Mystic Delgon, guide my hand."

O'Gan moved, but he was already too late. Darshall clasped the knife with her other hand and ripped upward, slitting her stomach, leaning forward as she turned her hands and angled the blade to the side. He caught her as she fell, smelled her insides and felt the warmth of the steam rising from her spilled guts, and he saw the instant that life left her eyes.

"I hope you'll be at rest," he said. "But it's not the end until every last one of us is dead." He laid her along the stone sill of the fountain and knelt beside her, chanting her down into the Black, trying to keep his mind from her story but all the time desperate to believe that she could no longer hear his words, see his pale face, smell his fear.

He left the square and headed back into the heart of Hess. He looked for shifting shadows on the way, but anything watching from the darkness kept to itself.

———

O'GAN PENTLE HAD been a Mystic for more than fifty years, but he had no idea how to command an army. That was the job of the Elders, passing orders down from the Temple to the upper echelons of the Shantasi forces, commanding them here, there, back toward the sea and out into the edges of the Mol'Steria Desert. True, he had trained warriors in his time and sent them into the world, condemning them to lonely vigils for absent magic. He often wondered where his charges were and what they were doing. Mystic he may be, but he had never traveled beyond the boundaries of New Shanti. He had read much about Noreela City, the Cantrass Plains and Long Marrakash, but he had seen none of it. The warriors he trained were destined to see the world, while he, a Mystic committed to the good of New Shanti, was tied to his land.

He had trained warriors, but that did not mean he could command an army.

They can't all be giving in, he thought. *They can't all be* killing *themselves!*

He hurried through the streets of Hess, hating every sign of the panic that had spread through the Mystic city. The streets here were mostly deserted now, many inhabitants having fled eastward toward where the sun should rise. Clothes lay trampled into the dust. A chair lay on its side beside an ornate iron door, and beyond the open door O'Gan could see the insides of a wealthy home, tables heavy with precious statuettes and floors carpeted with rugs woven by Cantrass Angels. Whoever had fled this place never expected to return.

He could barely believe what was happening. The city was retreating without any thought of protecting itself, listening without question to the mad mutterings of the Elder Mystics and panicking at the sight of their public suicides. And why not? They were held in such high esteem, and if they viewed death as the only escape, what hope could anyone else raise against this catastrophe?

O'Gan craved news from the north. Poor A'Meer, perhaps she had been making her way back to Hess with news of magic reborn and recaptured by the Mages. And if that was the case, then other Shantasi warriors could be making that same journey even now, crossing the dangerous Mol'Steria Desert or sailing across Sordon Sound, to find Hess abandoned, its populace running like sand rats from the jaws of a desert foxlion.

"We're not cowards!" O'Gan said. A man and woman huddled beneath a small lean-to darted away, startled from their hiding place. The man looked back at O'Gan, recognizing the garb but fearful of the barely contained rage in this Mystic's voice. "We need to stand and fight!" The man put his arm around his wife's shoulders and hurried her on. "You!" O'Gan shouted.

The woman stopped and shrugged the man's arm from her shoulder. She turned, and O'Gan saw the cool determination in her eyes. "The Elders are killing themselves," the woman said. "Mystic, I have respect for you, but I also respect their message. There is no hope for the Shantasi against the Mages, they say. How can we believe any different? It's a new New Shanti today." The woman lowered her head in brief deference to Mystic O'Gan and then hurried away with her husband.

"It is," he said. "A new New Shanti." He sat on a bench beside a tall hedge and rested his head in his hands. He needed food and water, but there were enough homes left open for that, and he would feel no guilt at the theft. He would need weapons too. His own roll of weapons was back at the Temple, but he would be able to find what he needed here at the edge of Hess.

He wished he could ask the advice of an Elder, but he already had their story. They were dying into history, hurried there by their own fearful hands. O'Gan, the dusk, the fight to come—that was the present.

Every moment wasted was one step closer to defeat.

O'Gan stood to prepare himself for the journey westward. There, he hoped, he would find enough of a Shantasi army to command.

Chapter 9

ALISHIA WOKE, BUT she found the waking world uncomfortable. Her vision was bouncing left and right, her stomach ached, her bones felt as though they were being forced together at the sockets, ground into place as though to merge with one another.

A pair of shoes moved in and out of her field of vision, heavy leather soles bound with donkey hide and tied with twisted reed. *A fledge miner's shoes,* she thought. *They're passed down from father to son. Rebound, rewound, the soles smoothed and shined by decades of use. They're part of a proud miner's possessions. That and the disc-sword . . .*

I've seen that disc-sword red with blood.

She was being carried. And there was something wrong with the ground. No plants, no moss, no soil or dirt, just bare rock, cracks and fissures free of soil or dust, surface smoothed by time. It looked silver in places, yellow in others, as though the moons were fighting for control of this strange land.

Alishia was not sure where they were. They had been heading for Kang Kang, but now Trey was rushing somewhere with her slung over his shoulder, and in his shadow there was no sign of the disc-sword.

I need to know where we are, she thought. *I need* . . . She closed her eyes and, like a babe in arms, the movement of Trey's journey across this weird landscape lulled her back to sleep.

———

FROM THE DARKNESS came the smell of burning paper and charred wood. There was heat as well, though it may have been her own breath. She breathed in, out, and realized that the burning also came from within.

Alishia opened her eyes. The library was still ablaze.

She chose a route between two tall book stacks. Flames erupted at various heights, eating a thousand lives and leaving many more in place. Perhaps those surviving would burn later, perhaps not.

She ran. She was not certain what she sought, but this library was no place to be sure of anything. She waved her way through a sheet of flames. They did not affect her, yet she smelled the charred stench of another moment fading away.

I wonder if that was someone I knew, she thought. She paused and turned around, reaching for a burning book, pulling it from the shelf, letting it fall open in her hands and seeing only three words before the fire ate them away: *never knew her*. She dropped the charred mess and it broke into dust.

She ran on, ducking through the flames and never fearing them. This was *her* place; they could not harm her here. The passage remained straight for some time, and though she passed a thousand books every few seconds, she knew that they were not for her. Something was drawing her toward a truth that she must discover.

There was the place below the library, the cave, but she had been there already and it provided only a warning. *Hope*, she thought. *I didn't see her when I was awake. And Trey was* running!

Something fell in the distance. A book stack or a wall, a floor giving way or a tower of loose books tumbling as fire ate away at their foundation. Alishia paused and turned, trying to decide which direction the crash had come from. Millions of books dampened the sound. She turned left and right but the noise faded away, and there was nothing to do but carry on running.

It's coming apart so quickly, she thought. *The fire spreads faster than I could have believed*. She jumped through another wall of flame and crashed into a pile of books, falling to the floor, barely feeling the impact.

One of the books landed beside her, flipping open at a page begging to be read. She closed her eyes. Closed the book without looking. Opened her eyes again and glanced at the spine: *A Heartbeat in the Heart of the Sleeping God.* She pushed the book away and it opened again, and she read of Hope in the belly of the beast.

Only bad could come of this. Trey was running toward something awful, and she had to wake to tell him, warn him, because only *bad* could come of this.

Touch its heart and Hope fades away, the line in the book said. The only line. The rest of it was yet to be written.

———

HOPE WAS A young girl again, exploring north of Pavisse on her own because nobody wished to play with a witch. There were occasional friends, but they kept their distance, as if she really could plant some dubious spell on them. She asked her mother why they were like that, and her mother would smile, her green tattoos twisting around her neck like a snake tightening to withhold her answer. *They're scared of you,* she would say. *They know what you can do.*

But Hope knew that she could do nothing, and her child's brutal logic revealed the truth: other children did not play with her because they thought she was a fool. Even a child knew that there was no magic. Hope was a fool from a long line of fools, and children did not suffer fools gladly.

She had been to these woods many times before. They were familiar to her, and safe. It was a fine day, the sun was warm and kind on her face, and the first of her many tattoos was healing on her right cheek.

She paused and smiled, and felt the tattoo do the same.

The forest was small but few people visited. The people of Pavisse had more to trouble themselves with than walks amongst the trees, unless the walks themselves were toward something relevant. Once, she had been in the woods when a man ran past. She ducked down but he had seen her. His eyes turned left, wide and fearful, and he watched for a couple of beats before running on. Hope remained hidden for a while until she heard the dogs, and then she stood and revealed herself to the militia so that she was not attacked. They did not ask whether she had seen the man, and she did not volunteer the information.

Another time, she had stumbled across a couple having sex. The man was old and gray, the woman younger than her, and Hope had kept a guilty watch on them for over an hour while they fucked, rested and fucked again. There was real passion between that old man and young woman, and Hope felt sorry that they had to come this far to be on their own.

Later that day she had told her god about them, and it had given her its customary silent reply.

She reached her god in the ground and knelt before it, almost touching its surface, almost feeling its coolness or warmth, its smoothness or rough skin, the stillness of death or the invisible vibration of life. She had never touched her god, and she never could. Gods were not for that.

She began to mutter invocations she had heard her mother using, words and sentences in a language forgotten by most. *It's the language of the land,* her mother had told her, and Hope's memory did its best to repeat the words as they had been spoken: the same tone, same intonation.

It's a machine, a soft voice whispered. It was her voice, but she did not like to listen. It told painful truths. *It's just a dead machine.*

Something tickled her hip and she slapped at her clothes. Nothing changed.

She chanted some more, bringing her hands so close to the god half buried in the ground that she could feel its gravity pulling her closer and closer. One day it would move, she knew. One day she would come here and present herself before this god, and it would rise, and she would become the first real witch since the Cataclysmic War had stolen magic away. One day she would remember the correct invocation from her mother, mutter it in just the right way, and this god would shrug off its layers of rust and moss, bird shit and decay . . .

It's just a machine, and you're wasting your time. The only gods are the Sleeping Gods, and they're just a story your mother tells you when it's too stormy outside for you to go to sleep . . .

Another movement against her hip, grotesque and familiar.

Hope looked around the woodland glade but the light was starting to fail. *Dusk isn't for hours yet.* A light blue haze rose from the ground, wafting around her knees. *It shouldn't be this dark.* She was farther away from the god (*dead machine*!) than ever before, and then the smell of pine and wellburr trees faded away, replaced by the dust of ages.

I only wanted a god to give me magic, she said, and her young woman's words woke her with their old lady's voice.

———

HER FINAL WORD faded away, swallowed by the walls. No echoes here.

The gravemaker spider flexed in her pocket. Hope had been lying on her side, and the spider had obviously been crushed from its hedgehock sleep. She sat up and reached into the pocket, grabbing the spider by two legs and letting it dangle before her. Its other legs clenched, its body rose, but it could not bring its fangs close enough to bite.

"I've been away," she said, and an endless amount of time may have passed. Nothing would have changed in here: the walls would still glow, the floors would still swim in that strange, opaque mist . . . and the thing on the pedestal would still be there.

She could not bring herself to look, in case there was an eye staring back.

Hope waved the spider before her, holding it at arm's length. "Shall we stand?" she said. She stood, still clasping the disc-sword in her other hand. She was shaking. Still she could not look at the Sleeping God. She thought of that young version of herself, worshipping the hunk of rusted metal and cracked stone in the ground, and she was ashamed. So long spent kneeling before old magic, while the true gods were older still.

Her legs shook. Her tattoos writhed of their own accord as her face twitched, nerves jumped. She needed to piss, but the thought of doing so here terrified her.

She almost looked . . .

The spider curled around her finger and scraped her nail with its fangs.

"Almost," she said. She dropped the spider, kicking it away from her, and watched it scurrying through the haze toward the pedestal. As it drew close, the Sleeping God entered her field of vision, and then she looked because there was nothing more to do, no more distance to travel, no more dreams to be had between that instant and the next.

She had spent so long imagining what this could be like, but she never believed it would be her.

"Wake," she whispered.

She could make no sense of what she saw. Her eyes took in the shape but her mind could not translate the vision.

"Wake for me!"

The shape remained motionless. It was the size of ten people curled together, limbs and heads and torsos twisted around one another. She could see no eyes, hear no breathing. *It* must *be alive*, she thought, but she was too insignificant to understand. She stood in the presence of a god, and all she could do was ask it to wake.

She took one step forward and there was no scream of outrage. She could look at the thing now, and though she was unsure of exactly what she was seeing, at last she believed her eyes.

Another step forward.

The gravemaker spider crawled up the side of the Sleeping God and sat atop it like a disembodied hand.

Hope held her breath. Stared at the spider. Felt her pulse throbbing at her temple, her chest, her thigh. Her heart thumped, punching her as if to draw attention to something here, and here, and *here*!

The spider reared up, baring its fangs, and Hope saw what lay around the base of the pedestal. The light in the huge cavern was weak, yet she could see the drifts of ancient dust. It was orange, like the flaking rust that had drifted from that old machine in the woods long ago, and fine as sand.

"No . . ."

The spider hissed as if it had heard her.

Hope moved three steps closer and nothing in the cavern changed.

Orange, like rust.

"*No . . . !*"

She looked around her then, because the cavern had suddenly become something else. Her mind tilted. She felt it, a movement that shifted her slightly out of this world and into another. She lost whatever precarious grip she had possessed on her own destiny and fell, slipping between the fingers of Fate and plummeting toward whatever end this new bastard world had ready for her.

"*No!*" She screamed long and loud, and then stepped forward to touch the thing she had believed would save them all.

The Sleeping God was not inside; Hope was inside the Sleeping God.

And on the tail of that shocking realization came another, a truth that hit her like fire and burned away her hope, shattering her mind with rage and grief and making real every fear she had ever felt.

This God was no longer sleeping. This Sleeping God was dead.

———

TREY REACHED WHERE he had seen Hope disappear and lowered Alishia to the ground. He shook with exertion, kneeling with the unconscious librarian and making sure her head rested on his leather bag. The ground was totally bare of anything here, just exposed rock with clean cracks and wider, deeper crevasses.

Hope had apparently fallen into one of these. And there was something down there, a punctured layer of some material that seemed a different color from the rock. It was curved, textured, and there was a hole in its surface close to the wall of the crevasse. He could have reached it if he lay prone across the ground . . . but he did not like the thought of what may rise from there. The catastrophe that had befallen Noreela had uncovered this buried thing, and Trey understood with complete clarity that this was something that should have always remained buried.

"Hope," he whispered, but she did not appear.

Moonlight sheened the strange surface, but it seemed to exude a luminescence from within as well. Trey did not like this light. It looked dirty, and he shuffled backward to avoid it.

The landscape was silent, save for a slight breeze blowing in from the north. It brought with it the smell of disturbed ground and uprooted plants. He was surrounded by a plain of rock, gray and dead and smeared with moonlight here and there. Shadows hid also, in deep places where the holes could conceal things far more mysterious, and far more deadly.

Really? he thought. *Is there* anything *more mysterious than this?* He leaned forward again and glanced into the hole . . . and then he heard the sound.

Muffled, distant and dulled, nonetheless it was a scream.

"Hope?"

Alishia stirred beside him, rolling onto her side and opening her eyes. For an instant Trey thought he saw clear blue flames within her pupils, and he glanced up to see whether the darkness had parted to reveal blue sky. But the dusk was as deep as ever.

" . . . her own book of madness . . ." Alishia said.

"Alishia?" Trey touched her face and tilted her head to the side, looking into her eyes and realizing that she was not awake at all. Her mouth was slack, her chin limp and her eyes reflected nothing of what he could see.

". . . Hope . . ." she whispered.

"She's coming," Trey said, and a frown creased Alishia's forehead.

The scream came again, and the miner recognized how it found its way to his ears: it was eaten and spat out again, an echo wending around subterranean corners and through cracks in the land.

Hope sounded terrified. *"They're coming!"* she screamed.

Trey shivered. What was coming? The Nax? Had she gone deep and found them awake? But if that were the case, she would be dead.

He should shout to her, guide her up, lean down into the hole, ready to haul her out of the ground and away from whatever pursued her. But he did not. Because of that look on Alishia's face, and the depth of the sleeping nightmare in her open eyes.

WHEN HOPE TOUCHED the object—the middle, the center, the giant dried heart of this old dead thing—it disintegrated.

The gravemaker spider still sat atop the fossilized heart as it came apart. The creature's legs thrashed below it where before there had been rigidity, and Hope knew how it felt. The whole world had been ripped out from under her. Reality, already struggling to maintain its tenuous hold on the land, had given way to nightmare. As the spider fell so did Hope's mind, both of them lost in a cloud of dust as the Sleeping God's heart came apart. It went to grit, sandy blood and a haze of history spinning around inside this buried corpse.

Hope tried to scream, but it came as a keen. She could not move. Her hand was still held before her, fingers splayed, their tips grayed with the God's dust. She drew in another breath and the dust coated her throat. It hurt when she breathed. It hurt when she thought. *Here is the history of the land . . . dead . . . dead and dry, like a corpse left out in the sun.*

The gravemaker spider appeared again. It had risen in the dust and re-created itself, and each dust particle began to mimic it. There were five spiders now, and fifteen, and a hundred, all of them crawling slowly toward Hope on the dust that webbed her vision. Still she keened, trying to scream past the grit that clogged her throat.

The spiders came closer. She should have never come down here. The people she had killed smiled in their secret graves, and she turned and ran back the way she had come. She used the disc-sword to haul herself up the slope of the Sleeping God's chest cavity, wincing at every hack and cut, digging in with the fingers of her other hand.

From behind her, the sound of sand falling, small feet rushing. She started to glance back but saw the air moving, so she looked forward again. She jerked the disc-sword free and leapt up, jamming it into the ground again and pulling with all her might, kicking with her feet, clawing with her other hand, and then she reached the rent and pulled herself inside.

The walls still glowed but the light was changing now, phasing out, flickering back in again and revealing nothing new.

Hope paused and listened for a miraculous heartbeat. But there was nothing other than the gravemaker spiders following her, born of dead dust. They sounded like the sea washing onto a sandy beach. There must have been a million of them.

She screamed and drove forward, coughing and spitting dust that turned into spiders.

She swatted at them as she went. Their bodies burst back to dust, fell apart as the disc-sword swung, and she felt the unbelievable weight of them forcing her on.

She emerged into the huge cavern and fell from the narrow crack, feeling solidified veins cracking around her. She stood and swung back, hacking at the shadows that had already started falling out behind her. The spiders screeched as they died. She had never heard a spider screech before. She added her scream to their death cries and backed away, trying to follow the path she had made earlier.

The spiders poured into the cavern like a wave of black oil. They ate what little light there was, giving off no reflection.

Hope stomped. Her scream was free now, her throat clear of dust at last, and she vented her fear as she turned and ran for her life.

Everything she saw or touched, everything she breathed in, was the Sleeping God. She was looking at its insides. Dry now, fossilized and dead; still, this was the most amazing thing she had ever seen in her long life. The most amazing, and the most dreadful. *If the Sleeping Gods die, what hope is there for the rest of us?*

"*They're coming!*" she screamed, feeling the dark wave lapping at her feet as she ran. The spiders crawled up her ankles, her calves, but they did not bite. *Perhaps they'll cover me, smother me, keep me down here to die and dry in this dead dry thing . . .*

And then the light began to change and Hope saw moonlight. She had fallen and crashed through the Sleeping God's skin, entered its body searching for its self, and now the chance that she would escape was here in this splash of yellow moonlight.

Death moon, lighting the way for me, giving me sight to see the spiders come and take me. They'll all bite at once and my heart will explode and my body will rupture and spread me across the stony flesh of this God, my fresh blood, my corrupted mind . . .

"Hope!" The fledge miner was up there, his head a shadow against the death moon.

Hope stopped beneath the hole and looked at the wave of spiders closing in.

"It's madness!" she shouted. "Madness, that's all that's left for us now!"

She thrust the disc-sword up into the dusk and felt it hit something hard.

The spiders struck her, lifted her body, and light left her world.

———

TREY COULD NOT sit back and do nothing.

He lay flat on the ground and pulled himself forward so that he could see over the edge of the crevasse. The hole in the strange surface was alive with sound. Hope's screams, the slapping of feet, the scraping of something metallic on stone . . . and something else. A hiss. A whisper.

Trey grew cold at the sound, as though he were hearing the breath of a Nax. *It can't be*, he thought. *I smell no fledge. This is no fledge mine. It* can't *be.*

Hope came into view and looked up, and for a moment he thought she was yellowed with fledge. The death moon splashed on her upturned face and filled her eyes, and he drew back because that was a Nax she was running from, it had to be; he could hear it approaching even now. The terror in Hope's drug-yellowed eyes told him that there was no hope at all.

Alishia shouted incoherently, her voice startling him out of his stupor.

"Hope!" he said.

She stared right up at him, the tattoos on her face tight and straight, pulling down the corners of her mouth, painting an image of madness that he could not look at for more than a heartbeat. *Whatever she's seen has destroyed her.* She shouted, and then the disc-sword was thrust up from the hole. He jerked his head aside and caught its metal shaft, careful to avoid the still-spinning blade. It was smeared with dust.

He pulled. Hope helped, hauling at the edges of the ragged opening and then jumping, reaching for the lip of the crevasse and dragging herself out, rolling, tearing the disc-sword from Trey's grasp and stepping toward Alishia. The witch stood astride the sleeping girl, glancing down, up at Trey, back down again.

Trey looked down into the crevasse. A gush of dust had risen from the hole, hanging in the air and starting to drift back down as though given weight by the death moon. Only dust. *She seems so terrified . . .*

He stood and faced Hope. "What did you see down there?"

"You're slow," Hope said. "You're weak. You're of the underground, and the underground is all dead, all gone, all history turned to fucking stone!"

"What are you on about? What's down there?"

"Nothing now!" She spat on the ground and stared at her mucky spit for a while, as though expecting it to come to life.

"Alishia said—"

"She's all that's left," Hope said, her voice softening. "The only hope for the world. And you . . . you're of the underground. Slow. Weak. Fledge rage taking you down."

"Hope . . ." Trey stepped forward, hand held out. He didn't know why. To take the disc-sword? To offer a comforting touch? The witch looked down at the sleeping girl, and when she looked up again her eyes had changed.

They were dead. Dry as stone, deep as the pit she had just emerged from, surrounded by the tattoos that seemed to contour her face around the two black eyes. "You're no good for her," Hope said. And then she lashed out.

Trey stepped back, but the disc-sword's blade was spinning and the witch knew how to wield it. She pivoted forward on her front foot and slashed from left to right, increasing the killing arc of the weapon. Trey's arm went down in a reflex action, and the sword passed through his bicep and into his chest.

It felt as though he had been splashed with freezing water. His skin opened and exposed his flesh to the night.

Someone shouted, and it may have been Trey. Blood warmed the skin of his arm, flowed down his chest and across his stomach.

I still can't feel the pain, he thought. *That's bad. That's shock. It's like ice water . . . I wonder how far I'll fall. I wonder what I'll see.*

For a while he was back in the fledge mines, because everything had gone dark. He was someone else communicating with his wounded body. He reached up and touched his own face, felt the pain and fear etched into his expression. Ran his hand down his arm to the ragged wound there. Across his chest.

She's opened me up.

But to what, he did not know.

The darkness swallowed his mind as well as his senses. As he drifted away, Trey felt the first hint of the pain that would welcome him were he ever to wake again.

PART TWO

Writing
the Future

Chapter 10

A THOUSAND MORE Krotes had arrived, and now it was time to march.

Ducianne left first, followed by her force of three hundred Krotes. Several flew, most walked, some crawled like snakes. They gathered at the western outskirts of Conbarma and then wound out across the plains, Ducianne at the column's head, standing on her stone-slabbed machine and whipping her bladed hair from side to side. Lenora sat on her own machine and watched them go. *Bring me the Duke's head,* she had told Ducianne. *I'm for Noreela City. Meet me on the way, or meet me there, in which case I'll have already taken it.*

And so the real war to take Noreela began. Lenora felt a thrill of history running through and around her; she was the hub of its stories and pathways. Things were closing in on her, and moving out. The past was ending at the tip of her sword, and the future would be built upon her actions. There would be stories and songs written about her, and her name would be uttered in awe. This stinking world had existed in a state of stagnation for three hundred years.

The next few days would see more change than any Noreelan had experienced in their lifetime.

Lenora fingered the ears strung from her belt. She knew most of them by touch. Here was the Krote who had come at her a century before, determined to usurp her as the Mages' most trusted warrior: Lenora had gutted him and sliced off his ear while he was bleeding to death in the snow.

And here, the large bristly ear from a wild creature they had found on one of the hundreds of small islands east of Dana'Man. It had lived in a commune of sorts, with roughly built homes, some attempts at crop growing and a range of basic weaponry. But it was more beast than human—not a race that could be incorporated into the Krote army—and Lenora and her fellow warriors had set about slaughtering its tribe for food and skins.

She ran her fingers farther along the belt, each dried and shriveled ear inspiring memories more powerfully than any smell or sound. Lenora was a creature of violence, and the feel of the knotted edges where she had slashed these ears from her victims set her heart racing. A woman from one of the tribes living in the glaciers of Dana'Man, a creature from the far northern shores of that damned place, a young girl who had come at her with a knife after Lenora had slaughtered her parents . . .

And then at the front of her belt, closest to the knot that held the leather tight, the still-soft ear of the watcher on Land's End. He had been the first Noreelan to die at a Krote's hand since the end of the Cataclysmic War. Lenora had killed him. That had felt good, and the ear belonged on her belt more than any other.

Soon there would be many more.

Her blood was up, and her dedication to the Mages made her proud. That distant voice may come and go, yet she had a land to subdue before she could pay it heed.

Lenora closed her eyes and banished her unborn daughter's shade deep in her mind. Its time would come, but later. Much later.

Now there was blood to spill.

THEY RODE SOUTH and passed through the cultivated fields surrounding Conbarma. Dusky light revealed diseased crops and trees, too far gone to have turned this way since the Mages cursed away the daylight. Lenora rode her machine along a rough dirt track between stone walls, but other Krotes rode across fields and through sparse hedges, kicking up the stink of rot from the ground. This was a crop that would never have been harvested. Lenora leaned down and plucked the fat head of a grass crop she could not identify. It was slick with decay, its yellow seedlings turned black and damp.

The fields soon gave way to wilder ground: the Cantrass Plains. Lenora had been here before. At some point in the next day she would cross the path she had taken three hundred years before, fleeing Lake Denyah with the Mages and retreating across Noreela to the foot of The Spine. She wondered whether she would know that place when she came to it, whether it would give her the sensation of having come full circle through life. Before, she had been running away. This time, she was on the offensive.

Lenora stood on the back of her machine and gave the order to increase speed. She was amazed and awestruck at the sight behind her. She had eight hundred Krotes with her, and for as far as she could see the landscape was alive with machines of all shapes and designs. The Krotes rode as if they had been born into this. Some had fashioned reins from rope or leather, preferring to stand as their rides loped across the landscape. Others sat back, sharpening weapons, checking quivers, greasing slideshocks, packing throwing stars, testing crossbows, or familiarizing themselves with their machines' various weaponry. Fires exploded here and there when engines billowed gas. Some of them growled, as though already a part of the fight, and others darted about as if stalking something.

Moonlight sheened their way. They leapt over tumbled stone walls, skirted around trees, crashed through hedges, and Lenora could see the shadows of flying machines against the darkened sky. She wondered whether they could fly high enough to find the sun, but it was a treacherous thought, as though she was denying the Mages' power.

The sun has gone, she thought. *There's no reasoning to that. It's gone because Angel and S'Hivez wish it so, and they are the most powerful things in the world. Let the creatures of Kang Kang rise against them, let New Shanti unite in a final stand, let the Sleeping Gods rise. The Mages have magic, and its power is dictated only by the limits of their minds.*

Lenora's machine vaulted a fallen tree, but she did not even need to brace her legs. The ride was as smooth as floating on water.

———————

THEY WERE MOVING fast, and several hours after leaving Conbarma they encountered one of the Cantrass Plains' shifting homesteads.

Lenora was astounded. She felt a flicker of admiration for the people who remained with this giant thing, trying to continue their ancestors' lifestyle. The energy and effort expended in moving back and forth across the Cantrass Plains surely outmatched any benefit they may gain. Perhaps it was a way of keeping madness at bay, like a man clearing a glacier a snowflake at a time. There was no final aim in sight because it was impossible; it was the process that took time and diverted attention from more serious matters.

The homestead was battered and dilapidated. The remains of rope bridges hung at its sides, their treads long since decayed and fallen away. Deflated water sacs were home to large gray fungi. Its roof had cracked and crazed, and even from close to the ground Lenora could see that large slabs of rock were missing.

The machine's legs had disappeared, and now its inhabitants pulled it on a carpet of logs.

A hundred people tugged on thick ropes, a hundred more pushed. Dozens of large cattle and a few bedraggled horses were attached in leather harnesses, whipped on by rovers standing on their backs. The machine moved minutely, creaking and cracking some of the logs underneath, and the people strained as they tried to find somewhere better. It was a monumental effort for minimal results, and Lenora wondered whether this same machine had been moving in the same direction for three hundred years.

She ordered the Krote army to halt and they watched for a while, amazed that none of the homestead rovers seemed to have seen or heard them. The light was poor, but the moonlight seemed to like these new machines of war, glinting from sharp edges and making their stony parts almost luminescent.

"How hopeless," Lenora said.

The rovers pushing and pulling their giant, broken home were all heavily muscled, and yet they appeared tired and weak. Their feet were large and flat, their hands knotted into stumpy pads. Lights burned in a few of the homestead's windows, and Lenora

wondered at the hierarchy that allowed people to remain inside.
The rulers, obviously. Tribal heads. Those with power or charisma,
who could command the others to do their bidding.

The machine moved a step as they watched. Many people sank
to the ground, while others dragged several stripped trees from the
rear to the front. They placed them behind the harnessed cattle and
horses, forcing them beneath the front edge of the homestead with
heavy wooden hammers. Then they walked back to the rear and
took up position again.

So here was the first real test. For three centuries the Mages had
plundered the tribes and races of the huge land of Dana'Man and
its neighboring islands, adding to their army, training it, instilling a
hatred of Noreela—a land none of that army had ever seen and
many had never heard of. Down the decades old warriors had died
and new had been born, until a large proportion of the army was
Krote through and through. Different toned skins, different hair,
some tall, some short . . . yet all Krote. Bred to fight. Born to kill,
and aid the Mages in their revenge.

Now Lenora would begin to see how dedicated this army could
be. The battle for Conbarma had been a fight; this would be a
slaughter.

Lenora turned around and spoke to the Krotes within earshot.
"It's a sad first challenge," she said, "but it's practice for your machines." She nodded, and half a dozen warriors moved forward.

The rovers saw them at last. Some stood upright and dropped
their ropes, rubbing their hands as if to massage some feeling back
in. Others turned and ran behind the machine. The men and
women whipping the cattle dropped their lashes, and the cattle relaxed, heavy ropes dipping into the grass, animals slumping to their
knees and baying in pain and relief.

A few windows in the machine grew dark as the fires inside
were extinguished.

Six Krote machines walked across a field of low, ropy plants,
and the screaming began.

A hail of arrows dropped onto the advancing Krotes from atop
the homestead, and they returned fire. A body fell to the ground,
arms and legs thrashing. Another slid down the side of the huge
structure and snagged on a rope, swinging there as blood darkened
the stone below it.

The rovers who had been pushing the homestead ran, and two machines went in pursuit. One of them flailed its long metal arms, harvesting the people. The other machine coughed a wide spray of fire before it, lighting the dim scene. It stomped across its burning victims, crushing them into the undergrowth.

The other four machines reached the homestead. One Krote started slaughtering the cattle, using a crossbow to kill individual creatures while her mount fired a dozen spiked balls at a time from rents in its fleshy hide. A rover leapt from one of the horses and came at her, fearless and mad. The Krote let him get close before putting a bolt through his mouth.

More arrows were slipping from shadows as those within the homestead recognized that they were under attack. The Krotes went inside.

Lenora sat back on her machine and watched the display. Any anxiousness quickly melted away, and she felt a sense of satisfaction. These rovers had been battling to survive for centuries, and their history would be wiped out in minutes. It could be the same for all of Noreela. The timescales would differ, perhaps, but the result would be the same. In a few moments these rovers' wraiths would be wandering with no one to chant them down, and their future would have been erased.

But that vision, Lenora thought, *with no room for survivors of any kind.* She shook her head. Symbolism. Angel was fond of it, and she had used its touch to show Lenora what she wanted for Noreela.

Lenora could sense the effort every other Krote had to expend to refrain from joining in. The stench of burning flesh filled the air, and it was a smell that most of them had not experienced for some time. There were some with her who had landed at Conbarma several days before—captains now, blooded with Noreela's first blood—but most of these warriors had not seen battle since long before departing Dana'Man. There *had* been fighting there, when the Krotes launched expeditions east or west along the seemingly endless island and encountered primitive tribes and settlements. And there were more ferocious enemies the farther afield they went, leaving the shores of Dana'Man and venturing out into uncharted and unexplored waters. On those unknown islands were unknown things, and some of them had offered a challenge.

But never anything like this. This was a slaughter. And this blood, spilled so easily, smelled of triumph.

Lenora breathed in deeply, and the last scream of a dying woman drifted away across the Cantrass Plains.

Scattered fires illuminated the scene, giving a deeper darkness to the middle distance. Bodies burned, spitting and gushing geysers of bluish flame. The windows of the homestead flickered like blinking eyes. The rear of the old machine seemed to blur and slip, and a great section of it melted away from the rest, the glowing acid flowing thick with dissolved rock, metal and flesh.

Sweet revenge? a voice said deep inside, ambiguous, and Lenora was strong, she could listen. The future was filled with vengeance, and one would feed the other.

With the shade of her daughter whispering to her, she led the Krote army south across the Cantrass Plains.

———

LENORA KEPT HER eight hundred Krotes and their machines with her. They split into four groups, maintaining contact with one another by means of small flying constructs, several dozen of which had split off from some of the larger machines and formed themselves from air, earth and rock. There was a hint of the shade's workings in these things, but they did more than simply flit through the air like bats. The first time one of them landed before Lenora on the back of her mount she cringed away, waiting for it to sprout arms and legs, a head or some other less obvious appendage. But it remained motionless, a thing the size of her fist with only a grilled opening at one end to mar its smoothness.

And then it spoke.

Since then Lenora and her captains had been in constant communication, though the landscape often meant that they were out of sight. They spoke of the battle to come with both eagerness and concern, but none of them considered anything farther ahead. None of them spoke of a time beyond war.

The ground trembled beneath them. The darkness parted for them, and closed again when they had passed. They slashed across the surface of Noreela, wounding it with their presence, and already there was blood drying on their swords.

———

JOSSUA ELMANTOZ HAD been walking forever. At first he had tried counting the days and nights, but the constant twilight had disturbed his perception of time to such an extent that seconds became minutes, and the only count he could rely upon was his own rapid heartbeat. It pummeled at his chest, speeding even when he tried to rest, as though keen to carry him ever closer to death.

He kept his hood up, rested his hand on the hilt of his sword, looked at the ground a few paces ahead of him as he walked on.

His moonlit journey across Lake Denyah had been strange. He had heard things he had never noticed out there before: creatures surfacing, hissing at the sky and sinking down again beneath the waves, leaving the spicy stench of something unknown drifting across the lake's surface. None of the rising things seemed interested in him. One emerged a hundred steps from his small boat, a black shiny shape. He stretched out low in the boat so that he did not offer such a large target—joints complaining, old bones wishing he were still at rest in the Monastery—and watched over the gunwale as the serpent twisted and wailed like a pained wraith in the moonlight. The life moon sheened its oily skin, stroking head to tail as it raised various parts of itself from the water. Then it floated on the surface before sinking slowly beneath, leaving barely a ripple to hint at its existence. Jossua sat up again, staring after the serpent, and he knew why he had never seen its like before. *That was not something of the Mages or the new magic, but it* was *a thing coveting darkness. A creature of the night previously hidden away from the sun, emerging now because of the constant twilight. The* Mages' *twilight.*

Perhaps there will be more.

He had continued on across the lake, sailing when the winds were in his favor, paddling slowly when they were not. He was a very old man, and he expected his heart to give out at any moment. But he was resilient. He had seen and been through much more than any other Monk alive, and experience had hardened his shade like petrified wood. His bones might be weak, his skin thin and his blood like water, but it was his single powerful obsession that drove him on. Even in this dusk, when color all but bled from the world, he knew that his face was a bright, angry red.

After Lake Denyah, he had entered into the mountain range of The Heights, a place that harbored many small, isolated settlements. The people who lived here rarely left, and knew little of what was happening elsewhere in Noreela. Jossua had not been here for over a hundred years.

The Heights was where he found the first body.

At first the corpse was simply a shadow amongst shadows, blending into the shaded landscape like any other rock, tree or deserted dwelling. But then the shadow showed its first hint of red.

The settlement he was passing through revealed signs of having been abandoned in a hurry. Front doors were hanging open, the streets were strewn with clothing, and here and there he found rotting animals that had been left tethered to stakes in the ground. He could make out the shape on the foot of the hillside now, distinct from other shadows, a shape he should recognize . . .

Walking through the village, he looked for clues as to what could have made the people flee. There was no indication that they had been attacked: no arrows in timber walls, dropped swords, bodies cleaved in two. There were no bodies at all, other than those of the trapped animals.

And that one ahead, on the hillside, something gleaming in one hand.

Jossua paused at the edge of the village, trying to gain a sense of what had happened. If there was danger in The Heights, he should know it for himself, because he had a long way yet to travel. *Far too long*, he thought, but he cast that idea aside. He had not been more than a dozen miles from the Monastery for decades, and now here he was embarking on a journey of three or four hundred.

I'll be like that, he thought. *That dead thing up there on the hillside. Left to rot into the ground. Purpose unfulfilled. My life ended as uselessly as it began.*

He could still recall parts of his first journey across Lake Denyah, the glow of the Mages' terrible power scorching the horizon, and the hundreds of people around him who would be dead within hours. Three hundred years ago, more lifetimes than he had any right to have lived. Yet here he was still breathing and thinking, and he had always believed there was purpose in that.

He always believed he lived for something more.

As soon as he left the deserted village behind, he knew that he was looking at a Red Monk.

Her hood had been torn away, along with most of her robe. The exposed skin was dark, and made darker by huge rents in her flesh. Dried blood was black in the moonlight. She had lost one arm and most of her other hand, her left leg was shredded like a gutted fish and her face was a mess of broken bone. The remnants of her hand were still curled around the hilt of her sword.

Jossua knelt beside the dead Monk, reached out, touched the back of her neck. He moved her cold head from side to side and lifted her hair. He was trying to see what had killed her.

Some of the wounds were from swords or slideshocks. Others were less easy to identify. The terrible trauma to her foot seemed to have been inflicted by something multibladed, or perhaps by teeth.

"What have you been through?" he said. But she had no answer, so Jossua stood and moved on, leaving the dead Monk to rot into the hillside.

He worked his way through the valleys of The Heights. He had neither the energy nor the inclination to climb mountains and traverse ridges. The valley was shaded from moonlight for much of the way, carved over time by the small rivers and streams that started high up and flowed eventually into Lake Denyah. He took water from the streams, rested by the rivers, and all the while he was amazed by the utter silence of this place.

Last time he was here, the mountains had been alive with noise. He hid himself away up on the mountainside, finding a small hollow in the ground sheltered from above by an overhanging rock and concealed from all sides by a growth of thick yellowberry bushes. From there he watched and listened, content to observe events rather than be a part of them.

Skull ravens had buzzed him, cawing into the sky as they touched on his mind and turned away. People worked on the valley floor, tending crops and hunting, building homes and damming streams to form fishing lakes. Their cattle bayed, wolves howled, children ran and laughed and screamed, and late at night the adults would sit around the village perimeter and light fires, keeping the darkness at bay and talking quietly amongst themselves. There was noise and activity, and Jossua had remained in his hiding place for seven days watching the village go about its business. The mountains were never silent. At night there were animals abroad, and the land itself seemed to breathe. There was still a rhythm to things even then, two hundred years after the Cataclysmic War had plunged the land into decline. The rhythm was upset on occasion, and the land sounded like an old man's breath on his deathbed . . .

but there was always more than silence. Perhaps it had been the sound of plants growing and dying.

Now the permanent twilight had started killing the plants. The inhabitants of these places had fled, and whatever once lived on the mountains seemed to be still, or dead. Magic's withdrawal had mortally wounded the land; it seemed that it had taken magic's reemergence to finally kill it.

A couple of miles farther on, Jossua found two more Monks, both of them dead, both bearing horrendous wounds similar to the first. He barely paused. He had known once the sun failed to rise that the Monks' cause was at an end, that the Mages had returned to claim magic for themselves. And he had known what this would mean.

But seeing the results of defeat was harder than he could have imagined.

———

HALF A DAY later he saw another Red Monk. This one was still crawling.

Jossua paused for a moment, unnerved by this, the only living thing he had seen in over a day. Perhaps deep inside he had decided that he would never see a living Monk again. Days spent making his way across Lake Denyah and through The Heights had engendered a sense of isolation, which finding the Monks' corpses had only exaggerated. Now something else was moving in this valley floor apart from him.

He knelt, tilting his sword so that it did not drag against rocks. The injured Monk was a hundred steps away, crawling so slowly that movement was barely visible. Jossua had spent long nights watching the moons vie for space in the sky, and he had often tried to discern their movements, wondering what it could mean that he only made it out if he closed his eyes for hours at a time. He had once believed that it displayed his disassociation from nature, an inability to perceive the tides of time which meant that he was remote from the land's true beat. Events of great consequence shifted with the speed of a waning moon, and Jossua missed it all because he did not have the ability to see.

He looked at the ground by his feet, trying to decide whether the shapes and shadows of moonlight in the loose shale meant

anything other than twilight. He shifted one stone with his foot and
nothing crawled from beneath its shielding mass. He moved another
and it hid only damp darkness. The shadows were motionless.

When he looked up again, the Monk had moved a step or two,
one hand reaching out as if to grab water from the stream still a
dozen steps away.

"You're still alive," Jossua whispered, not knowing what this
could mean.

He approached the Red Monk. It was another woman, robe
badly shredded and stained with blood and the muck she had been
crawling through. There was little left of her face. Bubbles of blood
formed where her nose had once been. Her hand clawed at the
ground, found a hold, then pulled. The fingernails had been ripped
out. She pushed with her feet. Her other hand was crushed and
stinking of rot, and Jossua could make out fresh blade wounds
where she had tried to amputate.

The bad hand would poison her blood, and she still had many
questions to answer.

"Lie still," he said. The Monk lowered her head to the ground
and sighed.

Jossua raised his sword and brought it down just above the elbow of the damaged arm. He severed the limb with one strike, and
the Monk twitched once and whined, the sound fading to nothing
as her body grew still. He kicked the stinking arm.

Jossua knelt and turned her head. She still had one good eye,
and he drew close and stared into it.

"I am the Elder Monk," he said. "You must not die yet. I need to
know what happened, and where, and when. You need to talk to
me now."

The Monk opened her mouth and hissed. Her tongue, gray
and swollen, scraped at her teeth, flexing aside as she tried to speak.
"Wa . . . wa . . ."

"Water," Jossua said. He refilled his canteen from the stream,
returning to the woman and letting a few drops touch her lips and
enter her mouth. She barely moved, though her tongue writhed
like a fat slug.

"Tell me," he said. "Where have you come from?"

The woman took several deep breaths and pushed herself onto
her side, looking up to the sky as though searching for the sun. "I
saw the sun set," she said, "and it never rose again."

"Where was this?"

"Machines . . . graveyard . . . a place where they died, but I saw them live again."

"And the Mages?"

The woman closed her eyes. "Took the boy from within a machine. Took him away. Darkness remained. That, and slaughter."

"Where was this?"

"Gray . . . Woods."

Jossua frowned and knelt back, trying to conjure a map of this part of Noreela in his mind. The Gray Woods lay to the east, a strange place bordering the Mol'Steria Desert. He had never been beneath the influence of their canopy, but he had heard the stories.

"You crawled that far?" he said. It was impossible. This woman would be dead within hours, and not all of her wounds were old and putrid. Some of them were new. He touched her chest and smelled his hand. Fresh blood, not rank.

The Monk shook her head, and her whole body started to jitter against the ground.

"What?" Jossua said. "What do you have to tell me?"

"Taken!" she suddenly screeched. "Taken and dragged and *shredded*!" Her good eye opened wide. It caught the death moon and shone yellow, echoing its shape and size in the sky.

"A tumbler?" Jossua asked.

The woman shook her head and snorted. Perhaps it was meant to be a laugh.

"Then, what?"

"No tumbler," she said. "Monster. God. *Demon*!"

"But it let you live."

The woman frowned and rolled onto her stomach, gnawing at drooping heathers.

"*It let you live,*" Jossua said. "Why?"

"Elder, we've lost," she said.

"Do you have a message for me?"

"We've lost, we've lost . . ." She twisted her head, small stones crunching between her teeth.

Jossua stood. "That is no message at all." He swung his sword and cut off the dying Monk's head. For a second her jaw still worked, and he wondered at her final thought.

He left the body to cool and walked on. *Monster . . . god . . . demon!* He looked up at the hillsides and along the valley, but then went back to staring at the ground a few paces ahead. If something came at him from the dark, perhaps it was best he did not know until it arrived.

Then perhaps it would give him its message in person.

———

JOSSUA HAD THE stolen page from the Book of Ways in his pocket, ready to be referred to once he reached Kang Kang. Though even reaching that place was not a certainty.

He passed through the heart of The Heights and found more abandoned settlements. He discovered other things too, which he knew were signs of the land's continuing decline. In one valley, a small forest had sprung up alongside the river. The trees' leaves still shone bright and healthy in the moonlight, though they had not seen the sun for several days. As he drew closer, Jossua realized why. He had believed they would offer shelter for a camp, and perhaps food for his supper. But he wanted none of this fruit.

Wrapped in each trunk was the body of a small child. It was as if the children had been held there while the trees grew around them, and now they were part of the trees, their arms and legs jutting from the bark in imitation of the great limbs sprouting high above their heads. The trees pumped blood and the children seeped sap. They must have been old, though their flesh was still pink and ripe, and their eyes glittered in the moonlight, following Jossua's progress as he paused and slumped slowly to the ground. Their mouths hung open, though no sound escaped their petrified throats. He could see the whites of their eyes like the inside of a burst wellburr seed. But these were like no trees he had ever seen before.

Jossua was tired, his old bones ached, his shoulder hurt from wounds received long before any of these children were born . . . and yet they disturbed him. There was something powerful about their stares, as though they knew much more than he, and he had to walk around the small forest and leave the valley before he could sit and rest in peace.

Monster . . . god . . . demon!

"Where are you?" he said to the night. "Come out of the shadows. If you're demons, I'm just like you. If you're gods, I won't believe until you show me. If you're monsters . . . well, I've taken

meals with worse than you. You can't bother me." He thought of the
mad Monk's fear as she had spoken, and those fresh wounds cut
through others gained days before in the Gray Woods. "You can't
bother me," he said again, but repetition added no strength to the
words.

Walking on, Jossua looked up into the strange twilight. No stars,
no clouds, only moonlight smearing the heavens and battling for
supremacy. The life moon seemed to be rising still, the death moon
lower in the north, yet the color that persisted was the pale yellow of
old fledge.

And at the thought of that buried drug, Jossua's next breath
brought a hint of its spice to his nose.

He paused and looked around. *No fledge mines in The Heights*,
he thought. He snorted to clear his nose and breathed in again, but
this time the scent was absent. Yet there was something in the night,
a consciousness colliding with his own but trying not to make itself
known. He looked left and right, searching for a sign, a shifting
shadow or the glitter of unknown eyes watching from the vague distance. Nothing . . . and yet for the first time in days, he no longer
felt alone.

He stood and spoke into the darkness. "If there's meaning here,
let me know it now. If this is just something looking for dinner, I'm
old and tough, and I won't go down without my sword opening you
from arse to mouth." Nothing responded, nor came at him from the
shadows. He breathed in and sensed no fledge, and cursed his aged
nose.

It was there, he thought. *Just for an instant, but it was there*.
Because there were no fledge mines in The Heights did not mean
that there was no fledge. It could be buried in deep veins never before found. Or perhaps fledgers *did* know of its existence but for
some reason had decided not to mine here. It was possible that a
whiff of the buried drug would make it topside on occasion, especially in times as strange as these. *I'm fooling myself*, he thought. *I'm
making up stories where there are none, and making excuses for things
I can never know.*

Jossua walked on, glancing behind now and then, certain that
there was now something else alive in The Heights other than him
and those monstrous trees. The ground was breathing again,
processes were no longer ended. But not all that lives is good.

Monster . . . god . . . demon!

"I think I know you already," he said. And even Jossua's bad old flesh felt a thrill at such presumption.

SOMETHING HAD BROUGHT those wounded Red Monks to The Heights. They had fought a battle in the Gray Woods—a fight that had involved the Mages and stabbing, clubbing things that could only have come machines resurrected from their deaths. They could not have come this far on their own, not bearing such terrible injuries. And something had given them fresh wounds bringing them here.

"A sign for me," Jossua said to the dark.

An hour later he saw another Monk, his body wrecked with terrible wounds both old and new. He put him out of his misery without asking any questions.

I'm following a trail, Jossua thought, *and the message will lie at its end.*

IT TOOK ANOTHER day to leave The Heights and find the end of the trail. Jossua guessed at the passage of time, estimating it from the periods between food and toilet rather than anything to do with the sky. Time was paused for Noreela, and it was only inside that Jossua felt it moving on. *I'm too old for this,* he kept thinking. The idea seemed to provide the impetus to go farther.

He saw three more Monks, two of them dead. The living one was sitting against a rock beside a dry riverbed, holding his sword in both hands and staring ahead as if challenging the death stalking him. His wounds were many, but most of them were old. He had lost a lot of blood but retained his red rage, hood still raised, robe pinned to his body by several snapped blades.

As Jossua approached, the Monk's attitude remained unaltered. The sword was still, his eyes open and dry. He was mad.

"I am the Elder Monk," Jossua said, but the Red Monk did not seem to hear. Jossua reached out and passed his hand before the seated man's unblinking eyes. Yet he was still alive, because Jossua could hear his ragged breathing, feel the heat flaring from him as though the red rage were fire.

Jossua clasped one of the broken blades and jerked it from the man's flesh. He shook once, but did not utter a sound.

The Elder looked at the blade. Short, curved, snapped at the base, it looked more like a tooth than a man-made weapon. *I've never seen a blade like this before except . . .*

"Except on a machine."

The man still did not blink.

"You're dying," Jossua said. Silence. He looked at the various wounds across the Monk's body. The man was sitting in a darkened circle of soil where blood had leaked and dried. The robe hid much, but Jossua had no reason to reveal this Monk to the night.

"If you're in no pain, I'll not kill you," he said. "Though there's no use for you now. Do you know that? Do you see? Were you there when the Mages came and defeated us?"

The Monk remained still and silent and Jossua left him that way, a living statue looking westward as though trying to see his way back to the Monastery.

Jossua was being watched all the way. Each breath he exhaled was taken in by something else, examined by an intelligence he could not understand. His footsteps played the beat of an alien heart, and there was always something beyond the next outcropping of rock, hidden in the darkness just out of sight, concealed behind the next mountain. The land no longer felt dead, but what life existed was strange and foreboding.

Jossua had felt this way before, and not so long ago. He was in the presence of something both terrible and great. Though he was the Elder Monk, and had seen much in his long life, still he knew his place. He walked with his head bowed, and not only because he did not wish to see.

The mountains shrank into hills, the valleys grew wider, and Jossua felt the things following him move closer. Standing in a wide fields of dead yellowberry bushes, he felt the vibration through his feet that signaled the end of his time alone.

"I know you," he said, but there was no bravery in his voice. Only fear.

———

THE SCENT OF fresh fledge accompanied a movement in the ground. Fifty steps away, on the hillside that showed no sign of harboring anything but rock, a wide swathe of yellowberry bushes waved, whispering in the dusk. Then they were tugged belowground, twigs and dead leaves bursting upward as though taken in and spat out by whatever was rising.

It was the loudest noise Jossua had heard in days, and he expected the land to object. But the Nax were more of the land than anything he knew. Noreela's heart beat in tune with their own slumbering souls, and they had been here longer than he could imagine. They were ancient as the rock, old as the mountains, and he had often wondered how complicit they were in each small step Noreela took through time. He had come to the conclusion long ago that humanity meant little to the Nax, sleeping their time away in fledge seams far below the surface of the land. Here and there were ghastly stories of miners disturbing their sleep—fledge demons, they called them—but Jossua doubted they would be disturbed if they did not desire it. Perhaps they were like the moons, existing on a different timescale to humanity, passing through life so slowly that their movements could never be properly discerned, their meanings and intentions subject to myth and legend rather than understanding.

Jossua still felt dread whenever he recalled his recent meeting with the Nax. Deep below the Monastery, time had stood still. And his question to them—had they driven the Mages out three centuries before—remained unanswered.

Now they were back.

The Elder Monk sank to his knees and bowed his head. He did not wish to see. He did not want to know. There was no true darkness aboveground, and when the Nax emerged he would see them, take in their forms while he felt himself observed and touched and smelled.

They've been doing that for days, he thought. *Steering me and guiding me to this place for a reason I cannot begin to understand.*

He listened to the sounds of tearing undergrowth lessen to nothing, and then soil and rocks tumbled into the ground. Fledge fumes drifted across the mountainside and Jossua breathed in, the drug's fresh touch providing a brief, vivid series of images:

The Monk lying dead, head parted from her body by my sword, and in her chest the bolts from a resurrected machine; another Monk, one I never saw, walking west through The Heights on stumps instead of legs, my face in his mind and the words of defeat on his tongue; the

*one I left sitting against a rock, propped there still with his sword held
out in front of him. Heart racing. Red rage scorching his face. Hunger
and thirst closing in, blood thinning, wounds seeping, rot spreading,
and he would decay to nothing whilst still staring ahead at something so terrible he can never let it go.*

And then a voice answered his visions: *We are the Nax.*

Jossua opened his eyes.

Shadows rose before him. He could make no sense of them and
for that he was glad. Their presence was a negative on the world,
voids rather than shadows, places that should not be filled but were.
They were so wrong that Jossua could barely see them.

Priest, the Nax said.

"Elder Monk," Jossua whispered.

Priest . . . Monk. What do you learn of the Nax?

Jossua thought back to his few brief years in Long Marrakash
before the Cataclysmic War, training as a priest and learning the
myths and legends of the land. "I . . . I can't remember," he said.

Priest . . . the Nax . . . what do you know?

Jossua squeezed his eyes closed against the Nax, tried to hold
his breath, but the tang of fledge oozed through his skin and touched
his mind again. He remembered—a rapid recall that played like
the pages of a turned book. "You're fledge demons," he said, keeping his eyes closed. "Sleep in the seams of fledge. Rarely seen, never
survived. Sometimes the digging machines woke you, and the machines stopped and the miners working with them vanished. Then
you go deeper. The fledge preserves you. Perhaps you are the
fledge."

The vision came to an abrupt end and Jossua opened his eyes,
shocked. The shadows before him drew back, letting in moonlight.
Jossua gasped. *The Nax*, he thought, unable to do anything but
stare at the thing standing before him, poised above the ground in a
place it was never meant to be. It dripped yellow dust, as though
shedding the death moon's light.

You know nothing of the Nax, the shadow said, and it uttered
something that may have been a laugh.

Jossua tried to stand and move away, because he did not think
his heart could survive this. There were other shadows on the hillside, other Nax prowling the dark and shedding the death moon's
light as soon as it touched them.

"What are you?" Jossua whispered.

We are waiting, the Nax said. *You wait with us. In Kang Kang
there is hope.*

"The Womb of the Land?"

The Womb is protected.

"What can I do to help?"

Unprotect.

"How?"

Learn our language. And suddenly his audience was over, and
the Nax had somewhere to take him.

Jossua felt something grab him around both legs. The touch
was nothing he could identify. Solid and soft, sharp and blunt, it
was as though the shadows had taken hold.

Will they keep me here forever? he thought, and then the shadows pulled.

He fell onto his back, reaching out behind just in time to prevent himself from being brained. Still, the breath was knocked from
him, and he was dragged up the hillside toward where the Nax had
emerged. They took no care over him at all: his robe was ripped
from his back, undergarments snagged on rocks or spiky plants, and
the jarring impacts soon caused Jossua to cry out in pain.

Monk, the Nax said, voice full of derision.

The Elder Monk clamped his mouth shut and weathered the
pain as he was dragged up the hillside. He looked up at the unnatural sky and thought of the Mages, and realized then that the Nax were
acting because of what the Mages had done. Filled with mockery
though they were, the fledge demons still had cause to guide Jossua
here, to them.

They spoke of Kang Kang and the Womb of the Land.

They spoke of hope.

"You need me," Jossua said, his voice shaking with the multiple
impacts his body was enduring. The Nax did not respond. The pain
became something else—an experience from another life, remote
from him now—and as the moons vanished and true darkness took
him, Jossua found a smile.

———

THEY TOOK HIM deep. To begin with, he felt the remnants of the
yellowberry bushes scratching at his body, then there was only darkness and the impact of rock and stone. His skin and flesh were

scored away. He found himself surrounded by fledge, the smooth, sandy drug soft after the sharpness of rock on his body. The Nax moved quickly, darting left and right, powering through the fledge and hauling him after them, taking him deeper and deeper. Jossua felt the weight of the world changing around him. The land above weighed down, the mass of rock sucking the blood from his body, draining him, stripping his bare wounds of loose flesh and filling him with fledge, more than was safe for a man one-tenth his age, and yet he smiled at the Nax, pleased that he felt no smile in return. They terrified him, but they needed him. In that he found comfort.

The Nax dragged Jossua until he faded from consciousness, carried away on fledge visions that made no sense to a dying man.

———

JOSSUA ELMANTOZ WAS over three hundred years old. He did not know how or why he had remained alive for so long, but he believed that it resulted from his purpose in life. It was his destiny to remain alive on Noreela to prevent the Mages' return. To do this, magic had to be kept away from the people and places of Noreela.

He had never considered the possibility of failure. He was confident in his task and those who helped him: the Red Monks, mad and strong and so committed to the life they led that they thought of little else. If commitment had been a force of nature, the Red Monks would have been unstoppable.

I'm a monster, Jossua had once thought, but only once. That had been a long time ago when he was a hundred years old. *I'm a monster. But perhaps it takes a monster to defeat one.* And so he had continued to gather other monsters to him, converting them and making them even more monstrous than he, and the Red Monks had waited in their Monastery like a blood bubble ready to burst. Their craze and madness became their life force, a throbbing insistence that death was no easy answer, and slowly their flesh and bones and blood took on the same stubborn defiance against the Black. *We'll all be chanted down in the end*, Jossua had once told the assembled Monks, *and it will be the greatest death chant Noreela has ever heard.*

And now here he was, his body broken and wallowing in fledge, his mind sent to see the truth of things, and the Monks' final song was barely even a whimper. Its echoes had passed across the land without touching a blade of grass or turning a sand rat's head. The Red Monks' wraiths were loose and mad, awaiting their elusive rest knowing that their whole lives had led to failure.

———

CLOSE TO DEATH, perhaps Jossua found life for the first time.

His body lay broken and bleeding beneath the foothills of The Heights, Nax sitting about him like shadows. So many open wounds let in so much fledge that his mind soared, passing through a mile of rock with no effort at all, and when he burst out into the Mages' dusk he reveled for a while, suddenly free of the decrepit vessel that had kept him chained to Noreela for so long. He was old and wise and mad, but with fledge driving his soul skyward he rediscovered that seed of youth, a naive curiosity that had somehow survived the centuries. For the first time in a hundred years he could remember the face of his fiancée as she cried him away to the Cataclysmic War. She had been so proud being betrothed to a novice pagan priest, and he had shunned her as he left. Perhaps he had been afraid, knowing that he would never return. Or maybe at that moment he had already found his purpose. The cruise down the River San had been like being born again, leaving behind the safety of normality and emerging into this new life of war, battles against the Krotes, everything that had followed. He wondered what had happened to his fiancée. She must have grown old thinking that he was dead. Perhaps she married, had children. And that thing she had placed in his hand, the cool metal of a brooch or other lucky charm . . . he had opened his hand without looking and let it sink into the water, drowning his past.

Spinning high over The Heights, Jossua tried to imagine where that charm was now. It would be buried in silt after so long, unseen from above, unknown from below. Waiting there for someone to find it again. Perhaps it would take ten thousand years, or a hundred thousand, and when it was eventually discovered there would be stories built around it, tales that could never be true because there were a billion different stories in Noreela, and he did not even know the truth about himself.

He sensed something to the east, a flicker in the stillness of the night. He floated that way and drifted lower to the ground, and there he found a dead Monk, his wounds home to insects and other crawling things. The Monk's wraith hovered over his corpse, mad and moaning and terrified of the mind that approached.

Don't be scared, Jossua thought, and the wraith stilled. *I've come to chant you down.*

He had no idea whether it would work. But he stilled his floating mind and shut himself off from the world, and as he imagined the words of a death chant he sensed the wraith fading to Black.

———

HE MOVED ON, traveling farther from his body with every second that passed. He found more Monks, all of them having died on their journey toward the Monastery. Their wounds were terrible, and their tenacity impressed him. He calmed their wraiths and chanted them down. Every few minutes he opened his mind to his own body and felt the agony of gaping wounds, content in the pain because it meant that he was still alive. He had never used fledge, and he spent an occasional panicked moment thinking that he too had become a wraith craving the Black.

The Nax wanted me, he thought. *They sought me; they* need *me. There is more to my life than this.*

He went farther, passing over a gray forest where things screamed and plotted, and he rose higher than ever to avoid their touch. There were many dead Monks down there—he could sense their wraiths wailing, staining on the gray like blood splashes on ash— but he could not bring himself to tend them. He could not save everyone. Whatever mad things inhabited those woods had the Monks for themselves, and Jossua would not think of them again.

He cast backward and felt his body beneath the ground, coughing blood into the fledge seam. The Nax were still there, heartbeats so far apart that they may as well have been dead. Waiting. Guarding him. And every now and then something would reach out and touch his skin, ensuring that his heart still beat and his blood flowed.

Jossua journeyed on, and soon he sensed a concentration of confused wraiths ahead of him, every one of them a Monk. He slowed, rose higher and then smelled something that almost made him turn around and flee the way he had come.

Down there in a large depression in the land, magic had happened, and it had left a residue of itself in the ether.

Jossua moved on, gliding up a slope and emerging above the bowl in the land. And there were the machines, still and dead yet scarred with fresh scrapes and scars. They were clean of vegetation. And there were Monks, hundreds of them lying dead and dismembered across the ground. He went to them, chanting all the while and feeling their wraiths slip gratefully away to the Black.

JOSSUA CHANTED LONG and hard, and with every Monk that left the world he felt more and more alone. *Am I the only one left?* he thought. *I was the first, many years ago. Am I now the last?* The awfulness of what had happened here pressed in on him, crushing his mind to a small, defensive point that he was terrified would blink out at any moment.

I'm still alive, he thought, and he felt the Nax touching his body a hundred miles away.

I still have purpose. They called for him and he left, chanting down the last few wraiths as he fled.

I will not yet admit defeat.

He felt the mockery of the Nax, stroking his rent flesh and reeling in his mind as though they controlled the drug. He prayed to the Black that whatever it was they were holding him for, he would find out soon.

THE NAX TOOK him out of the ground. He did not know how long he had been down there—it could have been a hundred weak heartbeats, or perhaps it was days. They dragged him as they had on the way down, but this time they cleaned fledge from his wounds as they went. He felt a hot fluid scorching his opened flesh, his face, his hands, and when a few crumbs of fledge fell into his mouth the fluid entered there as well. It was bitter and boiling, and he spat and gagged as more flowed in. He was forced through the vein of fledge without being able to absorb any of it. The Nax wanted him with his mind attached.

My body is almost dead, he thought. *What good is a body like this to them?*

Monk, the Nax said, and again he could hear the amusement in their voice.

"You need me," he said. In their silence, he found some measure of victory.

They emerged into the freshness of endless night. Jossua was
dragged across the hillside, the Nax hanging on to one of his feet
with a slick, warm touch. He looked up at the moons hazing the sky
and wished he were up there again.

You're a lucky Monk, the Nax said.

Lucky? Jossua thought, but the Nax said no more. *Lucky?* He
should have been dead, but somehow they kept him alive. Flesh
and skin had been scoured from his bones, his insides were open
to the night and his mind was trapped once again in this ailing,
weak, pathetic body. He had seen the Red Monks' defeat and
failure—he had smelled magic and sensed the Mages—and now
he was lucky.

Lucky?

But the Nax would not be drawn. They paused by a stream and
retreated into shadows, hidden away from the massive sky. They left
Jossua out in the open. He could feel the coolness of grass beneath
his back, though now it was faded and dry.

Noreela may be dead already, he thought.

JOSSUA ELMANTOZ—A few heartbeats from death, cold from
blood loss, pleading with the Nax to tell him what he was meant to
do—heard the thing before he saw it.

It was strange how darkness had silenced the land so much.
Even night creatures seemed to find no comfort in this endless
dusk. But when the rumbling began in the distance, some animals
made themselves known. Something small scrambled over his
ankle. He felt its scaly tail scrape across a deep gouge and then it
touched his other leg, passing over there as well, fleeing quickly from
the approaching sound. Another animal passed close by, and in the
distance there were growls and cries as things twittered their fear
into the dark. They all fled east to west.

The rumbling grew closer, a series of impacts interspersed with
brief moments of silence.

Tumbler, Jossua thought.

Do well, the Nax said in his mind, and for the first time ever he
heard something other than mockery in their tone.

The tumbler came out of the darkness and rolled Jossua Elmantoz into its hide.

IS THIS THE BLACK? Jossua thought. *The Black isn't supposed to hurt.*

He could sense wraiths all around. They feared him, and he was not sure why.

Am I dead at last?

Not quite dead, a voice said. *No use dead.*

Who are you?

Flage. I'm of the tumbler that has you, though you are not yet of the tumbler. The mind has chosen me to rise up and speak with you.

I don't understand.

The voice uttered what could have been a laugh, and it chilled Jossua to the spiritual core.

You're different, Flage said. *I'm here to tell you why.*

Chapter 11

A'MEER WAS SMILING down at Kosar, kneeling so that the sun
was behind her and throwing her into silhouette. She was beautiful;
her hair was braided as usual, and hanging to either side of her
head; her pale skin shone even in shadow. And she was laughing.
Many times since leaving Pavisse and settling in Trengborne, Kosar
had yearned to hear that laughter again, and now it was a balm for
his wounds, a tonic for his soul. He reached out, but she shook her
head and drew back, still laughing. He wanted to speak to her but
he could not find the words. He felt protective and jealous, wanting no one else to see what he was seeing now, hear what he was
hearing.

    A'Meer, he tried to say, but there was no strength to his voice.

    Her laughter faded, her smiled faltered. For a few seconds she
moved sideways so that he could see the concern on her face as she
stared down at him. And he realized then that his emotions toward
A'Meer were so charged because he knew that she was dead.

    She mouthed something, reminding him of the image the
mimics had shown him. That had been a representation of her at

the moment of death; this was beyond. And this time he knew what she was saying.

Trust the Monk.

———

THE RED MONK—Lucien Malini it had called itself, though Kosar had trouble attaching a name to such a thing—was sitting close to one of the dwindling Breaker fires. It had its back to him. He lay a few steps from the Monk, arms and legs free of the old machine now, his throat so painful and swollen that he could barely turn his head.

I'm going to kill you, Kosar thought, staring at the red cloak in the poor moonlight. That cloak was stained with splashes of A'Meer's blood, and whatever he dreamed her saying, she was still dead. *Soon, I'm going to kill you.*

The Monk raised its head, lowered its hood and turned around. It was monstrous, just like all the other Monks Kosar had seen over the past ten days. Its head was almost bald and its face was a mass of scars, old and new. Its eyes were black in the moonlight, its face shifting in shadows thrown by the fading fire.

"I don't expect you to trust me," it said.

"Good."

"I can help you. Circumstance has made us allies."

Kosar tried to laugh but it hurt too much. He raised himself up instead, turning and spitting into the dust. There was still blood in his mouth.

"This Alishia you spoke of . . ."

"I'll kill you before you can touch her."

"I don't seek to hurt her." Its voice was quite unlike any he had ever heard before. Gruff and hesitant, as though the demon was not used to speaking.

"I don't believe you."

"A Monk never lies."

"I don't believe that, either."

"Ahh. There's a dilemma."

Was that humor? Kosar thought. *Is it trying to seduce my trust?* He felt only disgust and rage at the Monk. It had killed A'Meer. Then it had tortured truths from him and expected him to ally with it when it chose to act on those truths.

"I'm going to kill you," he said again.

The Monk frowned and stood. "Then that's difficult," it said. "Because I *can* continue on my own to Hess, to tell the Shantasi of the hope there is in Alishia. The final hope to stand against the Mages. The Shantasi will kill me, but there's a chance that their Mystics will smell the truth in my blood. Less chance than if you presented the story to them . . . but a chance, at least."

"You're trying to *appeal* to me?" Kosar said.

The Monk shook its head. "I'm stating a fact. If you refuse to come, I kill you now in case you fall into the hands of the Mages' agents. You go for New Shanti, and perhaps with me to protect you, you'll get there."

Kosar coughed, swallowed, felt the tang of blood still in his throat. Even the thought of walking was daunting, let alone negotiating whatever dangers there may be between here and New Shanti.

"You sound hoarse," he said to the Monk. "Bet you've never said that much in one go before."

"Sometimes I talk to myself," it said. "I'm mad, after all."

Kosar was glad the demon did not attempt a smile.

He lay back down, wincing as the strain hurt his throat. Smoke from the fire gave the sky some texture, but the moons soon bled that away.

"So you're giving me two choices," he said. "Go with you and live, or stay here and die."

"Yes," the Monk said.

He closed his eyes and thought of A'Meer mouthing those words, *Trust the Monk*. Perhaps the demon had implanted that image when he gave Kosar the sleeping drug. Or another insect, cut into his brain while he slept to insinuate the Monk's desires into his mind.

"Of course," Kosar said, "there's choice number three."

The Monk remained silent.

The thief stood, flexed his hands and felt the familiar sting of the brands. "I could cut you to fucking ribbons now, shit in your foul heart and go on my way."

The Monk did not move. It still had a crossbow bolt in its shoulder. Its hands were dark with Breaker blood. The fire gave its skin a red tinge, and Kosar remembered the Monk in Pavisse that had fought on with slayer spider venom melting its veins.

"Of course, that would be unfair," Kosar said. "You're weak from the recent massacre. I have honor."

"So will you wait until I've recovered my strength?"

Kosar nodded. "It's only right."

The Monk looked down at Kosar's hands. "I can cure your brands."

Kosar splayed his fingers and looked down. "You can fuck off," he said. The brands were like speckles of burning coal on his fingertips. The blood glistened fresh, and when he touched two fingertips together the pain was exquisite. It was different from the pain in his throat, his back, his ribs; this, he was used to. It was familiar, and with familiarity came some sort of acceptance. The brands were a part of him, and after so long they had started to define him. They were as much a part of him as his eyes, his mouth, any other characteristic by which people formed their first opinions.

Kosar wondered what the Monk thought of them, but he would never ask.

"I really can," the Monk said. "If you ever want me to."

"A show of trust?" Kosar asked.

The Monk tilted its head slightly in what passed for a shrug.

I could pick up my sword, Kosar thought. *It's lying over there where that thing threw it. Its handle has known A'Meer's hand, and together we'll slay this monster and move on to Hess. A'Meer's message is fresh in me. They'll believe me when I get there. The Mystics will believe me.* He glanced across at the sword lying away from the fire, visible only because its blade reflected the dying flames.

"If we fight, you will die," the Monk said. "I am Lucien Malini."

"You told me that once before," Kosar said.

"I'm telling you again in the hope that you may listen."

"You want me to know your name? You want me to believe that you're human?"

The Monk frowned. "What else am I?"

"Demon," Kosar said, looking away.

The Monk was silent for some time. Kosar sat again and listened to the crackle of the dying fire; logs settling, sap popping, flames licking the sky lower and lower as though defeated by the dark.

"Our cause is a good one," the Monk said at last.

Kosar did not wish to enter into conversation with a demon. It would confuse him, catch him off his guard, make him believe that it was right to let it live and accompany him to Hess. It would be sly and devious, though right now it seemed only sad.

"No cause justifies what you do," Kosar said. "And you've already failed. Three hundred years of murdering innocent people and the Mages snatch magic from beneath your nose."

The Monk did not reply. It raised its hood and stared into the fire, face hidden from Kosar.

Now, Kosar thought. *I could snatch up the sword and take off its head. Kick it into the fire. Watch it scream without voice as the flames eat its eyes, its brain, boiling away the only true memories of A'Meer's death.*

But he still felt weak, and he had lost a lot of blood. And perhaps he would fumble the sword and the Monk would be upon him, accepting the implied decision and killing him before moving on to Hess.

"Do you really believe that Alishia is a chance?" he said. "Or do you want to kill her, as you tried to do with Rafe?"

"We tried to kill the boy to keep magic from the Mages. They have it now. You're right; the Red Monks have failed. But our cause is still my only reason for being. We could not prevent the bastard Mages from taking the magic, but perhaps I can help win it back."

Kosar turned his back on the Monk and lay down. He looked up at the dark sky, ribbons of smoke from the fires dispersing when they rose above the Breakers' ravine. *It's a long way to Hess,* he thought. *I'm weak. And the world is a dangerous place, more so now than ever. The Breakers proved that.*

He closed his eyes, decision made but not yet spoken.

Besides, he thought, *revenge can never grow stale.*

———

THEY LEFT THE ravine together, climbing the same cliff path they had descended several hours earlier. The Monk had disappeared for a few minutes before they departed, and when he returned he carried a spray of plants; heathers, leaves, a drooping flower and a soil-encrusted root. He made a paste and told Kosar it would help.

Kosar placed a pinch of the paste beneath his tongue, and by the time they made the climb from the ravine, his pain had faded to a dull throb. He should be stitched, he knew; the wounds on his back were pouting, inviting infection and chafing against his rough shirt. But there was no time. And while he was willing to accept the Monk's herbal pain relief, Kosar did not like the thought of the demon crouching behind him and stitching him together with sand rat teeth.

He ran his fingertips across the wound in his throat. The tiny curved teeth were still there, holding the edges of the wound together so the flesh could heal. *I may be dead before this is mended*, he thought. *And then I'll rot away with a throat full of sand rat teeth.* He giggled, the sound strange in the silent night, and he was glad that the Monk did not turn to share in the joke.

Lucien Malini had insisted on leading the way out of the ravine. Kosar had seen no reason to argue, and he'd rather have the Monk in front of him than behind. Behind them, all the dangers were dead.

Kosar paused on the cliff path and looked back down to the ravine floor. The giant machine was little more than a shadow, the fires dwindled almost to nothing and the Breakers were dark shapes spread-eagled against the light soil. The Monk had killed their children. No mercy. No qualms. It had been killing for so long that it knew no other way.

"I'm nothing to the Monk," he whispered. *I'm just part of its route to Hess, to the Mystics, to Alishia and whatever magic she may have in her.* He turned and watched the figure in red climbing out of the ravine, sword held ready in one hand. It reached the head of the path and turned, waiting for Kosar.

The thief moved on, splaying his fingers so the cool air could kiss his wounds.

———

KOSAR WAS CONTENT to let the Monk walk ahead. The Monk seemed to accept this. It led the way and Kosar followed, always keeping his sense of Kang Kang's presence to his right. If the demon tried to edge him northward away from New Shanti, he would know.

He chewed on the paste, welcoming the numbing relief. He did his best to ignore the suspicions that arose in his mind. Taking a drug from a Red Monk? Following it? Not questioning its route, its cause?

Trust the Monk, A'Meer had said in his dream. And while he was certain it was nothing *more* than a dream, he did not believe that A'Meer would betray him, even in memory.

Two hours after leaving the ravine, the land began to change. Heathers gave way to hardier plants, the ground cover of grasses and moss became patchy and the smell of the desert drifted in from the north. Heat rode on the breeze, even after several days without the sun. The smell of spice rode with it. *We're approaching New Shanti*, he thought. In all his years of wandering, Kosar had never been there.

The Monk stopped ahead of him, drew its sword, and its robe blurred as it became a confusion of swinging limbs.

Kosar dropped to one knee and drew his own blade, grateful for the weight of steel in his hand.

The Monk grunted and slipped onto its back, and shadows swirled above it.

Kosar stood, moved a few paces forward and then paused again.

The Monk lashed out. Something screamed long and loud, and another hack from the Monk's sword ended the cry.

Kosar could smell blood now, mixed in with the warm hint of spice, and he moved forward again.

"Stay back," the Monk hissed.

Kosar obeyed, happy to leave the demon to its fight.

What are they? he thought. *Skull ravens?* There were several shapes dancing around the Monk, darting in and away again, squealing as its blade found them, hissing as they attacked again. The Monk seemed to have limitless energy; the fight went on for some time, and Kosar could not help recalling A'Meer's tale of her clash with a Monk on the steam plains of Ventgoria. That had lasted a whole night.

The Monk screamed and turned, fell and jumped, ducked and sidestepped, and more shadows fell. It stomped them into the ground whilst continuing its attack.

Kosar sat, wincing when he reached out one hand to the ground and found sand pricking his fingertips.

The fight ended as quickly as it had begun. The Monk dropped one final shadow and stepped back, tripping over its own feet and landing hard on the ground. Kosar went to it, his sword drawn in case the things rose again. As he closed on the fallen Monk, he was not sure which to keep his eyes on the most: the Monk, its bloodied sword still pointing skyward; or the dead things on the ground, their shapes indefinable, their smell mysterious and potent.

The Monk saw him coming and stood.

"Sand demon," the Monk said.

"Just one?"

"They have many parts."

Kosar looked down at what the Monk had done. He could not identify any of the parts on the ground. There were long, thin shadows that may have been tentacles, one small round chunk that could have been a head. Flames seeped from some of the wounds, weak and blue, guttering and going out as Kosar watched. The Monk trod down on one of the larger flames and crushed it into the sandy soil.

"It was a strong one," the Monk said. "They usually don't come this far south. They stay in the heart of the desert, preying on those foolish enough to cross."

"How do you know all this? Surely you don't spend much time this close to New Shanti? The Shantasi hate the Monks."

"Everyone hates us," Lucien Malini said. "And I know because I spent a lot of my youth reading."

"At the Monastery?"

"Yes, there was a library there. Huge."

"Alishia is a librarian."

The Monk raised an eyebrow in surprise but said no more.

They walked on, moving together this time, but it took Kosar some time to say what was on his mind. "That thing would have killed me."

"It may not have revealed itself to you. Sand demons are not all of this world. They . . . span."

"But if it had so chosen, it would have killed me."

The Monk grunted. "They're very strong, yes." He nursed his left arm, chewing herbs and pressing them into wounds hidden beneath his robe.

I'm thinking of the demon as a "he" now, Kosar thought. *I can't let myself trust it.*

"It revealed itself to you," the thief said.

"As I said, everyone hates Red Monks."

They walked on, crossing land that was quickly turning to desert. *A hundred miles to Hess,* Kosar thought. *Maybe a little more.* He wondered what would happen when the Shantasi discovered him in the company of a Red Monk.

The Red Monk who had killed A'Meer.

Kosar stared at Lucien Malini's sword.

———

TREY WAS IN the home-cavern back in the fledge mines, alone this time, and there were a hundred fledge demons in there with him. It was dark and he made his way by touch, but whenever he neared the entrance to a current mine working, the pain came, so loud and brash that he scampered back into the cavern, hiding in caves, circling the great pillars and lying low in the Church.

The Nax made the darkness their own, creeping around him with every heartbeat. He could smell them, taste them on the air, and they were as alien to him as the topside he had never seen.

He moved across the cavern floor, dodging heavy points of darkness that signified a Nax. He approached another mine working and felt a different pain possessing the rest of his body: the agony of wanting. The scorch of the fledge rage lit up his flesh and bone.

Perhaps one of the Nax would save him? They were fledge demons after all, coated in the stuff, some even said they were made from fledge in its purest, most intense form. Perhaps one of the Nax . . . ?

He moved forward and the pain exploded in his mind.

For an instant, the home-cave was illuminated. The Nax were not ignoring him at all. They were gathered around him, some less than an arm's length away. They hung from the ceiling high above on threads of fledge, crawled on the walls of the cavern before him, slid up and down the wide column fifty steps to his left, all *staring* at him, surrounding him as completely as the darkness that quickly returned.

He opened his mouth to scream, but the Nax were the air.

He ran toward the tunnel once again, certain that its dark mouth was the only place where the Nax had not gathered. Heading for topside brought the pain again, lighting his way and displaying in a flash the hundreds of Nax lining his route. They reached for him as the light blinked out—limbs, wings, flaming tongues—but none of them could touch him in the dark.

He reached the mouth of the working and entered, running through the agony of his upper body.

It's the fledge rage, he thought, *torturing me more than the wounds Hope gave me, tearing me up from the inside, giving me nightmares when I'm already in one.*

He ran through the mines, cringing away from the walls of Nax that each flash of pain revealed. It was as though they saw him only when the pain came, but by the time they reached for him he had willed it down again.

The light became more rhythmic, the pain more regular, the claws of the Nax closer and closer to ripping into his dreaming flesh.

He saw himself through their eyes, with their minds. He was nothing amazing at all.

———

TREY OPENED HIS eyes. However terrible reality might be, he welcomed it.

He was cold. The sky was stained the color of stale fledge by the death moon. The life moon seemed to be fighting a losing battle, and Trey stared at it in the hope that it would grow.

His head thumped with fledge rage. A lump of it—a grain, fresh or stale, beneficial or fatal—would take the pain away. Fledge would carry him home, back to the place he should have never left. Sonda and his mother were dead down there in the ground, two miles below and hundreds of miles away from him, but at least he would have been dead with them had he found the courage to stay.

His arm and chest were boiling hot, freezing cold. Blood still flowed freely across his body, passed between his arm and his side, tickled his armpit, seeped to the ground and dripped down onto the thing Hope had recently emerged from. Trey could feel himself open to the night. He raised his good arm and laid it across his chest, and he touched the meat of himself there, parts he should have never felt. He stank of his own blood.

Hope killed me, he thought, and his mind recoiled. *No!*

He remembered the look on her face as she lashed out with his disc-sword. He had killed stingers with that weapon in the caves, and it had tasted Red Monk blood at the battle in the machines' graveyard. Now its steel was smeared with him, its handle spattered with his blood, and perhaps soon that would be the last of him.

No! he thought again. *Alishia* . . .

A terrible fear took him, a dreadful certainty. He moaned and rolled onto his right side. His left arm struck the ground, the slashed muscles denying him control. The flame of agony illuminated his night for a few seconds, but this time there were no Nax waiting for him. *I dreamed them*, he thought. *They're still my nightmare, even lying here like this.* He lifted his head and looked around.

He was lying where he had fallen, next to the hole in the

ground from which Hope had emerged ranting and mad. Alishia had been lying close to him when Hope came up, asleep or unconscious, and he searched for her now. Perhaps Hope had gone mad and killed them both. Perhaps she had found her thing in the ground wanting, and now she was raving across Noreela seeking her own demise.

But Alishia was not lying where he had left her.

Trey rolled onto his back again and looked left, biting his lip against the pain. No Alishia.

Had the witch killed the girl and tumbled her into the hole?

He rolled again, shifting himself around to try to see into the ground, but there was still no sign of Alishia.

I need to sit up.

It took Trey a long time to raise himself into a sitting position. Each breath hurt, every movement was agony, and he was starting to feel faint as blood loss darkened the dusk. But once up he could look around, and he was now certain that Hope had taken Alishia with her.

There's no way I can give chase, he thought. He was sure that he was dying. The pain scoured his soul, seeking to pluck it from his body, and if that happened he would be just another lost wraith waiting for someone to chant him into the Black. *There's no way I can go after her.* He looked south toward Kang Kang, those distant teeth set in the edge of Noreela. It had taken him an hour to sit up, and it would take him an age to go that far.

He tried. He managed to stand, swayed, biting his lip until he tasted blood, trying to chase away the faintness and find the stance that suited him best. He reached across his body with his right hand and grabbed his left sleeve. He lifted, head back so that he could look at the sky, and brought his slashed arm up until it was pressed across his body just below his chest.

He was crying. The tears carried a subtle taint of fledge and he licked them from his upper lip, knowing they would have no effect but welcoming their taste.

If I don't die from blood loss, the fledge rage will be waiting.

He braced his left arm against his body, popped two buttons on his shirt and pushed his hand inside.

Trey gasped and almost fell. He thought perhaps he could move like this. His legs shook and his thigh muscles felt as though they were ready to cramp, but he set one foot in front of the other, one at a time, avoiding shadowed areas that might hide a pit or a hole, and he took ten steps south.

That's how I can do it, he thought. *One step at a time. Concentrate . . . There, one step closer to Alishia. And another . . . and another.*

But however much he tried, however hard, Trey could not fool himself. He would be dead long before he reached Kang Kang.

――――――

TREY WALKED ACROSS the bare ground, craving grass and soil, bracken and heather beneath his feet. He was used to rock, but since coming topside he had realized that rock was merely the bone of the land. The living part of Noreela was what grew and lived upon it.

Where he was now, Noreela felt dead. The stone was cool and uncompromising beneath his feet. His blood splashed darkly across its surface, looking like holes in the moonlight. *At least there's life there*, he thought. But it would not last for long.

He had no idea how far he had come. He was concentrating too much on placing one foot in front of the other to judge distance, and his only gauge of the passage of time was the need to urinate. He stood still to piss, and ignored the exhaustion that threatened to topple him. If he lay down to rest he was doubtful that he would ever rise again; the bare, dead skeleton of Noreela would suck the life from him and he would lie there forever.

He felt the weight of that unnatural cloud above him, swirling so slowly that its movement was barely noticeable. He glanced up only once, but the sight made him woozy, its weight tugging at him until he was ready to fall. *It may come down*, he thought. *It may all come down again.* But even that fear could not increase his speed.

Then something howled in the darkness. It seemed to come from a long way off at first, but after a pause another cry sounded from much closer. Trey fell to the ground and crawled into a depression in the rock, fearing that the creatures would smell his blood and tear him apart. He had no idea what animals would be wandering here. If Kosar were with him . . .

But Kosar had left Alishia in Trey's care, trusting him with the girl because he knew that Trey thought highly of her.

Trey closed his eyes and thought of Alishia's beautiful face and

the dark, closed mind he had seen on one of his fledge trips. She
had been so much like Rafe; so much power hidden away. It was
confusing that someone so powerful needed protecting, but it had
been the same with Rafe, and he had seen the way that ended.

This won't be the same!

A creature howled so close that Trey could almost feel the
warmth of its breath. Another answered from the distance, and
another, and he realized why he had not been able to place where
the call came from: there were many of them, not just one. The
howls started deep, rising in tone until they almost disappeared
from his range of hearing. He could not tell whether they were in
pain or on the hunt, harmful or harmless. Whatever they were, they
sounded big.

Trey tried to hold his breath. The pain of his wounds was fresh
and bright, still lighting corners of his mind but revealing nothing
like the dream.

I've never heard the Nax, he thought, and the idea that it was
them out there made him gasp.

He caught his breath and held it again, terrified at the silence.

Something walked by. It was moving slowly, yet the footfalls
were rapid, as though it had more than four feet. He opened his
eyes and looked without moving his head, ready at any moment for
a shadow to fall across him and cut the moonlight from view. *I can't
fight. I have no weapon. I'm wounded and bleeding and weak. It's
hopeless.*

The creature paused and Trey heard the distinctive sound of
something sniffing the air.

No hope since the Nax attacked.

A low growl, rumbling behind a closed mouth.

*Something else controlled us with Rafe. So does something steer
me even now?*

The animal held its breath.

Whatever I do, it's destined to be.

Trey gasped in another breath, sat up and shouted as loud as he
could. Something whined briefly to his left and then dashed away, a
huge shadow bounding from rock to rock, multiple limbs slapping
down to accompany its squeals of terror. He shouted again, and in
the distance he heard similar sounds of fear from the other fleeing
creatures.

He screamed again, for himself this time, and with nothing to dampen the scream it echoed across the landscape, perhaps still traveling even when it had passed beyond his own hearing. He sat there panting, sucking in breath after breath to make up for his fear, and he liked to think that his scream would reach Hope, struggling with Alishia flung over her shoulder or leading the girl on foot. Perhaps his cry would make her wish she had remained behind to finish the job, instead of leaving him half dead. Or perhaps not. He thought of her eyes, her rambling, and decided that she was probably too mad to be afraid.

He stood again, easing himself to his feet and fighting the sudden nausea. He could not afford to lose any fluid or the meager contents of his stomach; Hope had left him with nothing, and if this stripped landscape extended much farther he would die from thirst.

Steady, his vision level, Trey started on his way once more.

——————

HE WALKED FOR a long time, still only counting one footstep after another. He reached a couple of hundred and started again, trying to forget how many times he had done so. He had come a long way. The mountains of Kang Kang loomed closer, approaching almost too fast, as though he were running rather than hobbling. They were taller than he had imagined, harsher, and their peaks glowed white in the moonlight.

Snow, he thought. He had never seen it. But somehow he knew that snow from Kang Kang was snow never meant to be seen.

His wounds hurt abominably, and the fledge rage blurred the edges of his senses, lodged behind his vision and hiding just below his perception of hearing. It would be so easy to curl up and let the rage smother the physical pain of his wounds. After that would be madness, and after that death, either from blood loss or from his failing heart. Fledgers in the final throes of withdrawal could make an easy choice: accept death, or fight. Most fought.

But his mother had not sacrificed herself so that he could lie down here and die. Maybe she had seen a purpose in his eyes. Perhaps it had always been there, or maybe their flight up from the home-cavern had made her see him in a whole new way. She had slipped away and thrown herself into a deep crevasse, ensuring that she remained underground forever. She had not been sad when she died; he had traveled to her, and she had told him that this was what she wanted. She was slowing him down. Without her, he would stand a chance of reaching the rising and going topside.

She had been right. And now there was something else slowing him down; his wounds, and the rage. If only they would leave him so willingly.

———

PERHAPS A DAY passed. Trey fought the urge to sit and rest, fearing that he would not be able to stand again. Many times he believed that he saw Hope and Alishia in the distance, but when he concentrated on the spot where he thought he'd seen movement, the shadows grew still once again.

They can't be that far ahead, he thought. *If Hope is carrying the girl, then she'll be moving as slowly as me, and if Alishia is walking, she'll be taking a child's steps.*

He saw a haze of shadows moving back and forth over the ground. At first he thought it was his failing vision, but when he stood still he could hear the soft whisper of their movement. They did not change direction to come toward him. They did not pause to stare. They drifted back and forth just above the ground, passing around and through one another without interruption, and Trey diverted around the place the shadows circled. He tried to see — leaned closer than he should, almost feeling a shadow touch his skin — but there was only a hole in the ground. Darkness made it impenetrable. By the time he had left the shadows behind, Trey was glad.

His wounds demanded attention. His bicep was split and still bleeding — movement ensured the wound remained open — and his chest was slashed to the bone. Sometimes he thought he could smell the beginnings of rot, but he put it down to his unwashed body and clothes, that slightly musty smell of age and decay. He hated to attribute it to the injuries. If the smell came from them, then his blood was turning poisonous, and he would be dead in hours.

My disc-sword has tasted Monk blood, he thought, but he tried to shut that from his mind.

He had no water or food. When he pissed, he caught as much as he could in his good hand and drank it, cringing against the taste but aware that he could not lose the fluid. He had learned harsh lessons from miners who had been trapped for weeks after rockfalls.

Drink your own piss, they said, *otherwise it's a waste. And eat your own dead, because if it takes weeks to be dug out that's all the food you'll have. At least then they won't have died in vain.*

Kang Kang loomed closer and larger than ever. Sometimes Trey thought he could reach out and touch its mountains, and when he tried, his fingers grew cold, as though buried in the snow capping their upper reaches. Even having spent his life deep beneath the ground, still he knew of Kang Kang. A *wrong* place, someone had called it. Kosar? Hope? He could not recall, but he trusted their words. It felt wrong even now, miles distant and all but hidden by this unnatural dusk. There was something both alluring and repulsive about the mountains, a sense carried in the air and through the ground. He could not make out exactly where that feeling came from, but it confused his already weakened mind and toyed with his fledge-teased senses.

He bent over and almost vomited, shaking his head to rid it of the smells, the tastes, the sounds.

And then he smelled fledge.

He knelt on the rocky ground, and something compacted beneath his left knee. He looked down, trying not to lose his balance— he felt disoriented, unsure of up and down—and lifted his knee. Mud, wet and slick.

He looked up and sniffed again, smelling fledge and feeling his whole body crave its touch on his tongue, its taste in his mind. His joints ached with the rage.

Mud?

And there before him, several hundred steps away, the ground began to show the darker patches of covering once more. He was almost at the edge of the desert of rock.

"Thank the Black," Trey whispered, and something close by responded with a hiss, and a touch of some vision on his mind.

He saw himself standing there alone and covered with blood, scared, abandoned, a fledger aboveground and as removed from his environment as he could ever be. And as he wondered how he could be seeing himself like this, the smell of fledge grew overpowering and he tipped forward. Before he struck the ground, something came between him and the rock.

Something hot.

———

HE WAS BATHING in fledge. He was underground—in a dream or reality, he neither knew nor cared—and around him the drug was crumbling, giving itself to his touch, finding his wounds and soothing them, pricking his tongue with its tangy freshness, setting his blood and his brain afire and readying his mind for any journey he wished to take. It was the freshest fledge he had ever encountered, as though he had found it not only before it was touched or mined, but at the actual moment of its creation. There had been much speculation as to what fledge was and how it came into being: it was grown by the Nax, it *was* the Nax, it was the fallout from Nax dreams. But the simple truth of the drug had often done away with such musings. It was like questioning the existence of air or the origins of water, questions both pointless and faithless. What mattered was that they were there.

Trey welcomed in another mouthful, chewing the perfect grittiness into a paste, swilling it between his teeth and below his tongue and letting it slip down his throat. It set his flesh alight and took away much of the pain. Something else touched his mouth, briefly but definitely. He opened his eyes but there was nothing to see, so he closed his eyes again and welcomed some more of the crumbling fledge inside.

He was moving, slipping through a seam of the drug as though he were a fledge demon, steered between rough stone walls and protruding rocks. The drug parted around him easier than it ever should have, coming apart before him and joining again behind. And it whispered all the time, giving him ideas and images that he would never have imagined himself.

The fledge rage retreated, defeated and petulant. He was happy to feel it go.

I can travel, he thought, and he set his mind free of his body, moving away and only glancing back once.

He obscured what he saw from his mind. The drug made it easy to do so.

Trey traveled, up out of the ground and into the cool dusky night. He spun and rose in the air, trying to decide which way to go. North would only take him back over the ground he had just traversed, and he had no wish to see that ruined landscape again. South . . . that would take him closer to Kang Kang, and while that was not a place he wanted to go, he had need to travel there. He must find Hope and Alishia, and make sure that the girl was still alive.

He moved through the air, a mind separate from body yet still inextricably linked. The ground below soon returned to normal, and he passed through the huge banking of uprooted trees, soil, rocks and dead creatures that marked the limit of this strange effect. He sensed little still alive in that pile of detritus: a sheebok here, a snake there, shaken and confused by what had happened and still trapped. They would be dead soon. He emerged from the other side of the mound into open air once more, expecting to find a normal landscape below him: trees and scrub, rocks and gulleys. Streams, perhaps, originating in the foothills of Kang Kang and venting out onto the plains. Even dwellings.

But what he found was anything but normal.

This was the edge of Kang Kang; its first small hills, its border region, pushing against the rest of Noreela like opposing poles on two swing-sticks. Trey paused high in the air, disoriented and confused for the few seconds it took him to level out and calm down.

The ground below looked like the diseased skin of a buried giant. Here and there soil had filled a hollow and given rise to small shrubs, grasses and trees, but most of what he could see was a pale, pitted surface, marred by conical vents gushing steam. The steam flowed southward toward Kang Kang, dispersing into a mist. The light from both moons reflected through the mist, casting shifting shadows on the ground below.

Trey dipped lower, moving into the steam to hover close to one of the vents.

He recoiled as a slew of images struck him, each with a distinct emotional impact. He wanted to cry and laugh, cower with fear and march on unafraid, but the visions were confused, their implications sensed rather than seen or felt. The instant he thought he had an understanding of one image, it flitted away to be replaced by another.

The ground was venting memories that Trey could not understand. He was glad. They tasted of painful histories, and right now it was the future that concerned him most.

The vent resembled a pustule on bad skin, except a thousand times larger, standing as tall as a man and its surface so stretched and tight that it was almost translucent. He wondered whether he would find any memories of the future inside, so he moved back down. But the vent would allow him no access. He moved around it and tried again, probing with his disembodied consciousness, feeling strong from the fledge but still unable to see inside this thing pouring memories from the land.

The flow from the vent's mouth was fast, tempting and hypnotic, and Trey had to force himself away. If he submitted to its allure, perhaps he would be lost in Kang Kang's memories until he became one of them.

And then, struggling away from the flue, he saw movement farther up the hillside.

Hope was dragging Alishia after her across the strange ground. The girl was struggling behind the witch, trying hard to keep up. Hope had a tight hold on Alishia's hand.

Trey closed in quickly, pausing above the witch and listening to her insane babble.

"All gone, all lost, come with me, come on, girl, keep up! We're nearly there, we'll find the place and the place will find us, and I'll be there when you're there. Forget the past, forget what happened here, don't *breathe* if that's what it takes, it's misdirection. Kang Kang fooling us into thinking it's still *alive* . . . Keep up, girl!" She tugged at Alishia's hand and the librarian began to cry.

Alishia was smaller than ever, her clothes hanging on her as though she were barely there at all. Her eyes were watery, dark rings beneath them, and the skin of her face looked sallow and sweaty.

What's happening to her? Trey thought. But he knew without asking, and without going closer, and without dipping into her mind to try to tell her everything was going to be all right.

She's dying.

Trey moved closer to Alishia and passed inside her, looking for that vibrant young woman he had known for such a short, precious time. But he found something else instead, a place that drove him away like steam from one of the land's vents: a burning library, books falling, blackened paper floating on the air, words and history of Noreela becoming ash and dust beneath his gaze.

"What's that?" the witch squealed, thrashing around her head with Trey's disc-sword.

Trey tumbled from Alishia and rose high into the air, looking only upward because he did not wish to know what down revealed. The dusk persisted, always dusk, and he stopped only when he became afraid that he would never find the ground again.

Trey returned eventually to his own body, finding it deep beneath the ground. And slipping back inside, he realized where he was, and began to wonder why.

———

THE NAX MADE hollows in the wide fledge seam and moved Trey ever southward.

The miner was more petrified than he had ever been before. His heart fluttered like a bird trapped within the cage of his chest. The fledge flooded his system and tried to calm him, but he could sense what was moving him. He could feel their shapes and forms, and they were wrong. He could hear their voices, words he could never know, and they were wrong. He could sense their minds around him, inviting him to enter, urging him to view things through their own world, and every touch of their thoughts was very, very wrong. Trey opened his mouth to scream but there was no air to draw into his lungs, only fledge. He inhaled anyway.

Soon, he was drowning.

Chapter 12

ALISHIA HEARD THE voice of Hope the witch, mad and raving and filled with selfish intent, and everything around them was wrong. She closed her eyes and found sleep again, a place haunted by the stink of burning.

Blue flames danced all around her, and whichever way she turned she saw only smoke, and burning books, and tall book stacks simmering as the histories they contained came under threat as well.

There's so much here, how can I ever find what I need? she thought.

What do I need to know?

She was worried about Trey, because she had read of his danger in a book that burst into flames. She was worried about Hope because the witch was hauling her ever southward into Kang Kang. And she was worried about herself. She felt that she had been handed some great task, but she could not find her way through it. She was lost here in this burning library, adrift in a place she should know so well. *If I'm to be told something, why do I have to go and find it?*

"Whatever I have inside me is much deeper than this place," she said, and she closed her eyes to see. But she could not. She probed with her mind, trying to discover the route back into that basement. Perhaps she had missed something down there? But she could no longer find the door. She dropped to her knees and scratched at the timber floorboards, using her nails to pry up a few loose splinters, widening a joint, prying and straining and finally snapping up a slat of wood as long as her hand. A burning page fluttered across the floor and slipped between the boards, and Alishia pressed her face to the crack to see where it went.

The page fluttered downward, barely touching the thick darkness below. She watched it for a long time, falling, falling, listening to the library destroying itself around her but never taking her eyes from that single falling sheet. And in the instant before it was snuffed out forever she saw shadows moving around it, closing in and starving the flame as though afraid it would reveal them for what they were.

Alishia sat back on her heels and gasped. *So deep*, she thought. *So filled with* things.

She stood and ran, an aimless sprint that took her into a warren of narrow passages. Around one corner she came across the worst destruction yet. Fire had eaten into the sturdy timber supports of a bank of shelving and much of it had given way, the fractured stumps of wooden columns charred and exposed like the library's ribs. Several dozen shelves had fallen, and thousands of books had tumbled into chaos. Many of them simmered, some burned and a couple of hundred had been reduced to little more than a ghost of their old selves, ashen shapes that fell apart beneath the weight of Alishia's gaze.

The librarian started climbing. It should have been treacherous but she seemed to find her footing easily, mounting the hill of books and standing at its summit to see what was on the other side.

In the library, a forest glade. She closed her eyes and frowned, feeling for an instant the movement of Hope carrying her ever southward. When she opened her eyes again she was still in her library, and before her lay the clearing. The trees all around were made of books, stacked up for trunks, twisted for limbs, torn for leaves. Between the trees and the actual clearing reality changed,

blurring from ripped pages to rough grass. Here and there a plant
showed both; a bush with twigs and leaves, book bindings around its
base and genuine roots protruding above the paper-strewn ground.

At the center of the clearing lay a wide, flat stone. It was dusted
with snow and the wind—perhaps birthed by the fires—had blown
the fine flakes into lines, shapes and pictures etched into its surface.

I don't know what that says. But with that thought came the realization that, were Alishia to go down into the clearing, its meaning would become clear.

She began descending the barrier of books, her feet stepping
unerringly from one firm foothold to the next. She held her hands
out from her sides for balance and thought of Kosar, the thief with
the branded fingers, and how he walked like this to prevent his fingertips scraping on his clothing. *I wonder where he is now?* She
glanced down at the books beneath her feet—perhaps one of them
held his story, or part of it, or whatever the future may have for
him—then stumbled and fell forward. She landed on her side in
the strange clearing, sitting up quickly and looking back, terrified
that she would be somewhere else entirely. But the library stacks
still stretched back from this place.

The grass beneath her hands was cold and brittle. There was no
daylight here, only the light of the fires, and it seemed to match the
strange twilight existing in the real world. *What's real and what isn't?*
Alishia thought. This *could be the real world. Everything else—Rafe,
Hope, Trey, Erv the stable lad and my library that the Red Monk
burned down—that could all be my imagination. Pages in my own
book. Ideas I never wished to have.* She stood, wiped her hands on
her legs and realized that the snow coating the stone slab was actually ash.

She blew the ash from the carvings in its surface.

At first the images and etchings made no sense at all. They
seemed to be a random collection of markings: strange letters and
obscure symbols, pictures of creatures she did not recognize, numbers written backwards. She blew more ash away, making sure that
she had uncovered everything in case the whole picture suddenly
came together.

Something grumbled deep in the library and shook the ground;
another stack of books tumbling to nothing. *And another thousand
people die,* Alishia thought, disturbed by the idea but certain that it
was true. High up where book stacks met in the haze of distance, a

massive cloud of fire and smoke erupted, jumping from stack to stack and encircling the clearing like a crown of flames. *Fire won't touch this*, she thought, tracing one of the etchings with a finger. As she followed the smooth carving, something stirred in her mind, a memory stretching its legs and unfurling. She frowned and closed her eyes, continuing to touch the same etching back and forth, and each completed circle made the thought stronger.

It was a memory of something she had never done. It belonged to something else. But it was becoming whole and clear, and she moved on to the next carved shape and began following it with the same finger.

Fire bristled high above her and several burning books struck the ground close by. One of them burst apart into a shower of flaming paper, and it took Alishia a few seconds to register the burn on her arm and the smell of singed hair.

"This fire can't touch me," she said, and as if to deny her words another burning page landed in her hair and set it aflame. She waved both hands and batted out the fire. She had scorched a couple of fingers, and her palm already held a blister the size of a tellan coin.

The rock called her back and she went. It was the knowledge she needed, and while the rock itself would always be here—wherever "here" was—she understood that her chance to read it would never come again.

Scared now, breathing harshly and feeling the baggy clothes hanging loose around her body, Alishia began to see what the rock had to say.

———

IT FELT AS THOUGH she was reading a book about the whole world of Noreela in the space of a few heartbeats, rather than the many lifetimes it should really take. She felt drowsy and sick with the information input, but ecstatic as well. Ideas floated through her mind, and they were like words in a sentence that had no clear meaning. *Birth Shade needs a seed*, she read, and everything else seemed to echo that thought, that image, building on the idea and giving it a history. She was filled with the joy of new life. Around the clearing were young trees and plants, budding flowers and a few fledgling birds and the fleeting shadows of ghost animals that would one day exist here. The stone slab itself was redolent with the memories of birthings, the antithesis of a sacrificial stone. Alishia could almost smell the fresh blood.

And though the images and name—*Birth Shade*—were there, she still did not fully understand.

I need help, she thought. *That's why I'm here, in this place that really isn't inside my own mind. That's why I'm exploring what Rafe left me with, because we need help, all of us, me and Hope and Kosar and Trey and the rest of Noreela. We need help or we're lost forever.*

She moved on to another shape, waving away drifting ash that burned when it touched her. She looked up at the cone of empty space above this strange clearing, and all around the towering walls of books were exploding into flames.

She traced more etchings, closed her eyes and thought, *Death Shade needs an offering of pain.* When she looked again the plants around her were withered and black, and skeletons of small animals shone in the firelight. Leaves rustled beneath her knees, dead and dry. The slab beneath her fingers was still bloodied, but now it was caked from sacrifice, strong blood that had sent a powerful message.

Alishia frowned, then suddenly cried as though everyone she had known was dead. But she could not move her hand away. To do so now would be like reading the history of the world and stopping three pages before the end.

I don't have very long.

She wiped her eyes and moved on to the final shapes on the flat stone, excited and scared at what their reading would reveal. *Birth Shade, Death Shade*, she thought, *but what does all that mean? Where's the seed . . . and where's the offering?*

She traced her finger through the speckles of ash within the final shape's smooth cuts, and when she came to the end everything changed again. The clearing around her became a moment in time, the plants alive and yet not shifting, small creatures pecking at the ground or grooming themselves with blood still in their veins, and thoughts frozen in their heads.

Her heart stopped.

Half-Life Shade needs the passion of life and the fearlessness of death.

Alishia fell back from the stone, rolled onto her back and stared up at the towering flames around the clearing. Her heart thumped again in her chest as if to remind her of life. She felt as if she had read a million books in one single sitting, but there was no great epiphany.

I've been reading the language of the land, she thought. *Birth Shade, it tells me, Death Shade, Half-Life Shade. And though Noreela has spoken, it's making no sense.* She stood and screamed: "It's making no sense!" And a shower of pages fluttered down around her head.

Alishia beat at the flames in her hair and on her clothes. Paper fell away, words blackening and disappearing before her eyes as though eaten by a shadow. "Shade?" she said. She wanted to save them all, but first she had to save herself. She dashed from the clearing and clawed at the slope of tumbled books, hoping that once back in the library she would be safe from the fire.

But what if this weight of new knowledge had made her more susceptible to damage? What if this place had suddenly ceased to be so welcoming? Perhaps she had been reading things never meant to be read—the language of the land was *for* the land, not mere people living upon it.

Alishia brushed a burning page from her back and rolled down the other side of the pile of books. She fell into a ball of flame, and the blue tongues stroked across her skin and seemed to salve her fresh burns.

She lay there for a while, listening to Noreela being unwritten word by word, instant by instant. What she had read in the clearing was important. But she knew that there was more yet to discover.

———

ALL OF HOPE'S talk of Kang Kang, the knowledge she held, the stories she had heard, the myths and legends that haunted squalid taverns and desolate rover camps, the screams of those who had been there dreaming about it still . . . none of it could have prepared her for being there.

She felt totally dislocated. Once she was a part of Noreela; now she was apart from it. This place was somewhere else. The feeling had been growing steadily, though to begin with she attributed it to hunger and thirst, the effort of rushing across the damaged landscape, the impact of her time belowground. It began as a feeling of growing apart from herself: her feet were a long way down, her hand holding the disc-sword impossibly far away. Each step took

forever and sounded like thunder, yet still she had the sense of rushing headlong into Kang Kang.

The ghost of the dead Sleeping God was chasing her all the
way. She felt it on her back, crushing her down far harder than the
measly weight of this shrinking girl ever could. Alishia was fading
away, a barely noticeable bulk that Hope shifted from left shoulder
to right. The Sleeping God . . . even its breath would have melted
her into the ground. Its ghost, its memory, its unrealized potential,
Hope carried all of these with her.

Sometimes she thought she heard it scream.

Hope moved on, climbing the first of the Kang Kang foothills.
In all her time as a whore and witch she had never managed to se-
cure a map of this place. It was mentioned in Rosen Am Tellington's
Book of Ways—and Hope owned one of the few remaining original
copies of that tome—and yet even that great mapmaker had found
these mountains obscure and unreadable. Some of those who
claimed to have been here spoke of mountains and valleys, lakes
and towers, holes in the ground and the ruins of races immeasur-
ably old and forgotten. Others spoke of fields of snow and glaciers
with no identifying mark between one place and another. Yet there
were rumors of a map . . . whispers of a man who had come out of
Kang Kang millennia ago with the lay of the land imprinted on his
mind . . .

Hope believed none of it. Kang Kang was not a place to be
mapped, nor even remembered. It was a place to avoid. Perhaps
shades lived here, and tumblers, and mimics, and other things that
no one should ever have to see. But this was not a world for people.

"No people," she said, looking up at the long slope before her.
The Sleeping God watched her back and Hope spun around,
Alishia's weight nudging her off balance and spilling her to the
ground.

In the distance, two moons reflected from the stripped-stone
landscape like a pair of staring eyes.

"Leave me alone!" she shouted. "You're dead and gone! Failed
me, failed *us*, and now you're just a fossil!"

"It's only in your mind," Alishia said. The girl rolled away from
Hope, sitting up and rubbing her shoulder where she had struck the
ground.

Hope looked at her suspiciously. "We arrive in Kang Kang and
you wake up?"

Alishia looked stunned. "We're in Kang Kang already?"

"As if you didn't know."

"Where's Trey?"

Hope glanced away, trying not to look at the disc-sword she had dropped but failing. Alishia followed her gaze.

"Trey?" the girl asked again.

"He left us. Fled back underground. Found a fledge mine, smelled his damn drug, and he betrayed us."

"No," the girl said.

"Betrayed *you!*"

"No," Alishia said again, her voice gentle but firm. She stared at Hope, and the witch did not like those eyes.

"We have to go on," Hope said. "No time to sit and talk, things to do, a place to find, and you . . . look at you . . . you're . . ." *Is she really as small as I think?* Hope thought. *Or is this just Kang Kang trying to fool me again? She looks like a child. Or perhaps she's far away.*

"I'm learning."

"Learning what?"

The girl looked away, up toward the mountains they had to pass through.

"You don't trust me?" Hope said.

"No."

Hope was not surprised. But neither, she discovered, did she really care. "It's watching me," she said. "The whole of Kang Kang, sitting here where it doesn't belong, and it knows I'm coming and it knows you're coming."

"I know," Alishia said.

"You know?" Hope stood over the girl, stooping to pick up the disc-sword. "What else do you know? What is it you're learning? Is magic in you? Is it there now, ready to come back and fight? *Give it to me!*" She moved quickly, pressing the disc-sword beneath Alishia's chin and resting her hand on the lever that spun the blade.

Hope, you stupid whore, what are you going to do now? Kill the girl? Take away any chance, any slight hope you may have of becoming what you've always dreamed of being?

"If you kill me, Noreela is dead."

"I don't care about Noreela," Hope said. She thought of the petrified heart of the Sleeping God, once filled with such wonder. "Noreela no longer cares for itself, so why should I?"

"There's more to the land than Sleeping Gods." The girl was staring at her over the blade, no fear in her eyes.

"What do you know?"

"Some, but not enough."

Hope shook her head and stepped away. "I don't *care!*" she said.

Alishia stood, and Hope saw how small she had become. She had the body and the height of a young teen, yet the attitude of someone with a whole world on her shoulders. Her eyes were those of someone ten times Hope's age.

"Come on," Hope said. "The longer we wait here, the more Kang Kang can plot against us."

Alishia's eyes drooped, she swayed, and Hope slapped her across the face. "Come *on!*" she said. She grabbed the girl's hand—it was hot, the skin of her palm bubbled as though burned—and pulled her up the slope.

———

THE GROUND CHANGED, as Hope knew it would, and she saw the first steam vent. It was the height of her knee, and emitting an opaque mist into the night. She veered away from it, walking across the slope for a while to avoid its exhaust. Alishia followed blindly behind her. The girl was stumbling and dragging her feet, but still she walked on, tripping now and then and sobbing.

Hope breathed in, felt the dry air turn warm and wet, and she had a brief, intense vision of a gigantic army marching toward a precipice a mile high. There were tens of thousands of soldiers there, many of them twice as tall as normal men, all wielding terrible weapons of death and destruction and illuminated from above by hovering globes of molten metal. She could smell the meat of them—rank and rotten, ready to be opened to the air—and hear their diseased breathing, and she had a very real sense that desperation drove them on. The cliff they approached was sheer, and she could see no way that they could climb it. From above, simmering through the night and making it suddenly daylight, great swathes of fire floated down and set the army alight.

Hope gasped and fell to her knees, spitting bitter saliva from her mouth and turning back to Alishia. "Did you see that?" she said. "Did you *taste* that?"

Alishia was kneeling, drowsy and pale. "I saw something," she said, looking around as though searching for a lost pet.

"It's Kang Kang tricking us," Hope said. "Trying to frighten us, kill our hope. Showing us what will never happen."

"I think it's already happened," Alishia said.

Yes, Hope thought, *it had a tang of memory to it.* She looked across the hillside at the flow of steam rising from the vent, slick like oil. A breeze whispered down from the mountains and the steam changed direction, but it danced with the breeze as though playing with it. "Let's go on."

As they walked uphill they saw more of the vents. These were taller than the first, their bases thicker, the stream of substance pouring from their open necks wider. Hope kept as far away from the chimneys as possible, her breath so shallow that she became dizzy and disoriented. She waved the disc-sword around her head, shouting at phantoms, and she never let go of Alishia's hand. *If I let go she might blow away,* she thought. *She's so small now, so shrunken. I can't lose her. She's my future.*

The funnels venting from beneath Kang Kang—a gassy drug, poison, memories—became less frequent the higher they climbed. *First line of defense,* Hope thought, and she waited for the second to appear.

"What happened to your hand?" she asked. Alishia had gasped in pain whenever Hope grabbed harder to pull her on.

"I'm learning," Alishia said. Or perhaps she said "burning." Hope was unsure, and she thought that repeating the question might give Kang Kang another small victory.

———

THEY FOUND A ruin. It was a tower, upended and thrown back against a cliff of ragged stone. Its walls were cracked but still clung together, and its base sprouted into a tree of foundation; globes of footings, buds of ground piles. They defied gravity and threw a shambolic shadow against the cliff. Around the tower's smashed head sat a jumble of giant rocks, as though the hillside had been impacted and shattered by something huge. One of the upside-down windows shone as the life moon reflected from some old thing inside.

"No one said it was always this way," Hope said. She paused a few hundred steps from the ruin and stretched, hands on her hips and shoulders pulled back. Alishia stood by her side, breathing fast, swaying.

"This could be from before the Black," Alishia said.

"Could be. Or it might have happened yesterday." But Hope could smell the age of this place, and when the moons struck the tower, it reflected old light.

"I wonder who lived in there?"

Hope looked higher up the ravaged hillside, trying to see where the tower had tumbled from. But it all seemed wrong. It had not fallen here, it had been thrown.

"I wonder who died," the witch said.

"We should go on." Alishia aimed east to walk around the tower and the shattered ground before it. Hope watched her go and suddenly wondered what would happen if she did not follow. She could go up and into that tower, make a home in its upside-down world and spend the rest of her time exploring its inverted history. Perhaps she would find something of significance, perhaps not.

It's of Kang Kang! she thought. *Nothing good could have ever lived there. No calm hands laid those blocks, and no peaceful hand tore them down.*

Hope closed her eyes and breathed in deeply, and as she exhaled she knew that there was something extra to the air of this place. Between blinks—when she thought her vision of the world was negated—she saw more than ever. Perhaps it was one of the legendary Children of Kang Kang, this giant shape stepping in and out of the fallen tower, in and out, as though unsure where it would find its final rest. Its outline was formed from a dozen bodies twisted together, arms waving and mouths gaping, eyes rolling and catching the reflection of an ancient death moon, as if the wraiths of whole families clung together for comfort.

Hope gasped and stepped back, keeping her eyes wide open. She hurried after Alishia, glancing at the uprooted tower as she went. When she eventually had to blink again, that shambling image was still there on the inside of her eyelid, weaker than before, fading with each successive blink, until those old wraiths were a memory once again.

———

SOMETIME LATER—Hope had no idea how long, because time here was skewed—they came to a wide crevasse in the land. It stretched along the skirt of the first of Kang Kang's true mountains, a river of darkness. They would have to cross it to continue their journey. That, or walk east or west until the crack in the world ended. Hope thought that perhaps it would never end.

"It's trying to stop us," Hope said. She sank to her knees and dropped the disc-sword, pressing her hands to her face to make sure her tattoos had not entered into the betrayal. She felt them just below her skin, twisted into confusion and fear, and she could not deny them. "The whole of Kang Kang is after us." She turned around and looked at Alishia where the girl stood behind her. Her eyes were hooded, their whites bloodshot and yellowed by the death moon. "Alishia?"

"We have to go on," the girl said.

"Of course we do, but—"

"There's no excuse not to go on," she continued. "We have to get there, I have to get there, and a simple hole in the world can't stop us."

"I've been into one hole," Hope said. She spat as far as she could, watching the spittle glint as it was carried into the ravine on the breeze.

"There's more than shadows down there," Alishia said, and her voice was suddenly filled with such fear that the hairs on the back of Hope's neck bristled.

Alishia sank to her stomach behind Hope, pressing herself as flat to Kang Kang as she could. Hope followed her example. She tasted the grass of this place—bitter, as though its dew were blood—and smelled the ground, and she knew it was dying. Venting its memories. Giving them to the darkness as though it had no use of them anymore.

"What is it?" Hope whispered, and the question could have so many answers.

"Shade?" Alishia said. Hope turned around and looked at the girl, but she seemed to be unconscious again.

The witch looked ahead, wishing she had some chemicala to light the way. But she had used the last of her tricks in the machine, trying in vain to save Rafe.

She would not let them snatch magic from her again.

How can I stop them?

Kang Kang could do its worst, but she was attached to this girl as a mother to her unborn child.

What can I possibly do to protect us?

Whatever came up out of that ravine—and something *was*

coming, she was certain of that—she would fight it until her last spark of life guttered out.

Because I've got nothing else left. Noreela is dead, but the girl can give me magic for the final days of my life.

A hundred steps away a shape drifted up from the rent in the land, darker than the shadows around it and more animated. This blot of darkness had independent movement; it did not rely on clouds crossing moons. It twisted and writhed higher, and Hope averted her gaze.

Shade? Alishia had said.

Hope pressed her face into the ground and held her breath, eyes squeezed closed, skin creased, tattoos almost burning as they illustrated her terror like never before.

She attempted to lose her mind. Ironically, mad as she surely was, her mind stayed with her, muttering its fears and suspicions. Much as she tried to drift away—to think of nothing—the here and now grabbed hold of her and refused to let go. Time had its claws in her, and it was slowly dragging her toward the gaping maw of its mouth. And it had teeth. Alishia fading away was one of them; this shade, risen from the ground of Kang Kang, was another. It must surely be of the Mages, and if it saw her, discovered Alishia, then everything truly would be over.

Hope chewed at the grass, hoping that it might have some drug-like quality that would stifle her thoughts.

She heard Alishia's breathing behind her, fast and irregular as though something pursued her in dreams.

The shade made no sound. *It's not of this world,* Hope thought. *Not even of Kang Kang. It's from somewhere else.*

She lay there, not daring to look up in case the movement attracted the shade, and waited for the end.

She waited for a long time. Perhaps she even drifted into an unsettled sleep, because for a while she was back in her rooms in Pavisse, fucking men and mixing herbs, telling fortunes and fulfilling deadly commissions. In all that sex for money, and poison for hate, there was an unbearable naiveté that she so wished she could rediscover. She had been just another witch for so long, and finding that pathetic farm boy curled up in a doorway in the Hidden Districts had been the best of things, and the worst.

She started whispering into the soil of Kang Kang, an old spell that her grandmother had once told her. It had been passed down through the ages from ancestors who had used magic for real, and though now its words were empty it had always held power for Hope. It was from this spell that she had taken her name, because uttering it was another expression of hope for magic's return.

Nothing changed. The words fell from her mouth and sank into the ground. And when she opened her eyes she was back on that bare hillside in Kang Kang, and the shade had gone.

───────

ALISHIA TRIED TO hide. When the shape had risen out of the ravine something shifted deep in her subconscious, causing her to retreat from the waking world and find her dreams again. She heard Hope's voice coming from far away, questioning what she was doing and asking what sought them. As if she didn't know. *She knows far more than she lets on,* Alishia thought. *She doesn't need me to tell her.*

In the burning library, she was no longer alone. There were no signs of an intruder, no smells, no echoes of something else walking these endless book corridors, and yet she knew that her mind was no longer all hers. Another presence was smelling this smoke from afar. Another consciousness perused these books' titles, and Alishia had felt something like it before.

Shade? she thought. And then she ran.

She had to hide. If the shade found her it would know her, and it would tell the Mages, and the time between now and the end would be short. With all the Mages' might and armies focused on destroying what little Noreela still stood for, one single person stood a chance. But if the shade saw the taint of magic Alishia carried, the whole emphasis of this war would change.

The burning library felt heavier and darker to her right, so she turned left, ducking beneath a tall book cabinet that had tilted to lean against another. She paused in there for a moment, wondering whether it would provide a safe enough place to hide. She ran her fingers along the book spines. *Sixteen Heartbeats in the Fledge Seam,* one was called. And *A Question for the Monk.* And *One Way to Appease the . . . .* The final two words of this spine had been scraped away, and the wound on the book looked new, the exposed card fluffy and white.

Appease the what? Alishia thought, and the book burst into flames.

From back the way she had come, she heard the sucking sound

of flames being smothered. She ran. *What smothers flames? Nothing. A vacuum. Emptiness.*

Turning left, right, trying to lose herself in the hope that she would lose the shade, Alishia thought of Trey and wondered where he was right now. She paused for a heartbeat to look at book titles, but they gave her no clues.

Something's playing with me, she thought. The idea that terrified her. This place was entirely random, a depository for every moment that ever was. And yet she had discovered that room beneath the library, books that related to her and those around her. And the woodland clearing; that wasn't random. That was planned. *Something's steering me. Something's always been steering me, us, all of us. And it's teaching me, and telling me, and making me know its language.*

Alishia reached a junction and turned left, changed her mind, headed right. And then she paused and attacked the book stack before her. Their pages fluttered as a warm breeze roared along the corridor. The sound of flames being drowned followed.

It's close, Alishia thought, and she scooped books from the shelves faster. Every binding she touched lured her in, but she resisted the temptation to pause and read. Though they might tell her much, their tales would hold her back, and then the shade would find her sitting among a stack of books, perusing the past of Noreela while it stole the future from her mind and took it away.

Some of the books she touched were warm, others cold. There seemed to be no rule dictating which burned and which did not.

The pile grew around her feet. After a couple of minutes she had cleared enough of a space to crawl into. She pulled herself through by grabbing hold of shelf supports and uprights, then pushed with her feet when she was far enough in for them to touch the shelves. She shoveled more books behind her, then found it easier to push at them instead. She was seeing rough paper edges now instead of imprinted spines; the books were facing the other way. *Another corridor,* she thought. *Maybe one I was never meant to see.*

One last shove and she fell out after a tumble of books. Another cough of flames extinguished, but this was from much farther away.

Alishia stood and looked around. She was in a space between stacks that looked like any other. To her right was flame; to her left, darkness. She chose that way.

Don't think of why, just lose the shade.

The darkness was not complete. High above her, flames reflected from the haze of smoke, casting secondhand firelight down at her. It flickered in sympathy with its source, and book titles on the shelves beside her seemed to change second by second.

As she turned the next corner, Alishia saw a ghost.

The Red Monk sat amongst a drift of broken books. Some of the page edges around him were yellowed and smoking, but he seemed not to notice. His hand worked at each tome, prising the pages apart and scattering them like dead butterflies. He did not appear to be reading anything: spines, covers or the text inside. He simply tore and scattered. His hood was thrown back to reveal skin so old and thin it was almost transparent, but though Alishia could see through him she found only darkness.

"You burned down my library," she said.

The Monk looked up and grinned. His teeth were black. His eyes were black. And there was no Monk there at all, only a void where something should have been—a shapeless hole that flexed and twisted in a confusion of movement.

Found! Alishia tried to turn but her body would not obey. *Leave me alone,* she thought, adding as much weight and menace as she could, hoping that the seed of magic she carried would aid her in avoiding this thing. But she felt weak and feeble, and she could do nothing as the first tendrils of something wholly alien kissed her mind.

She dropped to her knees and the shade vanished. It had barely touched her, its impact on her senses so slight that she wondered whether she had truly seen it at all. But looking around, realizing how this place now felt, she knew that whatever had been in here with her was now gone.

It saw something, she thought. *It felt something. It knows.*

She so wanted to go on searching, because there was more yet to be found. She reached out and grabbed a burning book, watching the flames caress the skin of her hand without harming her, and when she opened the tome it gave her a line that she had to obey.

Everything has changed. The witch needs to know.

———

ALISHIA WAS STILL unconscious behind Hope, eyes shifting as she dreamed. The witch looked around, hardly breathing, watching for shadows that should not move. The ravine was a line of darkness before her, but now nothing rose above it. Whatever had been there—a shade, a thing of Kang Kang, a trick of the eye—had gone.

"We have to move on," Hope muttered. She leaned over Alishia, whispering into the unconscious girl's ear, "We have to move on!" Alishia twitched but did not open her eyes. Hope nudged her, slapped her, started shaking the girl, seeing her face scraped against the ground but not caring.

Alishia woke then, eyes opening wide and head rising to look around. "Is it gone?" she asked.

"I think so."

The girl sat up slowly, touching her face where a stone had scratched it. She looked at the blood on her fingertips. "We've been seen," she said.

Hope gasped. "How can you be sure?"

"I can't," Alishia said, "not *sure*. Not *positive*." She gazed past Hope as though searching the darkness for some errant memory.

"So why say it? To scare me? To frighten me into taking you back to Trey?"

"Where *is* Trey?" Alishia asked, suddenly vulnerable and sad. It was strange to hear an adult voice coming from a body growing so young, and in that voice so much hidden wisdom.

"I told you, he's gone. Back underground."

"No, he wouldn't."

"He did! And if you want to reach the Womb of the Land you have to stick with *me*." Hope stood and stared down at the girl, trying to read her eyes in the poor light.

"What are you doing, Hope?"

"I'm taking you. I'm *helping* you."

Alishia shook her head. "You're doing only what Kang Kang allows."

Hope could feel the hatred pumping from the land, strong and repulsive. It made her skin crawl, cooled sweat on her brow, thumped pain into her heels. The ravine pulsed before them, as though darkness was the rushing blood of the land. She listened, but heard no sound of movement from in there. For a few heartbeats her visions swam; spots on her eyes, or giants stalking them in the distance.

"Nothing here is as it seems," Hope said.

Alishia stood, holding on to Hope's arm for support until she could stand on her own. They went east, hoping to find a way across the black ravine in that direction. The witch moved several steps ahead. She listened to Alishia following her, and after a while their footsteps fell in time with each other. If Hope had not known better she would have believed that she was alone.

Chapter 13

WITH NOREELA UNDER attack in so many ways and so many places, one scene appeared serene. It was a haunted serenity, because the endless dusk seemed to suit this place. Darkness had always been comfortable here: dark histories, dark times. Water lapped at the lakeshore a few hundred steps from the building. Usually there were larger waves, but even the waters seemed to have been muted by the stealing of the light. Boats nudged against their moorings as the lake lifted and fell in a gentle, hypnotic rhythm, like the slowing heartbeat of Noreela. Bracken lay slumped to the ground in the darkness, its greenery fading into the soil with the rest of the land's color. A few birds flitted here and there, but they did not sing. Something splashed, causing a line of ripples to spread from where the mystery creature had decided not to emerge. The darkness, perhaps, had changed its mind.

The building was huge, imposing. But no longer empty.

Beside the building sat a gigantic machine. Its wings were spread across the ground to either side, and several trees that had been uprooted by its landing lay splintered beneath its many feet. Its body swelled and shrank, swelled and shrank, and a mist hung around its various exhausts. Noses, perhaps, or mouths. One wing twitched and stripped the bark from one side of a living tree.

The machine was waiting. Its fleshy parts shivered, its metallic elements shone in the moonlight, its wings of wood and water and skin flexed and shifted, unable to find stillness.

Moonlight slid from the walls of the building and left it in darkness. There were windows, but they were pitch black. There were doors, but they remained closed. A gate in the building's front facade had been blasted from its hinges and scattered in a thousand charred pieces. Some of them still burned. There was no breeze to disturb the smoke, and perhaps it rose forever.

Inside the entrance hall, something had conjured chaos. A huge timber staircase had been smashed to pieces, and some of the debris still smoldered along with the remains of the gate. Stone walls had been scored as if by giant nails. Tiles had erupted from the floor and been flung against walls, shattering and leaving parts of themselves embedded in the stone or timber. Beneath the tiles and their ancient bedding lay the rock of the land itself, and even this had not escaped the fury of destruction.

The Monastery had stood for a long time, and it would stand for a long time more. But its inside had been burned by unimaginable power. Something had passed through here, eradicating all evidence of the Monastery's most recent inhabitants: the Red Monks. Robes were shredded, tables and chairs burned, food stores turned to rot, dormitories corrupted with feces and flame, kitchens stomped down as if by giant feet, and scars of the chaos marked every wall, floor and ceiling of the ancient building.

The Mages, in their wrath, could have easily destroyed the building itself. Their magic was rich and new and still being explored, and already they had powers that they had never before experienced. Maybe they could have tumbled walls and brought ceilings crushing down, but this had once been their home, before they were driven out and hounded from the land. The filthy Red Monks had taken it for their own, and perhaps the Mages could have touched the very heart of the Monastery and changed it completely, setting a seed of destruction to melt its stone skeleton, turning it into a lake of unstoppable fire that would spread over time; a year to reach Lake Denyah, five more to turn its waters to steam.

But they had come here for a reason, and their reason lay deep.

Past the steps and basements, deep down where tunnels had been dug by unknown things eons ago, that was where their true destruction would be wrought.

And that was where they would have their first real taste of revenge.

———

"CAN WE KILL fledge demons?" Angel said. "Oh, I think we can!"

The Mages stood at the junction of several tunnels, clothed in fire. Blue flames licked from their mouths, their crotches, their ears and eyes, and as Angel spoke, her words singed the air. The phrase became a distinct ball of fire, bouncing along the tunnels and disappearing into their depths.

She laughed, and coughed another fireball to follow her challenge.

S'Hivez was smiling, as he had been since their return to the Monastery. "We'll make our own demons to kill them," he said. "We can make a hundred!"

They had sent a sea of fire pouring along each tunnel they found, letting it find its own level. They listened for shrieks of pain but heard nothing. They melted the air, adding a magical slick of acid from their tongues that expanded and multiplied, flowing through paths of scorched air and disappearing along tunnels faster than a crossbow bolt. The Mages closed their eyes and waited for the psychic waves of agony, but none came. They were not concerned; not yet. Time was theirs. An easy victory would feel like no victory at all.

Angel and S'Hivez formed a machine from the rock of the tunnel walls, giving it drops of their blood and gasps of their fiery breath. It was more powerful than anything the shade had formed in Conbarma. Here they were using their newfound magic to its full, richer and far more potent than the taste they had left with the shade. A mockery of the things they sought to destroy, the machine tumbled down the deepest tunnel, scoring walls with molten blades and parting the thin skein of reality as it went. Its exhaust was a miasma of nonexistence that would wipe any living thing it touched from history and memory. A small tunnel rodent, blind and albino, was caught in the machine's breath. Elsewhere in the caves, a thousand more rats ceased to exist. Droppings disappeared from corners never touched by light.

And as one rat inhaled, the bite scar on its ear mended itself, a scratch on a protruding knob of fledge smoothed over, and a million lice, worms, spiders and beetles existed again, suddenly uneaten.

The strange machine went on, carrying its new molten body around it, seeking the Nax and preparing to exhale again.

"And more!" S'Hivez said, conjuring chaos from the ground before him. Angel laughed. The air danced with things that should not be. They were back in their old home, more powerful than ever, chasing down the bastard Nax that had driven them out three hundred years ago.

The tunnels were illuminated with the sick light of dark magic.

The Mages paused and listened, touching the rock walls, sniffing the air, searching for the dying agonies of Nax. Still they heard none. They made yet more machines and sent them into the depths. One turned rock to ice, another made fledge unreal, yet another froze moments in time, halting history in small pockets of timelessness.

And then, tired of waiting, the Mages started to descend farther, moving deep on constructs of stone and water. They passed through tunnels cauterized smooth by the machines they had sent before them. Angel pressed against rock and summoned her dark magic, melting her hand inside to feel the beat of the land. She closed her eyes and sought the machines they had sent down, placing them all in a multidimensional map in her mind's eye. Some had gone so deep that they had almost disappeared from Noreela entirely, while others had stayed shallow but traveled far. One machine—shredding the future and leavings shards of timeless vacuum in its wake—had passed beneath Lake Denyah, probing up and out in case the Nax had tried to escape that way.

"There's nothing," Angel said.

S'Hivez spread his hands and crunched his knuckles. "Then we go deeper."

They felt the weight of the land weighing down upon them. The pressures were great, but the Mages reveled in them. Blue flames danced about them as they moved. The stone around them came alive and died again with each breath, and their dark magic filled them, brimming from their eyes as tears.

They found a fledge seam that had been opened and destroyed by one of the machines. Angel paused and listened at its entrance, sniffing, smelling the peculiar taint of unmade fledge. That was all.

No echoes of a Nax's dying sigh. She frowned—something about the ruined fledge did not seem right. She shook her head and they moved on.

They reached another fledge seam, this one untouched by their machines. Angel saw why: the exposed fledge was stale and rank. She scratched at the drug, snorting a flame so that she could see, and the heart of the fledge was also stale. She cut deeper, stepping on chunks of the drug and cooking it to nothing with the heat from her heels. S'Hivez stood back and watched, still listening for messages from the machines they had sent deep and far. None of them returned; their tasks remained undone.

Angel stepped back and turned to her old lover. "They've truly gone," she said.

"No." S'Hivez shook his head and blue flame trickled from his eyes.

"Yes. They're not here anymore. The fledge is stale, and they've gone. But we *will* find them again."

S'Hivez closed his eyes and took a deep breath. It came out as iced air. "They've denied us our vengeance."

"Only for now," Angel said, looking around, trying to convince herself. "We've got forever to track them down."

"They're the Nax. They could go deep."

"We've more to do than this. There'll be time. There's *always* time. And besides . . ." Angel touched the rock of the land and let magic flow, turning stone to glass, illuminating it, letting visions flicker within its cloudy embrace. " . . . we have this. And we can always go deeper."

The Mages left the machines to stalk and haunt the tunnels forever.

———

THEY MADE THEIR way back up into the Monastery, emerging into its basements and pressing shadows aside as they climbed up to its ruined heart. There they found a shade cowering in a corner, invisible to those who did not know how to look. Angel conjured it to manifest before them, a silent void of potential.

It came, and Angel frowned. "This shade has something to show us," she said.

———

OUTSIDE THE MONASTERY, the Mages' flying machine flexed its wings and knocked over another tree. It shifted its body across the ground, and the movement caused ripples to rise at the edge of Lake Denyah a few hundred steps away. Eyes flickered open and shut across its torso, and mouths gaped to utter deep, piteous groans.

The first time the machine fell completely still and silent was when it heard the land-shattering screams of rage.

———

"SO TELL ME," Lenora said.

They were sitting beside Lenora's machine, cooking meat over a hastily prepared fire while a thousand Krotes did the same around them. Her force had swept through a village that afternoon, slaughtering almost everyone there and stealing their livestock for food. Lenora had granted an hour's pause to eat and drink. To her left she heard warriors drinking stolen rotwine from stolen tankards, but she knew that they would not drink enough to dull their senses. War was a sober business.

Ducianne smiled, jerking her head slightly to set her braided hair jangling. The sound was as much a part of her as her voice. "It was easy," she said.

"So I see." Lenora took another swig of liberated rotwine and looked into the dead eyes staring up at her.

Ducianne had ridden into their camp with the Duke's head impaled on the front of her machine. She towed his body behind, though by then it was little more than a hunk of meat and bone. Flies and flying beetles had landed on it as soon as she stopped, eating away the last of the Duke's flesh. Ducianne had jumped from the machine, prized the Duke's head from the spike and handed it to Lenora.

Lenora had accepted the offering of war with a smile. Ducianne always had been one of the most bloodthirsty Krotes she knew, reveling in slaughter rather than viewing it as a duty.

Now they sat eating and drinking while the Duke's eyes reflected firelight. *As fiery as he's been in years*, Lenora thought. *Lucky for us.*

"There were hardly any defenses at all," Ducianne said. "It was disappointing. Yet Krotes will be talking of the sacking of Long Marrakash for decades. I'll be in a song, Lenora." The Krote lieutenant grinned. "They'll write songs about me!"

The Duke had an unkempt beard, scars across his nose from

some old disease, and his teeth were black from a lifetime of rotwine. His eyes were open, cloudy and bloodshot, and Lenora was sure they'd been like that even before Ducianne sliced his head from his body. "I'm sure you had your share of pleasures in Long Marrakash," she said.

"Oh you should have been there . . ."

"So tell, don't tease. The defenses? The opposition?"

Ducianne drained her bottle of rotwine and leaned an elbow on the Duke's skull. "Few defenses," she said. "Little opposition. They were totally unprepared, and their fight was nothing to speak of. I sent a scout by air as we approached, and he came back with news of a few small embankments on the approaches to the city. Some militia hiding in holes, like rats. Most of them appeared drunk and unconscious. There were some road traps—holes dug and covered over again. But only on the roads, as though they expected us to march on them in line. In one or two places the scout saw more-determined preparations: fire pits, trip ropes, stores of arrows and bolts in firing stations in the trees. Just a few hard places in a belt around the city filled with hollows.

"We went straight through them. I took on a firing post myself, and the militia there couldn't even shoot straight! I rode in on my machine and their arrows fell around us, and none of them hit, *not one*. My machine took down the tree and I finished them hand to hand. There were three of them; one dead from the fall, the other two ready to fight because that was their only choice. No soldiers, these. They wore the uniforms of Noreelan militia but they were fat and slow and confused. Probably spent their time drinking and eating and fucking the whores in Long Marrakash. I killed them quickly and mounted again, and we rode on.

"It didn't take long to break the defenses and reach the city gates. We lost one Krote in that time, though I don't know how he died. His machine came on with us. Strange. It seemed aimless, as if the Krote had been its brain." Ducianne bit the cork from a fresh bottle of rotwine and took a long draft. "By the Black, this stuff is fucking evil."

"The city?" Lenora asked. She was eager to know, but also somewhat deflated. If Long Marrakash—home of the Duke, the supposed ruler of Noreela—had been this easy, then what of the rest of the land? Would there be any real fighting? Would the Krotes have a chance to prove themselves? Lenora could remember the rout during the Cataclysmic War, vicious and brutal and costly—a *real* fight. Back then, though, magic had been available to both sides, not only one.

She was a soldier; she did not want to feel like a farmer slaughtering cattle.

"The city," Ducianne said. "What city? Not much left of Long Marrakash now. A few arrows, a few crossbow bolts were fired at us, about as troublesome as flies to a hawk. The flying machines had landed inside, and their riders were already causing chaos, attacking militia buildings and spreading panic. I'd told them to decapitate as many as they could: there's nothing like a headless body or a bodiless head to send the fear of the Black into someone." Ducianne tapped her fingers on the Duke's forehead and laughed.

"The gates didn't take very long, though we lost a machine there. The militia had set up a fire curtain, and when the first Krote rode to the gate and started taking it down, the oil fell and ignited. One dead Krote, and the machine was made largely of wood. It ran away on fire. I never saw it stop, so perhaps it's still running, somewhere.

"Once inside, my force split up. I'd instructed them to stay in groups of ten and cause as much panic as they could. The whole city was echoing with screams, and I could hear the thud of heads parted from bodies. I took a few militia prisoner and tortured them. Asked them where the Duke was hiding."

"How did you torture them?" Lenora asked. She was enjoying the story; Ducianne always had been one for bloody detail, and right now Lenora could think of nothing better. *The whole of Noreela will swim in blood,* she thought, remembering the vision Angel had given her. But then there was a sigh in her mind—not her own—and the thought, *And with everything in Noreela gone, what of the victors?*

"With these," Ducianne said, pulling two thin, curved knives from her belt. "Had no time for pleasantries like acid, or spider venom, or crushing their balls with hot coals."

"I'm sure you made do."

"I worked on a different organ with each until one of them told me what I needed to know. Didn't take long. The Duke was living in a whorehouse run by the Cantrass Angels." She sliced meat from the cooking sheebok and ate, smacking her lips and washing it down with more rotwine. "There were fires all over by then!

Machines spitting arrows and blades. Corpses in the streets. Heads pinned above doors. I took a few myself, but I had an aim now: the Duke. And I trusted my Krotes to do what had to be done."

"By the Black, I can't wait to reach Noreela City!" Lenora said. She eyed her friend's second rotwine bottle, half-empty. She did not need a drunken lieutenant when they rode again soon . . . but this was Ducianne's hour.

"That will be a joy," Ducianne agreed. "I'm glad I'll be there with you. It'll make Long Marrakash look like a spit in a lake."

"I hope so," Lenora said, and from afar she heard the shade voice echo, *I hope so.*

"So I found the whorehouse at the center of the city. Those Cantrass Angels, Lenora . . ."

"They're a strange breed."

"Strange? One of them came out naked and started to worship a machine! The Krote cut her in two and both parts kept moving. Not conscious, not *doing* anything, but they shifted in the dust like two halves of a sea snake. I've never seen anything like it. Even the snow tribes on Dana'Man weren't that strange."

"The Cantrass Angels have a history that disappears in time," Lenora said.

"Well, they're extinct now. At least those who were in Long Marrakash. We killed them as they came out, and soon the ground was crawling with bits of them. Arms. Legs. Even with their heads off, their mouths and eyes moved for a while."

"The Duke?"

"I went for him myself. Took three Krotes with me. We killed the few militia inside; they were doped up on rhellim, fighting with hard-ons. How pathetic is that? So we went through them, and I carried a head in each hand when I entered the room where the Duke was hiding. He was a fat, naked, stinking old man. His sweat stank of rhellim, but even then his cock was limp as a landed fish. He was covered in welts. I think the Cantrass Angels had been whipping him."

"Did you talk to him?"

Ducianne smiled, stroking the Duke's cheek. "To begin with I was just going to kill him, but I came over all poetic. You'd have been proud. You're wont to poetic musings yourself, on occasion."

"What shit are you talking?"

"I've seen you." Ducianne's eyes glittered with humor. "You go into some other place in your head, more so since we've landed here. Poetic musings. Justice for Noreela. That's what you're imagining, I know."

"That and other things," Lenora said. *That lake of blood . . . nothing left . . . a victory with no rewards but revenge . . .*

Ducianne laughed and swigged some more rotwine. "So! There he was, this fat, stinking excuse for a man, his whores cut to pieces and his cock trying to hide from me. I dropped a head and drew my sword, but he couldn't take his eyes from my face. I smiled at him. He smiled back. He actually believed . . . well, perhaps it was the rhellim still in his system."

"Dispense with the buildup and tell me what he said!" Lenora sliced a chunk of meat from the roasting sheebok and took a bite. Hot, juicy, fresh; after so long on the barren Dana'Man, she might never get used to Noreelan food again.

"I asked him what he'd give me for his life," Ducianne said. "I told him who my masters were, though he already knew. And I told him I'd been sent by them to negotiate a surrender. I said that his militia were fighting fiercely and bravely all across Noreela, and that we were willing to accept capitulation rather than see endless bloodshed and slaughter. So . . . I asked him what he'd give for his life."

"And?"

" 'Take Noreela,' he said." Ducianne spat. "So I took his head. Slowly. He screamed until I hit his spine, then he just hissed. I held up his head and showed him his fat, repugnant body. Then I went outside and stuck it on the front of my machine. By the Black, I wish I could have found his crown!"

Lenora laughed, spitting meat into the fire and hearing it sizzle away to nothing. "Now, *that* would have been poetry," she said. "So, what then?"

"We stayed in the city for a few hours and enjoyed ourselves. Killed some more, let some escape to spread the word. We marked them all. From some we took a whole limb, from others a finger. Everyone that escaped bears the evidence of our visit. We met a little more resistance—a few bands of militia who gave us some sport—but they were no match for the machines. In total, we lost the wooden machine at the city gates and four Krotes."

"That's good, Ducianne," Lenora said. She looked around at the warriors celebrating by firelight, some dancing, other sitting and swapping stories as they drank. "I only hope we're up to the challenge."

"Of course we are! How can you doubt it?"

Lenora shrugged, instantly regretting her show of uncertainty. "Krotes are trained to fight, but this is a slaughter. They've experienced skirmishes, but this will be a sustained war." Someone laughed, someone else shouted. Lenora hoped the time would not come when she heard sobs or—worse—loaded silences mixed in with the celebrations of some future victory.

"Huh!" Ducianne drank more rotwine and looked away, angry or perturbed.

You don't know Noreela, Lenora thought. But she would never say it.

And yet, Lenora's own sword arm ached with the need to fight again. The village they had recently taken had offered nothing but bleating women and pleading men, and the children had died with a whimper. *Perhaps it really will be this easy*, she thought. *And if so . . . what comes later?*

Me, a voice said, softer than her own heartbeat.

Stay away, Lenora thought. *Just for a while, please stay away.*

"Do you know where they are?" Ducianne asked quietly.

Lenora shook her head. "They have their purposes," she said. "The Mages' time will come later."

"When there's nothing left of Noreela?"

"There's *always* something of Noreela," Lenora said, disturbed that Ducianne had verbalized her fears. And as she stood ready to order the march on Noreela City, she wondered whether she was only trying to convince herself.

———

THE KROTES BROKE camp and prepared for their journey to Noreela City. Those with flying machines took off, heading south to reconnoiter. Lenora ordered them not to land in the city until the ground force was visible from the walls and gates. The panic would be widespread then, the fear heavy, and a sudden assault from above would provide the distraction Lenora needed to drive her army through whatever outer defenses there might be.

What are we looking for here? Ducianne had asked.

Destroy the city, Lenora replied. *It's a symbol. We raze it to the ground and whatever backbone Noreela has left is snapped.*

There was much banter between Krotes, pledges made and wagers placed, and Lenora rode amongst them to give encouragement. And she in turn took encouragement. Many of Ducianne's Krotes were blooded from their victims in Long Marrakash, and they looked terrifying. *Is it really going to be this easy?* Lenora thought again. She ordered them to move out, and a thousand machines began their relentless march southward.

Lenora rode at the head of her army. She sat astride her machine and urged it on, faster and faster until she had to strap herself to its back to avoid being thrown. They emerged from the mouth of a large valley and entered an area of sparse woodland, most of the trees shedding their leaves now that sunlight was absent. Animals scattered before them, some escaping into holes or climbing trees, others being crushed beneath machine feet. The noise of the Krote advance was relentless: the pounding of metal, stone and timber feet, the gasping and grunting of machines drawing air or venting steam and other gases, the occasional shout of a warrior calling to a friend. The army was a storm front scoring across the ground, sweeping before it any pretense at normality or peace. Lenora shouted out, holding the leather straps tied to her machine as she stood and spun a slideshock around her head.

This is good, she thought. *This is what I'm here for. This is why Angel made me live!*

Make me live, that voice said.

Lenora nodded. *Soon.*

———

TWO HOURS AFTER leaving camp, Lenora heard a rumbling sound from above and behind. She turned in her seat, thinking, *It's them!* Most Krotes were looking back, weapons drawn, ready for battle.

Lenora saw the dozen shadows dipping from above, silhouetted against the death moon to the north. No two shapes were alike. A few seemed huge, others were quite small. Wings waved, while some seemed to fly by more arcane means. On the back of every shape rode an upright figure, clasping on to leather reins or waving a weapon around their head when they saw the stain of the Krote army beneath them.

The shade at Conbarma had been busy. Lenora had seen it take five times as long to make a flying machine than a walker.

She had left orders for the second wave to bypass Noreela City and head for the wilder places to the south, taking towns, villages and farmsteads wherever they discovered them still occupied. Once the city had fallen, their two forces would combine and head for New Shanti, where they expected to fight their fiercest battle.

"For a moment there . . ." Ducianne said. She had ridden her machine alongside Lenora's, sitting upright and still clasping a small crossbow in one hand.

"Scared?" Lenora asked. Her friend glanced at her and looked away again, and Lenora laughed. "I'm fucking with you, Ducianne. For a heartbeat, I thought it was them as well."

"But what a sight," her friend said. "I've seen hawks flying overhead a thousand times, but never anything like that. Never anything so *strange*."

"Everything's strange now," Lenora said.

Ducianne rode beside her for a while, staring after the shadows fading into the distance. The Krotes on the ground were riding hard and fast; those that had just passed overhead must have been flying at twice the speed of any hawk.

"We'll be at Noreela City in a few hours," Lenora said.

Ducianne smiled. "Then the fun begins!"

"I'm the first in."

"Of course, Mistress," Ducianne said, but Lenora saw the hint of disappointment in her friend's eyes.

"Ducianne? You had Long Marrakash." She nudged the Duke's head with her foot. She had speared it on a metallic horn on her machine's back, positioned so that it looked forward toward what they had come to destroy.

Ducianne nodded.

"Noreela City is five times the size of Long Marrakash. There's plenty for us all. But I'm the first in, Ducianne. I've been here before, and I have my own forms of revenge to find in this war."

"In the city?"

"That's where it begins," Lenora said. *And then it rolls on, and on.* She imagined her route south from the city to New Shanti, where they would kill some Shantasi, then west to Robenna. The time she had there would be long and wonderful. Ducianne had sliced off the Duke's head slowly so that he knew exactly what was happening. Lenora imagined doing the same to a whole village.

"By the Black, this is a fine time," she said, but Ducianne had already steered away.

THE HILLS TO the north of Noreela City were high, offering a fine vantage across the capital. And there was much to see. The city was ablaze with contained fires and lamps, its inhabitants doing their best to see away the dark and live out a normal day. The sky above the city was bright, and there was no sign of the flying machines that Lenora knew were there, waiting.

It must have been such a temptation. The city shone like a jewel in the land, a huge place beginning in foothills to the east and ending in a long, flat plain to the west. South of Noreela City were the Widow's Peaks, though they were too far away to see from here. The flood of firelight seemed to make the land around the city darker than ever before.

Lenora gave her orders, then rode down the hillside on her machine, a dozen Krotes following close behind. The rest of her force would wait for several minutes before commencing their own march down the slopes toward the city walls. By then, Lenora would already be fighting in the streets. More symbolism, which Lenora was growing to like: thirteen Krotes, challenging the whole of Noreela City. And the thousand machines that followed would make the defenders' hearts sink with dread.

The anticipation of the violence to come thrilled her. She hoped that they faced a real fight here, something more involved than the skirmish at Conbarma and the minor clashes they had fought between then and now. She was a warrior who welcomed a fight, but it was more than that setting her muscles aflame and her heart racing: for the first time, this really felt like Noreela. She was riding against the largest city in the land with the Duke's head speared on the front of her machine, and she knew that the only outcome could be victory. Right now, it was the process of winning that excited her.

Old wounds ached. Her shoulders and neck, stomach, right thigh and left ankle, her deformed scalp and pitted cheeks and left breast, all of them sang with the memories of how their scars had been formed. She thought back to the final few hours she had spent on Noreela three centuries before, and how vicious the fighting had been. Noreelans had been throwing themselves against the Krote army, driving it into the sea and using their own war machines to trample the Mages' failing magic beneath their feet.

"Things change," Lenora said into the wind. Her machine was running fast now, leaping down the hillside and sprinting for the long, open area that led to the city's large north gate. The gate was shut, and there were signs that a series of defenses had been erected before the walls.

She drew a sword, strapped a crossbow to her left forearm, checked the weapons on her belt, the braces crossing her chest and the quivers tied across her back. "Good! Fight for your land, you cowards. Give me something to dream about in the future." *Something to dream about as I make my way to you,* she thought, sending her words out and hoping they were heard.

She turned to check the Krotes charging with her. As instructed they were a hundred steps behind, driving their own machines hard to keep up. Some of their mounts gasped fire; others breathed ice. Blue sparks splashed from their rides' feet where they connected with the land.

They closed on the city and Lenora began to make out the individual defenses. Several rows of sharpened stakes faced outward, their tips fresh and pale. There were trenches—perhaps filled with oil—and large rocks, and a few humps that might have been trenches fronted by earthen bunds. She hoped that there were militia in those holes. That would bring blood a few heartbeats closer to her sword.

A hail of arrows greeted her as her machine crashed over the first line of stakes. The sound of splintering timber was deafening. An arrow sliced across her shoulder, another stuck her hip and shattered on the knives sheathed there, and then the men who had fired them leapt from a trench and ran for the gates.

She rode them down, leaning sideways to swipe at one with her sword. The others fell beneath the machine's legs.

The machine vaulted a trench which erupted into flames. Lenora closed her eyes against the heat and enjoyed the brief touch on her skin; it had been cold for so long that it felt like sunlight.

More arrows came and Lenora sent an order to her machine. It rose on its hind legs and presented its underbelly, and the arrows snapped and shattered there. She slipped from her mount's back, darted between its legs and jumped into a trench filled with several terrified militia.

"Please," one of them said, and Lenora laughed. By the time they gathered their wits, there were only two left standing, and Lenora dodged their clumsy attacks and felled them both. They were wallowing in their own guts as she climbed from the trench and mounted her ride once more.

She glanced back and saw the other dozen Krotes ride their machines through the wall of flames, and Lenora shrieked as she rode on, the cry beginning in the very heart of her.

This is life! she thought. *This is what you missed, my daughter.*

She stopped a hundred steps from the city wall. The fires lit the whole scene, yet something slipped over the wall and slicked to the ground, hunkering down against the ancient stone structure to blend with the background.

Shade? Lenora thought.

Guards of the gate peered at her from atop the high wall. They were petrified. She could instruct her machine to kill them and it would, but this was a symbolic moment that she could not let pass. She knew that the best way to defeat an enemy was to soften their minds before slitting their throats.

"I have something for you!" she called. "A final message from your Duke." She stood on her machine's back, tugged the Duke's head from its mount and held it up by the hair. "He says he's sorry, he's been busy fucking and taking drugs in Long Marrakash, but now he's back and so you have nothing to fear. Do you hear me, Noreela?"

A flight of arrows came her way, and her Krotes launched several fireballs from their machines. Something flared, someone screamed and the day was growing brighter with every beat of her heart.

A shadow shifted away from the city wall and crossed the ground toward Lenora. She frowned, disturbed, but she could show no fear.

"So who wants him?" she called. Silence was her response. "Here's a deal: Whoever catches the Duke, I'll kill quickly." She leaned back and prepared to throw the head toward the city wall.

The shadow rose before her, and she knew it for sure. *Shade!* The Mages had been here already . . . and they left something behind. It smothered the firelight for a few heartbeats, then passed around and through her, cold as the ice of Dana'Man, redolent of an emptiness she never imagined could exist.

Lenora gasped and swayed, and the shade disappeared behind her machine.

For a moment I was nothing . . .

Something shifted in her hand. The Duke's eyes had opened wide and his mouth was working, dry tongue protruding between lips like a fattened grub. His eyes turned to her and held her gaze.

She threw the head as far as she could.

What is this?

It sailed through the air, spinning toward the city wall.

Nobody caught the head. It disappeared over the wall, and a few seconds later screams rose from beyond.

She rode her machine toward the city gate. Arrows and bolts zipped down from left and right, liquid flame poured from above as they tipped burning oil, but her Krotes protected her. The machines launched a blistering attack on the defenders with discs and bolts, fireballs and something less fiery, but more destructive. One of them leapt onto the wall and hung there like a spider, its rider standing on its head and firing arrows up at the Noreelans. The machine plucked several militia from the wall and dropped them into their own burning oil.

From above came the sudden screams of diving machines. Shadows emerged from the glare over the city and rained fire and metal across its rooftops. Some of them attacked the defenders inside the north wall, while more explosions and screams sounded from deeper within the city. *Good,* Lenora thought. *Confusion for everyone.*

She reached the gate. Her machine reared up and battered the thick wood with its front legs. Huge splinters erupted outward, and soon she could hear the massive gate beginning to crack and groan.

In the reveals to either side, shutters snapped open and bowmen began firing. Lenora ducked and shot a crossbow to her left, hearing a man groan as he fell. She spun right, swinging her slide-shock and crunching the skull of the Noreelan on that side. She had an arrow through the flesh of her right arm, just above the elbow. She decided to leave it there; it would drive even more terror into her victims.

The gate cracked and fell, and her machine drove forward over its remains. She caught a brief glimpse of two men disappearing beneath the machine, flailing uselessly as its feet crushed them, and she paused for a heartbeat to assess the situation: before her was a wide road leading into Noreela City, barricaded several hundred steps along its length; to her left an alley barely wide enough for her machine, and just within its shadows lay the Duke's head, chewing air.

She turned right and rode, knowing that she would be met with a hail of arrows. She had to get away from the gate, leaving room to allow more Krotes to enter. And she wanted to spread her own destruction deep into the heart of the city.

I'm here, she thought. *I'm in Noreela's capital!*

She would circle around, back onto the wide road that led toward the city center, and attack the barricade from behind. Open up the main artery and watch the city begin to bleed to death.

Oh bleeding, she thought. *There'll be plenty of that. Plenty for us all.* And again, that memory of the Mages' lake of blood came to her, twisting the knife of uncertainty in her heart one more time.

A man jumped from a building and landed on the back of her machine. His sheer stupidity and bravery surprised her for a second, and he swung a heavy axe at her head. She ducked just in time, sprawled on her side and sent a message to her machine to stop. The sudden halt tipped the man forward, and he slid from the machine's back and became snagged on two of its limbs.

"You're a brave one!" Lenora shouted.

"You Mages can't win," he said.

"You're not even militia."

"It's the normal people of Noreela who'll beat you, just like before."

The man was still trying to rise, hefting the axe in one hand and using the other to claw his way back up the side of the machine. He saw something—the machine's eyes, its mouth?—and froze for a heartbeat in shock. Lenora cleaved his skull in two and kicked him to the ground.

She urged the machine on, turning left into a space between buildings. They rose two stories on either side, and the machine shattered balconies and smashed windows as it went. Whenever Lenora saw a pale face at a window she fired at it with a bolt or throwing star.

The alley opened into a courtyard with a fountain at its center and a group of militia trying to barricade themselves in. *Sport*, Lenora thought as she halted the machine and jumped from its back.

There were five militia, all men. "Any of you ever fought a woman?" she asked. They stared at her, utterly terrified, not one of them going for his sword. "I bet you have," she muttered. "After you've fucked, I bet you beat them, just to make you feel more like men."

One of them went for a knife and Lenora jumped forward, opening his chest with her sword.

Something whispered to her left and she turned, but there was no one there. *Is that you?* she thought.

Two men came at her but they were slow and scared. She moved back from their first sword swings then stepped into their killing circles, taking one with a knife in the eye and pulling the other close, smiling at him, dipping her head and severing the main artery in his throat with one bite. His blood tasted weak.

Is this the living I missed? a voice said. Lenora dropped the man and turned, seeing something flit across her vision as though it existed on the surface of her eyes. She tried to follow but a man ran into her, trying to knock her from her feet. She stumbled and turned, letting him fall then kneeling astride him. As she brought her sword down with both hands she thought she saw something reflected in its blade: a face, young and innocent and so familiar. She twisted the sword mid-swing and struck the man with the flat side. He cried out, nose burst and cheekbones crushed. Lenora looked past her machine, wondering where the vision had gone.

"Is that you?" she asked out loud, and the loaded silence seemed answer enough.

The man beneath her whined and Lenora pushed her sword into his chest.

The final militia man came at her, swinging a heavy mace on a long chain, and she sent a thought to her machine. A limb unfolded from its body and tripped the man, sending him sprawling onto the spiked ball of his own weapon. He screamed, tried to stand, and the machine planted one huge foot on his head.

"Not fair," he said.

"Fair?" Lenora told her machine to press down.

The courtyard was silent now, but she could hear the sounds of conflict from all around. A building falling, a flying machine expelling fire, a woman screaming, a machine whistling as it ejected a spurt of steam or gas at some unsuspecting enemy. Keen to rejoin the fray, she took an ear from one of the dead, then climbed onto the back of her mount. Her fury was rich, her mouth rank with sour blood, her sword wet with it . . . and still her unborn daughter was here, being with her and existing within her. *"Just a few more days!"* Lenora pleaded.

A shadow seeped into the courtyard over one of the makeshift barricades. It passed over and through the five dead men and then left as quickly as it had come, paying Lenora no heed.

The men began to rise. The one with the crushed head stumbled in a continuous tight circle, but the others picked up their weapons and climbed the barricades at the entrances to the courtyard, staring about wide-eyed. One of them saw Lenora and moved on, seeking different prey.

Lenora now knew for sure where the shade had come from, and who had brought it. "By the Black, how can we lose?"

As she rode her machine from the courtyard, sensing several terrified observers watching from higher windows, that voice started in her head once more, and for the first time Lenora heard something other than anger and neglect in its tones.

What is it that you wish for me? How can my unknown life be precious? the voice of her daughter said, and then as it dissolved back into the darkness of her deep subconscious, it left one parting comment: *This is not living.*

———

THE FIGHT EXPANDED, intensified and rolled on, and a thousand Krotes took their fill of blood. Soon after smashing her way through Noreela City's northern gates Lenora stopped thinking of it as the battle she had been hoping for; a battle was when two sides were fighting. This was a slaughter.

The level twilight made time almost impossible to judge. It could have lasted a few hours, or maybe it was a day. Much of the city lay in darkness where inhabitants had extinguished lanterns, but Lenora could smell burnt oil on the air. She and her Krotes lit up these areas, balls of fire cruising the streets and narrow alleys. Timber buildings provided excellent fuel, and Lenora's machine extended a long, thin limb from its underside and pumped liquid fire through windows, doors and cracks in walls. The buildings' windows lit up like the eyes of giants surprised awake, and soon the flames moved into their thatched or boarded roofs, heating stone tiles until they exploded, crawling into neighboring properties and catching them unawares. Fires spread as quickly as the killing. They became the signature of places the Krotes had already visited.

Many people fought, and Lenora was glad for that, but they were mostly untrained and resigned to defeat. Few of them came at her with anger or rage in their eyes, fewer still with hope. They blinked uselessly as they died on her sword.

Her machine took its toll of Noreelans. Lenora liked to kill them herself, but on occasion she was rushed by a dozen or more, and she took equal pleasure in guiding her mount through its own killing moves. It could only perform minimally on its own: it was her thoughts, her ideas, her action that drove it. Limbs flicked out and whipped across the chests of attackers. It kicked with one of its legs, spat fist-sized knots of molten stone that left smoking trails in the air, and vents along its sides opened to emit hails of razor discs, thudding into stone, wood and flesh alike. Some people went down fighting the machine, perhaps lost in the belief that this could only be a terrible nightmare. Others turned to flee, and these Lenora gave a slower death.

Her machine took occasional chunks of timber from collapsing buildings or stone from the ground and imbibed it, replenishing itself with its strange magic. It throbbed beneath her, and a bluish light bathed its legs for a few heartbeats at a time. Occasionally two of its eyes turned up to look at her, and though she felt their gaze she ignored it. *They're from* him, she thought. *From that farm boy. Long gone now.*

In one shop window, Lenora saw the reflection of a small girl, her face pale and eyes devoid of emotion. Lenora smashed the window with her slideshock and spun around, but there was only a dead tree standing behind her. She rode on and passed a fountain, saw that same girl beneath its surface, mouth hanging open as if in mid-scream. She turned away, thinking, *That can't be you.*

The shade had been busy. The dead were rising. She saw one of them as she rounded a corner, a shambling wreck of a woman with only one arm and a spear protruding from her throat. She wore simple clothes and carried a mewling dead child in one arm. She passed Lenora and her machine as though they had always been a part of this street, and disappeared through an open doorway into a small house. The spear banged the door frame on the way in, and as Lenora saw its bloodied tip disappear from view, she heard the first scream.

She drove onward, riding fast and stopping to fight only when there was no way past the enemy. She wanted to push through and cut the great Noreela City in two with her presence. That girl's face glanced at her from windows lit by the flicker of distant fires, and ponds and fountains reflecting the moons. The shimmer of her sword caught the child's reflection several times before being buried in warm flesh. *That's not you*, she thought, over and over again. *That's not you. You never were. That's not you. You never were.* It became a mantra, a beat by which she judged moments in time. She saw a lone militia slinking through shadows—*that's not you*—and took his head from his shoulders—*you're not her.* She held the head up but the shade must have been elsewhere. She looked into the man's vacant eyes and wished she could question his mind, discover where he had been going and whether the shade of an unborn girl haunted this city.

She haunts me and me alone, Lenora thought, but the idea had the voice she had given her daughter.

She killed a small group of fodder protected only by an old woman. "Why?" the woman asked, desperate rather than afraid. "Because you deserve it," Lenora said. She saw a shadow moving from the corner of her eye, a fire deflected by something that should not be, and she left the old woman alive.

Entering a large park at the center of Noreela City, Lenora found many people seeking shelter there. They were huddled beneath trees or behind bushes, listening to the destruction and gasping as a building collapsed, rocking the ground and sending balls of fire sparkling into the air. Lenora rode in quietly, keeping to shadows and listening to their voices. She found no strength here at all, no wisdom or bravery, only fear and hopelessness. They had already given up.

She passed through a collection of statue pedestals. There were fifteen in total, though none of them retained the statue they had been built to bear. The most that remained were two legs from the knees down, clad in worn stone sandals. Any writing that had once been there had been erased by time and neglect. Whomever these

statues honored—heroes or artists, writers or explorers—history had
long since forgotten.

Lenora told the machine to crush the pedestals, and the noise
caused a stir of activity across the park.

"You're all cowards!" Lenora roared. She jumped from the machine and ordered it to remain where it was. Strung an arrow in her
bow. Felt the weight of weapons on her belt, stars and knives and
slideshock still ready to take their fill of this night. "You hide here
like cowards, so expect to die like that too."

"Please don't hurt us!" a woman said from the darkness. Lenora
sent an arrow after the voice and heard a gasp of pain. A body hit the
ground, a man screamed in grief and anger, and the fight began.

Lenora knew that she was being foolish. As she ran here and
there, ducking sword swipes, making another corpse with her own
blade, she knew that she should have forged through this park on
her machine, let it do the killing while she thought on ahead. But
the absence of that voice in her mind was disturbing her. She would
have welcomed the absence were it not for the little girl she saw reflected in windows and ponds. *At least here there's nowhere to see
her,* she thought, but she was wrong. As she grappled with one man,
jamming a knife into his back as he hugged her tight, she saw the
girl's face in his eyes.

The shade passed through the park and bodies rose to continue
the killing. Wives gasped their relief at seeing husbands stand, then
screamed as they fell together. Children ran toward shambling parents, mothers smothered daughters and the dead soon outnum-
bered the living.

Lenora stood by her machine, certain that she would see a little
girl's form emerge from between the trees. She would hear her
first—there were more leaves dead on the ground than remained
on the branches—but the sounds of destruction were drawing nearer
every second. The skies to the north were alight, and sparks and
burning embers were drifting down all across the park. Lenora could
hear the fire's roar even from this distance.

South, she thought. *I should go south out of the city, find the
plains again where there is nowhere for her to stare from.* But there
were always the eyes of dying men and women, and the sheened
surface of her sword. Lenora knew that the girl was beyond her control. *I said soon,* she thought. *I said I'd find you and avenge you soon.*

Is this living? that voice said again, at last. *Is this what I missed?*

———

BEYOND THE PARK Lenora saw a girl darting from door to door, shadow to shadow. She urged her machine after the child, had it pick her up and deposit her on its back.

"Are you her?" Lenora asked. The girl was screaming, her dark skin livid with sweat, eyes wide with terror. "You're not her." Lenora threw the girl aside without even bothering to kill her.

———

SHE WAS STICKY with blood. It coated her from head to foot, settling on old wounds and seeming to burn its way in. New wounds added their immediacy to her pains: the arrow through her arm, crossbow bolt in her ankle, a cut to the side of her neck and a stab wound in her back, deep and painful and in need of attention. *You're immortal!* Ducianne had once said to her, many years before. *You're the one who came from Noreela with the Mages. Immortal, just like them.* On occasion Lenora wondered just how true this could be—Angel had touched her on that ship and brought her back from the brink of death, after all. But many times since then she had felt mortality closing in, and she often thought that the older she grew, the more difficult her death would be. Such an unnaturally long life must come with a price.

Maybe this is it, she thought. *Maybe on Noreela I'll be haunted into death by the shade of my unborn child.* She craved revenge on the people of Robenna more than ever, but as she fought her way through Noreela City she began to wonder whether vengeance could change anything.

The south of the city was more heavily populated than the north. People had fled down here during the fighting, or perhaps some of them had received word of what was to come. Riders from the north, maybe. Or maybe they simply expected the worst when the sun failed to rise.

Lenora lost her mind in a haze of killing. Fires erupted across her vision. Krotes rode by on their machines, red with reflected flames and blood. Some of them decorated machines with the heads of their victims, and one or two bore a dozen heads that still spat, rolled eyes, lolled tongues. The Mages' shade was everywhere in Noreela City tonight.

The militia were mostly wiped out in the north, but some re-

mained in the south, barricading themselves in thick-walled buildings with hundreds of Noreelans, thinking that perhaps the invaders
would pass them by for easier prey. But they did not understand the
Krotes. Machines punched holes in walls and pumped in fire, and
the interiors of many structures turned into firestorms, windows and
walls imploding as the conflagrations raged.

The living dead walked here too. Sometimes they seemed aimless, but when they found a Noreelan they went mad, scratching
and tearing with their hands, kicking, crushing, slicing if they carried a weapon. Lenora wondered what drove them, and she thought
perhaps it was jealousy. It would suit Angel's humor to use magic to
raise the dead to be jealous of the living.

The Krotes gave them a wide berth and let them continue on
their way.

———

NOREELA CITY HAD many hidden places. Not only did streets and
alleys cross and confuse themselves with courtyards and squares,
but steps and tunnels led below buildings, entering those unknown
areas beneath foundations where walls far older than the city still
stood and the languages written on the walls were long forgotten.
There were caves and catacombs even deeper, home to dropouts
and the dregs of society: fodder, fledge miners driven mad with the
fledge rage, Bajuman and criminals. These stretched the length
and breadth of Noreela City and perhaps farther, with entrances
hidden in the basements of taverns, houses and tumbled temples to
ancient gods. Many knew of these places, but few talked about them
openly. Some said that there were creatures guarding the entrances,
monstrous hybrids of wolf and snake that could move through narrow spaces, yet take off a man's head with one bite.

When the Krotes found these entrances, they closed them forever. But not before guiding a few of the reanimated dead inside
first.

———

WHEN LENORA FOUND herself at the city's southern gates there
were hundreds of Krotes already out on the plain, resting under the
light of the moons. Their machines steamed and clicked where they
cooled in the long grass. She passed through the remains of the gates
and welcomed the sudden cool breeze flowing in from the west.

The smoke was stinging her eyes and the constant stench of blood was making her queasy. She closed her eyes and breathed deeply, and when she opened them again there was a little girl watching her from a hundred steps away.

The girl stood still. She was wearing a white dress stained with a spray of blood across one shoulder. She stared, her hands fisted at her sides, her blond hair hanging in loose braids at either side of her face. From this distance Lenora could not see her eyes, but there was no smile. There was *nothing*. The girl stared as though she could not even see the burning city. "That's not you," Lenora whispered.

She rode on, lowered her machine to the ground and dismounted. She closed her eyes. *Not you*, she thought. *You're not here*. When she looked again the little girl was still there, and still not the thing haunting Lenora.

The old warrior looked around. To her left a Krote sat beside his machine, rubbing his hands with a scrap of cloth. He was breathing so hard that she heard it above the burning city. However hard he rubbed, the blood remained. Farther away, two more Krotes were standing before each other, not talking. One looked down at his feet, one stared up into the strange sky, both of them lost for anything to say.

Breaking through these stunned silences were the victorious calls and cheers of other warriors. Some rode across the fields on their blooded machines, others dismounted and shared stories of the slaughter. But it was the silent Krotes that troubled Lenora the most because she knew that, like her, they were looking inward.

A sudden queasiness hit her, bending her double as her stomach clenched and vomit exploded from her mouth. She spat, vomited some more, wiping away the mess and feeling it burning on her skin. There was blood in there, and perhaps some of it was her own.

And then something else arrived.

They're here! Lenora thought. And as she stood and wiped her mouth, the death moon was obscured as the Mages flew in.

Chapter 14

THE MOL'STERIA DESERT began surprisingly quickly: one moment there was more grass and heather beneath their feet than sand; the next, the only plants they saw ahead were occasional sproutings, like hairs growing from boils on an old man's face. The Red Monk walked ahead, stomping through sand and hardly seeming to notice the change.

But Kosar did notice. He had been smelling hints of the Shantasi spice farms for several hours now, and it seemed that walking on sand opened the desert to his senses. Heat hushed over him, still radiating from the deep sands even though the sun had been gone for more days than he could count. The sound of their footsteps was dampened, and the Monk looked like a red wraith floating ahead of him. Moonlight turned the ground gray. Kosar had never been to the desert, and the sense of danger was palpable. It was a place of unknown things that hid from sight behind the dunes or buried beneath the surface. Any of these things could be dangerous. *All* of them could be, and Kosar walked with one hand resting on the hilt of his sword. *Not that I could do much*, he thought. *If something like that sand demon rose against us, it would be down to the Monk to protect me.* He was tired, exhaustion wearing down on him and weakening his legs. He thought he had at least one cracked rib, a heavily bruised nose and cheekbone and a stab wound in his back that refused to stop bleeding. He chewed more of the paste Lucien had made for him, but the pain was tenacious. It found its way through the drugs.

The sand produced a strange heat. He could feel the warmth rising up from the ground and touching the sweat on his skin, turning him cold. But he could also feel the intense chill of the clear dark sky, threatening to suck heat from his body and leave him cold and dead. It would not take long for his corpse to be covered by the shifting sands. He wondered how many other luckless travelers lay dead beneath his feet, and he started watching the ground before him for protruding bones or mummified skin.

They walked from loose sand to hard, a compacted surface that was cracked from lack of moisture. Thin, spiky plants grew from these cracks, their pale roots exploring across the surface of the ground as well as below. In some of these roots Kosar spotted the skeletons of small rodents, wrapped tight. He wondered whether there were larger versions of these plants out there somewhere.

Lucien Malini kept a steady pace that Kosar knew he would not be able to maintain forever. He was thirsty and hungry, weak and tired, and he had no wish to die in the desert. A'Meer may have once walked these sands, and he did not want to melt away beneath her memory.

The Monk stopped. There was something to its left—a large, bulky shadow that seemed to be moving slightly, tipping from left to right. Kosar closed his eyes and opened them again, making sure it was not simply his heartbeat shuddering his vision with every thump.

Lucien turned and stared back at him.

Perhaps this is it, Kosar thought. *A sand demon ten times bigger than the last, and the Monk knows it's all over.*

"You don't look like you can walk much farther," Lucien said. He spoke quietly but his voice carried, unhindered by echoes.

Kosar shook his head, panting.

The Monk motioned him forward and pointed at the shadow with his sword. "We have transport," he said.

Kosar walked to the Monk. *This thing killed A'Meer,* he thought. He needed to remind himself of that from time to time.

Standing beside Lucien, he looked at the shape that sat a dozen steps from them. It was large, low to the ground, dark gray and still shifting from left to right. There were protuberances on both sides that appeared to be legs, and it seemed that its head was beneath the sand.

"What is it?" Kosar asked.

"I'm not sure of its name," Lucien said, "but I know it can get us where we need to go faster than walking. Especially with you like that." One nod at Kosar encompassed the thief's entire range of injuries and weaknesses.

"You made me like this," Kosar said.

"No, I saved you. The Breakers would have killed you in the end."

"So you killed their children as well?"

Lucien stared at him, his Monk's eyes dark pits in the scarred ruin of his face. "Breaker children are dangerous too," he said. "Just one of them would have bettered you in a fight."

Kosar looked at the large creature burrowing before them. It looked heavy—its back and sides were armored with scales or thick hide—and he could not imagine it moving quickly.

"You stay here," Lucien said. "I need to find something. This thing on its own can't move us, but given the right persuasion it will be fast and safe."

Kosar waved one hand at the Monk without looking, urging him away. Then he sat on the sand and stretched his aching legs before him, pulling back his feet and toes to try to work out the stiffness in his ankles. His face ached, his back was hot and his ribs spiked a sliver of pain through him each time he drew a breath. His heart was hammering with anger. *Stop!* it said. *Stop right now!*

"Can't stop," Kosar whispered. "There's nothing left to stop for." He glanced after the Monk disappearing into the gloom and then back at the large gray thing, its head still beneath the sand. "I wish I could bury myself away," he said.

The thing grumbled and groaned. Several feet shifted position and it dragged its head a few steps through the sand.

Kosar lay back. The ground gave a comfortable warmth, and that seemed to ease some of his aches. He stared up at the sky and wondered where everything had gone: no stars, no sun, just the death moon almost directly above and the life moon a smear to the left of his vision. Though his back was warm he could feel the coldness up there, sucking the heat from Noreela like the air taking warmth from a corpse. This land was dead already; there were simply those who refused to believe that.

Don't *believe it*, A'Meer said. Kosar frowned and opened his eyes. He had drifted off without noticing, finding sleep a strange reflection of being awake. He closed his eyes again and let his breathing slow down, and the memory of A'Meer was there, reading his inner thoughts in her own voice. Kosar was pleased, because he saw that below all the bitterness and anger and exhaustion, he still believed there was a chance.

He slept, meeting A'Meer in his memories, and when he smiled at her the pain in his broken cheek woke him again.

———————

WHEN KOSAR SAT up, the Monk was kneeling beside the desert creature. Lucien kept one fisted hand pressed against his chest, and with the other he was trying to prize the creature's head up out of the sand. "Some help?" he asked, and Kosar hauled himself to his feet.

"What are you trying to do?"

"Feed it these." Lucien opened his hand briefly to show Kosar several squirming shapes, each the size of his thumb.

"Why?"

The Monk sighed. "Help me raise it and feed it, then I'll have time to tell you while they start acting."

"You're poisoning it? Killing it? Or seeking the truth like you bled it from me?"

"Do you think this thing will know anything useful? We need a ride. Now help me, or prepare for a fifty-mile walk across the desert."

Kosar leaned across the creature's stretched neck and grabbed hold of the bony collar around the base of its head. Its skin was hard and smooth, abraded by decades of sand and possessing a dull shine. He had to curl his fingers beneath the collar to maintain a grip. Then he pulled. Lucien did the same, and slowly the creature's head rose out of the sand.

Its big eyes opened and blinked lazily. It looked left at Kosar, forward at Lucien, then it slumped to the ground and rested its scaly head on the sand.

"It looks about as lively as I feel," Kosar said. "You think this thing will carry us across the desert?"

Lucien opened his hand before the creature's face, displaying the squirming grubs. "Pace beetles," he said. "It will carry us. Go and sit down, use your belt and straps to prepare a harness. You'll need something to hang on to."

Kosar moved away from the creature, still doubtful. Its legs were short and stumpy and it seemed to want to bury its head beneath the sand again. He wondered what it had been eating down there, but had no wish to find out.

He heard the wet snick of the creature's mouth opening, then the stony sound of its teeth crunching down on the beetles. He sat down and touched his belt, then shook his head.

Pace beetles, the Monk had called them.

And then Kosar remembered the Pace that A'Meer had possessed, and how she had never been able to tell him about it. She had called it a secret.

"You know Shantasi secrets?" Kosar called to the Monk.

Lucien looked up, surprised. "Some," he said. "It seems you do too."

"Some," Kosar said. He touched his belt buckle and started to unthread it from his trousers. He had to untie the sword scabbard from it first. *Keeping that very close to me*, he thought.

"Monks read a lot," Lucien said.

"So have you been everywhere?"

Lucien fed another beetle to the prone animal. "Not me. But other Monks have, and they come back and write down what they know, and others learn. We all know the same things."

"Kang Kang?" Kosar said.

Lucien nodded.

"The Blurring?"

Lucien glanced up at him, dark eyes giving nothing away. "Monks have gone there."

"And?"

"They never returned."

"I've heard that things are undone there," Kosar said. The Monk did not answer, so Kosar finished extracting his belt and retying his scabbard to his trousers. The belt was thick leather, decades old and tougher and stronger than the day he stole it from a shop on the Western Shores. He fashioned a tight loop at one end which he could hang on to, and the other he left free, ready to fix it somehow to the creature's neck collar.

"Almost ready," Lucien said. "Come and tie your belt to its neck."

Kosar did so, wedging the belt tight into the creature's bony collar so that the looped end was free for him to hold. "What about you?" he asked the Monk.

"I'll be making my own handhold. It'll need a reason to run."

———

MINUTES LATER THE gray sand creature was pounding across the desert. Kosar hung on to its back, bent low so that he could hold the belt with one hand and its neck collar with the other. He gritted his teeth and squinted, trying to avoid breathing in the clouds of sand thrown up by the thing's six feet. Its legs had lengthened from its body, long and slender now instead of short and squat, and it ran with an almost graceful gait, hardly rocking at all. Kosar found the rhythm very quickly, leaning left and right to match the creature's slight sway and yaw. And below and ahead of him, its mouth opened again in a low rumble of agony.

It'll need a reason to run, Lucien had said, and behind Kosar the Monk was providing the reason. He sat facing the creature's rear, his short sword buried to the hilt in the animal's lower back. There was his handhold.

"Left," the Monk called, and Kosar tugged slightly on the belt, urging the animal to the left. It seemed just as confident on the soft sands of high dunes as it did on compacted ground. Its long legs ended in wide, flat feet, and they prevented it from sinking, lifting it high and fast up the sides of dunes. On harder, flatter areas its wide feet slapped down and threw it onward. Double-jointed knees dampened the major impacts, giving Kosar and the Monk a soft ride, and soon the rhythms became soporific. Kosar found his eyes closing, head nodding.

Time passed them by, and the creature did not flag. It grumbled now and then, groaned as Lucien twisted his sword or Kosar edged it a fraction to the left or right, but whatever the Pace beetles had given it did not fade away. Kosar noticed spatters of moisture on his face and thought it had begun to rain, but when he looked closer he could see that the animal was foaming at the mouth. He wiped a gob of spittle from his cheek; it was pink with blood. The animal moaned some more, its call starting to sound desperate.

"You're killing it," Kosar said. The Monk did not reply.

Always conscious of the movement, smelling the heat of the creature above the more subtle aroma of desert spices, hearing its pain but never sensing it slowing down, Kosar drifted away.

———

THE MOL'STERIA DESERT *is part of our border,* A'Meer said. They were outside the Broken Arm tavern in Pavisse, sitting on its crumbling windowsill and drinking Old Bastard from battered metal tankards. Kosar remembered the day well. It had been hot and dry, and he and A'Meer had drunk all day and fucked all night. It was at the time when their lives could have changed drastically. If Kosar had not packed and left three weeks later without saying why, the future would have been a very different place. *We have Sordon Sound to the north,* A'Meer continued, *and Ventgoria and the Poison Forests past that. And the desert itself . . . it's not the best of places, Kosar. It's dangerous. Shantasi warriors have gone out there and never come back. The desert is a whole world, and the surface you see is only a small part of it.*

So New Shanti is impregnable, Kosar said. Back then he hadn't known that A'Meer was a Shantasi warrior. He believed she had left of her own accord, and mixing with a Shantasi excited him. Many people did not like them. Few trusted them, and some called them whiters because of the paleness of their skin. Right then, he was beginning to believe that maybe he loved her.

She drank more ale. Her skin never darkened even in such intense sunlight. Her black hair was loose today, flowing down over shoulders that he would be biting and scratching later that night. This memory was a full, rich place, echoing with the future as well as that moment in time. She opened her mouth to speak, and for an instant she seemed to gape, echoing the mimic's representation of her.

Not impregnable, she said. *But safe.*

Then why did you leave?

She smiled at him. *Where's the fun in safe?* And he saw a wealth of experience and knowledge in her eyes that he knew he would never match.

———

ANOTHER TIME, ANOTHER place, another mug of ale. They sat on a quay beside the river in Pavisse, watching fishing boats bring in their meager catch and the fishermen haul them ashore. Some fish were dead and stinking already, while others were mutated. The fishermen carried small knives to kill those that were wrong, slicing them in two and throwing them back into the River Pav. They produced a slick of all that was foul with the land.

Look at that, Kosar said. He was more than a little drunk. His fingers were hurting a lot that day, and sometimes alcohol dulled the pain. A'Meer could do that too. She had a special way of soothing his fingers, and later she would do it for him. *Just look at that! People eat stuff from that river. Can you believe it? Would you?*

You eat sheebok meat, Kosar.

Yes, but the sheebok I see aren't all twisted up like that.

Aren't they? Many have three horns. There's a herd in a farm north of Pavisse with four eyes each.

But their meat's still fine.

Is it?

Kosar stared at her, and for a moment her wisdom annoyed him. She always seemed to know what was best. Perhaps he was *too* drunk.

Well, it's all we have, he said.

Yes. All we have. But maybe someday things will change.

Kosar spat into the river. A dead fish with beaks instead of eyes floated by. *Nothing will change,* he said. *Noreela is dying. There's a cancer in its soul, and it's dying.*

Think positive, lover, A'Meer said, and she leaned over and bled his anger with a kiss. *There's always hope. You just have to watch for it, and grab it while you can.*

———

HE DREAMED OF A'Meer for a long time. Sometimes they were honest memories of what had happened and how things had been, other times they were tainted with his knowledge of everything that would come to pass. She spoke to him and smiled, groaned as she bent over a chair, offering herself to him, and she gave him her wisdom and hope whether he liked it or not. Usually he did not. But it stuck, mostly in places he did not recognize. And even though each successive dream became darker with the knowledge of her impending death at the hands of Lucien Malini, Kosar reveled in these memories. It was as though he had been given one final moment with her. He made it count. *I love you,* he thought many times over, and her eyes lit up throughout his memory to show him that for her, the same was true.

———

SOMETHING BROUGHT KOSAR out of his deep sleep. He was watching A'Meer prepare a rabbit for cooking and then the rabbit grunted, loud and hard. He felt the dream recede and reality reassert itself around him, and another loud grunt forced his eyes open.

He was still lying atop of the creature, and it was running at full speed along the base of a low ravine. It dodged this way and that, passing around rocks tumbled from the ravine walls and leaping the long-dried streambed.

"Attack," a voice whispered. Kosar sat up, turned around and saw the Monk pulling an arrow from his hip. He hissed as the barbed head came out.

"Who?" But he did not have to ask. Ahead and to the right, halfway up the ravine's slope, A'Meer rose from behind a rock and fired an arrow at them.

Kosar was too astonished to duck. The arrow glanced from the animal's bony forehead and tumbled into the night. He searched for A'Meer but she had already vanished. He saw a flash of movement farther along the ravine as something crossed from right to left. He squinted, saw another movement from the corner of his eye and turned left to see A'Meer stepping into view. She raised a crossbow and fired, and below him the creature jumped and grumbled in pain.

"A'Meer!" Kosar shouted, confused by his dream memories, but he knew that he was wrong. These Shantasi were not A'Meer. Something flashed across the ravine a few steps ahead of the galloping creature, waited until they were close and then leapt onto its back. Kosar hardly had time to perceive the movement before a male Shantasi stood astride him. The warrior held one arm out for support and raised a sword in his other.

"We're here to see the Mystics!" Kosar shouted, but the Shantasi's eyes did not change. He brought the sword down.

Sparks flew as Lucien blocked the blow with his own sword. The Monk shoved hard and the Shantasi tumbled from the creature, disappearing in a cloud of dust.

"We don't have long!" Lucien said.

"We're no enemy!" Kosar shouted. *Red Monk*, he thought. *They'll see me with him and kill me without asking questions.* "Lucien, don't fight back," he said. He stood, holding on to his looped belt with one hand, knees bent as he braced himself on the running animal's back.

Two crossbow bolts whizzed past his head from different directions. He saw movement on both sides of the ravine, but he could not focus. *Using their Pace*, he thought. *We don't have a chance.*

"We bring hope," he shouted. "We need to see the Mystics! The Mages are here, but we have an advantage. Kill us and you'll never know what that was."

He saw something ahead, and for a moment it confused Kosar. Straight lines did not belong in this place. It was only a second before the creature ran into the taut rope that he realized what it was.

The animal's legs were snapped from beneath it, and Kosar and Lucien flew from its back. For a second Kosar was flying, then the ground pulled him down and he tried to curl in his arms and legs, folding his head in his arms, wondering whether his broken body could take any more abuse before giving out entirely.

He did not even recall hitting the ground.

———

"WHO ARE YOU?"

Kosar opened his eyes and stared up into the face of a Shantasi warrior. She was bigger than A'Meer had been, her pale face divided with a diagonal scar that ran from the corner of her left eye and sliced her lips in two. Her dark hair was cropped short.

"Kosar," he said.

"Thief?"

He nodded. She had seen his hands.

"Did you steal that Shantasi sword on your hip?"

"No, I was given it by a friend."

"What friend?"

"A'Meer Pott. A Shantasi warrior."

"And where is she now?"

"Dead."

The Shantasi blinked. "You travel with a Red Monk." There was more surprise than accusation in her voice, and Kosar thought, *Perhaps I stand a chance.*

"He's one of the last," Kosar said. Talking hurt. He tried to move, figure out where else he was hurt, but the Shantasi leaned in and pressed the point of a sword into the hollow of his throat.

"Move and you die! Now . . . the Monk. We're close to killing it, but my squad is intrigued."

"Don't kill him," Kosar said. "He's one of the last, and his meaning has changed."

"Magic is back. Dark magic. What meaning does a Monk have left in this world?"

Kosar realized that as well as angry and committed, this Shantasi was scared. "To fight that dark magic," he said. "To defeat the Mages. There's another hope, another chance for the land. The Monk and I have come here to meet your Mystics, and ask for help."

"You're speaking riddles!" the Shantasi said. She shouted something to the soldiers around her, a few terse words in their staccato language. Then she leaned close and Kosar could smell her breath, a curious mix of spice and staleness that gave him a sudden flashback to A'Meer.

"I hear your knives knocking together," he said. "A'Meer wore her weapons so that none of them ever touched."

The Shantasi blinked again, processing what had happened and what Kosar had said. He saw the doubt in her eyes, and the reluctance to believe. *We're not killers*, A'Meer had told him. *We're not a warrior race. It was thrust upon us.*

"How is Lucien?" he asked.

"Lucien?"

"The Monk."

The Shantasi glanced away, then back again. "Alive," she said.

"Will you give me a chance?" he asked. "Please? A'Meer died for magic, and I swear that it's not all over. The Mages have their magic, and I suspect their army is ashore and heading this way even now."

"We know that," the warrior said.

"Then you can help. I need to see a Mystic. To tell them. And they will know if I tell the truth, won't they?"

"They have ways of knowing," she said.

Kosar thought of the beetle in his throat and shivered.

"You're hurt," the Shantasi said. "I'll carry you."

"No, I—" Kosar went to stand but the warrior had already grabbed him beneath the arms. She knelt, lifted and stood with him slung over one shoulder.

Kosar groaned as his broken ribs ground together. "How far?" he asked.

"Not far." The Shantasi issued orders to the rest of her squad. Kosar saw at least eight other warriors, and he wondered how he and Lucien had ever survived. *They were trying to bring us down,* he thought, *not kill us. They were intrigued: a man and a Red Monk traveling together on the back of that desert beast.* The creature was dead, a still shadow back along the ravine. *If I'd been on my own . . .*

"What's your name?" Kosar asked.

"Nothing to you." The Shantasi started walking. Each step jarred Kosar's cracked ribs, and he was glad when unconsciousness took him away once again.

———

HE CAME TO when the Shantasi lowered him from her back and propped him against a rock. She was panting and sweating, but she still looked strong. He noticed that she now moved silently; she had retied some of her weaponry.

"Thanks for the lift," Kosar said. He breathed in deeply, and the inside of his nose prickled with the warm aroma of desert spices. The smell gave him an unaccountable sense of well-being. He looked around. Behind him rose a steep, short hill, shifting here and there where Shantasi moved across its face. Lucien was thirty steps to his left, sitting with his head bowed and his hood pulled down. Three Shantasi stood around him, arrows strung, belts gleaming with weapons. He looked like a helpless old man. He seemed to sense Kosar watching because he glanced up. Kosar looked away.

Ahead of him, the desert. He could see the silhouette of a spice farm. Distance was difficult to judge in such light, but he guessed that it was at least several hundred steps away, a complex network of rods and ropes high above the desert. He could see the shadings of leaves and the webbing of stems and stalks, and he wondered whether the desert spice could survive this dearth of sunlight. A'Meer had once told him about a harvest, how the Shantasi climbed through the supports and across the rope rigging to gather leaves and seed pods, and he felt suddenly sad seeing this farm empty and abandoned.

"Are the farms still alive?" he asked.

The big Shantasi woman wiped a slick of sweat from her face.

She followed his gaze, looked back at Kosar. "What do you care? Damned Noreelan, what do you give a fuck about us?"

"You're as much a Noreelan as I."

"Pah!" The warrior shook her head and turned away. "We make a new home for ourselves, and still it doesn't last."

"You've been here for so long," he said. "You're a part of the land."

The Shantasi turned back to him, her anger lessened now. She spoke to him like a child; Kosar was not sure which he preferred. "Thief, *none* of us are part of the land."

"So what now?" he asked. "I need to speak to someone. Can you take me to Hess? To the Mystic Temple? There's something—"

"There's hope," a voice said. Older, lower than the warrior who had carried him here. The Shantasi performed a brief bow with her head and backed away, leaving room for a man to squat on the sand before Kosar.

———

"IS THAT WHAT you came to tell me, thief? That there's hope? You ride across a desert of dying spice farms, under a twilit sky that hasn't changed in days, accompanied by a Red Monk that has enough wounds to kill a dozen Shantasi . . . to tell me there's hope?"

"The Monk is Lucien Malini. His being with me should show you that things have changed."

The man nodded. "Things have changed, for sure. The Elder Mystics have killed themselves, the others have fled deep into New Shanti. Hess is a city of ghosts and memories, and dead things that still move. Yes, things have changed." He bowed his head and fisted both hands together.

"I'm sorry," Kosar said.

The Mystic glanced up and smiled. He looked embattled and desperate, but the smile touched his eyes. Kosar could not help returning the gesture, because A'Meer used to smile like that.

"I'm O'Gan Pentle," the man said. "I think you've guessed that I'm a Mystic. A young one, comparatively." He leaned forward. "Are you a spy for the Mages?"

"No," Kosar said.

"Is there something in you?"

"No."

"Then the hope you bring us . . . tell me. I have hope of my own, and I'd be interested to hear whether they're of the same ilk."

"I need a drink," Kosar said. "And the Monk will need food and drink also."

O'Gan glanced across at the Monk, frowning. "Monks are our enemies," he said.

"Yes, they used to be."

O'Gan stared at Kosar for a long time. The thief looked down at his bloodied fingertips, but still he felt the Mystic's attention upon him. "Things have changed," the Mystic whispered. "Bring some water and food," he said, louder. "And feed the Monk."

"Mystic?" The Shantasi warrior sounded amazed.

"Feed it. And give it water. Things have changed, O'Lam."

The warrior nodded, gave the brief bow again and went to fetch food and drink.

"It was A'Meer," Kosar said. He was still staring at his hands, remembering how the mimics had shown him his lover's last moments. It was a painful memory, but one he felt he had to share now. It was almost like bringing her death home. "I'd left the others, I was *running away*, when the mimics showed me A'Meer. And that made it clear to me. It solidified what the librarian said, what Hope claimed, and—"

"A'Meer Pott," O'Gan said.

Kosar glanced up and saw the Mystic's eyes grow wide, staring at some past memory.

" 'Hope,' she said to me," O'Gan continued. "She spoke the language of the land, and she told me 'Hope,' but none of the Elders believed me. Their memories are tainted by what came before. They see only the bad. But there has to be good as well."

"There is," Kosar said, confused but invigorated. "Her name is Alishia."

———

HE TOLD O'GAN of Alishia, Hope and Trey, traveling southward for Kang Kang and the Womb of the Land. He told him of Rafe Baburn and what the boy had carried; their flight south; the pursuit by the Red Monks and their battle in the machines' graveyard. He glanced sideways at Lucien, trying not to imagine the Monk using his sword to end A'Meer's life. And finally he told O'Gan why he had come to New Shanti.

"They need time," Kosar said. "To reach Kang Kang and find the Womb of the Land. And they need protecting."

"And what happens if they get there?" O'Gan asked.

Kosar shrugged. "You're a Mystic. I'm just a thief. Don't you know?"

O'Gan shook his head.

"Alishia thinks she can do something," Kosar said.

"In Kang Kang? That's a bad place. They'll be killed before they get farther than its foothills."

Kosar closed his eyes. *I wish I could believe that isn't true,* he thought. *I wish I could believe that Noreela itself is guarding them and guiding them. But Rafe followed that voice in his mind, and still the Mages won.*

"There are no guarantees," Kosar said. "Nothing's written. We write history with every breath we take."

"That's a Shantasi saying."

Kosar smiled.

O'Gan nodded. "So, you came to ask us to march to Kang Kang with what's left of the army of New Shanti—leaving Hess open to the Krotes—and stop them from reaching this girl?"

Kosar nodded. "I've no way to persuade you," he said. "But I saw A'Meer, and you . . . ?"

"She was my student."

"You taught A'Meer!"

O'Gan nodded. "She was one of my first. I haven't seen her in over fifty years, and a day ago she appeared to me on the Mystic Temple. A vision. A ghost."

"Mimics," Kosar said.

"The Elders always told me that mimics are a myth."

"Myth or not, I've seen them, and so have you. And where are the Elders now, O'Gan?"

O'Gan's pale face actually seemed to take on a darker hue, and his eyes grew narrow. "You're in no position to demean the Elder Mystics." His voice was low and threatening, and Kosar knew that he was right. But times were changing.

"They've done that themselves," he said.

O'Gan stood quickly and walked away, heading toward the open desert and the shadow of the spice farm.

Kosar watched him go, wondering what all this meant. The mimics had shown him the way to New Shanti, and now this Mystic claimed to have seen the vision of A'Meer. *She spoke the language of the land,* he had said.

Kosar groaned, coughed into his hand, saw the splash of darkness in his palm that could only mean blood.

Leaning back, closing his eyes, he tried to shut everything from his mind for a while.

———

"WE'VE BEEN WAITING here for a day," O'Gan said. Kosar opened his eyes to see that the tall Shantasi Mystic had sat down beside him. "Waiting for the Mages and their Krote army to attack. I'm confused. I wish there were Elders I could commune with, but . . ." He shook his head, looked back out into the desert. "The spice farms are dying," he said. "That's sad. They've been there for a long time—over a thousand years—and they've never failed to provide us with a crop. They've weathered so much in that time, from drought to floods, and everything in between. Each year, thousands of Shantasi flood into the desert to harvest the spice, take it back and distribute it around New Shanti. It tastes nice, and smells good. It's used for treating some cancers, and it can guide the mad back to normality. It's the smell of New Shanti. Soon, the farms will be dead and we'll never smell it again." He looked at Kosar. "Your Monk told us that he killed A'Meer."

"I know," Kosar said.

O'Gan nodded. "And yet you still travel with him."

"Only for now." *Do I mean that,* Kosar thought. *Is there enough hate in me to kill the Monk, when all of Noreela is dying?*

"Revenge is a powerful driver," O'Gan said. "But it bears no reflection of what's needed and what is not. Revenge has no logic."

"The Mages are here for revenge," Kosar said.

"And they're having it. It could be that they've killed Noreela already."

"I still have some fight in me."

"Perhaps," O'Gan said, "although it looks as though you've been through enough fights. Can you fight without eating? The sun has been gone for a long time, and it may be absent for a long time more. It's growing colder. Plants are dying. When the plants die, the animals die. When the plants and animals die . . . there's nothing left to eat."

"I've seen the Mages," Kosar said. He was aware of O'Gan's sur-

prised intake of breath, but he ignored it and finished what he had
to say. "They want more from revenge than dead grass. They want
blood."

"They'll be having it as we speak," O'Gan said. "And they'll
come for New Shanti last because they know we're the strongest in
Noreela. At least, we were." He bowed his head.

"So is this all talking around what you've already decided?"
Kosar asked. "Are you staying here to fight the Krotes, or will you
come to Kang Kang? If the Mages get to know of Alishia—and they
have their ways and means—they'll go for her with all their army
and might."

"You could be mad," O'Gan said.

"I feel that way."

"You *could* be insane. I saw a man once—a trader—who believed he was a Sleeping God."

Kosar smiled. "I've seen the like as well. Usually with their face
in a bottle of rotwine."

O'Gan fell silent for so long that Kosar thought he had fallen
asleep. When he looked up at last he found O'Gan staring right at
him, as though trying to penetrate his skull and see whether the
thief told lies.

The Mystic nodded. "We'll come with you," he said.

Kosar's eyes widened. "Just like that?"

O'Gan shook his head. "No. Not just like that. I've been waiting for something to happen, and I think your arrival is what I've
been awaiting."

"Fate," Kosar said.

Again, O'Gan shook his head. "History. The Mages expect
Noreela to roll over and die before their greater power. I believe we
should take the fight to them."

Kosar closed his eyes and smiled. *Alishia,* he thought, *I really
hope you can do what you claim. I hope this is all for real. Because
all I want to do is curl up here and sleep, though I know I can't.* "How
big is your army?" he asked.

"I have almost two thousand Shantasi warriors, and an equal
number untrained."

"Four thousand. Do they all have the Pace?"

O'Gan raised his eyebrows. "A'Meer?"

Kosar nodded. "But she said she couldn't talk about it. Hinted
there was more."

O'Gan stood, smiling. "Good for A'Meer," he said. "The warriors have the Pace, and yes, there's more. If you live through this, thief, you'll be able to tell your children you saw the Shantasi at war. It's not something you or they will forget."

———

"HOPE, I NEED to learn more," Alishia said. "I've been told so much, but I still don't understand." She looked down at the burn on her palm as though truths were written there.

The witch glared at her. It had started to snow, and flakes hung in her wild hair like bizarre decorations. Alishia was cold. Her skinny body shook and shivered. She tried to hug her clothes tighter around her but they were too large, letting cool air in and allowing her meager body heat to escape. She was certain that if she reached inside and touched her chest she would find only ice.

"If you go back to sleep, you could guide it in! Whatever had you, whatever saw you, it could find you again and bring *them* to us!"

"I won't let it," Alishia said. "I'll hide. But I have to go, Hope, don't you see? Do you really know where the Womb of the Land is? Do you know where we're going, and what to do when we get there?"

Hope looked up at the mountains looming ahead of them, snowcapped and forbidding, and when she turned back to Alishia her anger was rich and strong. "*I'm* taking you to that place, no one else!"

"But you don't know where it is." She wanted to question what she had inside her but she could not reach it, not like this, not feeling the cold and misery closing in. *I need to go back in.*

. . . and I can.

"Hope, look after me," Alishia said.

"I am looking after you," the witch said, voice softening. She almost smiled.

As Alishia closed her eyes, she saw the witch's smile fade.

She sought the door back into the vastness of that library. Something jarred her, tried to pull her back, but sleep came quickly. Perhaps because the library craved her return, but more likely because she was too weak to remain awake.

Look after me, Hope, she thought, and the library was burning again.

IN THE LIBRARY, she did not feel so tired. Her body was still reduced, but being the size of a twelve-year-old felt more natural in here. She ran, and her girl's legs were long and slender and strong. Her dress fluttered about her, flattening against her stomach, and her hair bounced behind her as though freshly washed. She felt immensely liberated dashing between these cliffs of books, even though some of them were burning. Books had always been her life, and now here she was existing within the heart of Noreela.

But it's burning.

She skidded to a stop amongst a pile of ashes and looked down at the marks her feet had made. Shifting the ashes to one side with her foot, she could see the charred timber floor, and the jagged gap in between boards where several half-burnt pages had become jammed. Down there, below the boards and beyond those cracks, was something else.

Something trying to get in, she thought. *Something showering in the ashes of Noreela.* She shivered and ran on, not feeling quite so free.

She had knowledge inside her, but she was looking for understanding. She knew that it had to be in here somewhere. She had read the stone and heard what it had to tell her, but she needed something more.

Somewhere in here, she thought. *It has to be somewhere in here.* She ran.

IT FELT LIKE a long time, but it could have been mere heartbeats, before the flames around her suddenly went out.

Alishia gasped. All around her, the burning had ceased, and it felt like a held breath awaiting something momentous. She held her own breath, afraid that something would hear her.

A violent breeze brushed past her, carrying smoke in a swirling storm. *Something's been opened,* she thought, and then the wind stopped as quickly as it had begun. Smoke twisted in mad eddies as the air settled once again.

The fires reignited with an explosion that blew Alishia to her knees. To her left and right, and up and down, fire roared across her vision, and she thought, *This is it, this is the end, I'll be burned to ashes and mixed with Noreela's dying history.* But although the firestorm blew around and through her and took her breath away, still the flames did her no harm.

She stood, brushed herself down and realized that the fires were more widespread and more destructive than they had been before.

"Something came in," she said.

She was no longer alone. She felt a presence searching for her, seeking her through the endless stacks of history and the shelves of moments in time, and this was far darker than the mere shade that had spotted her before. This was something that had lived, not something yet to live. It was a thing with experience and knowledge and hate in its heart. It exuded such menace, and its purpose permeated the air as effectively as the eddying smoke.

"One of *them*."

Chapter 15

JOSSUA ELMANTOZ'S consciousness was like a weak ripple on a stormy sea. His wraith had retreated into the tumbler with the dozens it already possessed, but it was still linked to his body, trapped by that ruin of blood and bone. A Red Monk's hold on life is tenacious, and much as Jossua craved to sever that connection, he could not. Perhaps it was his own resilient mind fighting, or maybe the fledge the Nax had bathed him in. But he hung on to the dregs of existence.

He felt the pain of his body being ripped to shreds, even though he had few nerves left. He did not hear or see, but he sensed every impact on the ground, pressed into the hide of the tumbler as it rolled quickly along hillsides and through valleys. He could feel the wet bones of his skull and ribs crunching against other bones deeper within the tumbler, and a voice came from nowhere to say, *That's me.*

Flage, Jossua thought.

That's my body. Not much left; just a few broken bones. I've not had cause to pay it any attention for a long time. It's safe and warm in here, and the tumbler welcomes us, and my bones mean nothing to me now. But . . . it's almost nice. Nostalgic. Like redreaming an old, happy dream that you thought had been lost forever.

You were going to tell me, Jossua thought. *You were going to talk to me. And then you went quiet and I've been stuck here—*

I don't like you. Flage's wraith drew back, almost an eternity away from Jossua. *You're a Monk. You're a bad man, and your wraith knows that well.*

I'm not a bad man, Jossua said, but a slew of memories flashed before him and none of them were good.

I don't want you here. None of us do. But you're here, and the mind chose me to communicate with you, so I shall. Flage fell silent. Jossua had no way to judge the passage of time, but he felt his bones broken some more and the final shreds of flesh stripped away. The tumbler rolled on, passing through places that made little sense to Jossua's disembodied mind. He could sense a multitude of wraiths behind Flage, pressing back as though Jossua were a hole and they were afraid of falling in.

I can chant you down, Jossua said.

I don't need *chanting down! The tumbler is my Black.* Flage was angry and frightened. Jossua tried to find the wraith, but there was nothing for him to find. He was stuck in a limbo of pain and wondering, and he so wanted to beg Flage to tell him what he must.

But Jossua was the first Red Monk, and he would beg no one.

———

LATER, FARTHER INTO the place that made no sense, as the tumbler was climbing higher and higher, Flage came back.

I can tell you now, the wraith said, *and then I will speak to you no more. I was comfortable in here. And then you came and—*

I know! Jossua called. *And you don't like me, and don't want to have to do this.*

Flage was silent for a while, and then he whispered through what must have been a smile. *You're afraid.*

Yes.

You should be. You're not alive, Monk, nor dead. You're in between, and that's no place for any wraith to be. You're in a moment that shouldn't be, and it's so wrong that none of us can understand. You carry the finality of death with the reality of life, and you are to remain there for a while. Because there's a purpose for you yet.

You sound pleased, Jossua said.

I know what's to become of you. Flage said no more. Jossua called after him, cried, and in the end—heartbeats or eons into his incarceration in the tumbler—he began to beg. But Flage had returned to where he claimed to be happy, and all Jossua could do was wait.

———

HOPE CARRIED ALISHIA over one shoulder. The girl was lighter than ever, and the witch could almost forget that she was carrying anything other than a full shoulder bag. Alishia twitched in her sleep now and then, cried out and then fell silent. Hope paused regularly to check her breathing.

"You'll not take from me what's mine," she said, again and again. Alishia's breath was warm and musty and smelled of ash. "You'll not take what's mine!"

The witch found a narrow stone bridge crossing the ravine that she was beginning to fear ran the length of Kang Kang. She did not know whether the bridge was natural or made by someone or something, but she crossed anyway, glancing down into the depths only once. *There's no bottom to that,* she thought, *no ending. Only darkness growing darker.* Her skin crawled, her hair stood on end, her tattoos squirmed at the corners of her mouth, providing runways for tears.

If she stumbled, she knew that she would fall forever.

She reached the other side and started climbing into the mountains without pause. Alishia had been right, she did not know where she was going. But this was Kang Kang, and the Womb of the Land was here, and the only way to find it was to search.

The slopes grew steeper and turned from grass and bracken to loose shale. The snow continued. Sometimes it burned when it touched her exposed skin, and she wondered where the waters that formed this snow had risen from. Within every shadow she sensed eyes watching, yet when she looked the eyes closed. At any moment she expected the ground to give a heave, shrugging her from the slopes of Kang Kang. Sometimes her feet seemed to barely touch the ground, and she wondered whether she was repulsing the land or vice versa. She was an alien in this alien world, utterly unwelcome. The whole place watched her, silent and surly. Planning her demise.

Not long now, she thought, a mantra that drove her on. All that Hope had been was slowly filtering away. She had memories, but they grew vague—and the farther she went, the more her early life seemed to consist only of the old, useless spells her mother had taught her, the routes and byways of genuine enchantments. The fake charms and false potions became the affectations of another woman, a sad old soul whom Hope had once known. Her life before finding the dead Sleeping God had been a held breath, and now she was close to gasping herself awake.

It's all me . . . not long now . . . it's all me.

"Guide us in," Alishia muttered.

Hope nudged the girl with her shoulder, but she said no more.

The death moon lit an ancient path up the side of a mountain. Light snow defined its edges, melting on the path as though the ancient footsteps that formed it were still warm. *Should be writing my own Book of Ways*, Hope thought.

This place threw all of its hatred and distrust her way, making her flesh creep and her eyes water with every step she took. But over her shoulder lay the future. Hope had been inside a dead God, and she was mad enough to survive Kang Kang's worst.

———

TREY WAS AWASH with fledge, but he could not travel. His mind jumped and jerked, bored within its own confines and eager to reach out and seek more, but each time he tried to leave, the Nax held him down. The first time it happened he had been so terrified that he lost all pretense at consciousness for some time. When he next came around and tried to travel once more, the Nax came in again. He slipped back into his mind and let them hold him there, but he did not pass out.

They dragged him through fledge seams deeper than any he had ever believed existed. He felt the weight of the world above him, mile upon mile of rock and cavern and water, fledge and earth and the bones of long-buried things. But the Nax had him, and though they exuded scorn, they seemed to have purpose. He could not guess what it was, and hoped he would never find out. Perhaps he would be dead by the time they reached their destination.

He tried talking to his mother. If he heard her reply, then he would know that life had truly left him.

But the Nax kept him awake, and he felt every pull and tug as they steered him through seams of the drug. His fledge rage was long since satiated, but still he opened his mouth now and then to exhale old drug and breathe in new. It still surprised him that he was breathing fledge instead of air, but he did not dwell upon it.

Alishia, thought Trey. *I was looking after her.* But she felt a whole world away. Perhaps while he had been held down here by the fledge demons, time had moved on many years aboveground. Maybe Alishia and Hope had reached the Womb of the Land and done what they needed to do, protected by Kosar and the Shantasi army riding behind him. Perhaps the Mages had been driven away and light been brought back to the land. Kosar would be wandering again, a thief, a hero, looking for the fledge miner he had left behind in Hope's unstable care.

Or maybe Alishia had died before ever reaching the heart of Kang Kang, and the land was left to the Mages, and Trey was the last human.

He should cast out, travel through the rock and see what was happening. But the crawling discomfort of the Nax was ever-present at the edge of his mind.

They exploded from the fledge into open air, and Trey gasped aloud. The Nax had him by the arms and legs and he kicked and twisted, trying to get free. It was pitch black, yet he could sense the massive space around him, a hollow in the foundation of Noreela that dwarfed the home-cavern where he had spent his childhood. He coughed and heard no echoes. He shouted, vomiting a dry stream of fledge into open air. He did not hear it hit the ground. The Nax flew on, ignoring his struggles and shouts, and Trey calmed his mind and closed his eyes to the blackness.

Will you let me go down, if not up? he thought, and he cast his mind from his floating body.

This time the Nax did not interrupt.

Soon, he would find out why.

———

TREY FELL THROUGH the darkness, always aware of the position of his body way above. The Nax flew him across this great cavern, moving slowly, almost as if they wanted him to travel down and see where they were. *They're waiting for me*, he thought. He guessed that they could hear him, see him, know him, but he had consumed so much fledge—the youngest, freshest drug he had ever experienced—that he barely cared. *Let them,* he thought. *Let the monsters read me.*

We are the Nax, their voice roared, and Trey went spinning through the cavern.

Even traveling on a fledge trip, it took him several minutes to reach the ground. He probed outward with his senses and saw, smelled and tasted more fledge, built up from the floor of the cavern into towering structures. This drug was different from any he had ever known. It was molded and worked, broken down and then re-formed with some other substance that gave it a thicker, rougher texture. And it was old, giving off a sickening stale miasma that almost drove Trey away.

But there was something else that urged him closer. Beyond the fact that it had been mined and then remade, past the obvious age of these structures, his own probing mind found others.

They did not notice him. They were mumbling, adrift and mad. None of them traveled farther than a few steps from this timeless fledge city, and as Trey dipped down between stale minarets, columns and towers, he knew why.

There were people trapped down here. They were buried in the fledge buildings, a leg protruding here, a face there. They were a race he did not know. High foreheads; dark skin; long, protruding jaws; wide eyes that had once surely been intelligent, though now they wore the dull taint of time in their blindness. The horrible fact of their longevity impressed itself upon Trey.

Is it this for me as well? he thought, rising quickly from the city and shutting his senses to it. *Am I going to be imprisoned like these unknown people, trapped down here for centuries, so old that they must be from an age long forgotten?*

The Nax holding his body drew him in, pulling him across space so quickly that he was left reeling within the confines of his own mind. They offered no explanation or comment, but moved on faster than ever.

Soon they were buried in another fledge seam, traveling quickly away from that huge cavern, and Trey was glad.

South, he thought. *We're going south. I wonder if my whole future now is belowground.*

No future, the Nax rumbled a while later. But Trey did not know to whom or what they referred.

————

THE KROTE ARMY rode south. Noreela City was a hundred miles behind them, still gushing smoke at the sky, still echoing to the sounds of the dead searching for those left alive. Lenora had started following her own shadow, cast forward by the blazing city. Now her shadow was a vague thing once again, thrown left and right by the moons. Most of the time she was not aware of it at all. And that haunting shade was still with her.

She stared forward, still shocked at the arrival of the Mages, their appearance and the news they had brought.

————

THEIR MACHINE HAD landed heavily, spilling Angel to the ground. She rolled and ran, coming at Lenora as though meaning to run straight through her. S'Hivez remained on the machine's back. He was slumped down as though asleep.

What have I done? Lenora thought, panicked. She could feel the heat of Noreela City's demise on her back, yet Angel looked grim and fierce and . . . frightened?

"Mistress," Lenora said, kneeling and bowing her head.

"Get up!" Angel spat.

Lenora obeyed. Still she kept her head down, because she did not wish to see such rage in the Mage's eyes.

"Look at me," Angel said, her voice gentler. Lenora looked. Angel glanced over the Krote's shoulder at Noreela City, its stone walls glowing with fearsome heat. "You've done well," the Mage said, but Lenora could see in her eyes that there were matters more pressing than praise.

"Thank you, Mistress. What of the south?"

"The south?" Angel said, raising her eyebrows. "You think we've been to the south?"

"You flew in from that way," Lenora said. She could not meet Angel's eyes for more than a heartbeat without looking away.

"We went to the Monastery," Angel said. "There was something we had to do there."

"The Nax?" Lenora said.

"The Nax. But they're long gone. The basements and deeper caves are empty. But we met something else there. A shade spy came to us, and it gave news we thought never to hear."

"And this news . . ." Lenora started, pausing when Angel glared at her. "The Shantasi?"

"Pah! Weakling slaves who think themselves warriors. Why would I fear those whiter freaks? No, Lenora." She moved close and spoke into Lenora's ear. "Magic. There's still magic free, and it conspires against us."

"You have the magic," Lenora said, confused. "I saw you take it from the boy with my own eyes."

Angel glanced at Lenora's machine, parts of its flesh and bone risen from the corpse of the farm boy. "So you did," she said. "But a shade has found another. A girl, going into Kang Kang with a mad witch as her companion."

"No one else?"

"Just two of them."

"Then what threat—?"

Angel reached out and grabbed Lenora's shoulder. Old wounds and new came alight, pain burning into Lenora's body and skull, and Angel pressed her to her knees. Lenora tried not to scream. She closed her eyes and welcomed the pain as a friend rather than an enemy. It would be over soon and she would not remember exactly how it felt. Pain was a thing of the moment.

Angel brought her face close to Lenora's and waited until the Krote opened her eyes before she spoke. "What threat? Consider what threat we are to Noreela."

"We're *destroying* Noreela!"

"Yes, and I can taste its blood on your breath. But if a magic beyond our control returns to the land, the blade will be turned. The threat will be on us. It'll be the War again. And as you well know, Lenora, we didn't fare well the first time."

"But we *would* win now, Mistress." Lenora stared into Angel's eyes, past the agony of her shoulder and her fear of the Mage. Behind false beauty wrought by magic she saw the embittered old Mage this woman really was, mad with the need for revenge, insane with its hunger. And in those eyes, she saw the reflection of herself.

Angel eased her grip until her hand was merely resting on Lenora's shoulder. "You're a good soldier," she said. "And a friend, Lenora. Does that shock you?"

Lenora shook her head. "No, Mistress."

"Good. Then do this friend a favor. Drive south to Kang Kang. Take the whole army with you. Ignore everything between here and there. Don't be tempted by the towns, the trains of fleeing people, the farming villages. Take only what you need to eat, drink and rearm, and go for the eastern reach of Kang Kang. A mad witch and a girl, that's all you seek of Noreela right now."

"Shall I bring them to you?"

"Kill them. And with the girl, make sure her head is crushed into the ground. Feed her brains to your machine. Leave *nothing*."

"Mistress," Lenora said, bowing her head slightly.

Angel touched Lenora's chin and raised her face. "I suppose you want to know where S'Hivez and I will be while all this is going on?"

"No, Mistress, I'd never question—"

"I can't tell you," Angel said. "But we'll meet again soon."

"Kang Kang is a long way, perhaps five hundred miles. How long do we have?"

"Perhaps days, perhaps . . . heartbeats." Angel looked up at the darkened sky, as though expecting the sun to shine through at any moment.

"I will not fail you, Mistress."

"Thank you, Lenora. I'm leaving you something. It will build you more machines, to carry a different army." Angel left and Lenora watched her go, thrilled and relieved.

The Mage leapt onto her machine with unnatural grace. She leaned forward and whispered something to S'Hivez, but the male Mage barely moved. *He's somewhere else*, Lenora thought. As the machine lifted off, something slipped from a rent in its gut and moved toward the city walls. Another shade crushed a hole in reality. Lenora tried not to see.

Angel spared not a glance for the burning city.

"As though she's seen it all before," Lenora said. And she had. The Mages had been dreaming of this every night for three hundred years.

IN THE DISTANCE Lenora saw the lights from a caravan of wagons. They snaked across the foothills of the Widow's Peaks, heading south from Noreela City. As they closed in, the lights blinked out,

and Lenora could see hundreds of tiny shadows fleeing the wagons
and dispersing across the hillside. More helpless victims to slaughter, but she could not let anything distract her. Angel had been very
specific in her orders. And in a way, Lenora was glad. She had seen
a killing frenzy in some of her Krotes that she could no longer find
in herself, and it had disturbed her. Perhaps because of that voice
that spoke to her, that child, and the innocence she had begun to
hear behind its words.

The massed army of Krotes thundered on. Their machines ran
or crawled or flew, and in their midst, giant new constructs—formed
by the shade the Mages had left behind—rolled on wheels of stone
cast from the ruins of Noreela City. They carried great cages and
bowls, hollow globes and flattened shelves of rock, and packed into
these machines were thousands of Noreelan dead. Limbs waved
feebly, mouths opened and closed and drooled black blood. Heads
turned to see where they were going and to search for their uncertain futures.

What of their wraiths? Lenora thought yet again, but she did not
dwell on that. Wherever they were, they would be in pain.

The machines tore down dying trees and crushed them to
splinters. They churned the soil, ploughing under failing crops and
exposing the guts of the land to the dusk. A heavy frost glittered, reflecting moonlight and marking their way. They moved quickly,
and when they saw a large town burning in the distance they diverted slightly and told the Krotes there of their new aim. These several warriors boarded their flying machines and took off, heading
south toward Kang Kang.

The land shook beneath them, and Noreelans shivered in their
hiding places. But for now the aim of the army had changed. The
invasion was over, and the battle for magic had begun.

Chapter 16

THE SHANTASI WERE harvesting, though not spice. The spice farms were dying, but the warriors were out on the desert sands anyway, digging instead of climbing, ignoring the intricate webbings and shriveling plants in favor of excavating things from below.

"More Pace beetles?" Kosar asked.

"I expect so." Lucien was nursing his wounds, chewing the remaining plants from his robe pockets and packing the resultant paste in the holes in his arm, shoulders and body. He felt weak and wretched. He should be dead. Yet here he was, surrounded by Shantasi, and he had no idea what would come next. Perhaps he would go with them to fight the Mages and their Krote army. The idea of that thrilled him, driving his blood faster and inspiring a heat in his skin which Kosar must surely feel where he sat a few steps away.

On the other hand, the Shantasi could simply kill him. He had fight left in him, but he was not sure that he would resist. The more Shantasi he took with him, the fewer there would be to fight the Krotes, and the more chance there was of Alishia being caught and

killed. He hoped the Shantasi reasoned as he did and allowed him
to fight.

They had let Kosar come and sit next to him after the thief had
finished talking with the Mystic. With the Shantasi going about
their preparations, it felt as though he and Kosar were set apart.
Lucien sighed and pressed more paste into an arrow wound above
his left elbow. He flexed his arm and felt the damage to the joint,
but his blood had hardened there, fixed the fracture and turned
fluid again to lubricate the movement.

A Shantasi returned from the sands and dropped a leather bag
against a rock thirty steps away. He muttered something to O'Gan
Pentle, who was sitting on the rock, glanced at Lucien and Kosar
then went back out onto the sands. O'Gan continued watching the
harvest.

They had sent a dozen Shantasi east immediately after O'Gan
had made his decision. Their army was spread across the desert between here and Hess, and they were to initiate a chain reaction of
orders all the way back to the Mystic City. O'Gan expected the bulk
of the army to be with them within half a day, and then he said they
would head southwest toward Kang Kang.

"I see no horses," Lucien said. "No transport. That desert creature we rode on was fast, but will there be enough to carry four
thousand Shantasi?"

"O'Gan said they would move quickly enough," Kosar said. He
had drawn his sword and touched the blade to his fingertips, smearing blood across the metal and leaving it to dry to a crust.

"I could heal those," Lucien said.

Kosar looked at him. "You told me that before."

"I meant it."

Kosar touched the sword again and watched a bubble of blood
run down to the handle. "I like myself as I am," the thief said.

"The offer remains open."

"The offer is *closed*!" Kosar stood and walked away, sheathing
his sword and approaching the Mystic.

I killed his love, Lucien thought, trying to remember that fight
in the woods around the machines' graveyard. The rage had been
fully upon him then, and he could not recall much of the Shantasi
other than her ferocity. He'd had an idea that she had fought Red
Monks before, and the fact that she was still alive to take him on

had inspired an element of respect for her. But respect was weakness, and Lucien had triumphed. And from that moment on, his and Kosar's paths had been destined to cross.

He finished dressing his wounds, rested his arms on crossed legs and stared out across the desert.

———

THE BIG THIEF approached, walking awkwardly and holding his arm across his ribs. Behind him the Red Monk sat staring into the desert, hood hiding his grotesquely scarred face.

O'Gan feared the journey and fight to come. They had their means to reach Kang Kang, and they had their weapons and training, but everything else O'Gan was hoping for to help them in the battle . . . well, they might no longer be available. These were desert things that craved the sun.

"What are you gathering?" Kosar the thief asked.

"What do you think?" O'Gan recognized a naive intelligence in the man's eyes; they held experience, but his manner also displayed an ignorance of many things. Someone out for his own gain, not interested in information and learning. Before all this, at least. Now, seeing the wounds he bore and the hatred he still harbored for the Monk with whom he had ridden across the desert, O'Gan knew that Kosar was much changed. He wondered whether the thief even realized that he was a new man.

"Pace beetles," Kosar said. "Just another drug." He sounded disappointed.

"A'Meer didn't tell you everything," O'Gan said. "It's no drug. The beetles live a different time from our own. It's . . . complicated."

Kosar raised his eyebrows. "I may not understand, but I'm ready to believe."

O'Gan nodded and smiled. "They age a hundred years in their lifetime, yet they exist in our world for only a few months. Things are *faster* for them. By eating them, we borrow their time."

Kosar nodded, frowning. "And age faster in the process. We killed the thing we rode in on."

O'Gan nodded. "We can't use it too much. It hurts."

"Have you just told me a Shantasi secret?" the thief asked.

O'Gan stood, jumped from the rock and landed softly beside Kosar. He rested his hand on the man's shoulder and squeezed slightly, and he was pleased when Kosar smiled. *He's glad I believe him*, the Mystic thought. *Glad I'm ready to help. He sacrificed so much to get here.*

"I think," O'Gan said, nodding toward the Red Monk, "that our secret is already out."

"He said he read lots of books in the Monastery," Kosar said. "I think he was fooling with me."

"The whole history of the land is written in books, somewhere," O'Gan said. "Most of them will never be found, most have never been read. But they've all been written."

"Who's writing this one?"

"You, thief. Me. All of us."

Kosar nodded. "And to talk of the end?"

"The land is full of seers and prophets, visionaries and those who purport to know the future. But every next breath is the future. Every blink of your eyes marks your progress from one moment to the next, and you never know what you're going to see when they next open."

Kosar blinked. "You," he said. "The desert. The dying spice farms. I knew they'd be there."

"You *trusted* them to be there. But you never know for sure." O'Gan picked up a handful of sand and let it slip between his fingers, holding out his other hand beneath to catch it. Some grains he caught, others fell back to the ground. "You trust this sand to fall, but one day it may rise."

"I saw a river flowing uphill," Kosar said. "It turned and wiped out a whole village."

O'Gan nodded, dropped the remaining sand. "Between one blink and the next, the world will change."

Kosar sighed and sat down. He held his head in his hands, elbows resting on his knees, and groaned as his soft rocking motion aggravated his broken ribs. "I'm just a Mage-shitting thief! I don't need to be here. I don't deserve it."

"Does he?" O'Gan said, nodding at Lucien.

Kosar did not even look. "He calls himself a human."

O'Gan blinked several times in surprise, and each time he looked again, the Monk was still there. "Has he seen what we saw?"

"The mimics? I'm not sure. I don't care."

"Without him, would you be sitting here now?"

Kosar continued rocking, looking down at the ground between

his knees and groaning each time his wounded ribs shifted. It was almost as if he was welcoming the pain. O'Gan felt sorry for him.

"No," Kosar said. "Without him I'd have been dead twice over. He rescued me from a band of Breakers. Then he took on a sand demon, and—"

"The Monk fought a serpenthal?"

"If that's a sand demon, yes. Weird. Lots of parts. He said it spans, whatever that means."

O'Gan's stomach felt heavy, and his throat suddenly tasted of bile. He stared at the Monk and the Monk looked away, drawing shapes in the dust with one long finger.

"They're deadly," O'Gan said. "They live deep in the desert. Prey on desert animals, or lone travelers and small bands of traders."

"Don't they prey on you?" Kosar asked, looking up.

O'Gan shook his head. "Most Shantasi know better than to go into the deep desert alone."

"Well, we met this one almost before the desert began, back to the west. Lucien killed it. Took some time, and he got hurt, but he cut it to pieces."

"They *are* pieces."

"Smaller pieces, then. So yes, he's saved my life, but I don't like that any more than you."

"If you hadn't reached us, I would still be sitting in the desert with the remains of an army," O'Gan said. "Waiting for a sign. Waiting for hope to present itself."

"So you believe me?" Kosar said. "Even though I have these brands, and I travel with a Monk, you truly believe me?"

"You're a thief, but that doesn't make you a liar. And we both saw A'Meer."

"We saw mimics imitating her death," Kosar said. "They could have their own end in mind."

"I'm sure they do. They're as unlike us as a shade to a sand rat."

Kosar went to stand, cried out in pain and accepted O'Gan's helping hand.

"I can give you something for the pain," O'Gan said.

"More drugs?"

"Medicine. It'll not heal you, that's for your body to do. But it will dull the aches."

"I've got too many pains to dull," Kosar said.

O'Gan smiled sadly and squeezed the big man's arm. "The

physical pain," he said. "Any other is, I'm afraid, beyond my control."

Kosar nodded. "So," he said, "when your army arrives, how does it travel?"

"We have our ways and means," O'Gan said. Kosar frowned and looked at the ground. *He's heard that phrase before*, the Mystic thought. *Ways and means*.

Kosar grunted. "I only hope we're not too late."

———

ALISHIA RAN THROUGH the halls and corridors and cliffs of books, and for the first time ever they did not make her feel safe. She had grown up around books; her parents' house had been full of them, and when they died it had been a natural progression for her to become a librarian. She found them warm and welcoming, even those she had not read, and touching the spine of a favorite tome inspired memories more intense than smell or sound ever could. With every favorite book, she could remember where she had been and what she had been thinking when she read it. They were old friends, constant companions, and their worlds often became real in her mind.

Now the books were here to trap her. Some of them burned, some did not, but all of them were leading her toward the presence that had invaded this place. However fast she ran, in whichever direction, she seemed to be drawing closer to the terrible thing in here with her, one of *their* things, the Mages. A *part* of them.

The land whispered to her in its own tongue. That gave her comfort and instilled hope, even though the dark thing seemed to be closing in with every heartbeat.

I'm still incomplete, Alishia thought. *There's something else for me to find before I fully understand. And now more than ever, I'm running out of time.* Her legs were beginning to ache from the constant running. She was strong in here, almost tireless, but the younger she grew the slower she ran. And when she regressed even further? What then? Would the future of Noreela be balanced upon the back of a crawling, mewling infant?

She changed direction again, and the darkness still hung before her. She could hear it moving and expanding, and it bore the weight of a dreadful consciousness.

She rounded a corner, tripped over a fallen book and went sprawling. The thing was behind her now, crashing through a stack of books close enough to shake the floor beneath her, and ahead of her the floor had been smashed open. The hole was far too wide to leap. She shoved a book across the timber boards and watched it fall in, swallowed by the utter darkness almost before it tilted from this place into another. She heard its covers flapping like some fledgling bird still unable to fly, but she could see nothing.

Whispers in her mind, confused words in her own voice. *I can't hear!* she thought, and the words came louder. She frowned and closed her eyes, but however much she concentrated, the language made no sense.

Something thumped the ground, hard enough to wind her. She gasped at the smoky air, inhaling deeply when her breath returned, and rolled onto her back. She could see nothing, but she *felt* it, coalescing like a storm cloud threatening to never pass by. *It's almost got me*, she thought, and then the shelving to her left started emptying its books. They fell in regimented lines, some striking the floor around the ragged hole, most of them disappearing into it. They were swallowed and more followed them in, one or two catching fire just as they disappeared. Alishia crawled to the hole and stared in, watching stars of fire plummeting quickly into the abyss.

A book struck her shoulder, another hit the back of her neck, and she retreated from the hole.

And then a line of books struck and held. They hung impossibly over the darkness, stretching from one side of the hole to the other, curved like a stone bridge over a river yet nowhere near strong enough to maintain their shape. More fell and added to the bridge, thickening its ends and supporting its center. It was one book wide, and many volumes were already beginning to smolder.

That won't hold me.

The presence behind her was strong and heavy, its gravity a dreadful pull on her thoughts.

I'll break the bridge and fall into that darkness, and there are things down there . . .

The thing came closer, scouring books from shelves and turning them instantly to soot. Alishia could sense moments in time being wiped out as she waited: no smoldering, no burning, no warning . . . they were simply gone.

She placed a foot on the first book. It gave slightly, as though she were stepping on a thick bed of moss, but when she lifted her other foot, the book bridge held. She walked on, staring down at her bare feet and trying her best to ignore the impenetrable darkness beneath her. *One step at a time*, she thought, moving on, and on. The bridge flexed and swayed. Alishia held her arms out to either side to maintain balance. *The pit's like the ravine. Bottomless. Filled with things we can never know. It's so black . . .* It pulled at her, and for one terrible instant she started to lean sideways, her knee buckling and lowering her toward a fall that would never end. But she bit her tongue, hard, and the explosive pain and taste of blood drew her back.

So close! she thought. The presence chasing her came suddenly closer still, keen to benefit from her confusion.

But then she was across. The timber floor felt so good beneath her feet that she dropped down and kissed it, turning just in time to see the bridge of books tumble away into darkness. A *whole library of sacrifices*. But most of the books had not been burning as they fell. They were gone from this world, but they would still exist somewhere.

She ran, and for the first time she felt the distance between her and the invasive presence growing with every step she took.

Alishia laughed out loud.

———

HOPE HEARD ROCKS grinding together in the darkness. She followed the rough path into the mountains, and the mountains voiced their displeasure. Already she had dodged one fall of rocks, ducking under an overhanging ridge as they fell in a shower of shards and snow. They bounced around her feet like angry rats, rolling away as gravity took hold.

She swapped Alishia from her left shoulder to her right. Light though she was, the girl's deadweight was starting to cripple the old witch. Alishia's clothes were loose on her now, and her shoes had fallen off somewhere back down the mountain. Snow landed on her bare feet and did not melt away. Hope brushed it off, feeling the chill of the girl's flesh. "Don't you die on me now!" Hope cried, daring the grinding rocks to answer back. "Not now! Not when we're so close!"

The crunching of rocks had begun a mile back, just as the path began to twist its way up a steep slope. The snow was settling now, and before long the path itself would be obscured from view. The snow scorched the bare skin of Hope's shins. The route veered left and right, carved into the side of the mountain, and she wondered who had come this way before. She shifted snow to reveal the stone beneath, but there was nothing remarkable there, nothing to be read.

It sounded as though the rocks were talking. When she first heard the noise, basic and threatening, Hope had turned and started back down. The sound ground at her nerves as though she were trapped between the rocks, and the idea that they were communicating was almost too much to bear.

But then Alishia had cried out in her sleep. Just a small cry, but it was enough to see Hope on her way. "I'm here for her, not for you!" she shouted, and the snow fell heavier, and rocks grumbled their mirth as the witch climbed again.

High up on the mountainside, heading for the ridge stretching toward the next peak, the path suddenly ended. Before her, another deep slash in the land stretched as far as she could see from left to right. The opposite side was painfully close. She thought about it for a while, blinking snowflakes from her eyelashes, tensing her muscles to keep them warm, feeling Alishia twitch on her shoulder as something chased her through sleep. But it was just too far to jump. She could try, and perhaps if she had been three decades younger she could have made it. But she knew that she would fall. She and the girl would die far below, their death cries lost amidst the groaning of stones.

The ravine echoed with the noise. Things were moving down there. Hope closed her eyes and willed the sound away, but it only came closer.

Alishia gasped. Hope stepped back. Several large rocks rose into view out of the ravine, leaving stark scratches on its mossy sheer walls. When they reached ground level they halted, and rearranged themselves into a seemingly solid bridge.

"Is this your magic, girl?"

She turned and looked down the way they had come. Even though it was not snowing heavily, her footprints were already eradicated. *Kang Kang is wiping me out*, she thought. *And perhaps luring me in.* She looked back at the bridge and the dark ravine below. "You won't get me like that," she said, and gauged the leap again.

A sound roared in from behind. It was not thunder, or a landslide, nor was it some giant thing screaming in the dusk. Perhaps it was all three. Hope spun around and looked down the mountainside. The landscape was confused by the moonlight and snow, and it could have been her own panicked pulse that caused every shadow to throb with movement.

Alishia gasped again, and then uttered something that could have been a laugh.

The stepping-stone bridge hung over space. Hope tested the first stone with one foot, careful to keep her weight on solid ground. It felt firm. More grumbles behind her, whispers from below, and she pressed harder, expecting the rock to fall away at any second.

"Alishia?" Hope said. "Is this you? Is this what's in you?" She breathed in the girl's stale breath, tried to feel her heat, hoping that something of it would pass to her.

The witch stepped fully onto the first rock and held her breath. Nothing happened, so she moved on, eyeing the far edge of the ravine with every step, ready to leap should she detect any movement in the bridge. When she reached the other side she gasped with relief, and Alishia laughed in her sleep, and the rocks tumbled away. Their impacts reverberated from the ravine's sides for a long time.

The mountains started grumbling again.

"Not happy, eh?" Hope shouted. There was no echo. Perhaps the snow dampened it. Or maybe once the mountains held her voice, they would never let go.

The path started again, and Hope followed.

———

MORE FIRE THAT did not touch her, more burning books and memories erased, more of Noreela scorched away and crushed beneath the feet of the thing chasing her. *It's one of them,* she thought, *one of the Mages, a part of them in here after me. It knows I'm here because the shade saw me. And if it finds me and crushes me, kills me . . . is that it for Noreela? I'm just a little girl . . . am I really all there is?*

Around another corner, across an open space where old leather chairs and a scarred reading desk simmered with the promise of fires to come, and then Alishia was in between book stacks again, running her hands along spines and experiencing a flash of vision from each one because there was more she had to know. The land had told her so much, but not enough. *There was more she had to know!*

The thing behind her roared. It was so near that she could sense the coldness of it bearing down upon her, closing in from all around like a giant hand slowly closing around a small insect. As fast as she could run, this Mage-thing could move faster.

The floor before had given way again, leaving a wide chasm sharp with the teeth of splintered boards. More books already lay across this opening, another bridge to save her, and as she mounted it the bridge gave way and sent her down into the darkness.

Alishia screamed, flailing her arms and legs, and then struck stone. She was lying on the floor of a cave. It was illuminated by the flames of burning books—there were a few here and there, stuffed into hollows in the walls, though this was no library. This was a place below the library, and away from it.

She held her breath.

She could see the opening in the ceiling above her, the hole in the floor that the book bridge had failed to cross. Books and loose sheafs of paper were blown past the opening, driven by a sudden storm, so fast that they almost blurred into one continuous stream.

Something pressed in. She felt the air pressure change, rising as the thing came closer. Blood trickled from her ears and her eyes felt crushed. She started to shake.

It's here, she thought, *above me, right above me, right now.*

The storm continued. And then began to abate.

Nothing entered the cave.

And when total darkness came and faded again, Alishia dared believe that she had been missed.

———

HOPE FELL, AND knew that something was coming. It was a heaviness in the air, the sound of something smacking at the atmosphere and moving on by means of violence. She knew that she should try to hide them away—they were bare and exposed, an obvious blot on the plain white landscape of the path—but she could not move. Terror held her.

She shivered and grabbed the girl to her. Alishia was still asleep.

"No," Hope whined, hugging the girl tighter, appreciating the intimacy of human contact more than she ever had before, in all her years as a child with her loving mother, and the·decades she had spent whoring in Pavisse.

The thing grew closer, and then passed overhead.

Hope had to look.

It was huge. A shadow blotting out the sky as it passed them by, passing north to south, climbing into Kang Kang a hundred steps above the ground. She saw the two shapes upon its back, one upright, the other slumped down. She knew them, because she had seen them before.

Hope's heart stopped. Her life froze, and her mind thundered on.

Do I die now? she thought. *Now that they've found us, will my body give in and leave the girl to their mercy?*

The Mages' machine flew on, higher, dipping neither wing to bank back at her.

Hope's heart kicked in her chest and resumed its frantic beat.

Missed us! She could barely believe it. She cried into Alishia's neck, shuddering, welcoming the gush of warm breath on her cheek as the girl sighed in her sleep.

HOPE PUSHED FURTHER into the mountains of Kang Kang. She knew that her madness insulated her, but there was something else as well. A distance had grown about her and Alishia. It was nothing visible, nothing she could sense, but it was as if they traveled in a bubble of normality that did its best to hold back Kang Kang's influence. Perhaps it had even shielded them from the Mages . . . though Hope had already begun to wonder whether that had been a dream. She heard strange noises, smelled peculiar aromas and here and there she saw things that she could not explain, even in the confines of her madness. But their effects were kept at bay. She moved onward, Kang Kang existed around her but her ever-changing mind was still wholly her own.

"Mad and bad," she muttered, smiling. Someone had called her that years ago, a customer who had tried to leave without paying. Hope had thrown a powder across his back which raised red welts and left him itching for days. *Mad and bad*, he had called her, and she liked it now as much as she had then. *Mad and bad, that's me, and you stay away, Kang Kang, or you'll get a dose of the same.*

Rocks ground together, wind drifted down from the mountaintops like bad breath and Hope walked on.

She was changing shoulders more often, even though Alishia seemed to be growing smaller at an alarming rate. She was a young girl now, maybe the size of an eight- or nine-year-old. Her body had shrunk and changed, her face filled out and her skin was pale. The witch tried to dribble water into her mouth, but Alishia spat it out. She tried to feed her dried herbs from her shoulder bag, but the girl's mouth squeezed tight, rejecting food. Perhaps food would make her grow again. Maybe growing younger like this was a part of what magic had planned for her.

"Fuck fate," Hope said. She shouted it again, hoping for a response from Kang Kang, but nothing came. Only the rocks grinding, and perhaps that was a language in itself. She listened for repetition in the noise, sounds that might signify meaning, but there was nothing. Could she really ever know the language of stones?

Perhaps they'll be there, she thought. *Waiting at the Womb when we find it. Perhaps that's why they passed us by . . . . if I even saw them at all.*

As Hope reached the ridge connecting the first two major mountains of Kang Kang, standing in snow up to her calves and gasping the thin air as she tried to discern details of the landscape before her, Alishia started to speak. Hope could not understand, but she had heard the words before. She knew no meaning, but she remembered her mother and grandmother repeating them, passing them down through the ages even though their relevance had been lost along with magic.

"Just where are you, librarian?" she said. She was suddenly afraid of this young girl. As Alishia regressed into childhood and whatever may come before, so she seemed to be taking on more of magic.

Alishia spoke the language of the land, and they were words that Noreelan air had not heard in their full glory for three hundred years.

————

HOPE FOUND A bush of berries, and even though some of them seemed to possess the features of small faces, still she picked and ate them. They burst in her mouth, releasing a sweet, warm fluid into her throat. *They could be anything,* Hope thought, staring close at a berry the size of her thumbnail. *Poison fruit, chrysalis waiting to open . . . anything.* She nudged one and every other berry on the tree swung in sympathy. She picked more and filled her pockets for later. *Kang Kang just makes them look like that to put me off,* she thought. She popped a few more into her mouth and crunched them between her teeth, feeling for movement that should not be there but finding none. She worked her shoulder to get Alishia into a more comfortable position and started off again.

Hope headed into a valley where darkness seemed to lap at the edges. Moonlight did not find its way down here. She kept the disc-sword at the ready, squinting in the poor light to ensure she did not stray from the path. Even here it was still evident, and when she strayed she found that it was very clear which was path and which was not. Whilst on the path the noises she heard were subdued, the grumbling of Kang Kang talking in its sleep. But when she left the path and felt rough, virgin ground beneath the snow, the grumbling turned into a roar, and an avalanche of rocks came at her from hidden heights. She huddled down to protect Alishia with her own body, but when she looked up again the tumbling rocks had stilled, or vanished. The noise of their displeasure dissipated into the night, and she moved on.

The route fell and rose again, finding the easiest way through the valley, up to the ridge and over into the next valley. The mountains weighed down on either side, but snow was coming in harder now, obscuring whatever the moonlight might betray of their mysterious heights.

Time passed without measure. Hope melted snow in her hands to drink. The water tasted of something she could not quite place. She tried to drip some past Alishia's lips, but the girl's mouth pursed tight. Sometimes she sat on the path and cuddled the girl to her, crying and feeling tears freezing on her cheeks. She shared her warmth but received little in return: a sigh here, a whisper there. Occasionally Alishia would start talking again, those strange words unheard for so long, but their meaning was still inexplicable.

She thought of the Mages perched atop their monstrous machine, heading south, deeper into Kang Kang. *Not them at all,* she tried to convince herself. *They'd have seen us. They'd have killed us.*

Not them at all. An image from Kang Kang? Another one of its tricks? But not them . . .

Perhaps she traveled for a day, or two days, or longer. The mountains grew higher around her and Kang Kang pressed in, threatening her with a thousand deaths that it seemed unable to deliver. "Is this you?" Hope would ask, but the girl never answered. "Is this *you*?" she asked what was inside the girl. But magic, as ever, was silent.

———

SOMETHING CAME AGAINST them from the sky. It began as a heavy drone in the distance, turning quickly into a loud buzzing sound that seemed to confront them from all sides. Hope looked around in a panic, brandishing the disc-sword. The shadows appeared from the east, flitting in across the ground and casting themselves large with light from the death moon. Their wings blurred the air like heat haze. Snow was stirred up behind them, swirling in complex patterns. Alishia mumbled something and a strong wind blew up, originating somewhere far behind and below them and roaring up the valley. The flying things came closer, and Hope could make out their long legs and heavy stings, their wings, their heads dotted with a dozen eyes and trailing hair like an old man's beard. The wind rushed past Hope and Alishia, passing by within a few steps of where they stood without disturbing a hair on their heads. It struck the flying things, swept them into the mountainside, cleared the ground of snow. The buzzing stopped, and the wind died away as quickly as it had come.

Hope saw the broken bodies spilling steam. Some of them twitched, but none of them remained a threat. She turned and left quickly, thinking of magic, asking the question of Alishia yet again and receiving the same silence as response.

She wondered how the Mages had extracted the fledgling magic from Rafe, and briefly considered whether it would work for her.

And eventually she began to despair of ever finding the Womb of the Land. It was on the southern side of Kang Kang, she knew that . . . but how reliable could even that information be? It was a fact she had known forever but which she could not recall hearing or reading. *How* did she know? Was it part of the knowledge passed on from her mother, another witch who had never known magic?

She consulted the Book of Ways several more times, but its pages on Kang Kang remained blank and useless.

Her mind turned inward, obsessed with finding magic for herself and fulfilling her vapid life, and she continued following the path. *We're being protected,* she thought. *We're being led. The Shades of the Land will guide us in.*

Chapter 17

THE REMAINS OF the Shantasi army—those who had listened to O'Gan Pentle's rallying cry rather than fleeing east—now traveled southwest toward the foothills of Kang Kang, and war.

They moved quickly, many of them using their Pace and others riding beasts of the desert after feeding them Pace beetles. They maintained almost complete silence save for the *hushing* of thousands of feet. Here and there came the occasional clink of metals knocking together, but mostly the warriors had packed their armory perfectly, wrapping and tying and strapping it so that no weapon touched another. Those that did make a noise were probably the untrained Shantasi, the two thousand civilians who had remained with the intention of fighting rather than fleeing.

The desert was a sea of dashing shapes and glinting metals. The life moon reflected from thousands of pale faces, and the death moon caught freshly sharpened blades and the tips of arrows and bolts. A desert beast died here and there, ridden to the end of its time by the determined Shantasi, and amongst the great swathe of footprints they left in the sand were the occasional humps of dead creatures. The

Shantasi that dismounted would use their own Pace and run, or perhaps head off at angles from the army and catch fresh beasts.

The smell of Pace beetles seemed to permeate the air around
the army, and Kosar realized that it was the breath of the Shantasi.
He did not recognize the aroma—A'Meer had never smelled like
this—and he could only assume that they had eaten fresh beetles to
provide them with the boost they needed to travel so far.

Kosar rode the same species of desert beast he and the Monk
had ridden in on. Lucien sat behind him, bent low over the creature's back. Kosar was not sure whether or not he was asleep, and he
had no interest in finding out.

Two Shantasi warriors—a man and a woman—held leather
lines tied around the animal's neck shield to guide it onward.

Kosar was as amazed now as he had been five hours ago when
they departed. It had taken an incredibly short time for the army to
amass, and soon the desert between his resting place and the failing
swathes of desert spice was filled with Shantasi, resting after their
run from Hess or helping with the gathering of Pace beetles and
other things. Even then they had been quiet, their subdued talking
amounting to a background murmur that fought the slight breeze
for greater volume.

"These are all warriors?" he had asked.

"Most of them," O'Gan said. "There are many more, but they
went east when the Elders . . ."

"Panicked?"

O'Gan had not replied.

With the Shantasi still coming in from the east, O'Gan Pentle
had stood on a rock on the hillside and issued a rallying call that
had Kosar in tears. Here was a man, he realized, who had been forced
into being a general. A man who, though he was a Mystic and a
seer, had always relied on those above him to make such monumental decisions of life and death as he now faced. The fate of
Noreela was on his shoulders, and it was a heavy weight indeed.

As Kosar had watched him climb onto the rock, he thought, *He
looks so weak. Slow. Beaten already.* But then O'Gan stood, lifted
his head and smiled. And in that one expression Kosar saw no consideration of failure at all.

He had told his people of the threat they knew, and the many
likely dangers they did not. He beseeched them to stand firm and
strong. They were the slave race, he said, and the greatest vow any

Shantasi could make—to the people, or to him- or herself—was to never be a slave again. The Mages were enslaving Noreela and its people. They would imprison their bodies and steal their minds, kill their children and destroy the culture the Shantasi had built up for thousands of years. And in the end, they would wipe their history from New Shanti.

We are the triumph of our ancestors, he said, *and the memory of our descendants. Let us make it a proud memory. One of forbearance and determination, rather than submission and slavery. Today, fight for tomorrow, and make tomorrow thankful.*

The assembled Shantasi had cheered—one long, loud exhalation that echoed from the low hills and seemed to set the dying spice farms swaying on their massive frames. And then they had begun their journey, with O'Gan and senior members of his army planning as they moved.

Kosar was becoming travel weary. He had been on the move for so long that he craved a day and a night in the same place. Though it had been a comparatively short time since the Red Monks had invaded Trengborne and set everything in motion, the period between then and now seemed even longer than those decades he had spent wandering Noreela as a thief. *I've done so much more in the past few days*, he thought. *Lost a lover, lost my friends. Lost so much. What drives me on? Why is this so much to me?* It disturbed him that he could not answer, but he did not dwell on the question lest the true answer distress him even more.

Lucien had not spoken since setting off. He had settled down, resting forward on the creature's back, and a couple of times Kosar wondered whether the Red Monk was dead. But when he turned around he could see the Monk's hands moving, fingers fisting and unfisting as though trying to grasp something from the air as they moved.

We're running toward a battle, Kosar thought. He had A'Meer's sword strapped once again to his side, but what could that do against the Mages and their army? What was a sword against magic? He was terrified. He did not understand what still drove him on, and the idea of dying in the foothills of Kang Kang was terrible to him. *Not there*, he thought. *I don't need to die there.* He needed to save his death for somewhere else.

He had seen the Mages without their dark magic, and they had been terrible. *With* magic? He could hardly bear to imagine.

Several groups of Shantasi parted from the main army and
headed north into the desert. Each group comprised half a dozen
men and women, and they ran as fast as they could out across the
sand. They disappeared quickly into the dusk. Kosar watched them
go, and jumped as a voice spoke up beside him.

"We'll be within sight of Kang Kang soon," O'Gan Pentle said.
"We've been making plans, but it's difficult without knowing where
the Krote army will arrive. We can't dig in. We can't sit and wait. We
have to maintain mobility."

"Take the fight to them," Kosar said.

"And what if they pass us by?"

"I know where they will enter Kang Kang," Lucien said. Kosar
and O'Gan exchanged glances; neither of them wanted to look at
the Monk.

"Where?" O'Gan asked.

"North of the Womb, of course. That's where the witch and the
girl will be going, and that's where the Mages will send their army
to follow."

"I can't trust you," O'Gan said. "You're a Red Monk."

"I'll tell you what I know," Lucien said, lifting his head and sitting up for the first time. "Do with it what you will."

"Let him speak," Kosar said. "His cause is our cause right now,
you know that."

"He killed A'Meer," O'Gan said. That was cruel. He held Kosar's
gaze.

"He killed her when our causes were conflicting," Kosar said.

"You trust the Monk?"

"No, but I trust in his obsession. And he's never told me a lie."

O'Gan steered his creature away for a while, conversing with
several running Shantasi in their clear, clipped language. Then he
moved back alongside their mount. "So tell us," he said, looking
ahead.

"I know only of where the Womb is supposed to be: in the
southern reaches of Kang Kang, but close to this end. North of
there is where the Krote army will try to enter, if they know of the
girl by now, that is. If not—if their cause is still the destruction of
New Shanti—then we're going the wrong way."

Kosar turned and searched for a glimmer of humor in the
Monk's face. He found none.

"We have our scouts," O'Gan said. "We'll know soon enough."

More Shantasi veered away and headed north. "So what are they harvesting?" Kosar asked again.

O'Gan rode ahead and called over his shoulder, "I told you: weapons."

———

LATER, WHEN THE first hills of Kang Kang appeared in the gloom to the south, they paused for a rest. Kosar and Lucien sat beside their ride, watching the Shantasi slumping to the ground, glugging water, chewing on dried meats and panting at the cool air. Some of them steamed. No fires were lit and no camps were set, because they all knew that they would be moving on again soon. A few glanced at Kosar and the Monk, but they looked away quickly. Most of the warriors seemed absorbed in their own thoughts.

So like A'Meer, Kosar thought. He was watching a female warrior, taller than A'Meer had been but possessing the same long hair and sharp features. She checked her weapons while she ate; drew her sword, pricked her finger and resheathed it. She was unaware of Kosar's observation and he felt like an intruder, but there was something about the unconscious grace of her movements that gave him comfort. She was confident and assured, at ease with her weapons and unquestioning of the task they had been set. Kosar looked down at his hands and gave the warrior her brief privacy.

O'Gan came to them, flanked by several Shantasi, who glared at Lucien with barely disguised hatred. *Have they come to kill him?* Kosar thought, and he was surprised at the panic he felt.

O'Gan knelt beside Kosar. "How do you feel?" he asked.

Kosar shrugged, trying not to wince at the pains from across his body. "Fine," he said. "Never better."

"Good. I want you and the Monk to go south with a complement of Shantasi into Kang Kang. We're splitting in two: two thousand will remain here, awaiting the word of scouts and ready to move wherever necessary to ambush the Krotes. The other two thousand will go into the foothills, spread out and hide. If they get through us, they'll have another surprise awaiting them when they enter the mountains."

"How do you know we're at the right place?"

"I don't," O'Gan said. "But the going ahead is tough. A scout returned and said that twenty miles from here, the land has been stripped bare as far as she could see. Down to the bedrock. Not an easy route for whatever machines the Krotes may have."

Kosar nodded. "You're staying here?"

"I will lead the First Army. I assumed you and the Monk would want to accompany the Second. And if he . . ." O'Gan looked at Lucien and started speaking to him. "If you really know the location of the Womb, it would be best for you to be with the Second Army." The Mystic shook his head and looked down at the ground. "Who knows what may happen if they break through to Kang Kang? There are so many factors unknown: we don't know where the girl is, whether she's still alive, whether she and the witch even know where the Womb is. We know so little."

One of his commanders spoke in Shantasi, and O'Gan looked up again. "He's asking whether you can fight."

Kosar nodded. "I've learned a lot."

"Good. Well . . ." He raised one corner of his mouth in a sad smile.

"Thank you for believing me," Kosar said. "It doesn't feel quite so hopeless."

"You're a liar," O'Gan said, but his voice was light. He looked up at the darkened sky, then north toward where the Krotes might soon emerge from the night. "I never thought it would come to this," he said. "The bulk of the Shantasi fleeing. We were always the strong ones. If only we'd stayed together . . . if the Elders had faced their fears . . ." He looked away, shook his head, perhaps embarrassed at saying so much in front of this stranger. Then he looked directly at Kosar, and fear and doubt were obvious in his eyes. "We have absolutely no idea what we're about to face," he said quietly.

"You have your ways and means."

O'Gan nodded. "We do. You're right. And you'll see more of them soon. Good luck, Kosar."

Kosar nodded. O'Gan stood and walked away without looking back, and Kosar sensed that the Monk was about to speak.

"Silence," the thief said. "Can't you hear that silence? It means the land is dying, but for now it's just . . . peaceful."

A few minutes later the order came to rise, and the Shantasi army split in two.

———

SOUTH OF MARETON, Lenora sent scouts ahead of the Krote army. Several flew, several rode their machines hard across the landscape, and she told them to return upon first sighting of any Shantasi.

She was happy to admit her nervousness to Ducianne. The Mol'Steria Desert was to their left, a looming presence that wafted the scent of spice and the feel of great wilderness, and out there might be the Shantasi. Angel had dismissed them as pale-faced freaks, but Lenora knew that they were true fighters, and the most likely to offer any real resistance against the Krotes. But with her nervousness came a sense of keen anticipation. A *real fight,* she thought. *Not just a slaughter. Something worthy of what we've trained for.*

Don't forget me, a voice reminded her. But Lenora shook it off, saying, *Of course I can't forget you.*

In the midst of the Krote army rolled the great constructs that transported the dead from Noreela City. Their bodies had started to stink already, yet still they moved and squirmed, eager to fulfill the unnatural killing desires that had been instilled in them.

After a day's fast travel, the desert smells began to fade, and Kang Kang loomed like a massive hollowness ahead of them. This was when the first and last of the scouts returned. His machine limped on three legs; where the fourth had been was a gaping hole, dribbling foul innards that could have been blood or molten rock. The Krote upon its back was spiky with arrows, and his head was missing a great slab of scalp and flesh, exposing his skull to the cold.

"Shantasi . . . and . . ." he said as Lenora rode to him, and then he died and fell across the machine's back.

Ducianne appeared at Lenora's side. "Must have been a good fight," she said, glaring at the dead Krote.

"He's the only one to return. The flyers would have been here before him if they were coming back. But the Shantasi made an error letting him escape; they've lost their surprise. Whatever ambush they plan, we can be ready."

"They have something that can kill our flyers?" Ducianne asked.

"We can never think of ourselves as unbeatable."

"I do!" Ducianne laughed, then looked at the dead scout again. "So, we ride straight in?"

"No. Hold position here. Three hours, that should be long enough."

"The flyers?"

Lenora called the flyers' captain through the voice box, and they brought their machines down to land in a semicircle before Lenora. There were about thirty flying machines in all, some with wings, others with hollow appendages that gushed flame and gas when they were airborne. They clicked and creaked as their Krote masters awaited Lenora's orders.

"There are Shantasi south of here," she said. "Probably scouting parties, but strong." She waved her hand, dividing her force in half. "You, fly low and fast and take them on. Clear our way through to the main force. You, fly high for Kang Kang. You know your aim once you're there: the witch and the girl. Find them and kill them, and then we can fight the Shantasi at our leisure. But right now, that girl and witch are the priority. I know I'm sending you south on your own . . . and Kang Kang is no place to be. But we will be joining you there soon. Questions?"

A few warriors glanced at the dead Krote and his battered machine, and their own machines jittered like nervous horses. Some exchanged glances. But none of them spoke.

"Good," Lenora said. She watched sternly as her Krotes took off.

"Don't worry," Ducianne said. "Even among Krotes there are the strong, and the weak."

"It's not weak to be scared," Lenora said. An edgy silence had descended across the bulk of the Krote ground force. Some of them looked at the dead man spiked with arrows, while others made it obvious they did not want to see.

"Then what is it?" Ducianne asked.

"Sane."

"Ha!" Ducianne rode to the damaged machine, leaned across and pushed the dead Krote from its back. The machine wandered away, aimless and leaking fluids.

"You think the Shantasi know about the girl?" Ducianne said, talking to Lenora with the dead warrior on the ground between them.

"Of course. No other reason to come this far out of Hess, other than to try to keep us away from Kang Kang."

"Unless they're drawing us away from New Shanti. Or sending an advance force against us. Or trying to keep the fight from their Mystic city."

Lenora shook her head. "If they thought we were coming for them, they'd dig in at Hess. It's the gateway to New Shanti, and it has a hundred miles of desert before it. No. They know what our target is today."

"So now we hold back?" Ducianne's despondency at this idea was palpable.

Lenora watched the flying machines fading into the darkness, one group climbing high, the other disappearing across the scrubland toward the Shantasi waiting in the distance. "I think not," she said. "Let's ride hard and fast now. What do you say?"

"I say I'll get sick of waiting."

The order was given and spread through the ranks, and the machines formed three attack lines. The faster machines—those with longer legs or sleeker bodies—took the outside of the front line, ready to sprint forward and enclose the enemy. The second line consisted of the heavier, slower machines, and behind them came the new transports, groaning with the mass of Noreelan dead. The army moved out with Lenora at the head, brandishing a sword in each hand, proudly displaying the wounds of every one of her three hundred years, whispering to a voice that nobody else could hear.

Sometimes, that voice spoke too loud. *Is this it?* it said. *Is this the life I missed? Killing and blood? Mother, maybe they were right to purge me from your body. Maybe they knew what you would become.*

Lenora shouted to drown out the voice, but nothing could silence her thoughts.

———

O'GAN PENTLE STOOD within a circle of small rocks and, in an effort to calm himself, breathed in Janne pollen from the crumpled bloom in his pocket. He already knew the Krotes were on their way; the lookouts he had sent north had engaged an advance force and returned with the news. It was the manner of the Krotes' destruction that caused O'Gan's nerves to fray.

The lookouts had hardly been touched. They lost one of their number when a Krote machine fell on her, but other than that, their involvement had been merely to ensure the Krotes were all dead. Serpenthals had done the rest.

"Huge!" one of the Shantasi had said when describing them. "The largest I have ever heard of, let alone seen."

They must have come out of the desert, O'Gan thought, feeling the Janne pollen settle his nerves. He opened his mind to visions, but none came. He was not surprised; the plant had been on the verge of death when he picked its bloom. *Followed us, perhaps. Or led the way.* But he had never heard of a serpenthal appearing outside the Mol'Steria Desert, certainly not one of the size his warriors had reported.

"Took the first machine apart," the Shantasi said. "The Krote on its back was sliced in two. And then the rest . . ."

And now O'Gan breathed in stale pollen and prayed to absent visions that the serpenthals would act again. The Krotes they had destroyed were a small advance party, nothing more. There would be hundreds more on their tails. Perhaps thousands. And now surprise had gone.

"One escaped," a warrior had said. "The serpenthals seemed unconcerned. We put arrow after arrow into him, but he rode away upright."

The Krotes knew that the Shantasi were here, waiting for them, in exactly the right place. And O'Gan had little doubt that the full force of their attack would come soon.

He closed his eyes, reached out and pulled the circle of stones closer to him. They were meant to represent the unity of thought—back at the Temple they'd had the Janne plants themselves—but they were not working. "Because I'm the only one." He suddenly felt more alone than ever before.

———

"MYSTIC," A VOICE whispered. "They're coming."

O'Gan opened his eyes and stared into the frightened face of a young warrior. She bowed her head slightly, glancing down at the rocks set around his knees.

"How many?"

"Maybe fifteen, by air."

"High or low?"

"Low. The spartlets?"

"Yes, the spartlets." O'Gan stood quickly, brushed himself down and followed the young Shantasi out onto the plain. He passed dozens of Shantasi, all of them hunkered down on the ground, hiding themselves within its natural folds and creases. Some of them were gathered around piles of dried wood, nursing flame-sticks. The Krotes knew that they were coming up against an army. What O'Gan could only hope is that they did not know what this army had at its disposal.

"Let them make one pass," O'Gan shouted. "Give them confidence. That way they'll come much lower the second time."

"Mystic," the warrior said, looking away. She knew what the first pass would entail, and so did O'Gan. *War is sacrifice*, he thought. One of the Elder Mystics had told him that, before sacrificing himself at the first sign of war.

The warrior cupped her hands to her mouth. "Spartlets!" To their left and right a hundred fires came alight, and soon after the first small flames licked skyward there came a frantic clicking sound, like a thousand sticks being whipped at the air and broken at the same time.

O'Gan drew his sword and knelt. The fires made the darkness before them more complete. He did not see the flying machines until they were almost upon them.

"Not yet!" he shouted. The whistling, crackling sounds continued, louder than before, and more frenzied. *After this first run*, he thought. And the Krotes' attack began.

The Mages' fifteen warriors flew their machines low across the plain. They had already passed over the first few hundred Shantasi before they realized they were there, but then the shooting began. Arrows sleeked down in the dark, fired by the Krotes and ejected from holes and slits in their machines. Many wasted themselves on the ground, but a few found targets, and grunts and screams rose up across the plain. Discs whistled through the air. One machine gushed fire, a long slick that lit up the scene, flames dancing as Shantasi ran with hair and clothing burning. Their screams melted away with their lungs. Another came lower than the rest, trailing a dozen long chains adorned with hooks that bounced from rocks and stuck in soft bodies. Three Shantasi were picked up and carried away, their bodies jarring along the ground and leaving smears of blood. Others jumped out of their way, many using Pace to make sure they were not knocked aside by their own dead or dying friends.

The Shantasi returned fire, launching arrows and bolts skyward at the undersides of the intimidating machines. They had never seen anything like this. They had all read of magic, what it could do and how it aided the land before the Cataclysmic War. And they had all seen dead machines, before and after the Breakers had their time with them. But this was all new. Leathery wings flapped; metallic appendages swiped and cut; stone bodies deflected arrows;

fleshy organs expelled gases as the machines passed overhead and turned for a rapid second approach.

"Spartlets in five heartbeats!" O'Gan shouted. He had turned to watch the Krotes' return, lying flat on the ground with his sword resting before him on a sprig of dead bracken. Almost as soon as he shouted, the spartlets were released.

These were vicious creatures. Having spent decades as chrysalides beneath the sand, the touch of fire would burst their shell and set free the winged serpents within. Newly hatched spartlets were jealous things; any other species they encountered within their own airspace for several hours following birth would be set upon with claws and poisoned fangs. Though only the size of a man's hand, they had the fury of a desert wolf.

When the fire pots were uncovered, several thousand spartlets rushed skyward in screaming, whistling clouds.

The Shantasi hugged the ground and watched. They had never used spartlets on this scale before, and they had no idea what to expect.

The winged serpents spread out, ignoring one another and expanding across the sky. And as the Krote machines powered in a dozen steps above the ground, the spartlets converged on them, attacking machines and riders alike. Arrows vented groundward, and the fire-shitting machine gushed more flames. But in seconds the Krotes became too concerned with their own exposed flesh to think about engaging the Shantasi below.

A machine passed directly above O'Gan, the Krote on its back slashing at the air. O'Gan rose and hacked with his sword, catching a trailing tentacle and parting it from its home. The flapping thing fell to the ground, a spartlet attached and jabbing again and again with its freshly exposed fangs.

"At them!" O'Gan shouted, but the call was not needed. The Shantasi were on their feet, loosing arrows and bolts at the confused shapes. The sustained firepower of almost two thousand weapons gave the Krotes plenty more to worry about.

The fire-shitting machine collided with another, and they impacted heavily into a copse of dead trees. Fire rolled along the ground as the machine ruptured, and its thrashing limbs were blasted across the battlefield as huge, flickering shadows. The survivor from the other machine dashed from the fire and took on several Shantasi, cutting them down with a slideshock and several throwing stars be-

fore more came to their aid. They drove him down with sheer volume of numbers, and O'Gan saw glittering swords dulled as blood
smeared their blades.

Another machine fell farther away, rolling over the ground with
the crumple of folding metal. Its rider was crushed beneath it, but
the machine rose on unsteady legs, thrashing out with blades as
long as five men. Several warriors ducked beneath the blades and
went in close, their own swords at the ready. The machine glowed
blue, light burst from it in a pulse and O'Gan saw the skeletons of
the Shantasi crumple as the strange fire faded again.

He ran toward the machine with other warriors, sword and
other weapons at the ready.

There were a dozen machines still circling above them. Several
still poured hails of arrows or fireballs down at the Shantasi, but
mostly they seemed more concerned with the spartlets attacking in
droves. Another machine fell, its wings tattered, its rider drifting
away and striking the ground a few steps from his mount. Neither
rose again.

"Use poison sacs!" O'Gan shouted as he approached the heavily
bladed construct. It was starting to glow again, a blue umber that cast
strange shadows beneath its low stomach. "Don't get too close! See
if the poison will do it!" He stood back while three Shantasi lobbed
poison sacs in carefully judged arcs. One of them burst on the machine's slashing blades, but the other two struck its body, spraying
across several globes that could have been eyes. It dipped as it tried
to wipe the affected area against the ground. The Shantasi darted in
with blades drawn.

O'Gan readied himself to be wiped out. *Magic did that*, he
thought, running past the scattered bones of the original attackers.
But though the machine still glowed, the pulse did not come.
O'Gan and the warriors hacked at its underbelly, keeping close so
that they stayed within its killing circle, using Pace now and then to
move out of the way of its rolling body. One of them leapt onto its
back and buried a spear to its full depth.

The machine grew still, and they thought they might have won.

But then it went mad. As its end closed in, the machine began
to roll and thrash in a final venting of fury. The Shantasi on its back
was cut in two by a swinging blade, her head and shoulders tumbling to the ground and being kicked toward O'Gan by the machine's thrashing legs.

"Back!" O'Gan shouted, unable to take his eyes from the surprised expression on the dead woman's face. She ran a fruit shop not far from the Temple in Hess. *Not even a trained warrior, and look what she did.* Disgusted, terrified and shocked, still in that moment O'Gan believed that they could win.

They withdrew and left the machine to its death throes.

Where are the serpenthals? O'Gan thought. *Have they left us so soon?*

Across the battlefield, similar engagements were taking place. More machines had fallen, victims of the spartlets, and those still flying were doing so erratically. As O'Gan ran from the dying machine and the decapitated woman, he saw three more enemies tumble to the ground. They cut down Shantasi as they fell, and one machine exploded and cast a hail of deadly shrapnel before its blossom of fire. The Krotes who had survived the spartlets and the crashing of their machines took on Shantasi hand to hand, and several vicious fights were taking place. O'Gan went to join one of them.

Soon there was only one machine still circling, its rider hanging dead amongst its confusion of spidery legs, with spartlets pecking at his face. The machine seemed trapped in an ever-decreasing spiral, drifting lower and lower and casting globules of molten metal in a spray as it came down. A Shantasi screeched as he was caught in one spray, bringing his hands to a face that was no longer there. Another warrior dashed in and pulled him away, holding his hand tightly as he drew his knife across the mortally wounded man's throat.

The machine eventually crashed to the ground and thrashed its limbs for a time, but the Shantasi were content to stay away and let it die.

Fires raged where machines had come apart. Another exploded, a thumping detonation that knocked O'Gan from his feet even though he was several hundred steps away. A cloud of boiling gas was blasted out, searing and scorching everything and everyone in its path. Shantasi lay scattered around the destroyed machine, many dead, many more injured, and O'Gan turned away because he knew that he could not help.

Fifteen machines and their riders, he thought, *and how many have we lost? Two hundred? Three?*

After a while the sounds of combat ceased, and the moans of the dying began.

——————

O'GAN HAD NOT killed for thirty years. Now he stood with Krote blood on his sword. He wiped the blade on a dead Krote's leathers, blood gathering and flowing and catching the moons, and in it he saw the reflected shadows of spartlets still flitting above their heads.

Medics and Mourners moved here and there, helping injured Shantasi where they could, slitting their throats and chanting them down where they could not. O'Gan tried to shut the chanting from his mind.

"To me!" he called, and the Shantasi turned to face him. He climbed atop a dead machine, more than aware of the symbolism of his act as he rested his sword's point on the thing's ruptured back. A stink rose from within, curiously sweet and unpleasant. He breathed deeply and wondered whether all dead magic stank like this.

"This was only an advance force," he shouted. "The spartlets will spread and hopefully disrupt any more attacks from above, but the Krote ground army will be here soon. An hour, or a heartbeat, but they'll be here." He looked north, saw nothing moving in the deeper darkness beyond the burning machines. "We'll form two lines of defense. The first there, behind the largest burning machine. Its fires will blind them until they're on top of you. The second five hundred steps back. Use the dead as shields. The Krotes see a dead warrior, they won't expect a living one to rise behind it. We have more to send against them, and I hope that the land will aid us, and the serpenthals will rise again." He looked around at the faces before him, grim and pale, dirtied and splashed with blood. And he wondered whether they knew what he had already realized: this was suicide. They were gaining time, that was all, precious hours or heartbeats for the witch and the girl.

None of them even knew whether those two were still alive.

"I've led you here," he said, his voice falling on the last word. Most of the warriors probably did not even hear him.

"At least we're fighting!" someone shouted. A sword waved, then another. There were no cheers—they were too tired and frightened for that—but O'Gan looked out at his army, and everyone he could see in this poor light was looking back at him. Not down at the ground, or east, where temporary safety may lie: at him. He nodded and jumped down from the dead machine.

The Shantasi regrouped, arranging themselves in two defensive lines with little discussion. Whichever line they were in, they knew that they would be fighting Krotes again soon. Krotes on foot, or on machines, or maybe those flying monsters again, swooping down through the spartlets and launching arrows or fireballs or stranger weapons yet.

O'Gan went to the forward line, approaching the blazing machine that had exploded with such devastating force. He passed by dozens of Shantasi bodies without looking. He did not wish to see the burns. The warmth grew and it felt good; eased his tensed muscles, tempered his tiredness, and he shrugged so that his cloak sat easier on his shoulders. A hundred steps from the burning machine he paused, looked around and knelt down. To his left he could see warriors fading into the distance, thirty steps between them in any direction, the line ten warriors deep. Their faces were lit by the flaming construct. To his right, the same view. The Shantasi—warriors, and those untrained in battle—staggered their positions, some heading farther forward as though keen to be the first to engage the Mages' army, others hanging back. They all faced the same direction. Their faces were sweaty and grubby, determined, and none of them had sheathed their swords. There was movement here and there where other weapons harvested from the Mol'Steria Desert were prepared, but mostly the Shantasi sat alone. Crossbows were primed, quivers fixed tightly, hair tied back so that it did not get in the way. They checked the equipment strapping across their chests and around their waists, and some took weapons from dead bodies, careful not to look at the corpses' faces. None of them wished to see a dead brother, sister or friend.

They could pass us by, five miles away, O'Gan thought. *They could avoid the fires.* But he did not believe that would happen. His best hope was that they would not be able to resist the flames of battle.

He rested his sword on his knee, turning it this way and that so that it picked up the fire and reflected moonlight.

"Mystic, can you help us?" a woman said. O'Gan glanced to his left at where she lay on the ground, propped on her elbows and staring at him. She had wide eyes, and the pale skin of her face was smeared with blood from a head wound. She was no warrior. She held a single sword, and there was a pile of throwing stars by her left hand.

"I can offer you hope," he said.

She looked down at the dead grass, averting her gaze.

"I can tell you that what we do here is important."

"Suicide is important?"

O'Gan nodded at the burning machine. "We did well against them."

"No we didn't," the woman said, but there was no anger in her voice, and no embarrassment at talking to a Mystic like this. "I can see a hundred dead even from where I lie. When their real army gets here . . ."

O'Gan looked at the shadowy humps scattered around them. "I can't pretend you're wrong," he said, "but I can tell you that there's meaning to all of this. There's hope, and we'll fight for it every second it still exists."

"If it's that important, why did the Elders run? Why didn't they stay and fight? I saw them in the streets. I saw one of them dead by his own hand, and you expect me to believe there's hope?"

O'Gan nodded, holding the woman's gaze. She was strong, he realized, perhaps stronger than he. But equally, she saw no valor in sacrifice for an empty cause. "It's *not* an empty cause," he said quietly.

She glanced away again. "You saw those words in my mind."

"I read them on your face."

"So can you help us, Mystic?"

He hefted his sword. "I have this." He nodded up at the spartlets. "We have those, and more. And perhaps the serpenthals will deign to help again."

"Perhaps."

He fell silent, the woman smiled and they heard thunder from the north.

———

O'GAN'S PLAN HAD been to hide behind the glare of the massive fire. It was a good plan, but it stole sight from the first Shantasi line. They heard the advancing army, but they could not see it. They felt the ground shaking beneath them, but as much as they squinted or shielded their eyes, they could not make out anything. The burning machine turned the dusk beyond the battlefield into midnight.

The noise grew quickly. A rumble in the distance to begin with, like the sound of a storm rolling into Hess across the waters of Sordon Sound. Lightning scratched the sky, arcing from one point on the ground to another. The rumble soon turned into a roar, and the ground thumped to its beat. It grew louder and louder, assaulting the Shantasi's ears, vibrating through their chests, punching at them where they lay or knelt.

O'Gan gripped his sword tightly, eyes closed as he tried to judge distance. *If their machines are small, then they're almost upon us. If they are large, then perhaps they are still a mile away.* He had no way of knowing. The flying machines had surprised them all, and now he feared they would be equally surprised by what came across the land.

"Flyers!" someone shouted in the distance. O'Gan glanced up and saw the illuminated bellies of several more flying things, spartlets darting in, fire glinting from metal, bluish explosions ripping spartlets apart, the huge shapes ducking and weaving and fighting their way groundward.

The roar grew louder still, and O'Gan laid his hand flat against the ground. Small stones spiked at his palm as they vibrated from the massive impacts. He closed his eyes. "They're close," he said.

"They're here!" someone shouted.

O'Gan looked. Just beyond the influence of the firelight, the whole darkened horizon began to shift. More lightning sparkled from shadow to shadow, leaving bluish impressions on his eyes. Metal glinted, stone glowed pale and the Krote army rode in.

Several Shantasi charged the advancing army, firing arrows and flinging stars, whirling slideshocks around their heads and screaming defiance at the dark.

Suicide, O'Gan thought. He looked to the woman at his left. She smiled and stood, and he knew that he would follow.

Chapter 18

THE SHADES OF *the Land will guide us in,* Alishia thought, and at last she was beginning to understand. With understanding came a new level of hope. *But there's so much more to this.* She lay there in the darkness, smelling Noreela burning above her. Sometimes she heard thunder as the Mage crashed through book stacks searching for her, and now and then the ground vibrated beneath her as it came close and went away again.

When smoke and fire started to invade the cave, she knew she had to leave. That made her sad. It felt safe down here, enclosed within the foundations of the land. Perhaps she had been lost for a while. But now the fire and heat of destruction were reaching her again, and she thought about how the flames had affected her in the woodland clearing.

The climb was daunting, but as she began she realized that she had little weight to lift. She found handholds in the stone wall, pushed herself up with her feet, and after a while spent breathing in smoke, her fingers closed around a splintered floorboard. Burning pages floated down around her. One landed on her head, but her hair did not catch on fire and she did not feel the heat.

The Shades of the Land will guide us in, she thought, *but they will each need a sacrifice. Half-Life, Birth, Death* . . . Finding her feet again, she leaned against a wall of books and listened for the thing hunting her. There was a rumble from her left, but she did not think that was caused by the Mage's shade. Perhaps it was becoming more sly, fooling her with silence rather than seeking her through violence.

But she had felt its rage and its fear. She knew that it would not be able to remain silent for long.

———

ALISHIA DWELLED ON what the land had told her, and she wondered how any of this could ever come together. It had opened itself and allowed her to see so much, but in doing so it had displayed weaknesses that she had no wish to comprehend. *A sacrifice,* she thought, wondering what each Shade of the Land would consider a just payment to guide her inside the Womb, and why. And really, she knew, it was out of her hands. She was the delivery to be made. Whoever delivered her had far more on their shoulders than they could ever believe possible.

In the library, smelling past times being scorched from memory, she ran.

Thunder erupted behind her as a tower of books tumbled and she was almost buried, pages fluttering at her face and covers scoring her flesh. She sprawled to the ground and felt splinters enter her hands. The books pressed her down. One fell open before her and she read a few lines, but she did not wish to know.

Alishia clawed her way out from beneath the book pile, hearing and smelling some of the books erupting into flames behind her. She did not turn to see. The thing was closing on her, pushing its way through from the neighboring corridor where it had been hiding. It shattered the shelving, threw books before it, breathed on them and set them on fire. She did not look, could not afford to see. She was just a little girl. If she froze in fear then that would be the end.

Not just for me, she thought. *Not only the end for me.*

Another book fell before her, its pages blank and ready to be filled. And when this one burst into flames, she realized that even the future was quickly being eaten away.

With the land's knowledge now brewing inside her, she had become much more than a librarian of the past. She had become the author of the future.

"I'm just a little girl," she said, her vision blurring. She fell again and rolled onto her back, and she saw the thing closing down upon her, the great, consuming shadow that solidity denied and reality veered away from. The shade of a Mage, fearsome and furious. "I'm just a little girl!" Her tears cleared then, steamed away by fire, and something beat her across the face.

At first she thought it was gushes of flame, and she supposed she would burn here just like every other memory. Her head thrashed from left to right and her skin hurt, but her eyes still saw, unmelted in their sockets. The shade drew closer, a void in everything she could see and conceive. And even as she faded away and woke into the real world, she felt no triumph. She had escaped with knowledge intact. But she knew that the Mages' ability to find her, and their determination to do so, would be stronger than ever before.

———

"WAKE!" HOPE SCREAMED. "Wake, wake, wake!" Each word was punctuated by a slap to Alishia's face.

The girl could barely feel the impacts. She wondered why that was: the witch looked madder than ever, and she was not pulling her punches. Alishia tasted blood in her mouth, and another adult tooth fell out to leave a milk tooth in its place.

"I'm here," Alishia whispered.

The witch was panting, whining, looking around her more than at Alishia. Her hair seemed to be falling out in clumps, and her tattoos were twisted together into two violent ropes, buried into the corners of her mouth and continuing down inside. Hope looked as though she was dying, but she was as strong as ever before.

"Something's coming!" the witch said, bending and grasping Alishia's loose dress collar. "They passed us once before . . . if I didn't dream it. And now they're looking again!"

Alishia touched Hope's wrist, encouraging her to let go. The witch started, held her breath, stood and stepped back.

"Everything's looking for us," Alishia said. "Please help me."

"Where do you go?" Hope asked, grabbing Alishia's hands and hauling her upright.

Alishia swayed on her feet, clenching her bare toes in the

snow. Balance was not an easy thing to find. "Away," she said. "To the beating heart of the land. But I don't think I can be a visitor there again. Next time, if there is a next time, I think I may be trapped there for good."

·"You're talking in riddles!" Hope seemed ready to strike out again, but Alishia glanced at her and the witch shuffled away from her. *What does she see in my eyes?* Alishia wondered.

"Life *is* a riddle," Alishia said. She looked around at the snow-covered hillside, mountains rising before them, the sharp rocks that seemed to recede ahead of them to form a path through chaos. She smiled at Hope, not upset when the witch did not smile back. "We need to go."

Hope's face crumpled. She sank to her knees, shoulders shuddering with dry tears, hands clawing at her thighs through her rough dress. No sound left her mouth, but wind whistled between nearby rocks, giving voice to her wretchedness. "I don't know what to do," she said. "I don't know where we're going, or how to get there. I just don't know . . ."

"I know," Alishia said. She stepped past Hope and walked uphill a dozen steps. To her left a field of razor-sharp rocks scraped at the air, accompanied by an almost subaudible groan that crawled into Alishia's feet and set her flesh crawling. To her right, shadows danced where they should not, turning the falling snow black. Ahead of them, the way looked safe.

"So now *you're* leading *me*?" Hope said.

Alishia frowned as the ambiguity of Hope's purpose flashed across her mind. But she turned to the witch and nodded. "I still need your help, Hope," she said. *Birth Shade, Death Shade, Half-Life Shade, which can she be?* she thought. The witch stood and came to her, loyal yet deceitful, determined but driven by her own madness and need to be the magician she had always wanted to be.

Alishia walked on, troubled and overwhelmed by her new knowledge. She hoped that when the time came for revelation—for sacrifice—whatever she carried inside would offer a guiding hand.

———

TREY FELT A change in the Nax carrying him south. They had passed through fledge seams and caverns, plunged into underground rivers and melted through a lake of ancient ice, emerging unscathed on the other side. All the while the Nax had been there at the edges of his mind, awful and playful, taunting and superior. And then they became silent and serious, and he realized that they were carrying him toward something even more inconceivable.

Where are we going? he thought, hoping that they would answer. *Can I take myself? Will you let me go when we arrive?* He knew that they heard his thoughts—they were in his mind, cool and sharp—but there was no response. They had not spoken to him for what could have been hours, or years.

The fledge around him changed. It was a graded change, but he felt it straightaway. He had become used to being flooded with the drug, abrading his skin on the outside and soothing his muscles and mind inside. But this new fledge was sharp and cruel, pricking at his skin like a thousand sword points and forcing into his mouth as the Nax dragged him through, filling his stomach. He coughed through the drug and could not breathe, but he had not been breathing for some time now. How could he? He was buried underground.

What is this? he thought. Images started to play across his mind. They were too rapid to catch. These visions were not his own, and he could not understand their source: he was not casting his mind because the Nax would not let him. No single image stood out, because of their speed—it was as if they played on the insides of his eyelids as he blinked—but they presented a picture of things unknown, and terrible.

Kang Kang, a voice said, and the Nax had spoken to him again.

Kang Kang! Perhaps Hope and Alishia are here even now? Maybe they're waiting for me . . . though what can I do for them?

Trey did not dwell on what he might have become. The Nax dragged him through the fledge foundations of the world, and he did not breathe, yet he could think and reason like the old Trey. *I am Trey,* he thought. *I can't be anything else.*

The fledge in Kang Kang was different. It flooded into and through him and gave him those countless images from the minds of others. The Nax disliked it, but he did not understand how he could perceive their discomfort. They were not talking in his mind, nor were their nebulous bodies actually touching his. Perhaps their uneasiness was his also.

What have I become? Trey thought once again, and they moved him on.

Sometime later, feeling the weight of the world above him lessening and the kiss of cold air against his fledge-scoured skin, Trey heard the voice of the Nax in his mind one last time.

You are there.

––––––––––

IN THE DISTANCE, Kosar heard the sounds of war. Fires lit the horizon, explosion of blue light boosting the glare, and a steady rumble of destruction rolled across the landscape. It reached the foothills where he waited with the Shantasi army and echoed into Kang Kang.

"They can't last for very long," Lucien Malini said.

"They'll fight hard." Kosar did not like the Red Monk at his side; did not like him speaking words so plain; did not feel comfortable knowing that their causes had converged. But the Monk seemed to have become attached, staying at Kosar's side to protect or be protected. Kosar was hardly surprised; he had seen the way the Shantasi looked at Lucien. *They're right to hate him,* he thought. *And I have a right to hate him also.* He glanced sideways at the Monk, surprised that he felt nothing.

The two thousand Shantasi had reached the foothills of Kang Kang just as the first sounds of battle came in from the north. Their desert creatures were all but exhausted by then, many of them dying from the huge doses of Pace beetles they had been given. The Shantasi continued on foot. Kosar and Lucien's creature had survived, coaxed on by whispers from the Monk and Kosar's force of will. *I can't run,* he had thought, *I can't walk. I can barely crawl.*

They had spread themselves out across the foothills, moving east and west to take up positions. There was no telling exactly where the Krotes would attack. But their advancing army would be seen by the Shantasi scouts hiding on the plains, and they would be warned, and by the time the Krotes reached Kang Kang, the Shantasi would be regrouped and waiting for them.

"What do we have that can fight that?" Kosar asked. A mushroom of flame and smoke rose above the horizon, spreading slowly and pushing the darkness back toward the moons. It glimmered with blue light at its furthest extreme, like controlled lightning. At this distance it was smaller than the fingernail on his thumb, but it must have been huge to be visible from so far away.

"Very little," Lucien said. "Nothing. But the aim never was to win."

"No," Kosar said. "No victory today." He thought of O'Gan Pentle and the two thousand other Shantasi they had left behind, fighting and dying in those flames. Every flash of light he saw brought death, and he wondered which rumbling explosion heralded O'Gan's passing. He liked the Shantasi Mystic, and mourned the fact that it was war that had brought them together. "War," he said, as though amazed that the word could be spoken. The Red Monk did not answer.

And yet Kosar also remembered what O'Gan had said to him, and the harvesting of weapons from the desert. *If you live through this, thief, you'll be able to tell your children you saw the Shantasi at war. It's not something you or they will forget.* Perhaps the Shantasi had more at their disposal than anyone had yet seen. If so, they would have a chance to reveal it soon.

The explosions on the horizon made the darkness here even more extreme. It had begun to snow, adding to their misery, and Kosar's wounds were aching from the cold. Whatever drugs O'Gan had administered were wearing off. Perhaps when their effect had vanished altogether O'Gan would be dead, and Kosar would be receiving more wounds. His hand was stiff where a Monk had slashed it back in the machines' graveyard, his cheek and ribs were sore and the stab wounds in his back felt as though the blades were present there again, parting mending flesh and skin. There was a warmth at the heart of him—the dregs of O'Gan's drugs—but his extremities were cold, and soon they would be colder still.

Snow landed on his hand where it was clasped around the sword's hilt. It did not melt. He brought it to his mouth and breathed out, licking up the resulting water and tasting the filth of his skin. "I don't want to die," he said, and the feeling behind the words surprised him. It was as if someone else had spoken.

Lucien looked at him, scarred face shaded by his raised hood. "Death is not the end," he said.

Kosar snorted. "You can't know that!"

"I've killed enough to know."

"The Black? I'm sure you've never chanted anyone down. You kill and leave wraiths to haunt their place of death. Torture them. That's not the end I want."

"If the Mages win, Noreela will be no place to live for anyone or anything."

Kosar shook his head, not wishing to talk with the Monk about such things. He and A'Meer could have conversed at length, and he would have enjoyed it. It would have made him feel *better*. "Leave me alone," he said. "Don't talk to me."

"I'll protect you as well as I can," Lucien said.

"You? Why?"

"Because I don't believe your part in this is fully played out."

Kosar flipped Lucien's hood back from his face so that he could see his eyes. They were dark and watery, reflecting flames. "Don't you pretend with me," Kosar said. "Not with me. Not after what you've done and who you've killed." He lifted his sword and pressed its tip against the Monk's throat, leaning forward so that his weight rested against the handle. One shove would break skin and send metal into flesh. He closed his eyes and imagined doing just that, but he knew it would not be the end. The Monk was strong.

"You can kill me later," Lucien said.

Kosar opened his eyes. The Monk had not pulled away from the sword, and a drop of blood ran down his throat from where the tip had punctured his skin.

"After this is over, if we're both still alive, you can kill me then. But now I'm needed here as much as you. One sword could be the difference between winning and losing."

"There's no winning!" Kosar hissed.

"I don't mean here," Lucien said. "I mean there." He nodded at the mountains behind them, peaks hidden by the haze of falling snow.

Kosar lowered his sword and sat back, following Lucien's gaze. "They must be in there by now," he said. *I hope Trey is all right, and that Hope hasn't gone mad. I hope Alishia is still alive, and that there's still time.*

"Every second we gain them here could be the instant they change the world," Lucien said.

Kosar climbed the shelf of rock they had been sheltering behind and looked northward. To the east and west he could see Shantasi doing the same thing. Snow muffled the air and aided the semidarkness, but he could still make out their shapes, slung with weapons and glinting here and there when another explosion rose above the horizon, rumbling in many seconds later and making snowflakes dance off the ground.

Everything felt so hopeless.

———

O'GAN PENTLE, along with hundreds of Shantasi, charged the Krote machines attacking by land. Even before the two sides met, the air was filled with flying metals and streaking arcs of fireballs, and here and there jets of some mysterious liquid that melted whatever it touched: metal, rock, flesh and bone. The Shantasi returned fire, using Pace to dart left and right, confusing the Krotes and scoring many hits. Once a Krote was killed, his or her mount became confused, but still remained dangerous. Many Shantasi were run down by rogue machines.

The first line of charging Shantasi met the first wave of Krotes, and the fight turned to chaos.

Shantasi used Pace to dart behind the machines. Some bore bows and slideshocks, others leapt at machines and tried to scramble up their sides, knives clasped between their teeth or swords brandished in one hand. Most of them were shrugged off and trampled beneath metal or stone feet. Others gained the machines' backs, only to be shot down by the Krote riders.

One group of warriors unleashed a storm of flies from fat pouches on their belts. The flies remained close together, buzzing low to the ground until they encountered the staggered stone legs of one fighting machine. They rose, shifting in fluid sheets as the Krote waved his arms about his head. The cloud expanded and the individual creatures seemed to blur, and O'Gan fell flat to the ground and covered his head with his arms as the Shantasi fired several burning arrows into the swarm. There was a soft hiss and then a deafening explosion, and when O'Gan looked up the Krote had been blown to shreds. His machine slumped to the ground, limbs waving, broken legs clawing uselessly at the cauterized ground. Black specks drifted down beside it, dead flies or flesh turned to ash.

O'Gan stood and surveyed the battle. *It's all about time*, he thought. He glanced up and saw another flying machine spinning out of control as spartlets harried at its rider. *We can never defeat them, but we can* hold *them*.

Something burst from the ground to his left, a sound louder

than anything else on the battlefield, its impact harsher. O'Gan
flinched away. A machine bore down on him, a white spidery thing
with a dozen whips lashing at the air and fire belching from vents
along its sides. He raised his sword, ready to parry the first of those
deadly whips, screaming in defiance and certain that every second
he lived on could give magic that extra chance it needed.

The machine was a dozen steps away when it was struck in the
side. It slipped, scoring furrows in the soil with its braced legs, and
the thing that had come up from the ground launched into a frenzied attack.

Serpenthal! It was the largest sand demon O'Gan had ever seen,
easily the height and width of six men, and its many separate parts
worked as one as it attacked the machine. Whips were torn away,
the construct's body was ruptured and it gushed a foul black fluid as
its rider was plucked from its back. The serpenthal crushed the
Krote like an insect and dropped his remains into the mess of his
dying machine.

The Krotes' advance had been slowed. Machines still streaked
for the huge blaze beyond which a thousand Shantasi waited, but
many others were involved in vicious fighting. They cut down warriors with fire and fluid and arrows and discs, and the cries of the dying came from all around.

Another serpenthal appeared from the east and joined in the
fray, setting upon a bulky machine and ignoring the hail of molten
rock pumped at it from the machine's nostrils. Another, and another,
and O'Gan had never heard of so many sand demons being seen at
the same time. It made the battlefield a stranger place than ever.

Several Shantasi ran past him, one of them grimacing as he
tried to pull an arrow from his chest, and set upon a machine. It was
small and rounded, running on stone wheels that flickered with
blue fire. The Krote sitting astride its thin neck turned toward the
charging Shantasi, firing a slew of arrows and bolts that took down
three before the others reached the machine. They attacked, and
O'Gan went to their aid.

He darted left and right as he went, using his Pace in the hope
that the Krote would almost lose sight of him. O'Gan felt the drain
on his strength every time he used Pace, and he knew that this
would be a shorter fight than he had wished for. *But it's a braver suicide than many Mystics chose.*

By the time he reached the machine, the other Shantasi were

dead at its feet. He glanced briefly at the battle raging all around: a
serpenthal in a frenzy a hundred steps away; a Shantasi warrior releasing a toxic pallid wolf against one machine; Krotes slaughtering
anything that crossed their path. A group of Shantasi dead lay to the
north, and in the heat of a blazing machine O'Gan was sure he saw
movement in their limbs, a flicker in their eyes.

And then he faced the machine and its grinning Krote rider,
and he smiled back as he raised his sword.

———

LENORA RODE THROUGH the battle, buffeted by the screams of
the dying and the sound of arrows whipping through the air. The
darkness was lit by burning machines and bodies. The air stank of
fear and blood. An arrow glanced from a knot of scar tissue on her
neck and she laughed, realizing that she felt more at home here
than she had for a very long time.

A Shantasi tried to climb onto her machine, and Lenora let
him think he had succeeded before turning around and burying
her sword in his shoulder. "Meet my machine," she said, and a
dozen mouths opened in the side of her construct, biting into the
dying Shantasi as he slid from its back.

Two eyes on the side of her machine stared up at her, pleading,
blinking, and she turned away. *Haunt me, will you, boy?* she thought.
Well, no need. I'm already haunted.

Ducianne rode alongside, grinning from ear to ear. "This is the
life, eh, Lenora? This is the life we've always meant to live!"

"This is only their advance," Lenora shouted. "The rest will be
hiding past that fire to the south."

"Shall we send the dead against them?"

Lenora looked back at the huge machines bringing up the rear,
their cages alive with thousands of dead Noreelans. "Not yet," she
said. "There'll be much more than this."

"Do you think so? Do you think the Shantasi have more to
throw at us?"

Lenora glanced left at where a huge shadow fought with a machine. The two seemed evenly matched. It was a dark, twisting
thing that seemed to part and merge again with every movement.
She turned to Ducianne and shrugged. "Whether they do or not,
we're adding to our army all the time."

The shade was with them somewhere, flowing back and forth

across the corpse-strewn battlefield. Lenora had already seen several dead stand and begin walking south.

"This is the life!" Ducianne shouted again, riding toward a small group of Shantasi.

Lenora drove south, keen to take the fight onward. She passed by several dead Krotes and many dead Shantasi, and it was already apparent who was winning this battle. It had started a few hundred heartbeats ago, and the end was in sight.

I see through you, her daughter's shade whispered. *I feel through you, and I hate what I feel.*

"You don't know *how* to feel," Lenora said, but she regretted her words as soon as they were out.

You teach me everything you know.

"I feel."

For the dead? For the dying?

"Enemy dead, enemy dying!" Lenora launched a hail of blades from her machine, cutting down two Shantasi and the big yellow wolf strung between them. The creature's blood boiled in the air and sizzled as it struck the ground.

I want my mother, the shade said.

"I am your mother."

You're so different from the mother you could have been . . . Its voice faded, though no distance grew. Lenora felt it sitting in her mind, watching, feeling, and her scream could have been rage, or anguish.

———

THE BATTLE ENDED quickly. The Shantasi First Army had been determined and vicious, and the Krote machines cut down dozens at a time. Near the end many Krotes dismounted and took on the remaining warriors themselves, enjoying the chance for true swordplay. Fights went on for some time, the Shantasi already filled with the knowledge that they were the final few left alive. Lenora respected their tenacity; none of them dropped their swords and submitted to their fate. They all fought hard and died hard, and one or two even defeated one Krote opponent before being taken down by the next.

By the time the last Shantasi was killed, the transport machines were harvesting the first of the new living dead and dropping them into their cages.

Lenora ordered a brief halt, wanting to take stock of the fight and see how badly her force had been damaged. Ducianne rode back and forth gathering reports, and Lenora slipped from her machine and knelt on the ground, eyes closed.

"Leave me alone," she said to her daughter's shade. "For a while, please leave me alone. There's work to do here, and then I'll come for you." But the shade only retreated to brood silently deep within her mind.

"Mistress, we've lost thirty machines and fifty warriors. And all the flyers are gone."

Lenora looked up to her friend. Ducianne was frowning through a crust of drying blood. She knew that something was wrong. "That's not too bad," Lenora said. "Gather everyone here. We push for Kang Kang in an hour."

"Are you hurting, Lenora?"

Strange way to ask, Lenora thought. *Hurting, not hurt.* She stood and shook her head, sheathing her sword and stretching. Her old joints clicked, several new wounds cooling as blood clotted them shut. "I'm old, Ducianne, you forget that. I'm not a youngster like you."

Ducianne nodded and rode away. Lenora knew that her friend was not comfortable with Lenora's unnatural age, how it could be or who had allowed it.

Lenora stretched again and turned to her machine. It watched her, and was that condemnation she saw in those blank eyes, or merely the reflection of her own? "Your night is far from over," she said. She turned south and walked a few hundred steps in that direction, leaving the hustle of the Krotes behind and facing the true darkness of Kang Kang. *That's no place to be,* she thought, and a shimmer of fear passed through her. She was surprised, and pleased. Fear showed that she was truly ready to face whatever they found once they entered that range of mountains. *No place at all.*

Chapter 19

HOPE FOLLOWED ALISHIA, following the path. Sometimes the girl tired and Hope carried her, slung across both arms or resting over a shoulder. Other times the girl seemed to be the strong one, forging barefoot through the thickening snow, climbing ever higher. The path guided them, and Alishia seemed happy to allow that. Whatever she had seen—wherever she had been—Hope had no choice but to let the girl's trust carry them forward.

Many things in Kang Kang were strange, but the path wended its way between them. It was almost as though the path was outside Kang Kang, a tributary of normality carrying them through this place that should not be. They heard, saw and smelled things that defied explanation—the cries of children where there were none, great trees rooted in nothing, fruit stinking of blood hanging on those same trees' branches—but the path was always there, true and straight. Even covered with snow it was still the obvious route.

Hope had to tear and tie up Alishia's dress when it started to tangle in her feet. Her top as well, twisted tighter beneath the coat that could not be so easily adjusted. She became chubby around her stomach and cheeks, even though Hope had not seen her eat anything for some time. Her voice changed, but not the words. Alishia still spoke like an adult, and sometimes she repeated the things Hope had heard her muttering whilst asleep, the language of the land that she pretended not to understand.

She knows so much, Hope thought. *I'm due what she knows. It's coming to me, as I've always known it should.* She stared at the back of Alishia's head as they walked higher into the mountains. Occasionally the girl turned and smiled at the witch, and Hope always smiled back. She could feel the tattoos flexing beneath her skin, the coolness of Kang Kang seeping up through her shoes and into her bones, the windchill penetrating her clothing in an attempt to freeze her old woman's heart. But it had been frozen long before now, and her obsession kept her warm.

They walked across the sides of mountains, along ridges, down into valleys that held reservoirs of darkness and unknown things. Hope heard sounds from the darkness at either side of the path, growls, something chomping on something else, mournful tears. She ignored them, as did Alishia. That was Kang Kang trying to distract them from where they were going.

Then why is it also leading us? Hope kicked at the snow covering the path, finding only pebbles and stones underneath that told her nothing. Alishia paused ahead, turned around and waited, urging Hope on with a quick wave of her small hand.

"Not far," the girl said.

Hope's breath froze in her chest. "We're almost there?"

"Not far," Alishia said again. She frowned and looked at her bare feet, her large coat flapping at her shoulders as wind blew down from heights they still could not see.

"Lead on," the witch said. Alishia nodded and started walking again. She tilted her head to the side now and then, and at first Hope thought she was trying to prevent the ice-cold breeze from entering her ear. But then the girl paused at the summit of a long ridge, tilted her head and stared skyward.

"Not far at all," she said.

Hope did not want to disturb her. Whatever she was following, whatever led her, Alishia seemed to trust.

WALKING ALONG ONE ridge, Hope heard something high in the sky. It started as a whistling, thumping sound, like flying things slapping at the air with heavy wings. More buzzing things? She thought not. She searched for the source of the noise but saw nothing. It seemed to come from far away, but it was growing closer. *Got to hide!* she thought. *Got to* protect.

And then certainty struck her like a tumbler. "Alishia! It's them . . . !"

Alishia paused and tilted her head. She closed her eyes. When she opened them again, she smiled.

The noise changed. Screeches underscored the thumping of wings, and then cries, and the sounds of impacts that echoed from Kang Kang's solidity. They were still far away, but Hope sensed the change from controlled to alarmed. A splash of blue flame lit the sky briefly several miles to the southwest, spilling across the dusk like liquid fire, and for a heartbeat Hope saw many dark specks silhouetted against it. Chasing these specks were shadows that seemed even darker.

She felt the vibration of something striking the ground. More screams, more impacts, and a hundred heartbeats later the sounds faded across the hills. Hope blinked and exhaled her held breath, and it was as though nothing had even happened.

Alishia had already started walking again. Hope hurried to catch up. Whatever had flown flew no more. *Hawks?* she thought. *Machines?*

———

WHEN THE PATH began to fade away, Alishia feared that they were finished. Perhaps it had always been just another trick of Kang Kang, to lead them this far into the heart of the mountains and then leave them at the mercy of whatever might dwell here. She walked on anyway, determined to retain her confidence before the witch. Something rumbled higher up the mountainside, like a giant stomach contemplating food.

The snow began to clear.

A voice spoke in her mind, muttering words she did not know, and she gave those words to the air. The witch was glaring at her— she could feel her mad gaze simmering the air behind her—but Alishia carried on. Speaking the words was different from having them spoken to her, and Alishia hoped that soon she would understand.

She crested a ridge, looked down into a valley and knew exactly where those words came from.

"We're here," she whispered. She heard running footsteps behind her and the witch was at her side, kneeling in the thinning snow and looking down into the valley before them.

"Too soon," Hope said. "Not where it should be!"

"Perhaps it moved . . ." A voice spoke once more in Alishia's head, and this time she understood. "We can go down," she said. "They'll allow that, at least. But at the mouth of the Womb we have to stop and wait."

Hope could barely talk. "Wait . . . for what?"

"The offerings."

The witch was shaking her head, denying what she was seeing. But Alishia looked with a child's eyes, and she could believe.

———

THE VALLEY WAS bare of snow, green, lush with vibrant grasses and shrubs, spiked here and there with clumps of trees that grew two hundred steps high, their trunks forty steps around at the base.

"I can see," Hope muttered. "And they're not here."

A breeze blew across the valley and rustled its grasses, sending a wave from one side to the other. At its base a stream flowed, heading south and disappearing into the darkness of a ravine at the far end. The stream's source lay on the valley slope below them. A hole in the ground, hooded with a slab of rock and centered in a wide splash of bright blue flowers. Alishia had never seen those flowers, but she had read of the mythical birth-blooms that midwives had once carried as a sign of their profession.

"I can see," the witch said again. "It's done. It's happened; we've won!" She grabbed up a fistful of wet soil, pressing her fingers together until it seeped from her hands, muttering under her breath and frowning when nothing happened.

"Are you so hungry for magic?" Alishia said.

"Yes!" The witch stood and thumped the disc-sword on the ground.

"Nothing is won," Alishia said. "If only it could be so easy. So fair. But I don't think anything will be easy or fair ever again."

"But it's *daylight* down there! I can see the colors of grass and flowers, and the trees, and the stream flowing into the distance . . ."

"And behind us?"

Hope glanced back into the darkness they had traveled through. The truth dawned. "It's not really daylight."

"Not really. Something from the Womb, perhaps. Or the Shades of the Land."

Hope looked dejected, and angry. "And where are they, these Shades? Are they who you speak to when you slink off?"

Alishia shrugged and looked away, disturbed by Hope's antagonism. "*Something* whispers to me," she said. *From the library*, she thought, but she did not want to say that aloud. It was a special place, and she did not wish it tainted. "As for the Shades . . . I think we'll see them soon."

Alishia stepped from darkness into light, but it was not as comforting as she had hoped. There was no sun heating her skin, no blue sky above. This was not daylight, but simply an absence of night. The light rose from the grasses and flowers, the trees and ragged shrubs, simmering in the air and presenting the same blank sky as the twilight that had fallen across Noreela days ago. The sense of it silenced Alishia, and even Hope fell quiet as they walked down the steep slope toward the Womb of the Land.

When they arrived, Alishia sat down amongst the birth-blooms. They smelled gorgeous. She closed her eyes to rest.

When she opened them again the Shades of the Land made themselves known at last.

———

ALISHIA SEEMED TO die. One moment she was there before Hope, sitting down in the long grass and flowers and sighing as she took the weight off her legs. Then she fell back to the ground with a grunt.

Hope dashed to her side, cradled the girl in her arms, shook her, breathing stale breath into her mouth in the hope that it would bring her back.

But the girl was still and limp, and when Hope pressed her head to Alishia's chest she heard nothing inside.

———

SHE WAS BACK in that vast, endless library, but so much had changed. It was a silent place this time, with no tumbling book stacks or rampaging shades to steal away the peace. And all the flames had gone, because all the books were burned.

Alishia walked between two cliffs of shelving. She looked up, unable to see the top because of the gently drifting haze of smoke high above. Where the shelves had once been stacked with books, there was now only ash. A few pages remained here and there—the dregs of memories to yellow, crumble and finally fade away—but this place was no longer a library at all.

Alishia released one single sob and walked on.

She turned left and right, following the corridor between stacks and never once finding a whole book. Her feet kicked through drifts of ash. Some of them came up to her knees, and she wondered at the countless forgotten things around her. She could never know them, because ash cannot be read.

She realized that she was crying. A few tears dropped to the floor and darkened, sinking down and forming small pits in the ashen surface. She moved on, wiping her face because she did not wish to leave anything of herself behind.

She reached a reading area, with leather chairs and a low table piled with burnt books. She was not surprised to see a young man sitting in one of the chairs. She thought she recognized him. Someone from Noreela City, perhaps? A visitor to her library, someone she had regularly passed in the street? He smiled at her. Everything about him was familiar, yet just out of reach.

"We thought it would be easier for you if we presented ourselves like this," the man said, and she almost knew his voice. "Please, take a seat."

Alishia sat down, perfectly at ease. The man was quite young—perhaps the age she had been when this began—and his clothing was unremarkable. There was a constant smile on his face, but she noticed that it seemed not to touch his eyes. They were dark, and deep. She felt as though she could lose herself in there. They reminded her of that place beneath the library floor.

"I'm frightened," she said, no longer at ease.

"Don't be. We're not here to hurt you."

Alishia looked around, expecting to see more people stepping from the charred shadows.

"We're all here," the man said, touching his chest.

"You're the Shades of the Land," Alishia said, and the man nodded. "The Birth Shade," she continued, "and the Death Shade, and the Half-Life Shade."

Again, the man nodded. "You're a wise young girl."

"I'm not as young as I appear."

"Obviously. Strange. But we accept that, because it is." He stood and walked around the reading area, kicking casually at a pile of ash. "Human history has turned to smoke," he said, "and there's no future to be written. Not here. Not as things stand."

"I'm here to change that," Alishia said. "The Mages can't win. There was a boy, and they took him, and now there's me, and I have something of what he had . . . but not the exact same thing. I think I have a seed for something new. Something fresh."

The man still walked, looking down at his feet. Dust rose around him as he kicked through the ash. If he kept kicking perhaps he would obscure himself completely.

"We guard the Womb," he said. "We tend it. We are the soul of the land."

"You have to let me in."

"*Have* to?" The man looked up. That smile, so beatific yet still not touching his eyes.

Alishia fought hard not to avert her gaze. "I'm important," she said.

The man nodded. "Your sort are always so filled with self-importance. Always so *sure* that you're the only things of worth. Noreela is so much more than the humans who live upon it, you know."

"Like the tumblers? Nax? Evil things."

"*Different* things." The man sat down before Alishia once more. "There are spirits of the air; a whole world folded beneath the surface of Sordon Sound; a great, mad mind south of Kang Kang; people living much deeper than any fledge mine, so deep that they have no concept of the surface. There's *so much* I could show you and tell you, if only you could take it all in."

"I can!"

He shook his head. "You're still too human."

"But it's the whole of Noreela under threat from the Mages! You've guided and protected me this far . . . haven't you?"

The man inclined his head but did not reply.

"Why bring me this far and then—"

"Surely the witch brought you?"

"She brought me, and sometimes I brought her. But I think she's taken with her lust for magic."

The man touched his chin and stroked it, as though unused to having skin. "You've been through this place," he said, indicating the silent, dead library around them. "You've read the language of the land, and you read it well. You're intelligent. You know what we need."

"Sacrifice."

The man laughed out loud, shaking his head. His eyes were still dark. "Offerings, Alishia. Or keys. You have been helped, now help us. *Not* a sacrifice. We're Shades, not gods. You see so much black and white, with no shades in between. There is no true darkness or light."

"The Mages. There's nothing other than evil in them."

"They're human. They were normal people, once. One was a Shantasi Mystic; the other became his lover."

"Why are you doing this?" Alishia asked. She felt tears threatening, and she bit her lip to hold them back. She had no wish to show weakness before this . . . *soul. I'm talking to the land itself, and I'm speaking its language, and I'm too proud to cry for Noreela.*

"Because things are so different. The Womb has birthed many times before, but it has never been seeded from outside. We have never let anything *in.* Yet events roll, and new things happen, and new magic will arise from this. An *evolved* magic. And we are responsible. We're the soul of the land, after all."

"But why the offerings? Why can't you just help me?" The first tear slipped from Alishia's left eye.

The man watched the tear trace a path through the grime on Alishia's cheek. She felt his gaze upon her, touching her skin, and the pressure of his presence was too great to bear. She started to shake, and he backed away, merging into the shadows between two blackened book stacks. He became little more than a shadow himself.

"Because of that tear," he said. "Because humans suffer. And in suffering, you may at last find your soul."

And then he was gone, and Alishia was left alone in her void of burnt memories.

HOPE SAT BENEATH the false daylight and held the dead girl on her lap. The valley containing the Womb of the Land was silent compared to the rest of Kang Kang. Gone were the grinding of rocks, the hushing of shadows rubbing together, the breath of the wind and the calls or cries of things killing or being killed. An occasional breeze stirred the long grass and sent waves across the slopes, but it was virtually silent. Even the shifting grass chose not to whisper. The only definable sound in this strange valley was the sobbing of an old woman.

If she truly had seen the Mages passing them by back there in Kang Kang, then they had not yet found this place. She didn't know whether that was even important anymore.

She had been to see the entrance to the Womb of the Land. It was unremarkable; a cave, a small stream running from it. She had carried Alishia in her arms, and even thirty steps away she knew that she would not be able to enter. The shadows in there were too solid. She threw a stone and it disappeared inside, but she heard no echoes. She dipped her toes in the stream. But she would not drink of that water.

So she had moved away again, sat back down, and now she waited for what would happen next.

Alishia moved. Hope held her breath, grasped the girl tighter and looked down. The girl's face was still slack and pale, mouth hanging slightly open, but one of her eyelids had raised to reveal the dark half-moon of her pupil. Her eye turned, centered on Hope. Her lips twitched. Another adult tooth fell from her mouth, and a single tear left her eye. It ran a clear path down the girl's dirty cheek.

"You're alive!" the witch said. She hugged the girl to her, breathing in Alishia's breath and looking around to see if the world looked any different. *But we're here!* she thought. *We're at the Womb of the Land. Surely everything will change now? Surely the magic will come back and everything will be better?* But the very idea of that felt impossible. How could anything really be better, ever again? The witch felt the power of the girl in her arms, radiating out in waves now that she had returned, but Hope herself was still a false witch without charms or tricks. She was the last of her line, destined to die cold and alone. Even if Alishia fulfilled whatever vague destiny she had discovered, Hope would be no part of it.

She remembered rising from the pit of the dead Sleeping God and lashing out at Trey. A moment of violence, a flash of red in her

mind, and since then she had cast it deep, not wishing to dwell on
the fate of the fledge miner. Out of every bad thing she had done in
her life, that act had damned her forever.

"Do what you came here to do!" Hope said. Even though her
voice was low, still it sounded loud in this narrow valley. "Do it!
We're here, we're at the Womb, it's over there behind us and I can
see the darkness inside."

"We wait," Alishia whispered. "We can't get inside until . . ."

"Until what?"

"I'll know when." Alishia tried to sit up in Hope's arms but the
witch held her tight.

"It's right there!" Hope said. But she looked into the cave mouth
thirty steps away, and its darkness suddenly seemed more solid than
any of the rocks surrounding it.

"Be content with waiting and they'll let us," Alishia said.

"The Shades of the Land?"

"Yes, them."

Hope helped Alishia sit up in her lap, and for a while she knew
what it would have been like to have a child of her own.

———

HOPE SPOKE LITTLE, and for that Alishia was glad. The girl was
weak and frightened, her bones ached, her muscles knotted and
cramped and her scalp itched as her adult's hair turned into the
hair of a child. *I'm getting smaller and smaller*, she thought, and for
the first time she truly contemplated the eventual end of the
process. Would it hurt? She hoped not. But the parting words of the
Shades stayed with her. *And in suffering, you may at last find your
soul.*

They remained there for some time, waiting for something to
happen. Hope found the berries in her pocket and they ate them.
They were sweet and sickly, but they both relaxed when the fruit
seemed to fill their bellies and take away the cramps.

Alishia drifted in and out of a sleep so deep that it bordered on
unconsciousness. She expected to find herself in that giant, dead library again every time she closed her eyes, but she did not return.
When she awoke she could not recall any dreams.

As her mind drifted to Trey and what might have become of
him, she heard the sound of something approaching the valley
ridge.

"What *is* that?" Hope said.

It sounded like many feet hitting the ground at the same time, impacts gentle, their progress rapid. It began as a scratching in the distance, and within a few heartbeats it was right above them, threatening to force its way from the darkness surrounding the valley and birth whatever made the noise into the light.

The witch stood and brandished the disc-sword, but Alishia knew that it would have no effect against whatever was to come.

"It could be the Mages," she said. "Or it could be something come to save us all."

On the valley ridge above them, a shadow emerged from the surrounding dusk of Kang Kang.

────────

THEY'RE COMING. The words were whispered along the line from the east, and Kosar heard them and passed them west. *They're coming.*

The sounds of the battle in the north had ended an hour before, replaced by the dull, solitary whistle of wind finding channels between rocks. Snow danced across the foothills of Kang Kang, whipping into spirals here and there when the breeze became trapped. Some of these flitting figures seemed possessed of a strange purpose, and Kosar wondered exactly what he was seeing. Snow wraiths? Or wraiths in the air revealed by the snow? None of them came close to him, and they all faded away after a few heartbeats.

"I can't see anything in this snow," Lucien said.

"We'll see them, I'm sure. They won't be sneaking this way. They'll be *charging*." Kosar placed his hand flat against the ground. "Can you feel that?"

"What?"

"The ground is shaking."

"Noreela is afraid," Lucien said, and for some reason the comment gave Kosar a boost of confidence. *If the land itself is afraid, perhaps it will do something to help.*

A few moments passed and Kosar stared north, down the hillside and across the plains that ended at the fiery horizon. There was still no movement, and he began to wonder what the Mages' dark magic could do. Would it make the advancing Krote army invisible? Were they even now crawling carefully up the slopes before them, reaching out, probing with swords until they held every Shantasi warrior a slice from death?

The ground shook some more, and now there was a rumble to accompany it.

"That came from behind!" Lucien said.

"No!" Kosar turned, hefting his sword as though expecting to find a Krote standing behind him. Shantasi all across the hillsides were doing the same, breaking cover and finding new shelter that protected them against an attack from uphill instead of downhill. "This can't be them!" Kosar said.

"Then what—" Lucien's words were swallowed by the thunder of what came over the hilltop above them.

Tumblers. Dozens of them, maybe a hundred, pouring over the crest of the hill and bouncing down toward the remnants of the Shantasi army. Some of them were larger than any Kosar had ever seen, the height of three men, and they trailed spiked whips and barbed limbs behind them, slapping at the ground to adjust their downward path.

Scores of Shantasi shouted and turned to run down the hillside. Many more stood their ground and prepared to fight. Kosar knew that both courses of action would be hopeless.

"They've got the tumblers fighting for them," he said. This was the end. These things would snap up hundreds of Shantasi, then they would turn and come back up, then down again, crushing the warriors onto the hides and piercing their bodies with hooks and spikes. They would join the dozens of other corpses already carried by these ancient things, and their steady decay would match that of Noreela.

The lead tumbler reached the first of the Shantasi . . . and passed them by. Others followed, some of them bouncing over the shapes crouched on the hillsides, others swerving to avoid warriors standing ready to fight.

"Maybe they're running from something," Lucien said. "Something happening in Kang Kang."

Hope, Alishia and Trey, Kosar thought, but then another idea hit him. "More Shantasi weapons!" he said.

Lucien shook his head. "No one controls the tumblers. Not even the Shantasi, with their weird ways. Even in a time of magic the tumblers were always their own."

"You're an expert?" Kosar said. "Don't tell me . . . you read about them at the Monastery." He crouched down as a tumbler came close, thundering past faster than any horse could run. He caught a whiff of old rot and aged bones, and then it was away, leaving a pitted trail in the sprinkling of snow where its hooks and spikes had dug in. His heart thumped in his chest. He actually felt thrilled. "What are they doing?" he shouted at Lucien, raising his voice above the cacophony of the tumblers' charge.

Lucien raised his head above the rock. "We'll see," he shouted back. "They're heading north!"

The last of the tumblers passed by and continued down the slope, dodging Shantasi and plowing furrows in the damp ground. The bones crushed into their strange hides flashed yellow and white in the moonlight. They rumbled north across the plain, and minutes later Kosar saw the first blossoming explosion of a Krote machine meeting its end.

"In the name of the Black, they're helping us!" Kosar said. Shouts rose up from the Shantasi scattered across the hillsides, cheers and calls, and metal gleamed as swords and slideshocks were waved in celebration.

"They'll still get through," Lucien said. "The Krotes will sweep the tumblers aside, and they'll get through."

"But every second counts," Kosar said, and he laughed. Actually laughed. And it felt so good, he did it some more.

———

LENORA LED THE charge, riding her machine hard toward the first low hills of Kang Kang. She expected the second Shantasi attack to come at any moment. If they had any sense of war at all— and she knew that the Shantasi had found cause to fight many times through their history—they would have a second line of defense between here and Kang Kang, probably upon those first low slopes. They would have had longer to dig in and prepare defenses, and they would have seen the signs of their First Army's destruction. Anger and fear gave a soldier more power. Hate drove him or her harder. This coming fight would be more vicious, but Lenora was not afraid of that.

She *was* afraid of failing to fulfill the task given her by the Mages. And the more it spoke, the more she was afraid of that voice. It was telling her truths she did not wish to hear. The more it spoke, the more she felt her determination bleeding away. *Is this the life I've missed?* it said. *Is this all you have become?*

But I've become powerful, Lenora thought.

You'll become nothing.

And Lenora remembered Angel's vision of the lake of blood, with nothing left of Noreela.

She was suffering. To drown the discomfort, she sought the pain of others.

Her machine ran, untiring and eager to do her bidding. She thought, *Left*, and the thing veered to the left, dodging a small hillock with an ancient ruin scarring its summit. *Right*, she thought, and the machine curved right, leaping a dry streambed and landing so gently that Lenora barely felt it touch the ground. *It's like a part of me*, she thought. But the shade of her daughter, that was the part of her missing, the part she should be pursuing. *I don't want you*, she thought. And *I'll come to find you soon . . . Leave me alone . . . Stay with me.* Her thoughts were as chaotic as war, as random as an arrow striking her or missing altogether. Peace was something she feared she would never find, even when all the fighting was done.

And then she saw movement to the south.

Ducianne rode alongside her across a wide, flat expanse of dried marsh. "What in the Black is that?" she shouted.

Lenora knew. She had seen some once before in Robenna, years before she became pregnant. One of them had taken a child from the village. Even then, she knew that they were too different to ever understand.

"Tumblers," she said.

"So let's take them!"

"Ducianne!" Lenora shouted, but Ducianne goaded her machine on, riding directly at the advancing wall of tumblers that streaked toward them. They jumped here, rolled there, twisting and turning their routes to confuse the Krotes. But the Krotes' blood was up. All of them were tainted by battle, some of them bearing wounds, a few carrying the stumps of arrows buried in arms or shoulders. It would take a lot to panic them now.

"Ducianne!" Lenora shouted. "Attack together. Not on your own!"

Ducianne turned on her machine and grinned, pulling back slightly so that she fell back in line with Lenora. Other machines rode up beside them, forming a long, snaking line that advanced quickly southward.

"Don't be so keen," Lenora called.

"Well, I—" Ducianne shouted, and the first of the tumblers struck the front of her machine.

The joint impact was tremendous. The tumbler was crushed flat and shattered, lifting high over the front of Ducianne's mount and sweeping her from its back. Lenora glanced around in time to see her friend ripped apart, torso and head spilling in different directions amidst a rain of old bones, torn vegetation and new blood. The machine was split as well, its ruptured parts rolling onward in pursuit of Lenora, finally exploding in a geyser of blue flame as the magic that held it together failed and faded. Lances of cobalt light probed out, sparking here and there where they impacted the ground, and a ball of fire burst from the machine's dying heart.

Lenora faced forward again, and sadness at the loss of her friend was cut short by what she saw: a field of tumblers coming at her, stretching left and right as far as she could see.

The two main forces of machines and tumblers met. The sound was tremendous, a mixture of machines roaring, tumblers thumping at the ground, Krotes screeching and fireballs and other ventings finding homes. The ground shook and the air sang with the tunes of war. Very soon the two opposing lines had disintegrated, turning into a pitched battle that spread quickly across the dried marsh.

Lenora swerved left to avoid a tumbler and drove straight into another. She tried to pull her machine up short but its momentum carried it on, front legs extended to ward off the huge rolling thing. When they struck, Lenora was thrown forward. She grasped one of her machine's forelimbs, swinging around and kicking out at the tumbler. It started squirming and flexing, whipping at her with hooked limbs, but her machine unleashed a dozen spurts of flame from slits above its eyes. The tumbler's limbs were severed and fell burning between the battling giants.

Lenora took the opportunity to scramble onto her machine's back, ordering it to reverse as she did so. It tried, shaking with the effort, but was held tight. She leaned forward and hacked with her sword. The tumbler squirmed some more, trying to drive its barbs and hooks into the machine but failing to penetrate deep enough to take hold. Lenora sliced through its remaining limb, reaching farther and stabbing at its hide. She saw the bones of dead people in there, one recent skeleton smiling at her with leathery lips and waving a loose forearm.

Fire, she thought, leaning back and closing her eyes. The machine breathed fire and the tumbler lit up, rolling back and trying to extinguish its burning side by crushing it into the ground. *And more*. The machine coughed again, and the tumbler was aflame, crackling and spitting as its ancient insides ignited.

Lenora did not wait to witness the tumbler's demise. She rode to the giant machines bearing the cages of the dead, instructing their riders to release the cargo. Wooden limbs were lowered, ropes cut, metal chains severed, and a thousand dead Noreelans tumbled from their incarceration. They rolled from the body pile, rising dozens at a time and moving forward into battle. They passed by any Krote or machine they met, bearing down on tumblers already in their sights. Some carried swords and knives, others had fashioned clubs from thigh bones or spears from sharpened sticks. None of them possessed weapons that would hurt a tumbler.

But Lenora had not released these dead to attack the tumblers. She wanted to *smother* them.

She rode back into battle, dodging past the stumbling dead. Several tumblers ahead of her lit up from the inside as blue fireballs penetrated and exploded, their bone cargoes silhouetted against the flames. Inside, the bones were shattered and scattered, but those on the outside were more complete. Some of the tumblers seemed to scream, but the sound felt the same as the voice of Lenora's shade: in her mind, deep down. Wondering whether she was the only one to hear, she screamed back.

Lenora saw the first of the dead crushed into the ground by a huge tumbler. Several of them remained squirming in the dirt, but a couple were pressed onto the thing's hide, its barbs and spikes jutting from their already rotting bodies. There was little blood. The thing rolled on . . . and then stopped. It started to shake. Its limbs whipped back across its own body, hooking into the moving corpses and tugging away, as if to remove them. But they were stuck fast.

Through the shouts and shrieks of the battlefield, over and above the unremitting whisper of her daughter's shade, Lenora heard the tumbler scream.

It seemed to go mad, darting this way and that, skidding across the ground when the dead Noreelans were beneath it, but it could not scrape them from its outer skin. They were tattered now, barely recognizable as human, but the damage was done. As the tumbler came toward Lenora, stopped and turned away again, she saw a dozen nebulous shadows flung from it, thrashing through the air, landing, little more than a heat haze on the twilit battlefield. But the air was thick here—misted blood, smoke, the stench of the dying—and these shapes soon took form. Diaphanous, ambiguous, the mad wraiths darted away from the tumbler. One of them struck a machine and seemed to disappear. The machine paused. Its Krote rider stood, looked down and shouted, as if angry. And then the machine flipped onto its back and crushed the Krote, its flaming legs thrashing at the air like those of an overturned beetle.

Yes, Lenora thought, *this is when the fighting gets bloody.*

ALISHIA LOOKED AT the things coming down the slope toward them, and what they carried, and she was the little scared girl she so resembled.

"I can't look," Hope whispered beside her. "I can't *see*."

"What do you think we're seeing?" Alishia asked, though she already knew. She knew because Trey was there, suspended between these things like a baby borne by multiple mothers. He was naked, his skin smooth and soft and yellow.

"I don't know," Hope said, "but they must be gods."

Alishia looked at the things carrying Trey, but she could not make them out properly. She was not even sure how many there were. They seemed to shy away from the light, like a shadow fading the instant a lamp was lit. There but not there, a trick of the light and a truth of the dark. What she *could* see was terrible, but perhaps only because she expected it to be so: ragged wings, long limbs with reflections of hooks, blades and nails, and faces that seemed to exude pure sunlight.

"Oh no," Alishia said.

"What?" Hope was hiding her eyes, and she glanced up at Alishia kneeling beside her.

Alishia ignored the witch. *Here he comes*, she thought. *The man I saved, and look at him now. Look at him. An offering if ever I saw one.* He appeared to be dead, carried by the Nax from wherever Hope had murdered him, because surely they knew what this was all about. The Nax were gods, weren't they? Gods and demons both, more powerful than thought and more dreadful than the worst of nightmares.

Trey had feared them, and now he was with them.

They came closer, and as they brought Trey nearer, Alishia could see the gaping wounds across his arm and chest. The cuts pouted pale and fleshy, bloodless, flesh yellowed by fledge.

"Trey?" Alishia called, her voice incredibly loud in this place that held its breath. He gave no reaction. He floated down to them, carried by the shadows of the Nax.

"Don't look!" Hope screeched, and something laughed.

They reached the rock overhang above the Womb of the Land and made their way around it, bringing the naked, motionless fledge miner down the slope to where Alishia and Hope waited.

Alishia was suddenly cold and terrified, certain that this was happening and mortified by that certainty. She felt something probing at her mind and pushed it away; its tendrils were cool and utterly inhuman, and she had no wish to bear something like that.

Hope groaned beside her, pushing her face into the ground.

"Trey?" Alishia said again. She stood and stepped forward, trying her best to ignore the things that carried him. She knew that if she really scrutinized them they would manifest before her and allow her examination, but she did not know why. *Because I'm human? Because I'm me?* They had brought Trey here, and they must have their reasons. She only hoped that their reasons were in harmony with her own.

Trey opened his eyes. They were pure yellow, with no pupils or whites remaining. Alishia could not believe that they could see, but he turned to her and smiled, the creases at the corners of his eyes caked with fledge. He opened his mouth to speak but exhaled only a whisper of the drug.

Alishia felt something else prodding at her mind and she smiled, closed her eyes and let him in.

Trey!

Alishia . . . the witch, Hope, is that her down there?

It's her.

She attacked me. She's dangerous, and mad!

I know, Trey. She tried to calm him, mentally stroking his brow. *She's mad, but she always wanted what we need.*

What's happening?

I'm waiting to go in, but I don't know when. But if we have time, I think everything will be all right. That's what it's down to now: time.

Time, Trey said, and his voice drifted away.

He withdrew from her mind and smiled again, reaching out for Alishia's hand. She squeezed, and he was cool.

The things lowered him to the ground and moved away, fluttering across the grass, climbing the slopes and merging back into the dusk beyond the valley. Against her better judgment Alishia watched them, and it was only as they passed from light to dusk that she perceived their true form.

She shivered, and Trey squeezed her hand again.

"I don't know why I'm here," he said, voice hoarse and dry. His teeth were yellow, his tongue sat in his mouth like a fist of fledge and his eyes closed as he rested back on the ground.

Alishia knelt by his side and touched his face, turning him to her. "Trey."

He opened his eyes again and looked at her. "Another hillside, and this time I've found you. You really are just a little girl."

"I am," she said, her voice tinged with an age of unrealized wisdom. "Trey, can you cast? Can you travel? Can you tell me what's happening in Noreela?"

He sighed. "Now that they've gone, I think I can do anything. I'm more fledge now than man." His head tilted back, and Alishia let him rest.

She put her hand on his chest and looked down his naked body. *So strong,* she thought. *Perhaps I would have known him.* And then his heart started beating faster than should have been possible, and his eyelids were rolling as he went away.

————

HOPE TRIED TO approach Trey, but Alishia kept her away with a simple look. *You've harmed him once,* that look said, *how dare you come to him again?*

The witch walked toward the entrance to the Womb of the Land, squatting and staring into the impenetrable darkness. Her thinning hair drifted around her brows now and then, as though stirred by a breath from the cave.

It was only a few minutes later that Trey woke, sitting up and

crying out, his good hand reaching out to the darkness as if to ward
it off. "They're coming!" he shouted.

"Trey!" Alishia tried to calm him, but wherever she touched he
flinched away, never meeting her eyes, staring into a distance she
had no wish to see.

"They're on their way!" he said again. "They know, they're searching for this place, circling Kang Kang and *searching*."

"The Mages?"

"Yes, *them*." He looked at Alishia then, his yellow eyes filled
with tears. "Not long, Alishia," he said.

She put her hand on his shoulder and pushed him to the ground,
and she felt his heart slowing as she sat beside him. "There's water
here, and food," she said, touching his lips.

"I need neither." His breath smelled of caves and fledge.

"What else did you see?"

"So much. But all fragmentary. I traveled, and I saw so much.
All of it bad, Alishia. Noreela awash with blood. People dead, and
living, and many in between. A war. Men and women fighting machines and dying, and . . . other things fighting as well. For the machines or against them, I couldn't tell. Some things I can't see." He
frowned and closed his eyes, trying to remember or forget. "But I
saw *them*. I don't know how near or far, but they're above Kang
Kang and coming this way. Every heartbeat brings them closer, and
they *knew* I was seeing them. They *knew*!"

"By hawk?"

"A flying thing. Like a hawk but so much bigger." Trey's heart
was slowing even more, and Alishia moved her hand on his chest,
trying to rediscover its beat.

"I can't get into the Womb, not yet. There are Shades guarding it."

"The Shades of the Land?"

"How do you know?"

"You have such an innocent mind. Like Rafe. I slipped in, just
for a moment, and saw."

"Then you know what the Shades ask for. They want us to suffer. They say that way, we'll find our soul."

"I'm an offering," he said.

"It's the Half-Life Shade that wants you, Trey. You're all fledge
now, and . . ." His heartbeat had reduced to a few per minute, weak
flutterings as though a bird were trapped in his chest.

"I don't think so," he said. "Not that one. Another. Take me down."

Alishia dragged him down the hillside. He moved through the grass easily, as though fledge smoothed the way. Every time he exhaled, a haze of the drug blurred his features. *Another*, he had said. The Birth Shade? Was he changing into something else? Was it too much to believe that Trey was becoming much more of the fledge than any fledge miner had ever imagined?

Alishia stared hard at him, but he was still all there.

He could never be a Nax, she thought.

At the mouth of the cave Hope scuttled away, as though afraid of this naked yellow man. Alishia glared at her, then sat beside Trey, resting her hand on his chest once more.

"I should have died days ago," he whispered without opening his eyes. "This wound runs deep, touches the heart of me. And then they *took* me deep. The Nax saved me for this, but even so much fledge can't hold me back forever."

"What do you mean?" Alishia was crying now, because she *knew* what Trey meant, and she was about to lose her newest, greatest friend. There was no sign of movement in the cave mouth, but an awareness grew in there, as though it were an eye suddenly opening to the world.

Something came closer.

"I hope I can help," Trey said. "There's so much more to Noreela, Alishia. I saw times from before time! The Nax showed me, and I don't know why."

"Because memories are important," she said, thinking of the library and the burning pages falling around her like dying butterflies.

"Even though they can't last?"

"Especially then."

Trey closed his eyes and smiled. "I remember you," he said. Alishia felt one final flutter in his chest, and then his heart was still.

"Trey," she whispered, to speak his name one more time. This moment was how she wanted to remember him: brave and wise. And this final page of his life was new and fresh, untouched by the scourge of the Mages.

She cried. Her tears fell on his yellow skin and washed nothing away.

"He's dead?" Hope said. She stood behind Alishia, her shape casting no shadow across the prone fledger.

"Yes," Alishia said.

Hope started to say something but turned away, and Alishia sensed her retreating across the hillside.

The librarian sat with the dead miner for some time, never taking her hand from his chest. She did not feel him cooling. She sensed no change. The only difference was that his chest was still, not rising and falling, and the smell of fledge began to grow stale without his breath to renew it.

An hour after Trey died, the Womb of the Land changed. The Death Shade came, making the cave mouth darker than ever with its presence. It rose from the depths, becoming denser with every moment that passed, and Alishia remained with Trey instead of moving away. She feared it, but she was the reason it had come.

There was increased movement in the small valley. The grass began waving with no sign of a breeze, and several trees that dotted the hillsides flexed their branches as if stretching after a long sleep. Alishia saw Hope crouch down in fear as a cloud of green leaves sailed past her head, several of them becoming entangled in her wild hair. The witch thrashed at the leaves, cursing and screaming.

"Come and take him," Alishia said. The cave suddenly seemed closer than it had before. Or perhaps it had grown.

There was no great unveiling, no giant Shade emerging. Trey simply rose a handbreadth from the ground and flowed toward the opening into the land. His hands and feet dipped to brush through the waving grasses, but Alishia had the sense that the Shade was taking him with caution and love. He passed into the cave. The Death Shade swallowed him, and Alishia's final image of Trey was his pale yellow skin obscured from sight forever.

"Back below where you belong," she said. Then she stood and walked away, her bones aching, heart fit to break.

Chapter 20

I HAD NO WISH *to ever be close to you again*, Flage said. He had risen from the depths of the tumbler, and Jossua Elmantoz had sensed him coming. Jossua was blind and deaf and dumb, but this new sense of unbeing gave him greater sight than ever before. Much that he saw was loneliness. As the first Red Monk, he was used to that, but it had never quite felt like this. This was a solitude of the soul that he could barely stand, a sense of abandonment by not only other people and beings, but the land itself. He felt so far removed from everything he had believed in that he struggled to keep hold of his own mind. He imagined his life as a book and he kept reading it, again and again, so many times that he lost count. Every time it finished he started again, realizing that the true end was yet to be written.

I'm dead, but not finished, he kept thinking, and then Flage rose up.

Not dead, Flage said. *Not like me. Your wraith and your shade are still together.*

I don't understand . . .

And were you meant to? Monk! All you understand is murder and death.

You know so little, Flage. What were you? A farmer?

A rover.

I've killed rovers.

I'm sure you have, Flage said. He moved away, his voice growing faint, and Jossua called out to him.

I'm so alone!

Flage laughed. *We'd have you, if the tumbler mind asked. But it doesn't ask. It doesn't really want you, either.*

Why?

There are reasons. I don't understand them, but I know them. Enough to tell you that you won't be here for very much longer. We're almost somewhere.

Where?

Somewhere. Now leave me be, Monk. I hope you're cold out here. I hope you're lonely. Flage left, still talking as his voice faded to nothing. *I hope you find all the pain you've given . . .*

Jossua sensed the vastness of unknown space surrounding him, and he could still feel the impact of his broken body on the ground as the tumbler rolled onward. But he was alone once more.

Almost somewhere, he thought. But nothing came to tell him where.

———

KOSAR AND LUCIEN had joined a small group of Shantasi on a wide, flat rock. Most of them remained standing, still clasping their weapons, looking north at the strange battle out on the plains. Several more huge explosions had lit the scene. Most were true fire, but a couple of them gushed cool blue flame at the sky, like a fountain of ice rising from broken machines. The battle was a mile distant, but the fires provided enough light to make out individual combatants, both machine and tumbler.

A few minutes ago, one of the machines had disappeared within a swirling, twisting shadow, and Kosar had heard several of the Shantasi say *Serpenthal.* "The one you killed must have been a baby," he said to Lucien. He was sure the Monk's complexion paled.

They continued watching, but though many fires marked the

demise of machines, still there was a growing awareness that the
rolling forms of the tumblers were becoming fewer. *They're all
fighting,* one Shantasi said. *They're dying,* another answered. Kosar
guessed that both were correct. The tumblers were fighting and dying, and although every second gained would help Alishia and the
others, the Krotes would be on them very soon.

"What else can Noreela throw at them?" Lucien asked.

"What do you mean?"

"The tumblers. The serpenthals. What else? The land seems to
be helping itself."

Kosar nodded, watching another giant flower of fire rise from
the darkened landscape. *Another machine dies,* he thought, but the
idea brought little comfort. "When we were traveling with Rafe, the
magic helped us."

"At the machines' graveyard."

"Then, and before. Alishia isn't the same, but perhaps that help
will be there again when we need it most."

"You're relying on that?" the Monk said.

Kosar shook his head, not looking at Lucien. "We can't rely on
anything but our willingness to fight." He looked around at the
Shantasi warriors, their commanders organizing them into smaller
platoons and spreading across the hillsides in readiness. A hundred
Shantasi started down toward the plain, ready to spring an ambush
on the first machines that approached. "Going to their deaths," he
said, "and we don't even know what's happening in Kang Kang.
We're fighting for a sliver of hope, and we'll die for it."

"Better that than die for nothing."

Yes, Kosar thought. *A'Meer died under your sword for what you're
ready to fight for now.*

"Something's coming," a Shantasi said. It was O'Lam, the big
woman who had first tried to shoot Kosar and Lucien from the
desert beast.

"Machines?" Kosar asked.

"Don't think so. Mage shit, this dusk is so fucking annoying."

Kosar smiled. A'Meer would have spoken that way.

"Something coming toward us from the battle. Slow. Perhaps
Krotes on foot, or something else."

"Krotes on foot we can fight," Kosar said. He squinted, still unable to see anything.

O'Lam looked at him and smiled, stroking her cheek with the

tip of her sword. "Krotes on foot make me wet." She laughed, and Kosar laughed with her. *Yes, just like A'Meer!*

"Whatever it is, it'll be here soon," Kosar said. "Who knows what else the Mages have made to come at us?" O'Lam did not answer, and Kosar guessed she was probably going over the same possibilities in her own mind.

"Perhaps the damage is already done," Lucien said.

"Meaning?" Kosar asked. He was aware that the Shantasi warrior was paying attention to the Monk too, her face pale and grim.

"The Mages are here. This Krote army had traveled the length of Noreela. Who's to say what has happened? Perhaps there's not much of Noreela left."

"Are you always so fucking upbeat, Monk?" O'Lam said.

Lucien did not answer, and Kosar looked at the fires and explosions in the distance. There was a huge conflagration to the east, and it seemed to be growing all the time. Tumblers being burned, perhaps. Or something else. He knew little, standing here in the foothills of a place where no one should go, ready to fight a foe no one had ever seen. *Please, in the name of the Black, I hope you're going to do something soon, Alishia.*

But right then the prospect of success, of victory, of this endless dusk giving way to daylight, seemed so very far away.

A FEW MINUTES later, they discovered what was coming toward them from the battlefield. Refugees. They watched them stagger across the dying land, and as they came closer Kosar could see their vacant expression, eyes wiped clean by whatever terrible things they had seen.

Many of them carried weapons.

"Where do they come from?" Kosar asked. "No villages out there, not this close to Kang Kang. And they don't look in very good shape."

"Perhaps the Krotes brought them," O'Lam said. "Prisoners who escaped when the tumblers attacked."

"We should go to help them," Kosar said, but O'Lam touched his arm.

"No. They'll reach our front line soon. Then we'll see how much help they need."

They watched the shapes climbing the slope, walking on at a

steady pace. And it was only as they reached the first Shantasi line that Kosar realized what was so strange. They all walked alone.

"Something's wrong," he said. He cupped his hands to his mouth. *"Something's wrong!"*

The refugees reached the Shantasi and the attack began.

The first warriors were taken by surprise, and three fell beneath the weight of the attackers. Several more fought back, using swords and slideshocks on the first group of refugees, cutting them down and then backing away before the main body of people reached them.

The men and women they had cut down stood again—minus arms, slashed across the chest, one of them missing his head above his mouth—and continued their relentless walk.

"What in the fucking Black is that?" O'Lam said.

Kosar could only stare. The dead walked on, and it took him several more seconds to realize that the refugees were *all* dead, cursed back to life and driven on as fodder to weaken the enemy. "This is only the first," he said. "There'll be much worse than this."

"You've seen the Mages before, haven't you?" O'Lam said. "I heard you talking with Mystic O'Gan."

Kosar nodded. "Yes, I've seen them."

"What were they like?"

"In all the world, friend, that's the one thing you never want to know."

The fighting had begun in earnest now, and the walking dead were starting to make their way up the hillside. There were hundreds of them, perhaps as many as a thousand, and those not immediately engaged marched on until they found an enemy to fight. There was no apparent strategy or method to their attack, but their power lay in their numbers and senselessness. If they lost one arm, they would heft a sword with another. Kosar saw a woman lose her left leg to a Shantasi throwing disc. She pulled herself upright and hopped forward once again. It would have been amusing were it not so grotesque, and he was pleased when the same warrior took off her other leg with a slideshock.

The woman fell and started pulling herself along the ground.

Many of the dead quickly lost their weapons, dropped from senseless fingers or left lodged between an unfortunate Shantasi's bones. Yet still they came on, overpowering warriors by numbers alone. The dead did not move very quickly. They could walk but not run, turn but not leap, and the Shantasi had the advantage of Pace. But the dead were also difficult to keep down, and one mistake would cost a warrior dear.

One group of Shantasi retreated a hundred steps and hunkered down, taking bags from their shoulders, lifting flaps and directing a dark cloud of something at the walking dead. From this distance Kosar could not make out what the cloud consisted of—flies, gas? But when one of the Shantasi fired a burning arrow into its midst, the effect was staggering. The air lit up, a fireball that swallowed many of the dead and expanded dangerously close to the Shantasi lines. When the flames receded, many of the dead had fallen, burning into the ground. They still moved. Fanning the flames of their own demise.

"How much more do you have?" Kosar asked.

O'Lam did not turn to him. "Some," she said.

Kosar shook his head. "It's hopeless. We're fighting magic with swords and burning flies."

"No, we're fighting what the Mages can make of magic. They keep it to themselves, selfish. Don't give their army true access. That was their downfall three hundred years ago, and perhaps they'll do the same now."

"Perhaps?"

O'Lam shrugged. "We'll soon see."

Several Mourners that had come with the Shantasi army started chanting, approaching perilously close to shambling corpses and doing their best to send them down into the Black. Some succeeded; others did not. Kosar saw at least one Mourner fall, in need of chanting down himself.

When the first of the dead reached them, Kosar and Lucien stood their ground. They stayed close together in case they were rushed, and Kosar hefted the sword A'Meer had given him, sad that it would be tainted by flesh corrupted with bad magic.

"Every death for you," he said, kissing the blade.

A man came at him, ragged and dirty and bearing a terrible dry gash across his throat. As he lunged, Kosar realized just how badly the man stank. He must have been dead for some time.

Kosar dodged aside and lashed out, lodging his sword in the man's ribs. The man fell, turning as he did so, and the blade slipped from Kosar's hand. He went for the sword but the man struck out. He caught Kosar across the arm and raked his nails down to his hands, ripping through the thief's brands. Kosar screamed.

Lucien darted in and cleaved the man's skull in two, hacking at the twitching body until it could move no more. He stood on the dead man's back and tugged Kosar's sword free, handing it back to the thief.

Kosar nodded his thanks and stared past the Monk. "Behind you," he said. The Monk turned and went to work.

It was a short, vicious fight, but not very bloody. The little blood that did leak from these enemies was thick and black with corruption. Kosar recognized many of them as northerners, and from their clothing—well made, colorful—he guessed that some were from Noreela City itself. *And what of that city now?*

A few of them were from the Shantasi's First Army, freshly dead and risen again. At least in death they seemed to have lost their Pace, so although the fight was a mental challenge beyond anything the Shantasi thought they would have to face, they still had the better of their dead friends.

Don't let me see O'Gan, Kosar thought, over and over again. *Please don't let me see him. Not me, not him.*

Kosar grew tired very quickly. His old wounds hurt, and he received several new ones to add to the pain. He kept a tight hold on his sword, and several times he and Lucien found themselves fighting back to back. The dead Shantasi seemed to aim for them, as though targeting the Red Monk's cloak, and Kosar found himself fighting men and women who had been on his side a few hours earlier. Freshly dead, still they possessed ease of movement and strength in their limbs, and they retained much of their fighting skill. But they were far slower than before. He maintained his concentration and tried to keep his fear at bay, and soon the pile of body parts before him was as high as his knee.

And it moved. Torsos flexed, limbs twitched. He nudged Lucien and moved sideways, finding fresh ground.

The Monk fought hard, and even though Kosar heard him take several wounds, they barely slowed him.

He was almost starting to feel confident about the fight when he heard the first cry rise up: "The Krotes are here, the Krotes—" The voice was silenced. Dashing away from the dead attacking him, looking down the hill, Kosar saw a sight that seemed to still the blood leaking from his wounds.

The hillside was alive with machines, and awash with dying Shantasi.

———

ALISHIA FOUND HOPE shivering beneath a tree two hundred steps from the Womb of the Land. The old witch was staring at the ground, eyes wide, hands clasped together at her chest, her hair still bearing a few windblown leaves. She glanced up at Alishia's approach, and then down again.

"Trey's been taken in," Alishia said.

Hope held her breath. "Inside there?" She looked along the hillside at the cave.

' "He's part of my misery," the girl said. "Misery is humanity."

"Then it's time to go inside! See what's to be done. I'll go with you and—"

"You will never go in there with me," Alishia said quietly, and even though she spoke with a little girl's voice, the witch recoiled in fear.

"I brought you all this way," Hope said.

Alishia shook her head. "I can't argue with you. I don't have the energy."

"But I—"

"What's that?" Alishia held up her hand and stilled Hope with a glance. She had heard something, a rumble from far away or a whisper from closer by. Perhaps the Nax were still out there, trailing around the lip of the valley.

"I hear nothing," Hope said.

Alishia let out her held breath and breathed in again, and as she did so the sky shook. A single, thunderous explosion thumped down into the valley, invisible but for the shock wave that preceded it. Grass flattened, trees cracked, soil and stones jumped as if pushed from below, and Alishia felt her eardrums and eyeballs squeezed. She fell onto her side with a groan and tried to bring her hands to her ears, but her arms would not work.

"In the name of the Black, not again," Hope said. Her voice was pure fear. Alishia followed her gaze up the hillside.

A giant flying machine sat on the valley ridge, its grotesque head and the tips of its wings protruding from the darkness. It edged forward, as though testing the strange light in the valley. When it found that the light did not hurt, it launched, flexing its wings, stepping from the valley edge and gliding down just above the hillside. Upon its back sat two figures, humanoid yet so much larger in Alishia's eyes.

"It's *them*!" she said.

"They have magic," Hope whispered, and Alishia was disturbed by the awe in her voice. *What would the witch do?* she thought. *What would she give up for a touch of what they have?*

The machine lifted higher above the ground and drifted across the valley, flapping its huge wings once to lift it over the clump of trees beneath which Alishia and Hope sheltered. Alishia closed her eyes as the thing passed them by. Though there was no sun to block out, still its shadow touched them.

"They'll find us in minutes," Alishia said. "They'll take me and kill me."

"Then bring it up!" Hope said. "Let the magic in you find itself! Give me something to fight them with and I'll do everything I can to protect you."

"If I could touch the magic, don't you think I'd have done so before now?"

"To protect yourself from me?" Hope said, leaning closer.

Alishia shook her head. "You may be mad, but I'm not sure you'll ever be a danger to your one and only hope."

Another explosion came, thumping through the valley and shaking leaves from the trees above their heads. Alishia and Hope rolled on the ground, clasping their ears, squeezing their eyes shut, trying their best not to shout in pain. Perhaps that was what the Mages were trying to do: flush them out.

Alishia pressed her face into the ground and groaned.

The flying machine came again, flapping its wings this time and moving much faster across the valley. Its wing tips scored the ground. Daggers of blue light leapt from its sides and rear, piercing the ground and sending up geysers of soil and molten rock. More fear, more pain, to make Alishia and Hope flee their precarious hiding place.

"Don't move!" Alishia said. Hope lay beside her, hands pressed to her face. Blood seeped between her fingers.

The machine landed close to the Womb of the Land, its settling surprisingly gentle for something so large. Its wings rested down and touched the ground, taking on its contours and imperfections as they molded themselves to rocks, trees and dips. The Mages stood and walked down the wing closest to the Womb. Neither of them took their eyes from the cave. They carried no weapons, but Alishia knew that they needed none. As Hope said, they had magic.

"Now we'll never get in there!" Hope whispered. Her nose was bleeding, and a dribble of blood leaked from her left eye. Her tattoos had turned red, as if echoed below the skin by burst veins.

"Neither will they," Alishia said. *But the witch is right. With them there, I can never get inside. And something . . .*

"Alishia," Hope said, and for the first time the librarian heard a gentleness to the witch's voice. "You're growing younger."

"I know," Alishia said, but even then she knew what the witch meant. She was regressing faster. Drifting back through the years of her youth, breasts shrunken to hints of themselves, stomach bulging with a little girl's fat, eyes wide, teeth small, and in her mind everything she had learned of the land over the past few days seemed to be growing larger and more intricate with every breath she took. "Hope, I think I'll have to be there soon."

Hope crawled closer, and the witch seemed to be growing. "I could go," Hope said. "I could offer myself to them. Pretend to help. Say I know where you are. Maybe they'll touch me, give me something of what they have in exchange."

"You can't."

Hope was looking at the ground close to her face, frowning, her eyes flitting left and right as she turned over whatever dark thoughts she had.

"Hope, that's not the way," Alishia said.

The witch looked at her. "You're afraid for me, or of me?"

"Both."

Hope nodded and looked along the hillside at the resting machine. "Perhaps you're right to be," she said.

The Mages were approaching the entrance to the cave now, and they appeared to be holding hands. Where their skin touched, a pale blue light danced, streaking up their arms and tangling with their hair. There was no companionship or affection apparent in their touch; they did not look at each other. And as they came within a few steps of the cave, the light between them started to grow.

"They're going to seal the cave," Alishia said. She closed her eyes and thought of Trey being taken inside, and even with everything she had learned she had no idea what was within that place. A simple cave, perhaps. Or something far more.

"Something's coming out." Hope touched her hand.

The darkness of the cave mouth was expanding, extruding into the weird light of its valley. Its edges were vague, the shape constantly changing, but it grew as it came, as though all the darkness from beneath the ground were forcing upward. As it projected farther, the shadow split in two.

The Mages took one step back and then lifted their clasped hands in unison, ejecting a splash of blue light that struck the two shapes where they were still joined at the ground.

The land vibrated with the impact. For the briefest instant, the two shadows were lit from the inside, and Alishia did not understand what she saw. How light could reveal deeper darkness, she did not know. For the moment they were lit—surprised by the blast of magical light, perhaps, or simply absorbing it as best they could—the Half-Life Shade and the Birth Shade seemed larger than everything else. They dwarfed the valley, made a mockery of the expanse of Kang Kang, and they drove Alishia's newfound knowledge of things down to a speck of inexperience. For a moment they were everything, and then the magical light faded and the Shades fell upon the Mages.

"Come on," Alishia said. "We can't stay here. We have to move closer to the Womb, and when the chance comes I can go inside."

"But the offerings," Hope said.

"Maybe I can slip by without them knowing." But Alishia knew how foolish this idea was. The two remaining Shades might be fighting the Mages, but their prime purpose was defending the Womb of the Land. It was Noreela's potential, as were they. *I'm the offering for the Birth Shade*, she thought. *I can think of nothing else. Yet the Half-Life Shade? Hope? How can she be that? She's an old witch without magic, but she's very much alive.*

Alishia darted from cover and moved low across the hillside. She sensed Hope following her, and for once she took heart from that. Perhaps the witch really did have goodness at the heart of her, hidden away by decades of bitterness.

The two Shades danced in the air above the Mages, hiding the sorcerers from view much of the time. Their darkness pulsed and changed, spurts of shadow spinning out and turning like a whirl-pool, sucking in the light and expanding some more. Fingers of darkness probed the air. Others dipped down to the ground far from the fight, searching cracks and dips, stealing behind rocks, and Alishia was certain that the Shades were seeking her out.

She ducked behind a fallen tree and held her breath, closed her eyes, expecting the human manifestation of the Shades to speak to her again. He remained silent.

Hope dropped down beside her. "I can't see them anymore!" she said. "Maybe they're defeated. Maybe the Shades have crushed them down!"

"I can't believe it would ever be that easy," Alishia said. Another jarring explosion agreed with her, thudding up into her hip and shoulder and shaking her insides.

"Mage shit!" More blood spurted from Hope's nose. Her left eye had become totally bloodshot, turning this way and that as though fascinated with this new take on the world.

"Come on," Alishia said, readying to stand again. The witch grabbed her arm and held on tightly.

"Don't run blind, Alishia," she said. "You don't know what's happening, or what to do when you get there. Wait."

"For what?"

Hope shook her head, exasperated. "Don't you think the land will provide? Those Nax arrived with Trey, and that was far from co-incidence."

"No one pretends to know the Nax," the girl said. Her own voice fascinated her—so young, so full of wisdom.

"And yet they intervene," Hope said.

"And you?" Alishia said. "When you cut Trey down, did you think you were serving the land?"

Hope shook her head. "Only my own madness."

Something screamed. The sound began deep, rising so high that Alishia thought her skull would break. The fallen tree they were resting against shook and split along its length, spitting a shower of dead beetles and wood slugs down onto Alishia's head and shoulders. She bit her lip to prevent herself from crying out. The beetles were light as a breath, their clear wings spread from their resting position on their backs as though they had tried to fly from death.

"The fight's moving," Hope said, looking over the top of the cracked trunk.

Alishia shook her head and brushed at her shoulders as she knelt beside the witch. The dead creatures fell apart at her touch. *Like old, dry books caught in a fire.*

The Mages had retreated back to their machine, and were now standing on its back fending off the two Shades of the Land. The Shades attacked from either side, flashes of darkness darting out like negative lightning. The Mages held handfuls of blue light, and every time the Shades came at them they used the sickly illumination to cauterize the darkness into a light ash. The air around them was thick with it, and it had begun to coat the machine around their feet like a layer of fresh snow.

The Shades moved like mountains, and the Mages fought back.

One of the Shades changed tactics. Instead of attacking the Mages, it assaulted their machine, melting across the ground and sending tendrils of shadow beneath the construct, then expanding again, lifting the machine up. It pumped more of itself under the machine, shrugging off the thing's defenses: fireballs faded, arrows passed through and molten metal spattered on the hillside and steamed back to solid.

The Mages almost lost their footing. The female jumped and landed again, screaming a curse as she unleashed a stream of blue fire directly between her feet into the machine.

It exploded. Whether or not the Mage had intended this, the effect was devastating: The machine's shell came apart under a ball of fire, chunks of metal and stone, flesh and bone spinning up and out into the air, streaming blue flame and smoke behind them. The two Mages went with it, visible for the first couple of seconds but then engulfed as their clothes and hair ignited. The ground beneath the machine erupted as though pushed from below, and soil and rock were powered out sideways.

Alishia and Hope ducked as the first of the debris struck the other side of the fallen tree, sending timber splinters carving over their heads. A wave of heat stole their breath, and the fringes on Alishia's dress began to smoke. Hope patted at them, hissing as the skin of her palms blistered.

The roar of the explosion rumbled back and forth across the valley.

Alishia looked again. Hope grabbed at her but she shook the witch off. "I have to see where they went!" she said.

The entire slope below the Womb of the Land was ablaze. Green grass was black, lush trees were bare trunks, their leaves fluttering through the air, smoking and bursting alight when the heat finally dried them to nothing. The small stream had vanished, steamed away to nothing.

A ball of smoke and fire boiled into the sky. The construct was in pieces across the valley. Some of them burned, others seemed to be melting into the ground, disintegrating into their constituent parts of flesh, stone, metal and other material. Alishia scanned the ground around the site of the blast, hoping against hope that she would see the Mages burned to a crisp: charred bones cracked and coming apart just as their monstrous machine broke down into nothing.

The Shades had vanished. The Womb of the Land was as dark as ever, shunning the blazing fires that should be lighting its insides. *I'll be there soon*, Alishia thought, and she hoped that they heard.

Something shifted before her, less than thirty steps away. At first she thought it was part of the machine, warping and cracking under the tremendous heat, but then it stood.

And laughed.

The laughter extinguished the flames licking at the Mage's eyes. Its tongue flipped out and lapped up the remaining fingers of fire. It ran its hands down the length of its burnt and disfigured body, and wherever they touched flesh was renewed. The Mage rebuilt itself touch by touch, and by the time it reached its eyes, Alishia was already turning away.

"There you are," the Mage said, its feminine voice as out of place as a shadow inside fire. "We've been looking for you everywhere. You—and this place—have taken a *lot* of finding."

Something struck Alishia from behind. She fell and rose again, and heard a scream as the ground rolled away beneath her.

———

HOPE REMAINED HUNKERED down beside the fallen tree. Dead beetles dusted her legs. The dried husks of wood slugs fluttered around her feet in the wafting heat from the blaze.

She hugged herself, trying to crush away her fear.

The Mage screamed again, a venting of rage and frustration that set Hope's tattoos squirming and lifted every remaining hair on her head into a filthy halo. She wanted to scream herself, but that would give her away. *And then she'll be here,* Hope thought, *the Mage, that madwoman, and she'll have me for her vengeance.* So she bit into the fleshy part between her thumb and forefinger, tasting blood and concentrating on the pain rather than the scream.

The tumbler had come in from nowhere and snatched Alishia away. Three more followed, the last one running across Hope's foot. Its spikes and barbs missed her, its weight held up on other whiplike limbs. It had left her alone.

She bit harder and closed her eyes and the Mage shrieked one more time, the sound receding as she ran after the fleeing tumblers.

Hope risked a look. *Alishia!* The girl was visible, pressed onto the side of the lead tumbler, her loose dress flapping in the breeze as the thing bounded down the hillside and across the base of the valley.

Alishia, she's gone, all that potential stolen away!

The girl spun around and around as the tumbler rolled, but it did not crush her into its hide.

Of all the ravages of fate, all the whispers in the Black, why this and why now?

The other three tumblers slowed as the female Mage ran after them with unnatural speed. Her hair streaked out behind her, yellow and beautiful, and her feet pounded clots of mud from the ground.

Because they're trying to help?

Hope caught her breath and dropped her bleeding hand from her mouth. She closed her right eye and saw red through the left, as though viewing a cloud-streaked sunset. The Mage neared the first tumbler and it swung around, reversing almost instantaneously to come at her. She barely broke her stride. A stream of blue fire burst from her chest, coughed up and out with a sound that reverberated around the valley. The tumbler rolled away, on fire. It struck a tree and became entangled in the vines that drooped from the lower branches, and soon the tree was an inferno.

The tumbler carrying Alishia disappeared behind a swathe of thick smoke, and the Mage gave chase.

Hope looked back at the Womb of the Land. The cave entrance

stood dark and indifferent within a wide expanse of burning debris. As smoke drifted toward the darkness it changed direction, blown left or right by the cave's invisible exhalation.

Where is he? She remembered the male Mage from their fight aboard the flying machine, in those final moments when she had still believed that Rafe had a chance. Unlike the female Mage, he had worn his monstrosity with pride. "Where are you?" She scanned the remains of their giant machine, eyes chasing shadows thrown by the flames. "I could help them," she whispered, testing the words in her mouth. She did not like them, nor what they intimated, but she had said and done many bad things in her life.

Nothing moved. Hope climbed over the fallen tree and started picking her way across the hillside, dodging the remains of the machine, stepping over a pool of jellied blood, skirting a scorched circle where something had melted into the ground.

I could help them, she thought. *If it gave me what I want, I could help them.* She paused and looked to the sky. "But what in the Black would that make me?"

The voice that responded in her mind surprised Hope to a halt. *A liar.* The voice of her mother.

"There's more to this than me," Hope said, louder than she'd intended, and it was as if her words held the power to change.

Something else came into the valley, and initially Hope thought she was seeing reflections thrown onto drifting skeins of smoke. But then from the corner of her eye she made out bloody red smudges flitting through the air, drifting low to the ground as they made their way out of the darkness and into the light.

A shape appeared before Hope. It rose from a squat beside the entrance to the Womb's cave: a ragged skeleton, unhindered by vanity or the need to reflesh its burnt self. The male Mage.

He roared a challenge, and the Nax flew directly at him.

———

WITH THE CONSTANT spinning, bumping movement of the tumbler, Alishia passed out. Her senses faded, though she was still aware of where she was and what was happening. She could smell no fire, yet still it burned. She could not hear the angered screeches of the Mage chasing her down the hillside, but she knew that she was there, reclothed in flesh and filled with more rage than ever before.

Alishia thought that the Shades might take this opportunity to talk to her, but the man did not appear. She searched for the library but she could not find her way.

Hold on tight, a voice said in her mind. *The end is almost here, and we have what you need.*

Who are you?

I was Flage. Now I'm one of many. And you are the hope we still have.

I don't understand . . .

That doesn't matter. Almost there. Hold tight. We have everything you need.

Chapter 21

LENORA RODE THROUGH the battle, dealing death here, avoiding it there, and something was happening to her. An ache in her groin; a feeling in her long-barren womb that she had not felt since her dead child was born in Kang Kang's foothills hundreds of miles to the west. It was a hollowness aching to be filled, and though she could not accept that feeling, neither could she deny it.

Mother, her daughter's shade whispered, and Lenora asked, "Are you talking to me?" *Mother,* it said again, *why do you deny me?*

"I don't deny you!" Lenora ducked below a hail of arrows and rode away, rather than taking on those who had fired them.

Then come for me.

"I always said I would, but I have something—"

Something to finish, the shade said. *Mother . . . you have a part in its ending.*

"I do!" Lenora threw a star and watched it slice through a Shantasi's exposed throat. She felt nothing; no glee, no sorrow. Her machine seemed to be looking at her, but when she glanced down she could see nothing in its eyes.

Her womb ached with wanting, and Lenora shook her head, angry. "On *my* terms," she said. She rode on, and her daughter whispered, and a sudden splash of blood across her chest made her retch.

WHEN THE MACHINES came, everything changed. Until then the Shantasi had been fighting well, cutting down the shambling dead and making sure they stayed down. It was demanding physically and mentally, but they were up to the task, and even Kosar had sensed a change in the Shantasi. Whereas before they had been resigned to defeat, they had now started to believe they stood a chance.

The machines and their Krote riders changed that. They stormed in from the north, still fending off a few rogue tumblers that had managed to avoid destruction, and when they hit the first lines of Shantasi they cut the warriors down almost without breaking their pace. The tumblers rolled at the machines and bounced away again. Shantasi darted left and right, using Pace to try to keep out of reach. And the lead machines drove on, bypassing the first of the Shantasi to fight those farther uphill.

When the first machines reached the last line of defense they turned around and started battling their way back down.

Their lines shattered, the Shantasi took on the machines in a free-for-all that had only one possible outcome.

Kosar and Lucien emerged from behind their sheltering rock and entered into the fray. Down the slope to their left, a small machine lay on its side, several legs torn away by Shantasi slideshocks. The Krote still sat astride his mount's back, and its remaining limbs whipped at the air, decapitating one woman and slicing a man across the thighs. A warrior drew an arrow against the Krote, but a fist-sized chunk of metal flew from the machine and crushed his chest before he could fire. He fell, the bow and arrow trapped beneath him.

"I'll go for that!" Kosar said, pointing. "You try to keep this bastard thing distracted." Without waiting for a reply, Kosar ran. He kept low, skirting far around the machine to keep out of range of its limbs. He checked left and right, making sure that no other Krote was closing on him. If that happened he would have little hope; he did not even have the Shantasi Pace to enable him to outrun some of the machines. He clutched A'Meer's sword and wished she were here with him. *Stop thinking and start fighting,* she would say. So he ran, attention focused on the fallen Shantasi with the bow and arrows.

Behind him, he heard Lucien roar. He did not turn to see why.

He reached the fallen man and tugged the bow from his grasp, trying not to look at the ruin of his chest. Then he rolled the body onto its side and grabbed a handful of arrows from the quiver. The man let out a groan.

Kosar fell back and pushed himself away, shouting out in surprise.

He sensed the Krote's attention move on to him. He ducked just in time to avoid being struck across the head by one of the machine's spinning limbs. He rolled backward, rolled again and came up into a kneeling position.

Lucien was hacking his way closer to the machine. A limb struck him on the arm and knocked him sideways, but he stood again and swung his sword. It met a metal whip and sparks flew.

Kosar strung an arrow and aimed at the Krote. The Krote turned back to him and raised his hand, fisted and pointing at Kosar.

Crossbow on his wrist, Kosar thought, but he could not let it upset his aim. He took a deep breath, let it out and loosed the arrow.

The Krote's bolt scored his cheek as Kosar's arrow found its mark. The Krote fell back, dying, and the machine paused in its fight, slumping down onto its belly as if relieved of a burden.

Lucien grinned at Kosar, his red face lit by fires springing up across the hillside. Kosar smiled back and breathed deeply. He could smell the fleshy fuel of those flames.

The Monk backed away from the machine and came to Kosar's side. "Where now?" he said.

There were fights all around them. Up the slope Kosar saw a group of Shantasi harrying a machine while another warrior closed in from behind. She carried something in her arms—it looked like a rock—and she dodged several of the machine's flailing limbs to place it against the construct's side. The Shantasi turned and fled, leaving the Krote swinging his sword and raging at their cowardice.

The rock came to life. It glowed, like molten stone, and quickly ate its way into the machine, spitting a hail of bloody stone dust above it. The Krote looked down just as his ride reared up, and as it fell on its side the Krote was trapped beneath its stiffening limbs. Three Shantasi darted in and finished the Mages' warrior, and the glowing stone ate its way fully inside the stricken machine.

"A young grinder," Lucien said. "I wonder how they took it from its parent."

"O'Lam said there was more, but not much." The darting shapes of Shantasi using Pace caused smoke to swirl and eddy across the hillside. Another explosion blossomed around a machine as a swarm of flies was ignited. A yellow wolf—Kosar had heard of the pallid wolves, but never seen them—loped across the hill and leapt at a Krote astride a machine, spitting acid and showering her with venomous blood as the machine sliced the creature in two. The Krote screamed and died on her mount as it ran rogue.

He thought of Trey, Hope and Alishia, and closed his eyes in a brief plea to the Black. *Let them be all right.*

Someone screamed close by, a long, loud wail that ended suddenly with the sound of metal cleaving meat. Kosar did not look for the source of the cry. "It's hopeless," he said.

"It always was," Lucien said.

Around them, the battle played out across the lower slopes of darkest Kang Kang. Perhaps the mountains watched and smiled, enjoying the fresh blood spilled and sucked down into its soil. There could have been eyes on its higher slopes observing the explosions, ears listening to the screams of dying men and women, noses breathing in the stench of blood and soil, cooking meat and insides. Or maybe they had no awareness of the fight at all; the most important battle for three hundred years, meaningless to a range of mountains that defied eternity.

A group of Shantasi joined Kosar and Lucien, several experienced archers among them, and they set on a machine. The Shantasi used their Pace to distract the Krote, while the archers drew a line and brought him down with arrows to the chest and back. The Krote slumped over and shouted, giving his machine one final order, which it obeyed without hesitation. The resulting blue-flamed explosion, fueled by dark magic, melted everything it touched.

Lucien grasped Kosar's arm and pulled him down behind a dead man, falling on him and screaming as the blue fire rolled overhead.

As the explosion subsided it was replaced by the screams of the injured. Kosar shoved Lucien from him and stood. The Monk sat up slowly, shaking, and then Kosar saw his back. The red robe had been burned away, along with much of his skin and flesh. The white of bones was visible here and there, pale and stark in the moonlight. No blood; the wounds were already cauterized.

"Lucien . . ."

"I can fight!" the Monk spat. He stood, screamed and ran at a machine coming their way, brandishing his sword, ducking at the last moment and hacking at one of the machine's thick legs.

Kosar went to fight with him. Any moment could be his last, and soon one moment would. But he was enraged now, encouraged by Lucien's strength, inspired by the ferocious Shantasi fighting and dying all around. And just when things became hopeless, the land rose up one more time.

THE SOLDIERS EMERGED from the ground. Three of them to start with, manifesting as blank, black shadows, flexing to form individual features, taking in moonlight and giving out a sense of power that sent a chill down Kosar's sweaty back.

"Mimics," he whispered, thinking of the last time he had seen them. They had changed his course of action, encouraging him not to flee and leave the fate of Trey, Alishia and Hope to chance. Now they were here again, and he could hope once more.

"Lucien, step aside!" he shouted. The Red Monk glanced back, saw what was forming out of the ground and moved away from the machine. A Krote stood on its back, a battle-axe held in both hands, mouth open in a challenging shout. When she saw the new soldiers, her jaw fell, and she brandished the axe at them.

She sees a true enemy, Kosar thought. *And she's scared.*

The mimics flowed at the machine. The construct formed a massive scythe from a molten limb and swung, but the weapon passed through the mimics with a splash, and they went on as though untouched. When they reached the machine's hips they melted, poured upward and re-formed on its back.

The Krote faced up to the three strange soldiers, and though there was defiance on her face, Kosar saw that she was already prepared for defeat.

The mimics pressed in, merging with her so that she looked like a freak with three half brothers. When they came away, the Krote's face and chest disintegrated into a flow of dissolving flesh.

More shadows were rising. The ground was crawling around Kosar's feet, every speck shifting in a different direction. He felt dislocated. He looked at Lucien to gather his bearings and the Red Monk was swaying, hood still sheltering his face. Kosar walked to him, glancing down to see mimics part around each footfall. He nudged the Monk.

"Lucien!"

The Monk looked up. His face was red, eyes glowing with some inner light that Kosar had no wish to dwell upon. What anger, to produce such a look. What *rage*.

"Let's go," Kosar said. "This can't be happening everywhere, and others will need our help."

They started making their way out from the forest of shadow soldiers. The mimicked soldiers did not walk, they *flowed*, moving over grass, stones and bodies. And whatever unfathomable minds worked inside these things were focused on one thing: finding Krotes and killing them.

A mimic shape rose beside Kosar, forming faster than any he had yet seen, and he recognized its face. It was O'Lam, her features altered by the vicious impact of the spinning disc that had killed her. Kosar paused while the mimic moved off, then looked around until he spied the body of the dead Shantasi. He went to her, knelt and touched the back of the woman's shattered skull, and closed his eyes to offer a brief chant. He had only ever chanted a wraith down once before.

"There's no time for that," Lucien said.

"You leave me to do what I have to do!" Kosar replied, angry that the Monk had intervened. "We need a Mourner here."

"And if there's any victory in the next few hours, we'll get many. In the meantime, it's those that are still alive we should be helping, not the lost wraiths of those growing cold."

"You're all heart."

"I'm a Red Monk."

They moved on together, and mimic soldiers *hushed* past them whenever another machine was spied. They passed one construct sprouting half a body where a Krote was melting away. The machine itself was under attack as well, bindings tearing, the arcane

building blocks of its form failing. Limbs fell, stone disintegrated
and brief fires erupted at its heart until the mimics starved the flames
of air. Not only was this a slaughter, it was a very precise, clean
slaughter. For some reason that made Kosar uneasy.

At last they emerged onto grassland not crawling with mimics,
and here they found the true battle still under way. Kosar glanced
back, wondering at the extent of the mimic help, and it was like
looking at reality unbecoming: machines were melting, their Krote
riders already coming apart, and blue fire disappeared in a flash.
The whole landscape was blurred and uncertain.

"I don't see how this can go on," Lucien said.

"What do you mean? Noreela is helping us! The serpenthals,
and the tumblers, and now the mimics. What do you mean?"

"Look," Lucien said. He pointed across the hillside with his
bloodied sword.

The ground was covered with the dead and dying. Machines
stalked here and there, dishing out more death and, occasionally,
finding it themselves. Several machines stood dead in a circle, the
result of some unknown attack, but their Krote riders had escaped
their fate and were now fighting the Shantasi on foot. The clang of
swords, the spark of metal meeting metal, drifted across the hill.
And from one extreme of the battlefield to the other, the dead were
rising again.

"Mimics," Kosar said, but he knew immediately that he was
wrong. These were the dead readying to bear arms against their
Shantasi kin. Among them, oozing like a slippery memory, a stain
on the hillside.

"That's a shade," Lucien said. "The Mages have given it something, and for every Shantasi killed we have a new enemy."

"That's unreal," Kosar said. "That's *unfair!*"

Lucien laughed. It was a strange sound, so unexpected and unusual on this field of death and undeath. The Monk actually bent
over and held his stomach, his burnt back exposed to the air and
glistening in the moonlight where the cauterized flesh had started
breaking down. "We're all going to die," he said. "And you . . . think
that's unfair?"

Kosar was angry at first, but then he smiled.

Neither of them heard the machine rush them from out of a
haze of smoke. It stomped Lucien to the ground, pressed down on
his throat with one heavy stone leg, and on its back the fearsome

Krote stood and smiled. "Glad to see you think war is so amusing," she said. "You could almost be one of us." She touched the machine's back and it balanced all its weight on one leg, crushing Lucien's chest and neck, parting his head from his body, squeezing out his final breath in a haze of blood and spit.

———

THAT FELT GOOD, Lenora thought. *Red Monk fighting with the Shantasi!* she sent to her machine, and it ground its foot some more, turning its stone heel until it met mud wetted with blood.

"You're no Shantasi," Lenora said, looking at the man cowering before her. She frowned. Something about his features, his hair, the smell of him . . . "I know you," she said.

"Last time I saw you, I made you fall," the man said. "I'm Kosar. And you've just killed another friend of mine."

"You were friends with a Monk?"

Kosar glanced down at the mess beneath the machine's legs, up again at Lenora. "He was against you. That makes him my friend."

Lenora slid from the machine's back and landed astride the Monk's remains. She drew a sword and thrust it down into his chest—these Monks were tenacious, and she wanted to take no chances—and then stood and faced the defiant man. She felt those eyes behind her, watching. "Do you recognize my machine? See any familiar features?"

Kosar did not glance away from her face. "It's a monster," he said. "As are you."

Lenora shrugged, and she bled. She had gathered several more wounds to wear alongside those from so long ago, and even her old scars were aching again, singing with the memory of their creation. "You were traveling with monsters," she said. "That witch, with betrayal in her eyes. That boy, carrying something awful. That girl . . ." She frowned, but tried not to show her doubt.

"Rafe had magic. It would have been *good* for the land." Kosar spat on his sword. "And why the *fuck* am I even talking with you?" He darted at her, sword swinging up toward her stomach.

Lenora sidestepped and cracked him on the temple with her sword handle. He groaned and fell, fingers splayed in the bloody muck around the dead Monk.

Kosar stood and turned on her, and in his eyes Lenora saw pride, and determination, and a confidence that belied his situation. She had seen the tumblers and fought one off. She had ridden through the gray haze rising from the ground, and it came apart before her machine. The swirling sand demons were still fighting the Krote's rear guard back on the plain, and ahead of them lay Kang Kang and the girl with her brains crushed into the dirt. But for a moment, this man unsettled her more than anything she had yet seen of Noreela. For a moment, he made her feel mortal.

"What surprises do you have left?" Lenora said. *Come with me,* the voice of her daughter whispered, and Lenora closed her eyes for an instant, trying to put the voice back down.

Kosar laughed. He saw that she had a weakness. Lenora tried to grin, but a pang of pain in her womb turned it into a grimace.

"Are you hurting?" he asked.

Lenora had been asked that recently, by Ducianne. And as she went at Kosar she realized that, yes, she was hurting. Soon, perhaps, she would find out why.

———

HOPE COULD NOT move. To her left, Alishia had disappeared in the grasp of the tumbler, rolling downhill and into the smoke that was drifting across the valley from the ruined machine. The female Mage, reclothed in flesh and rage, had gone in pursuit of the tumblers. Her screams still echoed around the valley. Before Hope, the male Mage was fighting the Nax. And Hope was trapped between them all, apart from the action, unable to do anything but watch.

Though grotesquely burnt, the Mage still possessed enormous strength. The Nax circled him like wisps of red smoke, gushing fiery breaths, lashing out with bladed appendages and spiked wings, bounding from the ground and trying to confuse him with their rapid twists and turns. But the Mage fended off every attack, his own limbs moving faster than Hope could see. The fight was vicious and brutal, every move a death strike, every counter a desperate defense.

Hope felt useless. In this clash of monsters she was nothing, a human smear on a battlefield the likes of which Noreela had never seen before. The Cataclysmic War had been humans against the Mages and their Krotes. No tumblers, no Nax. Just the humans, as though the land had been content to leave them to clear up their own mess.

Something had changed this time, and Hope was glad.

She looked around the valley, trying to spot the tumbler that had carried Alishia away. She was desperate to believe that the tumblers had come to help, but it was still a stretch of the imagination that she found difficult to make. This was Kang Kang. Bad things happened here, and perhaps this was fate's final cruel twist in their wretched story: so close to saving the land, then whipped away by a tumbler and never seen again.

But the Mages want *her dead,* Hope thought. *So why run after her when she's in the grip of a tumbler? No escape from them. Never.* She saw hints of movement between drifting smoke across the valley, and she tried to project its path, looking at a clear spread of hillside and waiting for something to arrive.

She saw them; two tumblers, one with a flash of gray cloth that must have been Alishia's dress, and the Mage running after them faster than was possible, her feet leaving smoking wounds in the hillside. *She must have dealt with another tumbler,* Hope thought.

The Nax emitted a horrendous roar, filling the valley with a voice that killed grass and shriveled leaves. They went at the male Mage again, converging from different angles and driving into him. He flexed his chest as they came, as though filling his lungs for a scream to counter their own. But what came from his mouth, eyes and ears was far more than a scream. Hope saw it the instant before she ducked below the trunk once again, a shock wave of solid air that expanded out from the Mage's head and drove everything before it.

Hope covered her ears and opened her mouth. The shock wave struck the fallen tree, shattering what little remained, sweeping up a cloud of dead insects and wood fragments and adding them to the wave of debris. She glanced up in time to see a flash of red pass directly above her. Its limbs trailed, and it seeped smoke and fire as it went. It landed fifty steps away and rolled in the disturbed soil, burrowing, disappearing below the surface even as the male Mage's defiant laughter followed the terrible shock wave he had unleashed.

Hope groaned, but barely heard. Her hands were wet with blood from her ears, and something clicked in her chest as she breathed. *I'll die here if I don't move,* she thought, but the only way to move was to stand. The Mage would see her. And old as she was, bitter and mad, she realized that she most definitely did not want to die.

She rolled to her side and peered around the end of the broken log. The Mage was standing to the side of the cave mouth, arms still held wide, head back, mouth open as though sucking in the scent of victory. His body was ruined from the fire, but Hope had never seen anyone appear so strong.

From down the slope Hope heard the female Mage scream again.

The two remaining tumblers rolled uphill into the blazing remains of the flying machine. They jumped and bounced, landing in areas free of fire and machine pieces. The lead tumbler still carried Alishia pinned to its side. Her arms waved, and one leg bent and straightened with each revolution. From this distance she still seemed whole.

The tumblers passed the wreckage, and Hope realized their intention.

They were aiming directly at the cave.

The female Mage appeared from out of the smoke. She screamed and raged, coughing out another burst of blue fire. The tumbler to the rear intercepted the fire before it could strike Alishia, spinning in a circle as the flame melted its way inside. Hope heard distant screams, and she knew they did not come from the Mage.

The final tumbler, Alishia spiked to its side, rolled quickly toward the Womb of the Land.

"S'Hivez!" the female Mage screamed, still running but realizing now that she would not reach Alishia in time.

Hope stood. "Here I am, you piece of shit!"

S'Hivez spun around to look at Hope.

The tumbler flitted behind him, carrying Alishia with it. It entered the darkness of the cave.

Hope closed her eyes.

———

JOSSUA ELMANTOZ KNEW that the tumbler now carried someone else. Someone *alive*. But he could no more communicate with them than he could with Flage.

He could sense the tremendous sense of potential present there. He could smell the stink of magic, and there was nothing he could do to purge it from this world.

If he were alive, Jossua could have fought. If he were dead, perhaps he would have attacked from the inside, because the wraith of a Red Monk would be as tenacious as the soul of one still alive. But he was neither. This first Red Monk, one who had seen the Mages from Noreela's shores three centuries before, refused to give up on life and would not accept death.

When the tumbler went from light to darkness once more, Jossua felt himself plucked away by something more bewildering than anything he had ever encountered. In that thing he found a shadow of acceptance, and a respect for his obsession. Its strange voices chanted him somewhere wholly new.

Chapter 22

WE'RE THERE, FLAGE SAID. *Now you can open your eyes.*

I'm not sure I'm able, Alishia said. *Everything's spinning. Everything's changing.*

It's due to change some more. We've been let inside, and I think you need to see.

Alishia opened her eyes to darkness. She could feel herself being transported in uncertain steps down toward a warmth, and a light. She could sense this light but not yet see it. She tried to lift her hand to rub her eyes, but could not move. Her whole body pained her, and she felt things stabbing into her leg, her shoulder, her hip. These things flexed with every movement, and she bit her lip to prevent herself from crying out.

Can you see? the amazed voice of Flage said. *Can you see the light?*

"Yes," Alishia replied, and her voice echoed.

Good, Flage said, and he faded away.

Alishia now could see the stone ceiling of the cave passing by above her. The light increased with each jarring movement, and soon she could make out cracks in the rock, spiderwebs, pale green moss spotting here and there. *Where's that light coming from?* she thought. *And why is it so warm?* She sniffed for a fire, but the only smell was one of old dampness.

She felt the roughness of the tumbler beneath her. It stopped and rolled gently to the side, and as her feet touched the ground the sharp things invading her body withdrew quickly. She cried out and fell on all fours, hair framing her face and hiding the surroundings from view. For a while she was glad. She stared at the stone floor and saw ancient human footprints, a thousand or a million years old, marking a route in the dust that led up and out.

Where am I?

No one and nothing answered. The sleeves of her dress swamped her hands and she felt cold and exposed in the huge garment. She looked down at herself and saw how small she had become.

What am I to do?

Still no answer. She looked up at the great tumbler that had brought her here, and crushed into its side were the remains of a Red Monk. Its hood was wrapped around the shattered remnants of the skull. All flesh had long since been scoured away, and her shock was only slight.

She sat back and turned her head, ready to take in everything else. *The Womb of the Land!*

Here was potential. Here was a library of blank books yet to be written. Here was the future awaiting discovery, and in her there was the future's seed ready to plant.

Alishia blinked slowly, trying to digest what she was seeing.

The cave was quite large, and perfectly spherical. She sat in an opening at its edge, and the walls rose around her in a flawless curve. It was warm, though there was no sign of fire. The air was damp, the walls slick with moisture, and as she moved her hand across the ground she felt the warmth of it.

"I'm Alishia," she said. Her voice came back to her, one name echoing into a confusion of noise that could have contained every word ever spoken. She said something else, something personal to her, and the resultant sound was the same. Whatever idea she gave birth to in here held the potential to grow into anything.

She stood slowly, uncertainly, and she was amazed at how light she was. How old could she be? Eight? Six? Younger? She put her hands to her face, pleased at the familiarity of the touch. "I'm still myself," she muttered, and the echoes said she could have been anyone.

Alishia stepped from the tunnel entrance onto the slope of the sphere. Moving down toward the lowest point of the cave, she glanced back, surprised to see that the tumbler had withdrawn. She had not heard it leave. *There's so much more to them*, she thought, but that idea probably applied to much of Noreela. "So much more to everything," Alishia said, and this time her words carried no echo, their meaning clear.

As she walked slowly down the slope she felt herself changing, regressing faster than ever. The dress slipped from her shoulders and she left it behind, though she was not cold. This place was welcoming and safe. It was a place of comfort.

Something appeared back at the entrance tunnel, a dark shape that drove back the strange light emanating from the walls. "Soon," Alishia said, and the Birth Shade withdrew. It was ready for its offering, and she was ready to make it.

At the lowest point of the cave there were hollows in the ground. They were shapes she recognized. Some had been used, their glossy texture turned rough, veined trace works in their sides gone to dust. *I wonder which one was Rafe's*, she thought. Others were fresh and clean, dips in the land filled with promise.

She chose one of these, sat close by and brushed her fingers through her hair. It came out in clumps. She tried to stand again but her legs would not hold her, so she crawled those last few steps and settled herself into the hollow.

She was not surprised to find that it fit her perfectly.

THE LIBRARY THIS time was whole and undamaged, but it was also characterless, and every book spine was blank. There was a reading area, and all the furniture was new and untouched. The leather chairs were fresh and unworn, the unmarked table carved from wellburr wood. No books sat on the table waiting to be read.

There was nothing with Alishia in the library: no rampaging shade, no man, no fire eating away at every moment in history. There was only her. She had the very real sense that she was waiting here for something to happen. And while she was waiting, she might as well read.

She left the reading area and entered the towers of books. She was only a baby, yet her mind was full, and in this dream her child's legs would carry her anywhere.

She walked for some time before gathering the courage to take down a book. She climbed a shelf to reach it; the spines were all the same, the blank books uniform, but she knew that this particular tome was the one she needed.

Hugging the book against her chest she walked back to the reading area. Here and there shadows were appearing on book spines. They were not yet whole words, but their potential was deafening.

She hauled herself up into the reading chair. It was far too large for her, but still she managed to lay the book on her stubby legs, open the cover and stare at the first blank page.

Alishia closed her eyes and something left her forever.

When she looked again, the page was no longer blank. She began to read of a new moment in time.

The land begins to heal . . .

———

THEY WOULD BE on her and she would be dead.

Hope kept her eyes closed, hands by her sides, suddenly willing to accept death with dignity. She would not fight. It had been a long time in coming, and in her final moments she had helped.

If I look, I'll see that thing coming at me. Angry. Enraged. Ready to exact weak revenge by spilling this false witch's blood.

She heard a roar, the sound of something hard striking something soft, and in the screams from the Mages she made out the dregs of words. They formed little sense. The Mages were mad, but unlike her their madness was deep and irredeemable.

At last, Hope could keep her eyes closed no longer, and when she looked, the Mages were battering at the entrance to the Womb of the Land. The Shades had returned, three of them this time, growing from the cave mouth like giant trees. They seemed to shrug off the abuse of the Mage's magical weaponry. They absorbed fireballs, deflected shock waves from the male Mage, opened shadowy arms to collect hatred and fury and closed them again, swallowing everything meant to do them harm. Each Shade was huge and unchanging now, as though they had recently been fed. And Hope could not help but pick up on the optimism being exuded from these shadows of nothing.

Nothing can touch them, she thought. *The Mages, with all their dark magic and three centuries of hate, they can't* touch *them!*

The male Mage turned and stared directly at Hope. His eyes were blazing red coals, narrowed to slits. His mouth opened and displayed long teeth, made longer because his gums had been burned away. He growled, and it rumbled from the earth and into Hope's bones like an earthquake.

She closed her eyes again. *And now he'll turn on me.* Something warm touched her face and scalp, and for a second she thought that he was at her, hot breath caressing her as he decided how best to kill. But then she realized that the heat felt good, and familiar, and the one word echoing in her mind as she opened her eyes again was *Alishia!*

———

KOSAR PARRIED THE Krote's first sword swipe, ducked below the second, and then the land began to bleed.

"Alishia!" Kosar shouted. He looked to the east, and the foothills of Kang Kang were silhouetted against an orange and red sky, their slopes and peaks cut in stark relief against the lightening sky, and the glow was spreading up and out like a growing bruise, seeping through the Mages' dusk from the ground up. Smudged lines of sunlight stretched across the landscape, reached at the sky, probed behind the mountains.

And then, like a giant birthed anew from the fading land, the curved head of the sun started to rise.

Cheers rose across the hillside, and the noise of battle lessened as warriors—Shantasi and Krote alike—paused to take in the incredible sight.

Kosar glanced at the female Krote. She was watching as well, and the amazement on her face slowly melted into what could only be relief. The fresh sun stroked across her scarred scalp and bloodied shoulder, and her few remaining teeth glittered as she smiled.

Kosar looked to the east again. He felt the fledgling heat of the sun on his skin, and it was like dipping into a warm bath. Wisps of fine cloud scratched the sky red. It was the most beautiful thing Kosar had ever seen.

"You've lost," he said. "Your filthy Mages are dead, and you've fucking *lost!*"

"So magic me away," the Krote said. But Kosar could see the

strange look in her eyes—part confusion, part relief—and when he raised his sword again she merely glanced at it before turning away.

A hundred mimic soldiers melted back into the ground. The surface flowed northward, down the slopes of the battlefield and out onto the long plains that led toward whatever was left of Noreela. Kosar mourned their passing, but he realized that their purpose was fulfilled. What happened to the few hundred remaining Shantasi, and their Krote enemies, was of no concern to the mimics.

"Going home?" Kosar shouted after his enemy. "Fleeing again?"

The Krote turned and stared at him, and Kosar began to regret his words. "I have more things left to do," she said. She gazed around the field of battle, the piles of bodies, the shambling dead and weary living, the Krotes and machines, the Shantasi cheering here, regrouping there, all of it now lit by the sun rising triumphant. "Do what you will. My time is moving on." She mounted her machine and sent it a command.

Kosar screamed at the Krote, "I made you fall!" She glanced at him again, dismissive, then rode away. He threw A'Meer's sword. Its bloodied blade glowed red in the sunlight as it spun at the Krote woman's head. It hit her neck and bounced off, rattling from the back of the machine and dropping beneath its stone legs. She did not even turn around. The machine stomped on the sword and moved on.

As the Krote and her machine seemed to shimmer away down the hillside, Kosar realized that he was crying.

———

KOSAR PICKED UP his sword, amazed to find it undamaged even by that monster's weight. Unlike Lucien. He felt little at the death of the Monk; no sadness, and certainly no delight. Lucien had killed A'Meer, but her murderer had been a Red Monk, not a man. Perhaps sometime in the future Kosar would have time to dwell upon what that meant.

He went to war again. With sunlight flooding the hillside—its heat and rays fresh and energizing—the fight became that much easier. The Shantasi used the confusion of dawn to regroup and change tactics, forming into four large circles, fighting their way up the slope. There were more pallid wolves to send against the Krotes, and a dozen young grinders were attached to machines confused by the dawn. They chewed and melted their way through stone and metal alike, eating out the hearts of these unnatural constructs.

The Mages' warriors lost something as day dawned. Whether it was a true sense of purpose or the confidence of victory, their fighting became less effective. Conversely, the Shantasi had gained so much more. These were the inhabitants of New Shanti that had refused to flee. These were the warriors and farmers, the poets and carpenters who had taken up arms against the aggressor, instead of following their Elder Mystics' lead and accepting defeat. It was confidence that fueled them now, and perhaps a hint of pride in knowing what they had already achieved. Both gave them strength and grace.

In between attacks, the Shantasi glanced skyward and smiled. The warm sun—free of Kang Kang now, and rising confidently above Noreela once more—smiled back.

There were no more serpenthals to aid their fight. The surviving tumblers had also disappeared from the battle, rumbling east and west along the mountain range. Many remained on the plains, the smoke of their pyres forming a dirty brown cloud that drifted slowly to the east.

It quickly became apparent to the Krote army that this was not their hour. Some of them turned and fled back to the north. Others dropped their weapons and stepped forward to surrender, a sense of weary relief on their faces. They were cut down by the Shantasi. This was not a battle where mercy held much meaning.

Kosar fought on. And hours later, as the sun peaked and scorched any remaining shadows of dusk from the land, he felt an urgent calling from the south. *Alishia*, he thought. *Trey. Hope.* He had been away from his friends for too long. He needed to know whether any of them were still alive.

———

HOPE WAS WHISPERING to the ground.

The words she used were old, and to many in Noreela they would have no meaning. But she came from a long line of witches, both true and false, and a witch could never forget the language of the land.

She spoke to the soil, stroked the grass, glanced up at the sky yet again to see where the darkness was being eaten away by the sun.

She buried her fingers in the soft ground and touched the roots of the grass. She felt things down there caressing her fingertips, cold and old.

Her tattoos widened across her face as her mouth fell open, and suddenly she knew.

She rubbed her hands together and pooled magic in her palms. She laughed, sniffed her fingertips and smelled way past the soil, down to the depths of magic and what it could do, what it *would* do. And she realized just how blinkered the Mages had always been.

When she stood, she knew that they would be close. The female Mage was tall and thin and beautiful, but such beauty remained far from her eyes. The male was still ruined from the fire. In the sudden daylight, his scorched black wounds were grotesque, but his eyes were bright and undamaged, glittering orange as though still filled with the fire that should have killed him.

"Hello," Hope said. She laughed again, and it felt good.

"I know you," the male Mage growled.

"I don't think so," Hope said. "I've fucked a lot of people in my time, and I'm sure I'd have remembered someone as ugly as you." She was completely unafraid, even though she knew that this would end in her death. Her life might stop here, but it was complete, fulfilled, and she felt the true blood of her ancestors coursing through her veins for the first time. *I could heal his burns,* she thought. *I could see her future, I could cast myself from the here and now, pass through the land and arrive wherever I wished. I could do all that and so many other things, but the first is something I owe. And I owe so much to so many.*

"You mock us?" Angel asked.

"Mockery is no answer to evil," Hope said.

Angel spat. "I *see* you! You've got evil hiding in you, just as surely as you have those markings on your face. Shall I pull them? Rip them out to see what they drag from your depths?"

"I can live with my own wrongdoings," Hope said. "But don't you see what else I have?"

"You're a witch," S'Hivez said.

Hope nodded.

"A witch," Angel said. "How cute."

"You've lost," Hope said.

Angel frowned and S'Hivez glanced at the sky.

"A brief setback," Angel said.

"No," Hope said, shaking her head. "You've *lost*. And you never even knew how to win. You ply your bastardized magic, but true magic is the language of the land. You never knew how to listen to it. And you will *never* speak it."

"And you, a sad old witch with no magic, can say this?"

"Oh I have magic," Hope said quietly, and she muttered words from ancient memory.

The ground below the Mages split open. They shouted in surprise as they fell, trying to cast some dark spell at Hope that fizzled to nothing. Angel coughed a blue fireball that sputtered out beneath the strengthening sun. S'Hivez threw a shock wave that parted around the witch and killed trees, flattened grass. Hope muttered a backward phrase and the shock wave reversed, slamming into S'Hivez, knocking him back, and behind her trees came back to life and grass stood up.

Hope felt the limitless power of the land thrumming inside. Her heart thundered in her chest, blood pumped so fast that her eyes and ears began bleeding again, but the pains were all good. They were good, because they meant that she was doing something right.

When the hole was deep enough to cover the Mages, Hope reversed her words, and the stone sides began to close in.

Angel rose, levitating from the hole, but Hope smiled and the Mage fell back down. S'Hivez screamed, and deep below his feet a cave opened up, rock crumbling and soil pouring in.

Hope frowned and spoke faster.

The stone sides of the hole were crushing Angel now, but S'Hivez, much of his frame stripped of flesh, scurried down into the cavern beneath his feet. His last look he spared for Angel. Hope could not see his eyes, did not catch what passed between them, but as the female Mage started screaming, S'Hivez slipped away.

She felt the Nax return to the valley before she saw them. She cringed, their senses existing for a few heartbeats in her mind. And then two of them whipped past her and darted into the crack, passing Angel and disappearing after S'Hivez.

Angel screamed. For a moment Hope considered mercy. The ground was closing in slowly on the Mage, pressing her face against rock, gripping her torso and legs and head, and the scream was one of true agony. But there were only three more words left to say.

Hope looked to the sky and spoke to the new daylight.

Angel's screams were cut off as the sides of the hole met. A weak blue light sizzled across the ground and faded away. With one final crack, the top of Angel's skull popped up, and a flow of brain matter sparkled in the sun as it pattered down across the grass.

Hope closed her eyes and the noises came to an end.

"Lost him," she said. "After all that, I lost him." But with the Nax on his trail, the escaped Mage would not survive for long.

A while later she lost so much more, as she knew she must. The magic leeched away, leaving her an old false witch once again, but this time she was no longer sad. Alishia had planted the seed of magic and it had lent itself to Hope, just for a while.

Someday soon, the seed would bloom.

Chapter 23

THE KROTE MACHINES had already started to die.

Most of the surviving Shantasi went north, pursuing the fleeing enemy and preparing to meet the future waves of Krote warriors that must surely come. There would be more fighting, for this war was far from over, but at least now it would be on equal terms.

Fifty warriors went east, back to New Shanti, where they would arrive victorious, ready to gather and lead the full might of New Shanti's army north to aid the rest of the land. There would be issues to resolve, and blame to be meted out. But the politics would wait until after the Krotes were once again driven from Noreela.

Kosar persuaded a Shantasi captain to lend him twenty warriors to take into Kang Kang. None of them were keen to go, but they were buoyed by the sun's reemergence, and many of them had seen Kosar with O'Gan Pentle. The thief had taken on something of a mystical quality himself.

THEY TRAVELED FOR a day and a night, camping deep inside Kang Kang and lying awake, listening to noises that none of them knew and imagining creatures that no one had ever seen. The next morning, tired and drained, one of them almost put an arrow into Hope when she wandered into their camp.

———

KOSAR AND HOPE sat away from the Shantasi, cooking a rabbit over an open fire and drinking water.

"It's not so bad," Hope said, nodding up at the mountains. The peaks were smeared with snow, the lower slopes wet with rain. The sun had risen again that morning. Kosar would never take the dawn for granted.

"The tumblers helped us fight the Krotes too," Kosar said. Hope had relayed her story in one long talk, staring into the flames, stroking and sniffing her fingertips. Kosar had touched his own fingers—brands sore from the fighting—and listened.

"Did you see the Nax?" Hope asked, eyes wide.

Kosar shook his head. "That doesn't mean they weren't there. It was confused. And when dawn came, it got more confusing still."

"How so?"

"Some Krotes fought on, some didn't." He thought of the scarred female warrior riding away, saying that her fight was moving on.

They ate the rabbit in companionable silence, both so loaded with questions that neither really knew where to begin. At last, the beast little more than bones in their hands, Kosar asked the question.

"Where will you go?"

He saw how the witch had changed. Her tattoos were still there, forbidding and angry, but a darkness had lifted from her eyes. For the first time ever, her name seemed to suit. "Back through Kang Kang," she said. "I'll avoid the Womb of the Land, though I doubt I'd even find it again. And then, into The Blurring."

"But there's nothing there," Kosar said.

"How do you know?"

"Well . . ."

"It's called The Blurring because it's never been mapped," Hope said. "And if the male Mage does manage to evade or defeat the Nax, that's where he'll go."

"What makes you think that?"

"His ex-lover is dead, his magic weakened, and when whatever Alishia planted is birthed, it'll be driven away completely. If I need to, I'll be able to fight him on equal terms. He has nothing left to live for, but somehow I don't think an old monster like that will lie down and die. So, my guess is that he'll go south. Away from everything."

"Toward nothing."

"Maybe. But if he survives the Nax, I'll follow."

"Why?"

"Magic *chose* me, Kosar! Just for an instant, but it *chose* me. And now I owe . . . so much." Hope licked meat juice from her fingers. "Besides, who knows what's there? I heard rumors that a mad Sleeping God is awake down there. And other stories, all of them fantastic. So much to see and discover. And I don't think Noreela's for me. I did things . . . I hurt people . . ." She did not finish, and Kosar did not wish to pursue that route.

"You?" Hope asked. "Where are you going?"

Kosar raised his eyebrows and smiled at the witch. "In all honesty, I hadn't even thought about it." *This is when she asks me to go with her,* he thought. But the witch stared back into the flames, a strange look on her face.

"Well . . ." she said.

"Well what?"

"Kosar, while you're thinking about where to go, I can do something for you. You'll maybe hate me for this. I wouldn't blame you if you did, but I can do this now, and I want to, and I insist you let me."

"What the Mage shit are you talking about, Hope?"

"Give me your hands."

"Why?"

"Those brands. I can cure them. If you'll let me."

Kosar looked down at his bleeding fingertips, made more raw since dusk fell. He had a dozen other wounds on his body, but now these seemed to hurt the most. "How long have you known you could do this?" he asked.

Hope looked away. "Quite some time."

"Oh." He fisted his hands, but remembered the change he had seen on her face. And it was no longer the time for hate. "Here," he said, and he showed her his fingers.

LATER, HOPE WRAPPED his brands with strips of cloth torn from her already ragged dress. The Wilmott's Nemesis root was burned and powdered, and she told him to keep the wrappings on for two days. "False magic," she said, smiling at him.

"Not for much longer."

Hope wrapped the last finger. "It'll stay sore for a while," she said, "but the bleeding should stop soon, and they'll have a chance to heal. Try not to aggravate the wounds. No wars for a while."

"I'll do my best."

"I can do those as well." She touched Kosar's neck. He had almost forgotten about the wound there, pulled shut by sand rat teeth.

"Lucien did that."

"A Red Monk stitched you up?" Hope pulled the teeth out one by one, dabbed Kosar's throat, nodded in satisfaction. "He did a good job."

"There was so much more to him," Kosar said. He touched his throat and winced.

After a pause Hope asked, "So have you decided?"

He shrugged. "I'm a wanderer," he said. "Perhaps I'll just wander and see where I end up. But first I have to visit where A'Meer died. Maybe I'll find her wraith. Maybe I can chant her down."

Hope nodded, her face severe. "It won't be easy for a long time, Kosar," she said. "The Krotes are still in the land, and there's no saying they'll just turn tail and flee. They might regroup and fight. Without the bastard Mages to lead them, perhaps they'll have their own designs for Noreela."

"I know," Kosar said. "But as you said, there'll come a time when whatever Alishia seeded comes to fruition. Who knows what the new magic will be like? Perhaps the Shantasi will build their own machines then, hunt down the Krotes. Whatever happens, those Mage shits will lose."

"I hope so."

"I know so."

They stood, kicked out the fire and returned to the group of Shantasi. The warriors eyed Hope warily, but the story of what had happened was already on their lips, and Kosar also saw a level of respect for the witch in their glances.

They gave Hope plenty of food and water, some new clothing and a bow and arrows. She also had Trey's disc-sword, newly sharpened and sheathed in a make-do leather scabbard. Kosar thought it suited her well.

Hope and Kosar shared an awkward hug before parting.

"Take care," Hope said to the thief, and that surprised him for a while. Here she was readying to journey into the unknown, and *she* told *him* to take care.

But later, as he gratefully made his way out of Kang Kang and headed back toward whatever remained of the Noreela he knew, he began to understand.

Chapter 24

SHE RODE HARD, moving by night and hiding by day. During the second night her machine ground to a halt, leaking fluids and stinking worse than the dead. She dismounted, walked to the machine's face, ready to stare one last time into its eyes. But the eyes she wanted to see—those that would reflect her own guilt at what she had become—had closed for the final time.

Lenora started to walk. On that second full day she kept walking as the sun rose. It was not so bad. Three centuries bearing the cold in Dana'Man, and however many long days merged into one night in the fight for Noreela, had left her craving the feeling of sunlight on her skin. She burned, but that was fine. The sun seemed to soothe her many wounds, old and new.

She was approached by a band of rovers traveling east to west. She hid behind a rock as they passed a few hundred steps away. They were singing and laughing, and she saw several couples rutting in the back of an open wagon, passing bottles back and forth and cheering at the sun. Light danced on their sweat-sheened skins.

Lenora supposed there would be many across Noreela celebrating the sunlight, in many different ways.

Now and then guilt pressed down on her for abandoning the Mages' cause with barely a backward glance. But the small voice growing louder calmed that guilt. *Come to me, Mother,* the voice said, and it seemed wiser and older than it should. *Come and find me.*

"I'm coming," Lenora whispered.

THAT NIGHT SHE slept, and dreamed a dream that would change everything.

She was in a huge library, shelves so high that she could not see their tops, corridors long and winding and confusing. The shelves were stacked with books, but however many she took down, she could find none with more than a couple of pages of writing. There was so much blankness here, and so much potential. She walked for a long time, and occasionally she saw a figure disappearing around a corner ahead of her. It was a small girl, naked, running like a toddler but glancing back with the look of someone carrying the wisdom of ages. Perhaps this was the same apparition that had haunted her in Noreela City, reflected in the swipe of her sword blade or the eyes of those she killed . . . or perhaps not. The same long hair, but a different shade of brown. The same eyes, but this one showed no fear, nor condemnation.

You're not her, Lenora thought, *but maybe you could be.*

She followed the little girl, trying to catch her, but she was always a dozen steps behind. The girl was not afraid . . . but she was not yet ready to be caught.

Lenora came to a space in the library set aside for sitting and reading. The girl was ahead of her, dashing across the open space. And before she disappeared between book stacks she swapped a glance with a man standing there—a look of recognition, and a smile.

The man stepped forward and guided Lenora into a comfortable leather chair. She was tired, and grateful when he told her to sit. She had been running for so long.

We've chosen you, he said, *because healing is needed.*

What can I heal?

The future.

I don't understand. Lenora was agitated and afraid, but there was something soothing in the man's voice, and something so confident and comforting.

A whole new magic, born of humanity.

What will it be like?

The man smiled. *That's where the wonder lies in this: none can know until it arrives.* He held out his hand and the small girl emerged once again from the shadows. She was smiling at Lenora. And Lenora looked into those eyes, and recognized them.

You are *her.*

———

SHE WOKE UP panting, hands pressing down on her abdomen, and she lay there for a while as the sun rose and her heart calmed.

———

AS SHE WALKED she grew heavier, and she feared it was weakness grinding her down. *I'm an old woman,* she thought.

You're my mother, the shade of her daughter said.

During the third day she found a dead Red Monk leaning against a tree. The leaves had died and fallen, all but hiding the dead Monk from view. Lenora twisted the stiff body out of its red robe and took it for herself. It hid her weapons and shielded her skin from the sun, and it seemed to make her going easier.

That afternoon she saw a machine running across a distant hillside on long, unsteady legs. There was no rider, and she watched until it disappeared over the horizon, swaying madly from side to side.

———

LENORA LEFT KANG Kang, and at some point she must have passed the place where she gave birth to her dead daughter over three centuries before. She cried for that whole day, her sobs doing little to hide the voice whispering to her from the hills, the plains, the places where countless old bones lay.

———

SHE REACHED ROBENNA three days later. Her stomach was swelling, though she denied the impossible truth of that, and as she crested a hilltop and looked down into her old village, she had the shattering sense of time moving on.

Robenna was deserted. It had been for some time, probably decades, and many of the buildings had gone to ruin. Plants had subsumed some, while others had fallen victim to the elements and tumbled into useless piles of stone, timber and mud. She tried to find the place she had called home but that had been far too long ago, and even these old buildings were new to her. She recognized the square, and the path of the stream, and the old stone bridge was the same. It was Robenna, for sure, but it was no longer her Robenna.

Even if the village had been occupied, she doubted she would have ever touched her sword again.

She decided to stay.

That evening, sitting beside a fire in what had been the village square, her daughter's shade spoke to her for the final time: *Thank you, Mother.*

She felt the baby kick.

———————

DENYING THE PRESENCE inside her was pointless. Lenora did not understand, but she quickly became calm and accepted what was happening. *I'm an old woman*, she thought, but the baby kicked and her one undamaged breast grew, and there were moments when she could remember what it had been like before she became a Krote. Those years wandering around Lake Denyah were clear to her once again, and the shame and guilt she had felt then became familiar once more. Finding a place in the Mages' burgeoning army had been the start of something new, but now, with so much history behind her, that moment in her memory felt like the beginning of something old.

Though she would always carry the scars, Lenora was no longer a Krote.

She made herself a home in one of the least damaged buildings, collected wood from the ruins for her fire, cleaned the well and drew clear water. With careful tending, some of the vegetable gardens began to show signs of life. A splash of blue birth-blooms came into flower around the village, and several trees unfurled tentative buds.

One morning, rising early from a dream that disturbed but did not scare her, Lenora walked out to the stone bridge and sat on the parapet. She had fled across this same bridge three centuries before, poisoned and driven from the village for falling pregnant out of wedlock. She touched her stomach and felt movement.

As she watched the sunrise, she thought of a name.

ABOUT THE AUTHOR

TIM LEBBON lives in South Wales with his wife and two children. His books include *Face, The Nature of Balance, Changing of Faces, Exorcising Angels* (with Simon Clark), *Dead Man's Hand, Pieces of Hate, Fears Unnamed, White and Other Tales of Ruin, Desolation, Berserk*, and *Dusk*. Other recent publications include *Hellboy: Unnatural Selection* from Simon & Schuster, plus books from Cemetery Dance, Night Shade Books, and Necessary Evil Press. There are more Noreela novels coming from Bantam, as well as two novels in collaboration with Christopher Golden. He has won two British Fantasy Awards, a Bram Stoker Award, a Shocker, a Tombstone Award, and has been a finalist for International Horror Guild and World Fantasy Awards. Several of his novels and novellas are currently under option in the United States and Great Britain.

Find out more about Tim at his website, www.timlebbon.net.

Visit the dedicated website for *Dusk* and *Dawn* at www.noreela.com.